WARRIOR'S TRUST

M.M. CHROMY

SIDELINE
THUNDER
PRESS

For my dear friend, Laura Comotto— You are loyal, kind, and always persevere. I'm so glad God saw to it that we became friends.

SAM

T he heavy thump of bass from music pulsing inside the bar matched my heartbeat as I ran. Only when I was halfway across the rear lot did I realize my best friend Leigh no longer sprinted beside me. I spun and saw her blocked by two humanoid demons of a size we'd never seen. They towered over Leigh by at least a foot. She snarled when one of them, an ugly orange-skinned bastard, punched her ribs.

Attack Leigh? Hell no. I gritted my teeth, wiped the sweat from my palms and wrenched my recurve bow, Azira, from her case on my back. I grabbed a white-tipped arrow from my quiver and nocked it. Leigh was moving in and out of my line of fire, but desperate times called for desperate measures.

Mr. Orange Nasty would die first.

I steadied my breath and drew on the Heavenly Power blazing in my veins. The white metal arrowhead glowed. When I had a clean shot, I took it.

And missed.

"Sonovabitch," I growled, snapping out of my archer's

stance. The demons stalked around Leigh, throwing punches and lunging at her with surprising speed. *These guys are faster than anything we've seen before.* Leigh dodged and parried, with her longsword, Fury, ablaze.

"I've got this! Go find the other one——" Leigh hissed.

I'd been chasing a third demon, but lost track of it when Leigh engaged the other two. My Warrior instincts found him in the dense trees lining the parking lot. I was downwind and could track him by his sulfuric scent and hear him among the oaks.

Darting to the canopy of trees, I scanned my immediate area. A flash of movement drew my attention to the right. I caught a glimpse of muscular shoulders before the demon blended back into the dark cover of oaks. A stick snapped somewhere to my left. I drew another arrow and nocked it before creeping forward into a small clearing.

Dickhead is taunting me. I'd never known a demon to possess this much finesse. This new type was big, agile, and cunning. *Who the hell are they?* As much as it pained my precious ego to admit it, we were woefully unprepared for this fight.

I heard my stalker move again. *Enough of this.* I tapped my Power. My body tingled, heat seeped into my veins, my senses sharpened. *There!* Moonlight glinted dully on the demon's smooth, black hide just ahead of me.

"I see you, asshole," I muttered and raised my bow. I said in a louder voice, "Cut the bullshit. Come out."

He growled and stepped from the shadows.

Holy Heaven. Mr. Big-Ass-Demon made his buddies look puny. His biceps were as thick as my thighs. From his bare feet to his hideous face, he was every inch a weapon. I swallowed the lump of dread in my throat. *I don't think I can take him on alone.*

"Stay calm," my inner Warrior whispered. Her gentle warmth washed over me, bolstering my courage.

"You can do this. You can do this. You can do this." I chanted to myself while taking aim at the center mass of his torso. I loosed my glowing arrow, praying it found something vital—preferably a major organ, artery, or vein. I wasn't picky.

The huge demon ducked sideways and the metal tip nicked his beefy bicep. "Think that'll stop me?" He chuckled, wiping two fingers at the bloody cut.

"Maybe," I bluffed, tightening my grip on Azira. My hand trembled. "Why don't you come find out?"

He bolted toward me. Heavenly Power roared through my body. I jumped out of the way. He grabbed my right wrist and crushed it until Azira tumbled to the ground. He spun me around, wrenched my captured arm behind my back, and yanked me close to his chest. He smelled like hot tar.

"You're coming with me," he snarled into my ear.

My breath caught. My stomach clenched. *He's too strong.* Sweat dripped down my forehead stinging my eyes.

"Don't quit," my inner Warrior said. Her kind warmth overrode my fears.

"I'm *not* going anywhere with you," I snapped. He groped for my other arm, but I swung my elbow down and back. My fist smacked his groin. I slammed my boot heel onto his bare toes. Pain doubled him over and I threw my head back into his chin.

The demon's grip slipped and I wrenched myself away. I spun and punched him in the nose, the gut, and landed an upper cut under his jaw before swooping to pick up Azira. Then I got the hell out of there.

I sprinted and hid behind an old Florida oak, peering around its impressive trunk. I pulled three arrows from my quiver, stuck two in the ground, and nocked one. He snorted, clearing the blood from his nose, and sniffed the air.

They can hunt by scent? I pulled in a steadying breath and exhaled slowly. Power pulsed bright in me. My vision sharpened, focused on this one demon. *They may fight back, but so do I.*

"Playing games, little Warrior?" He ambled forward. "I have all night."

I shot the arrows, one after another. Two missed but the third slammed into his hefty thigh.

Dammit!

He howled. I nocked another arrow.

"Is that all ya got, pup?" He jerked out my arrow and threw it down. Black blood soaked his camo cargo pants.

"You're nasty," I said.

"And you're mine."

"Not if I can help it." I drew and aimed.

At that moment, Leigh screamed. *Holy mother of—* I flinched as I released, and my arrow went wide.

The black behemoth hit me head on and sent me flying.

I lost Azira.

I twisted, trying to break my fall, but landed hard and cracked my head on a rock. Adrenaline flooded my bloodstream, but I couldn't get up. My right arm wouldn't take my weight.

"Get up!" my inner Warrior thundered.

"I can't." The ground spun and nausea rolled through me. I closed my eyes to keep from puking. *Stay alert!* I forced my eyes open and saw black feet, pleased to see two bloody toes on the left one.

"Samantha Fife, you're wanted by my master."

"Well, shit," I muttered, shoving myself to my knees,

gasping from the pain in my ribs and right arm. The earth still tilted. I touched the back of my skull and my fingers came away bloody. I squinted up at him. He smirked and cocked his head.

Why isn't he attacking me? What's he waiting for? "I don't have a damn clue what you mean," I said.

"I was told to keep you alive. However, my master didn't say anything about what condition you needed to be in upon delivery."

I wanted to offer a snarky retort, but nothing came. All I could do was gawk up at this ginormous beast, my false bravado gone. If he hadn't been told to keep me alive, I was sure he'd have squashed me dead.

"You're weak, little Warrior. I'm almost disappointed."

"Sam! Down!" Leigh's voice pierced my pain-filled fog.

I dropped flat on the ground. *Thank God, Buddha, and every celestial being in between,* I was never so happy to hear her voice in my life. I heard her running toward me. Then Fury, still magnificently glowing, sailed end-over-end into Mr. Big-Ass-Demon's chest.

Instead of bursting into ash as demons usually did, his form flickered. Shock contorted his ugly face and he winked out. Fury fell with a *thunk* on the ground near me.

Well, that's different. My brow furrowed. *"Did he go back to Hell?"* I asked my inner Warrior.

After a moment, she said, *"I'm not so sure."*

Leigh dashed over to me, plucked up her sword, sheathed it, and slung Azira over her shoulder. A slash across her cheekbone seeped blood.

"Oh my gosh, look at you!" Leigh gaped in horror as she neared me.

My arm throbbed like a hot fire poker. Every breath

sent pain rocketing around in my rib cage. I had a wicked case of double vision.

"You screamed. He threw me. I'm bleeding. He was so fast," I rambled. To my embarrassment, my words slurred.

Leigh knelt next to me, gripping my good arm. "Shhh, it's okay—"

"He knew my *name!*"

"It's okay. Sam, he's gone. I killed him. At least, I think I did. I don't see any ash. That's weird."

Leigh's reassurance, coupled with mellow warmth from my inner Warrior, calmed me.

Still cataloging my injuries, Leigh asked, "Can you stand?"

I grimaced. Everything hurt except my teeth. "Not on my own," I admitted.

Leigh slipped her arm around my waist. "On three. One, two, three." Together we rose to our feet. "Have you even looked down at yourself?"

"Not yet." I met her gaze and bit my lip. I was grateful to be alive. I whispered, "Thank you." *For having my back. For getting my weapon. For saving my butt. For being my partner. For putting up with me. For being my best friend.*

She smiled, her only acknowledgement of her heroism tonight. But worry faded that smile. She nodded toward my arm. "You're pretty banged up."

I looked down. Ivory bone flecked with blood poked through the skin of my upper arm. *This is a first*, I thought. My body started trembling and the fingers in my right arm went numb. *And this is real bad.* I swallowed back the bile rising from my roiling stomach.

"I think—I'm gonna be sick."

"Sam, you're in shock. Breathe through your nose. We need to immobilize your arm before riding home."

I focused on the word *immobilize* and broke out in a clammy sweat.

"Sam, this *will* hurt. Please don't hit me. Can you stand on your own while I get a splint?"

"Help me to that tree." When we were beside the oak, I slumped against it. "Go on. I'm not going anywhere."

"I'll be right back," she said, jogging toward a fallen limb. Leigh broke off two sticks and returned. "Ready?"

"Nope." I shook my head. *Bad. Move.*

"This'll only take a minute and then we head home." Leigh pressed one stick to the outer side of my broken arm, making me yelp. She guided my left hand up and said, "Hold this."

Leigh positioned the second stick, wrapped both with her belt, and the splint was done.

"Damn it!" I gasped through clenched teeth and fists.

"Sorry. Had to." She grimaced with me. "Let's get you home. Have Judy work her magic." She looked me up and down. "By the way, you can turn it off."

"What?"

"Your Power. You're still in your holy clothes."

"Oh. Yeah. Thanks." I closed my eyes and realized that letting go of my Heavenly Power was a helluva lot harder when I was in this much pain. The energy went dark and my white uniform morphed back into my khaki pants and polo shirt. When I dropped my connection to the supernatural, a fresh wave of agony crashed over me. *Holy Heaven.* I swayed in Leigh's embrace. She tightened her hold.

Leigh guided me to the edge of the parking lot. The bar was still lively inside, its patrons unaware of what had happened behind it. Divine Intervention kept human eyes from seeing either us or the demons.

Leigh summoned our Guardians and two horses materialized from the foggy darkness. They trotted toward us, their horseshoes crunching on the gravel. The chestnut headed straight for me, his coat a deep copper-red. Leigh's mount was a dark dapple grey. Both horses stopped in front of us.

"Samantha. I felt you break." The chestnut's mental voice was filled with distress. He touched my cheek with his muzzle, his warm breath comforting me. I gasped when his light touch triggered a fresh round of pain.

"Maximus Prime." I leaned against him, letting him hold some of my weight. *"Buddy, I'm so glad you're here. I'm way more than hurt."* I fumbled for one of the straps on Max's neck as a sense of queasiness rolled over me. "Leigh, I d-don't think I should be riding."

Leigh slipped Azira into the pack behind her saddle. "I don't think you should, either. Can you sit in front of me on Thad? Max will tag along."

"Do as your Warrior Partner tells you to," Max said. *"We will not let you fall. Thaddeus is capable."*

"I'll do whatever gets me home and in Judy's healing hands," I said. I took an unsteady step toward Leigh. Max supported me because my legs shook. The edges of my vision started to go black.

"Samantha!" Max stiffened. He resisted raising his head since I clung to his neck, but I felt every one of his muscles tense.

Through tunnel vision I saw Leigh speaking to me though her words didn't register. She reached out her arms.

"What is happening?" Max's apprehension turned to panic.

"Stay with us, Brave One," my inner Warrior pleaded.

My knees buckled and I crumpled into a heap at Max's hooves.

Everything went dark.

2

SAM

T he rhythmic rock of Thad's walk woke me. My eyes fluttered. Leigh's arm supported me as we ambled up a familiar tree-lined, dirt driveway.

Home.

I lifted my head slightly, ignoring the throb of pain radiating from the back of my skull. A moan escaped me before I could stop it. Every step Thad took was pure torture. Breathing took all my attention.

"Hang in there, Sam," Leigh whispered.

"You are awake." Max breathed a sigh of relief. *"Excellent."*

The path gave way to a clearing where a paved circle drive butted up to the Shaw's farmhouse. I winced when Thad stopped. Max bristled at the younger horse's less-than-gentle halt.

"Judy!" Leigh raised her voice. "Sam's hurt real bad. I would've called, but—"

"What the devil happened?" Judy pattered down the porch steps.

Leigh gave a quick recount of our night, but I found it

hard to follow the story. While she spoke, I focused on the short, round woman with curly silver hair. The porch flood lights wreaked havoc on my vision. I closed one eye but kept the other fixed on Judy.

She met my gaze. Her brown eyes studied me with clinical objectivity and she *tsked* her tongue when she saw my arm.

"Don't move her just yet," Judy said, pressing her fingers to my wrist pulse. "You did a number on yourself this time, Sammy."

I tried to say, "Well, it wasn't my fault," but it came out as a jumble of nonsense.

"Save your energy, child." Judy turned from us. "Andrew, my love, please help Leigh get Sam into the house."

I felt a new set of hands on me a moment later, holding me in place as Leigh dismounted. Andrew's hands were safe, comforting, and strong. He wouldn't let me fall. Leigh and Andrew worked together to pull me from Thad's back.

Holy hellfire—every pain receptor lit up like fireworks. I cried out in agony and let loose incoherent cussing.

"You got her?" Andrew asked Leigh. His voice held authority and calm assurance, but it was the Irish lilt in his words that soothed me. I stopped shouting.

"I'm good," Leigh assured Andrew. He settled my weight into her arms.

"I'll work on her on the dining room table," Judy said.

"We're almost there," Leigh said while she climbed the steps. "Judy'll get you something for the pain."

I tried to speak, but Leigh hushed me. Once we were inside, she laid me on Judy's stout dining room table and slipped a chair cushion under my head. She then busied herself clearing the chairs from the room.

Andrew placed a hand on my left shoulder. He wore

blue and white pinstripe pajamas and his white hair flopped in his grey eyes. I met his gaze, alarmed by his frown. Bernard Andrew Shaw shifted from Adviser to the Warriors of Light to concerned grandfather. He leaned down to kiss my temple as he'd done since I was a small child. It didn't matter if I was two or twenty, he always greeted me this way.

Judy hurried in, arms loaded with medical supplies. "Leigh. Be a dear. There's a pile of items I couldn't carry in one go. Fetch them for me."

"Yes, ma'am."

"Someone sent them after me," I said, or rather tried to.

"Saints preserve you, child," Judy cut me off. "Hold your tongue. No one can understand you."

Shivers shook me and Andrew spread a blanket over me while Judy filled a syringe with amber liquid.

Life Elixir! I'd never needed an injection before.

"This'll make you right as rain by morning, my girl," Judy said. She swabbed alcohol inside my good elbow and gave me the shot.

Leigh deposited the items Judy asked for, then stood next to Andrew. Judy lifted another syringe into my line of sight, this one filled with a clear liquid.

"Morphine," Judy said, and swiftly administered that as well. "You'll be out in just a moment." She smiled benignly and smoothed my hair back from my forehead. "I'll fix your arm then. Rest now."

The last thing I remembered was Andrew kissing my forehead.

MORNING LIGHT POURED through my bedroom window, its brightness subdued by white linen curtains. I rubbed my eyes and stretched before rolling over.

"Damn," I groaned at my stiff, protesting muscles. *What time is it? What day is it?* I ran my hands over my face before taking a quick inventory of my body. Clear vision. No headache. No stabbing pain. Zero nausea.

Life Elixir injections were miraculous.

"I need coffee," I muttered, swinging my legs over the side of the bed and reaching for my cell phone on the side table.

It was just past six-thirty on Thursday morning. My normal wake-up time was five. Someone had turned off my alarm. I smoothed a hand down the front of the over-sized green T-shirt I wore. Someone also changed me out of my bloody clothes.

My money was on Leigh for the small comforts. My kind, considerate, dutiful best friend. Thank God she'd only sustained a cut on her cheek last night. Despite her assurances, I shouldn't have run off. I should have stayed and helped her. I shouldn't have provoked the biggest demon of the three. I should have waited for Leigh before engaging him. If she hadn't saved me when she did, I'd probably be in the hands of God-knows-who.

I remembered the black behemoth's snarl, "Samantha Fife, you're wanted by my master."

Who is this Master? I shivered and noticed I was clutching the sheets. *Who has the power to control demons?* And not just any demons, either. Huge, steroidal demons with orders to hunt me down. I swallowed hard and stared up at the ceiling. That black gigantor demon kicked my ass so thoroughly I'd needed an *injection* of Life Elixir. He'd rendered me utterly useless—a first for me.

I shook my head. "Coffee before any more questions, Fife."

I undid the bandage on my right arm, tossed the wad of bloody gauze into the wastebasket, and ran my left hand over smooth skin. It was as if the break had never happened. Not even a small scar remained. I stood and dropped into a loose fighter's stance. I made a practice punch combination.

"Hooboy," I groaned when my tight muscles protested. While I loved being a super-powered, enhanced Warrior who kept humanity safe by fighting whatever Hell threw at us, I hadn't enjoyed last night's assault. Nor could I recall the last time I'd been as terrified.

I rummaged through a pile of clean clothes on top of my dresser for leggings and a fresh shirt. After pulling my hair back into a ponytail, I was ready for coffee, breakfast, and my morning run. I shambled through the farmhouse to the industrial kitchen. The fluorescent light bouncing off stainless steel appliances made me squint. To my delight, the coffee pot held a fresh brew.

As usual, my favorite mug sat next to the pot. *God bless Judy.* I poured the second-best elixir of life into my cup and replaced the carafe. Cradling up my mug with both hands, I turned and rested my hips against the counter. Breathing in the rich aroma, I sipped and wondered where everyone else was.

"Morning, sunshine." Leigh smirked, a knowing glint in her hazel eyes. She sat by herself at the breakfast bar with a plate of eggs, bacon, and an English muffin with a newspaper in front of her. Leigh's wet brunette hair was twisted up into a claw clip. "You look worlds better than the last time I saw you. Judy does good work."

"Judy and Life Elixir." I shuffled over and perched on the bar stool next to her. Caffeine arrived at my brain. A hot shower was tempting but I wanted to stick with our routine. That meant a small breakfast and a run before I could enjoy that hot water.

"How do you feel?" Leigh looked back down at her paper, splayed open to the Local News section. There would be no mention of what happened last night. Divine Intervention, and all.

"I feel like I took on a demon three times my size and, thanks to you, lived to tell the tale." I snagged her English muffin. "How did you manage to survive your two?"

"Rose guided me through."

Rose. My brow furrowed. *Who was Rose again?*

As if hearing my question, Leigh rolled her eyes. "I've told you about her. She's my——" Leigh's lips pursed and she tapped her fingers on the counter. "Rose is to me as your 'inner Warrior' is to you."

Oh, *that* Rose. I'd asked mine once before, but I was horrible with names. My conscience jabbed me. I'd never bothered to get to know her the way Leigh had done with Rosewyn. Maybe I wouldn't have gotten my ass kicked so badly last night if I had. Maybe I needed to get a little cozier with mine.

"What was your name again?"

"Leticia, Brave One." I swore I felt her give me a slow smile.

I nibbled on my English muffin, mulling over her name. Leticia. *"Can I call you Letty?"*

"If that's what you'd like." She seemed amused. *"Calling me Warrior Sam for the past two years worked just as well."*

"Are you teasing me?"

"Never."

"Helloooo, Earth to Sam!" Leigh snapped her fingers in front of my face. "You with me?"

"Absolutely." I blinked and hid my embarrassment behind a sip of coffee. "You were saying?"

"I said, when I found you last night, it looked like you and that demon were having a conversation, which was odd. What did he say?"

"Funny you say that." I ran a fingertip along the rim of my mug. "Where's Andrew? He needs to hear this, too. I only wanna tell this story once. It's a doozy."

"I haven't seen him this morning. Judy's running errands." Leigh tilted her head. "Hear *what* exactly?"

At that moment Andrew strode into the kitchen and put on the kettle. He set his briefcase on the counter.

"Leigh already gave me her account of what happened last night while we tended the horses. Please tell me yours," Andrew said.

"The demons, sir, they were strong, fast, and better trained. Huge, too," I said.

"The one that attacked Sam was toying with her," Leigh said. "He could have killed her, but that didn't seem to be his intent."

"That's because he had instructions to capture me alive and take me to his master," I said.

Andrew's eyes widened and his jaw tightened. The kettle started screaming. He swore in Gaelic and whirled to turn off the stove. He muttered to himself in the Old Language. He stood with his back to us, palms pressed to the granite countertop, his shoulders tense. He took measured breaths.

"What precisely did this demon say to you?" Andrew faced us, abandoning his tea making. "Did he give you his name?"

His name? Andrew had never asked for this kind of information before. "No," I said, "he failed to mention that. All he said was that I was a wanted woman. Didn't mind roughing me up a bit in the process."

"A bit?" Leigh squeaked.

I shrugged, not about to admit I'd been thrown around like a rag doll, and met Andrew's gaze. I'd known the man since I was in diapers. He'd been there for every major milestone in my twenty years. Hell, he'd even gifted Max to me. The nervous tick in his cheek was his only tell. Andrew was stressed.

"What are you not saying?" I asked.

"I'm hesitant to tell you at present," Andrew said. "It will be hard for you to understand."

He turned and pulled a travel mug from an upper cabinet. He popped in a tea bag and poured boiling water into the cup.

The suspense was killing me, but I knew better than to try and assert myself with Andrew. Peppering him with questions, despite my overwhelming curiosity, wouldn't get me answers any quicker. I hoped he felt my laserbeam gaze boring a hole in his back while I broke off bits of English muffin and shoved them into my mouth.

He took his time fixing his tea. Three hundred years later he finally joined us at the breakfast bar.

"Andrew, please tell us what's going on," I pleaded, glancing at Leigh. She'd folded up her newspaper, her fingers resting on top of it, and studied him.

"How is she so calm?" I asked Letty.

"This Master wants you, *not her. Perhaps you're more scared than you want to admit?"* she asked.

My nostrils flared. *"Maybe."*

"Do you trust me?" Andrew's eyes were on me.

"What kinda question is that?" I dropped the remains of the muffin. "I trust you with my life."

"Then trust me when I say you will have all the answers to your questions soon."

For the love of all things cryptic. I smiled and gestured for him to continue.

With my unspoken promise of good behavior, Andrew said, "I'm leaving this morning. Call it a business trip."

"What?" I gasped. "Why? Where are you going—"

Andrew held up a stern hand, his grey eyes hard. He was Adviser Shaw right now.

I bit my lip to keep from interrupting him. Leigh sat up straight and clenched her teeth.

"Samantha." Andrew sighed, his shoulders sagging. His eyes softened, and a haunted look passed through them. He looked *ancient.* "Because of what Leigh reported last night and you confirmed this morning, I'm leaving immediately. Every minute I spend here puts us all in grave danger."

I chugged some coffee to ease my dry mouth.

"Breathe deep, my Brave One," Letty said. *"Hyperventilating won't help the situation. You trust him. Let your Adviser do his job."*

I closed my eyes, inhaled deeply, and took another sip of coffee. My inner Warrior was right, so I swallowed my frustration, along with the bitter brew, and waited.

"I'll only be gone a couple of days. Keep to your routine. Train in the morning. Go to work during the day. Hunt for demon infestations at night. Stay sharp."

"What happens if we run into more of the same kind from last night?" Leigh asked.

"Keep Sam close. You go where she goes. Stay with her like a shadow." Andrew picked up his mug and briefcase. "Don't fight alone."

"Yes, sir." Leigh smoothed out her newspaper. "You promise you'll tell us what's going on when you get back?"

"I swear it," he said before hustling out of the kitchen.

I watched him go, struggling to keep my mouth shut, resolved to do as my inner Warrior suggested and trust him. It was prudent to keep my thoughts to myself, but I couldn't squash the little seed of anger in my confusion.

Who the hell wants me? Someone bad, someone strong, and someone who I knew nothing about. Why wasn't Leigh on this guy's radar, too?

Demons preyed on human chaos, coaxing them into crime, debauchery, and sin. From fear and guilt to anger and bitterness, demons fed off the pandemonium they incited. All that stood between Hell and humanity were Leigh and me.

If this Master wanted me, I wouldn't go without a fight. The demons would *not* take me alive. And I'd kill many as I could on my way out.

3

SAM

Searching for my favorite pair of running shorts, I jerked open a dresser drawer. In my agitation, I pulled it all the way out and dumped the contents on the floor.

"Get yourself together, Fife," I muttered and pressed the heel of one hand to my forehead and held the empty drawer in the other.

While I could have used any of the umpteen pairs of workout pants I owned—hell, three pairs were right by my feet—I wanted my black ones. I shoved the drawer back where it belonged and flung the clothes into it.

I rooted through the rest of my room and found my beloved shorts, wrinkled and buried, at the bottom of my closet. I also put on a hot pink dri-weave running shirt, ankle socks, and my neon purple running shoes with lime green laces. I still felt disgusting. I longed for a shower but it would have to wait. Resigning myself that clean teeth would have to suffice, I grabbed my cell phone, closed my door, and headed for the bathroom.

I looked into the mirror and fumbled for my hairbrush. Stormy blue eyes stared back at me. *Good God.* I had dark purple smudges under my eyes and my pathetic blonde ponytail listed to one side. I pulled the elastic band from my fine hair, raked a brush through it, and tied into a high top-knot on my head. I scrubbed my teeth, wiped my face, and was done.

Walking past the door on my right, I saw it was slightly open. That room had been vacant since Harper left. The door stayed closed except during Judy's monthly dusting spree.

A lump formed in my throat. I paused to listen, really *listen*, tapping into my Warrior power.

The farmhouse made the comforting groans and creaks of an older home, and the kitchen faucet dripped. But nothing came from the room beside me. I closed off my Power and tapped the door further open.

The crisply-made bedspread was wrinkled where a black duffle bag sat on it. There were fresh footprints marring the vacuum tracks on the carpet. I swallowed hard. Nothing else in the room had changed. Everything was neat, straight, and sparse. No pictures hung on the blue walls.

Harper's here?

"Sam, are you ready?" Leigh called from down the hall. I froze. "I'll meet you outside," she said.

Damn! I closed the door, leaving it cracked as I'd found it, and leaned against the adjoining wall. I took slow breaths with my eyes squeezed shut. *Why didn't Andrew warn me?* My heart thudded. *Why is Harper here?* I rubbed my clammy palms on my thighs.

"Sam!" Leigh yelled from the back door. "What the heck are you doing? Come on!"

I willed my feet to move and met her on the elevated veranda of the back porch. The farmhouse sat on twenty acres of Florida land wild with southern live oaks, bald cypresses, and sable palms. Cicadas screeched and birds chirped, filling the air with their morning songs.

"Sorry, I—" A fifty-pound blur of brindle and white slammed into my knees. "Bear!" I squatted, enveloping the squirming pit bull, who was desperate to lick my face, into a firm hug. "Hey, kid," I murmured, scratching behind his jaw. He grinned, ears flat and tongue lolling.

"You're the only one he greets that way," Leigh said, giving him some love. He licked her hand. And her wrist. And her thigh for good measure.

"I did save him from a couple demons and a terrifying feline. He knows who's got his back." When I'd brought Bear home that night, he'd been a mangy skeleton with skin. I thought I'd have to bargain to keep him, but one look at the pathetic dog and Andrew caved. "Are you running with us today?" His tail thumped the deck.

"Hey." Leigh grabbed my sleeve after we'd stretched. "How are you?"

"Fine," I said.

Leigh made a skeptical noise in the back of her throat. "Sure you are. You're a mess. I see it in your eyes. You've got that *look*."

I sighed. "Can we talk about this later? I need this run."

"No, tell me now." Leigh crossed her arms. "Are you mad at Andrew because he wouldn't give us any answers?"

I pursed my lips and shook my head. "No. I can't be mad at him. I'm a little irked he's leaving. Where's he going that's so important?"

Leigh tilted her head. "Don't deflect. Is it about getting beat up?"

My eyes narrowed.

She tapped her chin. "Hmm, I'm getting warmer. The Master, then?"

I hissed through my teeth.

"Ha!" Leigh laughed without humor. "I'm right. Spill it, sister. *Then* we can run."

"Fine." I checked my laces. "Why me? What's special about me? I'm no one."

"You're a Warrior of Light. That makes you pretty darn special," Leigh said.

"So are you." I punched her lightly on the shoulder. "But this Master isn't after you. Even though you killed three demons. You did all the heroics last night. I just got myself broken." I checked the treads of my sneakers for stones.

"You don't know this, but once that black demon got you alone, the others stopped trying so hard. It was easy to take 'em out. Andrew thinks it was a trap to isolate you."

"It felt like that to me, too." Rehashing how I felt wasn't improving my jitters. I wasn't accustomed to fear and helplessness, and now Harper was lurking around the farm somewhere. Bear whined and pressed himself to my leg. I gave him a reassuring scratch on the top of his head. "You know what? I don't want to deal with this right now. Are we gonna run?"

"Sam," Leigh chided, her hazel eyes kind. "I know you're scared. This whole thing has you spooked. I get it, but you're not alone. You got me."

For a brief moment, my guard dropped. My eyes burned with unshed tears and I sniffed before snatching Leigh into a tight hug. I let her go just as quickly then bolted from the deck, leaping over the five stairs. Bear bounded after me as I sprinted away.

"This conversation isn't over, Fife!" Leigh shouted as she trotted down the steps.

"Yes, it is!" I yelled over my shoulder.

Leigh caught up with me within seconds and, as usual,

she set the pace, and I picked the route. The tree canopy provided dappled shade from the brutal Florida morning sun. Our feet kicked up dust from the worn path.

Bear zoomed past us, pouncing after anything that jumped, be it a sand toad, grasshopper, or one of the billion lizards that called our tropical climate home. He never caught one.

I focused on breathing and form, and my worries faded. The exertion, the tension, the power—they freed me. I could just be.

Our run covered five miles in thirty minutes and ended at the gym built in the center of the property. I thought about blowing past the building, extending our run, but that only delayed the inevitable. I couldn't run from my problems forever. Following Leigh's lead, we slowed to a walk when the gym came into view.

"Did that help?" Leigh asked, bumping my shoulder with her own.

"I'm a new woman. That's what I needed." Some days her five-foot-ten frame and long, dancer legs chewed up the miles. While I was fast, it took effort to keep up with her on those days. Today she set a punishing pace.

She smiled. "Busted."

"But maybe a small bit appreciated." I held up my thumb and index finger an inch apart. "Did you see anyone in the house this morning?"

"Beside you, Judy, and Andrew? No. Why?" Leigh asked, arching an elegant brow.

I scrunched up my nose. "No reason. The light was on in the Harper's room."

"Andrew probably went in there when he was packing. He stores some stuff in that closet. Might've forgotten to turn off the light," Leigh said.

"Maybe," I said, opening the metal door for Leigh to

enter before me. *I doubt that.* Not much got past Andrew and the man hadn't owned a duffle bag in my entire life.

Once we were inside the gym, I stopped and breathed in the smell of sweat, pine, and blade oil. To my left, a wall of mirrors stretched the length of the building. On the opposite wall, ordinary weapons ranging from swords and battle axes to daggers and maces hung with precision. We practiced with all these non-Warrior weapons as part of our training.

At the far end of the gym stood archery mounts waiting with clean targets. *Did Andrew have time to set these before he left?* I smiled at the gesture. It was my job to prep my own targets.

I loved this gym. I loved running. I loved the morning. I loved our routine. I even loved the barn chores that would come after our training. This was home and we were safe on protected ground. For the first time since I woke up, the tension in my body relaxed.

Nothing could hurt me or blindside me here.

"You are twelve kinds of distracted today," Leigh said. "You sure you're okay?"

"Yeah. Fine," I muttered, passing by Andrew's modest gym office. The door was closed. He never closed that door. I stood there, body in the direction of the lockers, head turned to stare at the one-way office window; all I saw was a mirror, but whoever the occupant was could see me.

No way it's him. I stepped up to try the knob.

"Sam!" Leigh called over her shoulder. "We don't have all day."

"Right!" I jogged the rest of the way to the lockers.

After we'd changed out of running shoes, we gathered in the center of the gym where a white duct tape sparring circle had been laid out. I nestled earbuds into my ears, scrolled to my personalized Warrior training playlist, and thumbed the shuffle button. Running with music was distracting, but I did require tunes when shooting. My music tastes were eclectic and I enjoyed not knowing what would play next.

As I leaned forward, stretching out my hamstrings, one of my favorite Bryan Adams songs hit its climax. I stood upright, threw my arms out to my sides in airplane arms, and sang along with all my worth.

Leigh gave me a closed-mouth smile as she eased into another stretch.

"Sing with me!" I grabbed one of her shoulders.

She shook her head, laughing, but I kept singing, not letting her go. She rolled her eyes, still smiling, and joined in. The song was almost over when Leigh stiffened, and all traces of good humor washed away. Her eyes were focused over my shoulder, toward the gym office. Her brows furrowed, her lips mashed into a line, and she tilted her head.

I inhaled and the spicy scent of sandalwood and cloves hit me.

No, no, no, no, no. I prayed no in every language I knew, which wasn't many, that the person behind me wasn't Harper. But I knew better. Even after six years, there was no mistaking his scent. Miranda Lambert started crooning that she was better off without a heart. I ripped the earbuds from my ears.

"Samantha," he said.

His voice was just as I'd remembered it—a rich baritone, controlled, with a hint of wild. I whirled and dropped into a fighter's stance. My chest heaved and my panic mounted as I glared into the deepest blue eyes I'd ever known. They were dark as sapphires and just as hard. His eyes were slightly bloodshot, as though he were exhausted.

He was a wall of muscle, like a rugby player. His broad shoulders strained his light blue T-shirt. There was nothing soft about him. Even his brown hair was cropped short and sharp.

A red haze glazed my vision. I *never* expected to see him again. Nor did I want to. My heart sputtered painfully. "This isn't happening," I whispered.

I blinked, hoping when I opened my eyes that Harper had been an apparition. Only he still stood there. A frown tugged his lips, but I chose to focus on his nose. It had a bump where it had been broken and reset in a hurry.

"What the hell are you doing here?" I snarled, finding my courage.

"It's nice to see you, too," he said, crossing his arms over his muscular chest.

"Let me rephrase the question." *Breathe, Fife, breathe.* "What the *fuck* are you doing here?"

"Holy crap! Sam!" Leigh gasped. "What the heck?"

I tried not to swear around her, and I never dropped the f-bomb, but seeing Harper had short-circuited my good graces.

Leigh recovered, stepped around me, and offered her hand. "Leigh Kestler."

"I know who you are," he said, not taking her up on a common, perfectly civil greeting.

"Asshole," I muttered.

Leigh let her arm drop, quirked an eyebrow, and snorted at me. She shook her head then turned back to Harper.

"You have my name," she said, "but I don't have yours. That puts me at an uncomfortable disadvantage."

"His name is Harper Garrett Tate," I snapped, not taking my eyes off our visitor. "He's a pompous, cold-hearted *traitor*. And you should remember him."

"But obviously, I don't."

"Answer me, you bastard!" I stabbed a finger at him. "Why are you here?"

Harper had shattered my fourteen-year-old heart. He left without warning or reason, and never looked back, not even sparing a glance in his rearview mirror. I was fracturing all over again.

He arched a dark brow. I wanted to punch his nose and re-break it. Eight million times.

"Easy now," Leigh murmured. She threw out an arm to keep me from advancing toward him. "Stand down," she said in the same low tone.

I debated smacking her limb out of my way, but she was only trying to diffuse the situation. Damn her. Damn Andrew. And damn me. Relenting, I stepped back, baring my teeth like a feral animal.

"I'm sorry, Harper," Leigh said. "Would you please explain what's going on?"

Is he smirking or snarling? I couldn't read him at all. *What is he thinking?*

He looked away from me, meeting Leigh's eyes. "Pops called last night. Said he needed me to come home."

"Oh," Leigh breathed, comprehension dawning. "You're *Harper*-Harper. I didn't recognize you after all this time. My apologies."

I could see why she didn't remember him. Leigh hadn't spent her summers with the Shaws, or her after-school hours at the farmhouse. Her family hadn't gone on Fife-Shaw vacations to the Appalachian Mountains. It wasn't her heart that he'd ripped out.

In Leigh's defense, there was a different air about him from when he'd abandoned me. His posture, his demeanor, had changed. He was comfortable in his skin, standing there like he was the most dangerous person in the room.

Long gone was the jovial boy who'd taught me how to ride a bike, catch a fish, and change a tire. Before me stood a darker man who knew exactly who he was.

"I warned Pops this was a bad idea." Harper shook his head. "That's just like him that he didn't say anything to you. Why would he make anything simple?"

I wouldn't be talking to Harper. I didn't trust myself. Anything I said wouldn't help the situation. I stepped back, putting Leigh closer to Harper. She nodded.

Clearing her throat, she said, "So Andrew asked you to come back and—"

"Oversee your wellbeing and Warrior training while he's away."

There was one problem with that request. Harper Tate wasn't a Warrior. He may have been adopted by Andrew and Judy. He may have been trained in every Warrior skill possible, but the man was *not* a Warrior of Light. He wasn't an Adviser. He was simply human. Nothing special. And *I* certainly didn't need him.

"You can leave." I notched up my chin, planting my fists on my hips.

"Afraid I can't."

"Lord, help me," Leigh breathed. She pinched the bridge of her nose.

"Samantha, whether you like it or not, Pops felt the need to place us in this situation without your permission. While I don't want to be here, I cannot leave. I gave him my word that I would remain until his return. I won't fail him."

Heat flared up the back of my neck and my cheeks burned. "I hate you."

Anger or hurt—or both—sparked in his eyes. A muscle in his jaw jumped. "I know. But leave it outside the gym."

"So I can punch you at dinner?"

"Such a temper," he said. "Why has Pops allowed you to be this emotional? His soft spot for you is unfortunate."

"I don't see how it's any of your business to know what Andrew does and does not let me do."

"Brave One, calm down," Letty said. *"Andrew put him in charge and you cannot challenge that. Harper is qualified."*

"Qualified my ass," I huffed.

Harper rubbed his eyes, then ran his palm over his mouth. "Hate me all you want. That's your business. But in this gym, you will rein in your temper. Someone could get injured."

"What's gotten into you?" Leigh asked me under her breath.

"Later," I hissed through clenched teeth.

The day had taken a sudden downward turn, and it had started so well. I'd rather go round two with the demons from last night than be in the same room as Harper. Demons, I understood. Every fiber of my being snapped with electricity, and I instinctively reached for my Power.

"No," Letty commanded. The surge of heat I'd normally feel when tapping into my inner Warrior never came. *"There is no real threat here. No demons. Think."*

All the words I wanted to say came out of my mouth in one unintelligible sound that was more snarl than speech.

Leigh gave Harper an apologetic smile. "I'm sorry."

"Stop apologizing," Harper said. "You aren't the one acting like a child."

"We kinda had a rough night." Leigh offered a conciliatory shrug. "The gym is probably exactly how you remember it, but do you want me to show you around?"

Why is she sucking up to him? "He knows where everything is," I snipped. "And he can show himself right out the door."

"Ignore her," Leigh said. "Just give her some time."

"I'm fine," Harper said. "And she's not wrong about the gym. I'm well acquainted with the place."

"No!" I shouted. They both looked at me like I'd lost my marbles. Maybe I had? I was losin' it. Definitely irrational. Seeing Harper, smelling Harper, and hearing Harper was like ripping a scab off a festering wound. He'd been my hero. And the kicker was that he had every right to be here, possibly more so than I. It had been his childhood home after all.

"I'm going to shoot," I said. "We need to be at work by ten, so let's not dick around." *Kiss my ass, Tate.*

Approaching the wall of targets, I realized Andrew hadn't set them up for me. When had he had time? Harper did it. I thought about ripping them down, but that would have been a waste of perfectly good targets. Selecting a plain longbow, I grabbed a quiver of arrows and crammed my earbuds back into my ears. Kelly Clarkson was belting out how some dude had done her wrong and she'd never again fall for his bullshit.

"How appropriate," I muttered, strapping on a wrist guard. Azira never snapped back, but a normal bow's recoil stung like fire.

I squared myself into my archer's stance and reached for that Warrior place in my mind, the one where instinct took over. Letty released her choke hold on my connection to my Power and it seeped warm into my veins. She didn't speak or offer any words, and instead, gave me a solid mental foundation to stand on.

Without giving Harper one more of my precious thoughts, I proceeded to unleash a rapid fire of arrows. Smooth. Swift. No hesitancy. *This* was why we trained every day; to hone the Warrior on the inside. My arrows slammed home into the bright red bull's eye, my grouping impeccable.

I was flustered, fragile, battered, wounded, and miserable. Letty, however, was focused, calm, and disciplined. She'd always be a bigger badass than me.

4

HARPER

I watched Samantha plant a perfect group of arrows in the red in less than three minutes then growled in frustration.

"Harper, I'm sorry——" Kestler said.

"Don't"—I cut her off—"fucking apologize for Samantha."

"She prefers Sam," Kestler said, as if clarifying her best friend's name was habitual. "And I'd prefer that you not speak to me that way, I'm not the one you're mad at."

I glared at her. Kestler took a small step backward, but it was more to improve her stance than to retreat the way most people did when I glowered at them. Then again, Kestler wasn't the average human.

I sighed and stared at the skylights. *Breathe in, breathe out.* Samantha had a talent for pissing people off, though I knew she had a good reason to be angry. I'd known that this reunion wouldn't go smoothly. Pops's silence hadn't done either of us any favors.

"You've got to let *Samantha* take responsibility for her own actions. She has to grow up some time." I studied the tall woman before me. "Do you always cover for her impetuousness?"

Kestler furrowed her brows. "I don't cover for her."

"You do."

Her perfect posture put her at eye level with me. She crossed her arms, a mulish gleam in her eye. I turned my back on her, focusing on Samantha instead, and heard a low grumble from the Warrior behind me.

Pops knew my presence would be like gasoline on Samantha's fire. I'd hoped she'd have outgrown her earlier feelings. My parting words had been cruel, but I'd intended them to hurt, to make it easy for her to hate me. I'd had to get away from here, and it had nothing to do with her. I only wanted her to forget me.

"Grab a sword, Kestler," I said, not looking at her.

Samantha was no longer a scrawny tomboy with perennial dirt smudges on her face; she'd been replaced by a beautiful, lethal Warrior. What hadn't changed was that her stormy eyes still crackled with lightning when she had strong emotions—and they were a raging squall right now.

I'd have to figure out a way to get her to trust me. I sighed and glanced back at Kestler.

She hadn't moved. Instead, she'd crossed her arms and notched up her chin. "What did you mean when you said I cover for Sam?"

Didn't I ask you to go get a sword? The disobedience needled me more than I'd expected. I met Kestler's pointed gaze and sucked my teeth. *Try not to be a complete asshole, Tate.*

"Do you find yourself explaining away Samantha's behavior when she does stupid shit? Do you chalk it up to Sam just being Sam?"

Kestler shifted her shoulders as if I made her uncomfortable.

"The answer is yes, by the way." I didn't have time for Kestler to not own up to her shortcomings. "You enable her."

"I do not!" she shouted in an immediate protest. Her lips puckered as she collected her thoughts. "Did Adviser Shaw tell you what happened last night? Sam could have *died*."

"Ma's got a special cocktail for that kind of thing, no?" I winked to provoke her.

Her chest puffed righteous indignation. "Judy had to knock her out to fix her arm before the Life Elixir could heal it over incorrectly." Kestler boldly stepped in my direction. "And then we find you here. She's obviously not over what happened. You didn't have to needle her like that. Maybe cut her some slack instead?"

"Enough!" Irritation rippled down my neck. "You're *still* fucking enabling her. It'll bite you in the ass one day, Kestler."

"She's my best friend." Kestler's shoulders sagged, hand pressed to her heart. "How can I not defend her?"

"Emotions cloud judgment," I said out of rote. Pops hammered the phrase into me as I grew up. He'd been relentless in my training from an early age. "I told you to select a sword. Do not ignore me again."

I strode over to a walnut sword rack, grasped the third hilt from the right, and withdrew the weapon from the stand. It was a simple broadsword with a hefty pommel. The grip fit my hand as if it were made for me. *Hello, old friend.*

"Sure, she could do well with a bit more discipline," Kestler said with a half smile. "But Sam's always worked better with a loose interpretation of a plan. Everyone's different, right?"

"Are you deaf?" I asked quietly. "Select a goddamn

sword, Kestler." I pointed the tip of my blade to the middle of the gym. "And meet me in the sparring circle."

It had been a long drive from Savannah, Georgia to Riverview, Florida—one that allowed me to dwell on my past too much. Lack of sleep, dealing with Pops, and Samantha's reception had shot my remaining patience to hell. Kestler's obstinance—however unintentional—was the last straw.

Her hazel eyes narrowed at my order, but she went to the rack without further argument. "What are we doing?"

"Just meet me in the center." I stalked off.

As I waited for Kestler, my attention wandered once more to Samantha. She jerked arrows from one of the targets I'd set for her. When she turned, her eyes met mine.

Shit.

Samantha flashed me a malicious grin, flipped up her middle finger, and spun on her toe to continue with her target practice. I snarled silently.

Yeah, fuck you too, Sam. I paced around the taped area, anger simmering. "Kestler, how long does it take to pick a fucking sword?"

Kestler glared at me and snatched a slim katana from the rack without looking. An anticipatory grin grew as she stalked over. I struck at once when she was within range and lunged forward. Kestler twisted to the side. My blade missed her, a whisper away from her torso.

I attacked with an overhand strike, bringing the sword toward the top of her shoulder. As my sword came down, she brought hers up, and the ring of clashing steel filled the gym. The sound of metal-on-metal centered me and I slid into the relaxed focus Pops had honed in me for years. In this clarity, I could study the Warrior before me.

Kestler flicked her wrist in a circle, trying to disarm me. While she was fast, I read her quickly. It was a basic move

Pops drilled into me ad nauseam and I wasn't surprised she chose to use it. I flung my sword hand up, ducked low, and kicked her feet out from under her. In 'Pops's rules of sparring, this move was dirty. Her back slammed on the mat. I plunged my blade downward, stopping inches from her heart.

Kestler's face went white, the tendons in her neck flexed, and she parried a second too late. Her eyes filled with indignation and her cheeks flushed red.

"What the heck was that?" She smacked the flat of my sword aside, rolled out of the way, and sprung to her feet. "How 'bout you not take your crap out on me?"

"I'm perfectly calm." I returned to my side of the circle. "Ready?"

Kestler's kenjutsu stance was perfect. I advanced, attacking from the top a second time. She blocked me, so I reversed the direction and swung underhand, which she also countered. She danced and parried my strikes, but she never took the offensive. Her footwork was light and precise, each stroke efficient. Her breath came easily, and I suspected she could do this all day.

Why won't she attack? What is Pops teaching these girls? Was he soft on them because they were women? That made no sense to me because my surrogate father didn't discriminate when it came to gender. Perhaps Pops still considered them children, even though he had started my training at a much younger age. Had he stopped getting into the ring to personally train them? Was he too old now?

After several minutes of fighting, while I mulled over the curiosity of Andrew Shaw, Kestler seized her moment as I moved past. She spun and tapped the tip of her katana between my shoulder blades. *Fuck. She's good.* I froze and dropped my sword point down and out. Surrender.

I turned to face Kestler and saluted her with my sword,

the only acknowledgement that she'd bested me, before I engaged her once more. She moved with liquid precision, following the flow of battle and deflecting my blade with lithe grace.

"The fuck, Kestler?" I barked, as the flat of my sword struck her right hip. "When you strike from that angle, you leave yourself open. It's like you want a demon to kill you. Does Pops train you to ever strike first?"

"Yes," she snapped, swatting brunette strands of sweaty hair from her face. "And he has me practice those techniques on him. He still gets in the ring with me." She would defend the man, just like she defended Samantha. *Loyal to a fault.* I was aware of how hypocritical I was in this. When Pops said jump, I still did, even when I hadn't spoken to the man in years.

"Prove it," I said, getting back into position.

She struck fast with her katana, unleashing a ferocity she'd not been using before. It was quick. It was grace. And in a real fight, it would be lethal. All I could do was block each slash, dodge her advances, and skip away.

And then Kestler was in my space. I was trapped. My next-move options left me vulnerable. Before I could run through my possibilities, she rammed the butt of her sword onto my left hand. My broadsword clattered to the ground. My breath hissed in and I snatched my fingers into a fist.

"Are they broken?" Concern filled her hazel eyes.

She was holding back. She's damn good. "No," I mumbled, shaking out my hand.

Kestler's hair was wild from the fight, her T-shirt damp with sweat. But she was barely winded. "Sorry, I didn't mean to hurt you."

"Never apologize when you've done your job well," I said.

"Thank you. Sam and I have to be at work soon."

"Right. Jot down your schedule." I picked up my sword. "We'll meet back here tomorrow."

After returning my blade to the rack, I leaned a shoulder against the wall, crossed my arms, and watched Samantha shoot. Somewhere in the hurricane of emotions and undisciplined behavior, she'd found a quiet place inside for focus and precision. Even now as she timed the release of an arrow with her breath, it was controlled.

In the past six years she'd gained about three inches in height and put on substantial muscle. Her balance was effortless, and the significant weight of that bow didn't faze her. She was stout like a gymnast, her power in her shoulders and legs. The speed of her nock, aim, and release cycle impressed me. This was part of her symbiosis with her inner Warrior.

Why did Pops train her as an archer? Samantha was built for close-quarters combat which would use all the power in her body. It was a shame that Pops only had two Warrior weapons to offer them.

Samantha pulled her last group of arrows from the tattered target, unstrung her bow, and racked her weapons. When she met my eyes again, there was a flare in her nostrils. *Ah, still pissed. How can I convince her to work with me?* She hurried into the locker room and I went to the office.

I sat in a beat-up leather desk chair and opened Samantha's folder to the ten-page report Pops had left for me. *Kestler wasn't kidding.* Samantha had sustained three fractured ribs, a deep laceration to the skull, a grade 2 concussion, a compound fracture of the humerus, and grade 3 contusions.

"Jesus," I muttered, leaning back, the chair squeaking as I did. The paramedic in me wanted to know how the hell she was up and functioning this morning. The part of me that Pops trained for the Warriors of Light knew

Samantha was a full-fledged Warrior, which altered her DNA. She was much more durable than the damaged humans I treated as a first responder.

I flipped through the photos of Samantha's injuries. I didn't flinch until I got to the compound fracture of her arm. The gruesome torn muscle and splintered bone gave my seasoned paramedic's stomach a bad turn. *Damn.* I rubbed a palm over my mouth and turned to the next page.

Two words, right at the top, stopped me cold. I gripped the folder tighter, bending the stiff cover. *Greater Demons.* Pops hadn't mentioned Greater Demons during our phone call. I snapped the report closed and slammed the folder down on the desk—pens in a ceramic cup rattled, and the computer monitor blinked to life. I took several deep breaths, waiting for the adrenaline buzz in my limbs to fade.

"Son of a bitch!"

I flinched at the memory of my father's desperate pleas as they turned into tortured screams—a Warrior who never screamed. His scream was suddenly silenced and I heard a shrill, icy voice filled with rage and promised violence. I didn't see the Greater Demons who killed my parents, but I heard everything hiding in that closet. Pops found me still huddled in the pantry. He gathered me into his arms, trying to shield my eyes from the carnage, but I saw what had been done to my mother—her blood pooled on the white tile of our kitchen.

Even now, safe in Pops's office all these years later, I struggled to breathe. My skin flashed hot then cold. My head spun. I clamped my arms across my chest and hunched forward.

Pull yourself together, man. What can you see? Anything. List them. I lifted my head. Across the office was a filing cabinet with a small potted fern on top. Pictures hung on the wall above it. A fist-sized stain marred the carpet. The office door was ajar.

Nausea bubbled in my stomach.

Focus. What can you touch? I forced my palms onto the desk. Samantha's file lay in front of me. The computer mouse fit in my right hand, and I clutched a pen in my left. Still, my heart raced. *What can you hear?* The dull thump of old water pipes in the wall, the tick of the clock, the quiet hum of overhead fluorescent lights. *Smell?* I let out a pent-up breath and then inhaled the scent of sweat and floor polish from the gym.

Fuck me. It had been years since I'd had such a vivid flashback. Calmer now, I reopened the file and continued reading, dismissing the residual trembling in my hands.

According to what Pops had written, neither Samantha nor Kestler knew about this classification of demon. He'd only told them about Lesser Demons. *Why the hell hadn't Pops told them about Greater Demons? Why withhold that kind of information?* Sheltering them was one thing, but keeping them in the dark about a vicious enemy was almost grievous. They had no clue.

If Greater Demons were gathering, there had to be someone controlling them, which was more terrifying than the beasts themselves. A greater evil than these demons existed. One with the ability to bind the strongest class of demon to their will.

This was why Pops needed me. This *was why he hadn't told me why he was going to Ecuador.* How typical of the man to not give the full picture. If Greater Demons were at large again, some serious shit was going to happen, the only question was when. Pops had no choice but to leave. He had to gather the survivors from the last great massacre. I *now* understood the weight of my adoptive father's urgency.

I heard conversation and saw Samantha and Kestler walking past the one-way office mirror on their way out of the gym. They had transformed from deadly Warriors to young women headed to work. Goofing around, Kestler shoved Samantha's shoulder, their laughter filtering through the cracked door.

Just how much did they know about the Warriors of Light? What did Pops tell them? Given their ignorance of Greater Demons, the girls surely didn't know the history of their predecessors. They had no idea this was an emergency and fucking Bernard Andrew Shaw hadn't told them the whole story of who they were.

Anger prickled along my neck and I snapped the report closed. It wasn't my place to say anything. My orders were to manage their training and monitor events. But these Warriors deserved to know what they were facing.

"Gimme a sec," Samantha said to Kestler, "I'll be quick!"

As the door eased open, I slipped her file under a couple magazines and leaned back in the chair.

"Oh!" she gasped. "You're still here."

I raised a brow and nodded once. "Did you need something?"

"I came in here for a—" she mashed her lips together and hurried past the desk to a mini fridge sitting behind me. She crouched and snatched a bottle of iced coffee from the top shelf. She slammed the fridge shut, rattling the microwave on top.

Samantha faced me, coffee in one hand, the other clenched at her side. "To be clear, Tate, I don't want you here."

"I know."

"I can take care of myself."

"Perhaps." I had protected her from bullies, human and demon alike, when we were children, back when I could see the supernatural and she couldn't. I'd do the same now, even though she was a Warrior and I was not.

"I don't need you."

"Pops begs to differ." I wasn't trying to pick a fight.

She glared at me. "He's delusional!"

"Do you really think that?" I asked, keeping my tone level.

"No!" she snipped and took a step back. "I don't want to even breathe the same air as you."

"But here we are." I didn't want to goad her. I remembered what I'd just read and bit my tongue.

"I still hate you," she whispered.

"So you've told me." I gripped the arms of my chair until my knuckles turned white. *Don't let her get to you again.*

Samantha stomped from the office, slamming the door harder than she'd closed the fridge. A framed picture fell from the wall.

I scrubbed a hand over my short hair and stood up. I picked up the photo from the floor. It had been taken on a Shaw-Fife vacation when we'd visited Badlands National Park. Samantha was thirteen. I was seventeen. We'd stood on either side of Pops, and his arms were draped over our shoulders. We grinned together in front of the fierce, eroded desert landscape.

I'd left about a year after the photo was taken, and my parting words, intended to force her to forget me, had done terrible and lasting harm. She had no idea it hadn't been about her at all.

"You have every right to hate me," I told the Samantha in the photograph.

5

SAM

My little Honda Civic vibrated, engine revving, and speedometer pegged at eighty-five. I had a white-knuckle grip on the steering wheel while flying down I-75 toward my exit. The trees on either side of the highway were a green blur.

Harper. I glared at the road beyond the windshield.

"I get why you're upset," Leigh said from the passenger's seat, "but might I suggest you keep it under eighty? We don't want a speeding ticket, right?"

"This is Florida. Speed limits are a suggestion." However, she was right. I grunted and let off the gas.

"Wanna talk about it?"

"No."

"Okay, but—"

"How could Andrew do this to me?" I smacked the steering wheel. "And Harper had no business being so rude. He didn't even shake your hand."

"That's true."

"It sounded like that ass—er—jerkface took his anger into the ring with you. What a dick."

"Language, Sam. And I doubt he'll be making that mistake with me again. We came to an unspoken agreement."

"And why insist on calling me Samantha? He knows I hate that." To my surprise, tears burned my eyes. I pinched my trembling lips together.

"Are you gonna be alright?" Leigh asked.

"No!" I ran a hand through my hair. "Yes!"

"I'm sorry that Harper gets to you like this." She tapped my thigh with the back of her hand. "Don't give him the power to hurt you."

I snorted. Being around Harper made me feel weak and wounded, small and insignificant. He'd been deliberately cruel to me when he'd left. I'd shed my last tear over Harper long ago, but his sudden appearance shocked the hell out of me.

"Did I tell you I called him once?" I asked. "About a year after he left. Hung up after three rings. Judy took his leaving hard. She would cry at random times. She couldn't sleep, so she'd bake things in the wee hours of the morning. Andrew talked even less than he normally does and was constantly distracted. He would take me to the middle school instead of high school unless I reminded him where we were going." *And I'd lost my hero, my first love.*

"No, you didn't tell me that. I remember we ate a lot of junk food and binge-watched a lot of action movies that summer."

I laughed through my nose. "I know you hate those, but you never complained."

"My first steps toward sainthood," Leigh said.

I floored the Civic again so I could pass a fuel tanker. "Today was supposed to be Cam's last day, too." I had a one-month rule when it came to dating and my current boyfriend had passed his expiration date.

"Oh, really?" Leigh's brows shot up. "But you really like Camden. He's already gotten a two-month reprieve."

"I can't cut Cam loose until I can sort through this other crap." I neared exit 250, flicked on my blinker, and merged into the far-right lane. The exit ramp snaked around to the light at Gibsonton Drive. "I had everything planned so well, too. We were gonna have lunch today and I was gonna tell him how amazing he was. Kiss him. And then tell him it was over. That it was me, not him. But now I can't."

"What is it about Camden that none of the other guys had?" Leigh asked.

"I haven't dated *that* many."

"Seriously? You're a serial dater." She pointed out the windshield. "Watch the car in front of you."

I mashed on the brakes, swearing under my breath so she wouldn't hear.

"I'm not that bad," I protested. *So what if I liked to flirt?* The light turned green and I eased off the brake.

"The way your dating life works now fits our lives perfectly. You keep some guys around for a few days, maybe a week or two, but your limit is one month. No question, no exception. You made that rule and I approve. We're Warriors. We don't live by human law. We fight demons. With medieval weapons, might I add."

"Jerk!" I yelled at a jaywalker and swerved to dodge him. "What I'm hearing from you is that I *should* end it today?"

"I'm saying, be careful." She sighed. "He's not as durable as we are."

If I were being honest with myself, I didn't *want* to break up with Camden. He'd somehow gotten past my stalwart defenses into my squishy girl feelings. I wanted commitment but had no right to ask for that. For the millionth time, Leigh's concerns were valid. I grunted again, ignoring her warning, and flipped on the radio. Classical blared from the speakers.

I flinched and fumbled to turn down the volume. "When did you change my station?"

She laughed, looked straight ahead, and wore a Cheshire-cat grin.

"Wench," I muttered.

IT WAS ABOUT mid-day when I stomped through the rear door of the feed store with murder on my mind. I joined Leigh behind the square, three-sided sales counter situated at the center of the store. "If one more egotistical, sexist, backwoods bro speaks to me like I'm a delicate little flower, I'm gonna lose my Jesus."

Leigh handed change to Ms. Harrison then glanced at me with a quirked eyebrow. "What happened?"

"Don't let them boys get to you, Miss Fife," Ms. Harrison said, her voice crackling with age. She was a Milton's Feed & Tack regular and our token crazy cat lady. Her face sported wrinkles-on-wrinkles and she wore gaudy rings on every finger. "They don't know nothin', missy. Dumb as rocks they is, especially when it comes to common sense."

Ms. Harrison stuffed her money in a cat print wallet. "You girls be good. See you next week." She shuffled to the door, with her fuzzy green slippers in place of real shoes, wild purple moo-moo dress billowing, and frizzy white hair poofed in all directions. I suppressed a smile.

"What happened?" Leigh asked again once Ms. Harrison was outside.

"Freaking Mr. Ruther's idiot son, Adam," I growled,

hopping up onto the stool beside Leigh. "I was loading feed into their truck and he swooped in and took what I had in my hands. Told me he could do it quicker and didn't understand why Mr. Milton had a 'nice lady such as yourself' doing the loading.' So I did what any self-respecting woman would."

Leigh shook her head. "You used your Warrior Power didn't you?"

"I used my Warrior Power." I grinned. "Just a little. How else would I be able to carry four fifty-pound bags of grain at one time? Should have expected this, really. Adam's ego is wounded because I turned him down for a date. Several times." I still had a boyfriend. For now. Loyalty was in my DNA.

Leigh said, "Andrew got us this job to teach us to acclimate with the general public so we can balance our abilities with everyday life. This means dealing with guys like Adam. Four bags is bragging."

I snagged a cheese puff from an open bag on the counter. "I know. But you should'a seen the look on his face. It was worth it."

Leigh rolled her eyes. "Mr. Milton left a *to-do* list for us in his office. I split it down the middle." She shoved a piece of paper into my chest. "If you need me, I'll be reorganizing the halters in the front."

"You're not the boss of me!" I yelled after her. She tossed a dismissive hand in the air as she walked away. I read over my list and slid off my stool. "Let's get this over with," I muttered, heading to the supplements aisle to restack the salt blocks.

An hour later, my last task from the list brought me back behind the counter to organize the catalogs. I stared down at the haphazard mess of binders with folders and papers sticking out.

"Gross!" I pinched the corner of a baggie filled with moldy carrots and tossed it into the trash. "We work with slobs." While I could be labeled a messy person myself, I had standards.

I was taping up a menacing note that said I would slash the tires of the next person who destroyed my handiwork when the front door chimed.

"Hi! I'm behind the counter," I called. "Be with you in a moment!"

Silence. Whoever had walked in paused on the other side of the counter. Rising from my crouch, unsure what to expect, I met a familiar pair of gorgeous green eyes. They held a heady mix of pain and passion that I'd never get enough of. Not in one month. Not in three. *Never.* The owner of these eyes was surfer-fit and tanned, his blond curls sun-kissed.

Camden Bennett, whom I intended to dump today, held a large coffee cup in each hand. He'd stopped at my favorite coffee shop.

"Ohmygoodness." I leaned over the counter, grabbed a fistful of his designer polo, and planted a kiss on his mouth. "What did I do to deserve you?"

He chuckled. "Just be your splendid self."

I'd met Camden when he came into the store three months ago looking for food and advice for the hyacinth macaws his late grandfather had willed to him. I'd known nothing about macaws but connected him to the right people. Then I gave him my phone number, in case he had *any* questions. Camden called me a few days later and asked me to brunch. As he now bought feed exclusively from Milton's, my relationship with Camden was good for business. Rick Milton needed to give me a raise.

I sipped from the cup he handed me. A spicy mix of espresso, milk, honey, cinnamon, and a hint of cayenne hit my tongue. "You brought me a Bee Sting? You're officially my favorite person."

"Sam's favorite," he mused. "I like the sound of that."

"Don't take this the wrong way, but why are you here? Are you breaking our lunch date?"

He set down the second drink and brushed strands of my hair behind my left ear. "I was on my way here to pick up feed for the boys. But my executive chef called while I was on the road. One of my prep cooks slipped in the kitchen. Busted his head. I have to go be a good restaurant owner and make sure all of the incident reports are filled out and filed correctly. So yeah, I have to postpone our lunch."

"This is my consolation prize, then? You're placating me with a caffeinated beverage?"

"Did it work?"

"Hmm," I mused. "Probably."

"To make it up to you, I'd like to take you out on Saturday night. We'll go to an expensive restaurant. It'll be a real-deal date."

I gaped. *I didn't see that coming. Stupid, Fife. I wanted* to say yes. When I opened my mouth to say no, what came out was, "Cam, you know my rule."

"I'm not asking you to marry me, Sam. Let me take you out. We'll eat some amazing food, go for a walk on the beach, look at the stars." He hooked my chin with a knuckle and tilted it up. "Let me treat you like my girl-friend. You deserve more than you're letting me give you."

Well, damn. I averted my eyes down to my coffee cup, feeling this relationship's expiration date shift further out yet again. "Sure, but I—"

"Is that a yes?"

"It is." My hard-and-fast rules missed the curve and piled up in the weeds.

Camden kissed me, making my heart race. The front door chimed and I broke away, wiped my lips, and glared at him. His eyes glittered with mischief.

"Welcome to Milton's," I called to the newcomer, not looking away from Camden. "Can I help you find anything?"

"Hi, I'm looking for a specific hoof packing poultice," a woman answered. "My horse has an abscess and my vet—"

"Coming," I said in my cheery Customer Service voice. I stepped out of the counter area, pointed at Camden, and said, "Don't leave yet."

"I can wait a few." He smiled. But he was twiddling his car keys and I remembered he was in a hurry.

I led the woman to the medical section of the store. Leigh returned from the warehouse area and joined Camden at the counter.

"Cam, good to see you. Need anything for the birds?" Leigh asked.

I forced my attention back to my customer and passed her a tub of medicated clay.

"Have you heard good things about this product?" she asked.

"Excellent reviews. I've used it on my own horse. Do you need vet wrap and pads?"

"I do. And some apple cookies because he's three-legged lame and really cranky."

"So that would be the twenty-pound bag, not the 12 oz packet, then," I said, picking up the brand that Max loved.

"You are so right," she said. We walked over to the check-out counter and piled her purchases next to the register.

Leigh sipped from the second cup Camden brought and I realized the barista had written Leigh's name on it.

Camden's placating strategy included appeasing my best friend. Leigh was delighted. The crowd around the counter woke the store's orange tabby, Buster, and he glared as he stalked away to find a quieter place to nap.

Leigh rang up the sale, and the lady declined my offer of assistance with her goods. She headed out the front and a bizarre flicker disturbed the air to the right of the door. *What the hell was that?* I froze and focused on the spot, my heart rate jumping. An oblong, pearlescent portal hung in midair between the parrot food and the dog kibble. It yawned wider as I watched it.

I elbowed Leigh and nodded toward the portal. She glanced up and blinked, then her eyes flicked to Camden. *Never play poker with this woman,* I thought. Camden studied me with one eyebrow quirked up. I smiled, but he knew that I was horrible at hiding things.

"Everything okay?" he asked.

Any proper lie died in my mouth when a blood-red demon sauntered out of the portal, which snapped shut behind him. I'd never seen a demon in a tailored, formal black suit and fedora. His white shirt lay stark on his crimson skin. I didn't know that his kind could carry off that look. *Demonic dignity. WTF.*

The demon's presence triggered the familiar heat of my Warrior Power. Adrenaline sharpened my senses. My muscles went taut.

What do I do with Cam? What if a customer walks in?

The demon strolled along the far wall, stopped at the grooming tools and turned his black gaze on me. He smiled and pressed an index finger to his lips as if we shared a secret. My battle readiness slammed into place and a healthy dose of fear chilled me. *Defend Cam.* I reached for my bow.

"*HOLD!*" Letty commanded. "*The boy cannot see him.*

Divine Intervention can only go so far. If you draw on your Power he will see you, not what you're fighting. Think of the consequences. The demon has not attacked."

I exhaled. *"Is this the Master?"*

"No, this is just a powerful demon. He may be working for the Master, however."

Whoever he was, strutting around in broad daylight took audacity. I elbowed Leigh in the ribs again.

"I *know*," Leigh hissed through clenched teeth.

Mr. Enigma winked at me and then he turned his attention to Camden. He pointed his index finger and mimed a shot at my boyfriend's back. He winked at me again and continued down the far wall. The portal reopened next to the vaccine fridge. He stepped into the shifting mist and the opening swirled closed behind him.

"What're you looking at?" Cam asked, twisting to look behind himself. "Everything alright?"

"Cat," I gasped. "Mouse."

As if on cue—God bless him—Buster vaulted onto the counter and ambled toward his cat bed licking his lips.

Leigh *tsked* and said, "Buster is just doing his job, Sam. That's why we have a store cat."

"Right!" I hauled in a lungful of air. *That demon just threatened my boyfriend. My sweet, considerate,* human *boyfriend.*

Camden put a reassuring hand on my arm. "You sure you're alright? I didn't think you were the squeamish type."

"I'm not."

"Do you need to sit?" he asked.

"I'll take her to the office and get her some water." Leigh put her arm over my shoulders and gently pulled me along. "Sometimes the circle of life is hard on Sam. We'll only be a minute."

I let her guide me to Mr. Milton's office. She shut the office door and we spoke over each other in our rush.

"What the fire-fart kind of demon was *that?*" I asked.

"We need Andrew." Leigh ran her fingers through her hair and paced the office.

"Where did he come from? Where did he go?"

Leigh silenced us both with a hand. "You first."

"Yes, we need to speak to Andrew. Last night we got brains and brawn, now we get a dapper assassin? What demon has a tailor, for Heaven's sake?" I pulled out my phone and hit Andrew's number. A robotic female voice told me that the mailbox for this number was full. Andrew never cleared his voicemail.

I hung up. "That demon freaking *smiled* at me. He knows he's holding all the cards. And his power triggered me so fast I almost drew Azira. Letty shut me down. Did it feel like that to you?"

"Not like you did." Leigh chewed on the inside of her cheek, grimaced and said, "We should tell Harper."

"No."

Leigh rolled her eyes. "Adviser Shaw put him in charge—"

"No. Andrew told him to watch out for us and continue with our training. He did not make Harper the boss of me. I'm not tellin' him anything."

"As our trainer he needs to know."

In Leigh's mind, Harper was the logical choice since our attempt to reach Andrew had failed.

As usual, she had a valid point.

"Fine. But I'm not calling him."

"Okay, I'll do it."

"Mr. Enigma came to taunt me." I swallowed hard. "And Cam."

Leigh was quiet for several excruciating minutes. "I think you're right. Until we figure what to do, keep him close." She plowed ahead before I could interrupt her, "I think Mr. Enigma can direct his power toward someone specific. I saw him, I was concerned, but he didn't trip my Warrior to the point where I drew Fury. He wasn't focused on me at all, only you and Camden."

"They're going after Cam to get to me. How am I supposed to keep him safe? I'm a terrible liar," I reminded her.

"I've got your back. You're not in this alone. You can do this. Now go out there and be your normal charming self."

6

CAMDEN

Camden turned his Audi onto Madison Street, the
tires of the sporty coupe sounding like popcorn on
the oyster shell road. He'd spent the hour drive from
Milton's Feed to Sorcerie, his beach-front restaurant,
mulling over his curious visit with Sam. He'd been thrilled
she'd agreed to a real date, but something in the store had
spooked her and he wanted to know why.

Red and blue lights flashed through the palmetto leaves
as he turned into the restaurant's driveway. Emergency
vehicles filled the parking area near the entrance: two
police cruisers, an ambulance, and a white van with the
medical examiner's official seal on the side.

"What the hell?" Camden muttered. *All this for a head
injury?* He reached for his cell sitting on the charger and
turned it on.

He parked between the two cruisers. Yellow crime
scene tape stretched across the porch steps. Camden
ducked under the flimsy barrier and bounded up the stairs.
His huge macaws, Watson and Holmes, shrieked in their
aviary from within the restaurant, rattling the front

window. Three strides from the front door, a uniformed cop blocked him.

"Sir, this is an official crime scene. Unless you're the owner, I gotta ask you to leave," the officer shouted over the shrill squawks coming from the macaws.

"Get the hell out of my way," Camden said. "I'm the owner." He raised his hands and stepped back from the twitchy cop.

"I need to see your ID. Sorry, sir, procedure."

Camden wrenched his wallet from his back pocket and flashed his license. The cop grabbed the wallet in a firm grasp and studied the details. At twenty-two, Cam knew he was young to own such a prestigious business. He suppressed the urge to call for one of his employees to verify his claim.

"If you let me in, I can get the birds to calm down." Beads of sweat gathered between Cam's shoulder blades then ran down his spine. He forced himself to take a deep breath and exhaled slowly.

"Thank God," the cop said, handing back Cam's wallet. He tapped his com and said, "Detective Jones, I'm sending in the owner, a Mr. Bennett." He opened the front door for Cam.

Camden stepped into the large, bright foyer and whistled to his birds in their spacious enclosure, placed to greet customers as they entered the restaurant. The ruckus ceased.

"Easy, boys, easy," he murmured. Holmes stopped his frantic flapping and clambered down the manzanita branches to reach Camden. Watson clung to the aviary's ceiling and would take much longer to settle, but at least he stopped screaming. Camden plucked a slice of dried mango from the treat box and passed it to Holmes.

Sorcerie's Executive Chef, Renard Bisset, a robust man

with olive skin, dark hair, and a large nose hurried to Camden's side. "Oh, thank God," the short man prayed, crossing himself. "I couldn't get them to settle. They see you and, boom, silence. We couldn't hear ourselves think in here."

"What happened? Your text said Javi hit his head? My phone died after you texted me that Javi hit his head, and that he was okay, so I made a pit stop to see Sam." Camden saw the grief on Renard's face. "Just how bad is it? Did someone do this to him?"

"Mr. Bennett." Another man entered from the dining room. He was a head taller than Camden, clad in a crisp navy suit. "Detective Bill Jones—" he extended his hand, but Camden ignored it.

"Renard," Camden said. "What's going on?"

"Sir" —the chef's voice cracked. "Javi died."

Camden stumbled backward, groping for the white foyer bench, and sat down hard. "How? What? Dead?"

"There was a second accident. I tried to do CPR—" Renard pressed his fist to his mouth, blinking back tears.

Camden stared at his distraught chef. Javier Martinez had been a Sorcerie employee for a year. The guy was never late, lived with his sick mother, and paid child support.

"Sorry to press the issue, Mr. Bennett, but we need you to identify the body so the coroner can do her job. We can talk in your office when we're done. Let's start in the kitchen." Jones gestured for Camden to lead the way.

Camden's confusion morphed into dread as Renard led the way. He opened the swing door to the gleaming kitchen; light bounced off of the white tile and stainless steel fittings. A forensics tech snapped photos and measured distances between appliances, typing the information into his tablet. A woman crouched next to a sheet-covered mound right outside the walk-in refrigerator. She rose and extended a hand to Camden. "Dr. Kelly Rourke, medical examiner."

"Camden Bennett. Owner," he said, shaking her hand.

"We're sorry for your loss, but as Bill has probably told you, we need you to confirm the deceased's identity because you weren't here at the time of his death."

Identify the body. Medical examiner, Camden thought. *In my own damn kitchen, no less.*

Camden had never seen a dead body except at funerals. He had no clue what condition Javi's body was in under the sheet. *I can't do this,* he thought, shaking his head and taking a small step back. "This can't be happening."

Bile rose in his throat. Part of him wanted to call his mother and have her handle this situation. She was co-owner, after all. However, that would be a shit show, and he knew it. She'd find out sooner, rather than later, and the thought of summoning her sooner made his insides shrivel.

His mother would be furious.

"I don't envy the position you're in, Mr. Bennett. Let me know when you're ready," Dr. Rourke said.

Renard put a firm hand on Camden's back, the small gesture reminding Cam he wasn't in this alone. Despite his mounting trepidation, he'd never been one to run and hide. Camden needed to be strong for his staff. They needed his leadership. He hadn't been there when Javi died but he and his staff were a solid team.

Camden approached the covered mound on the floor, apprehension rising to nausea. He clutched the aviator sunglasses hooked in the vee of his polo shirt.

"Let's do this." He had to step around sliced vegetables scattered on the tile to reach the body.

Dr. Rourke pulled back the sheet. Javi lay flat on his

back. Cam noted the small man's impeccable white cook's coat, black slacks, and non-slip shoes. Standing over Javi's body brought on a fresh wave of sickness. His employee's head tilted at an unnatural angle. Javi's eyes were open and glassy, his lips blue, his skin ashy. Camden's stomach heaved. He bolted to the sink and vomited. He braced his hands on the counter and leaned over the basin, waiting for a second wave. Renard passed him a bright white towel.

"First dead body?" Dr. Rourke asked.

"Yeah," Cam rasped. He splashed cool water on his face, rinsed out his mouth, and took the towel.

"Hate to push you, Mr. Bennett, but I need confirmation," Jones said from behind Camden.

"It's Javi." Cam cleared his throat. "Javier Martinez." He ran the towel over his face again, mortified that his hands trembled. *How did Javi break his neck? We can't open tonight. I'll have Renard call the guests with reservations. Oh, God.* Camden flinched. *My mother.*

"Mr. Bennett," Jones said.

"Yes?"

Jones pointed a pen at the security camera mounted across from Javi's prep station. "I'll need to see the relevant footage."

"Sure." Cam shook himself and tossed his towel into the sink. "Follow me."

As he, Renard, and Jones passed through the dining room, Jackie O'Ryan, Camden's sous chef, caught his eye. She gave him a low wave and a sad smile. Camden stopped. She sat at a table by herself, a glass of water in front of her. Cam's four other prep cooks were each seated alone at a table. A cop interviewed Jackie, scribbling her responses in a notebook.

"I would prefer you wait on the questioning my staff

until I've reached our lawyer," Camden said to Detective Jones.

"This is standard procedure for suspicious deaths. As Mr. Bisset said earlier, this was a freak accident. We only need their statements to corroborate with the surveillance video. I assure you, no one's in trouble."

"Even still, they should know. One moment, please." Camden sent Sorcerie's attorney a quick text about the incident, requesting immediate assistance. When he finished, he led Jones through the dining room to the office. He froze at the door, his hand resting on the knob. "Renard, has someone called Javi's mother?"

"We wanted to wait until we heard from you. We can go see her later," Renard said.

"Good. Thank you." Camden unlocked the door. He gestured the two men in before bringing up the rear. "It'll take a moment to pull up what you need. Please make yourself comfortable." Jones nodded and settled into a chair. Renard stood behind Cam's shoulder as he activated the security software.

"You couldn't access the footage?" Cam asked Renard.

"I no longer have a key to your office." He stuffed his hands in his pockets. "Your mother took it from me." His voice was so low that Camden strained to hear him.

Camden met Renard's eyes. "She what?"

"Said it was a security risk." The chef shrugged as if it didn't matter; the severe frown he wore suggested otherwise.

"Oh, for fuck's sake. You carry Sorcerie credit cards." Cam ran his right palm over his face, a headache throbbing behind his eyes. He sighed. *The woman will be the death of me.*

"Is your mother involved with the restaurant, Mr. Bennett?" Jones asked.

"My mother and I are business partners. She doesn't handle any of the day-to-day. She's the financial backer."

Jones pulled out a pad and pen. "I'll need to speak with her anyway."

"No problem." Camden grabbed a business card from its holder and held it out. "Let me give her some warning before you contact her. She can be difficult, especially when it involves her business ventures."

Camden focused on locating the correct time stamp for the footage. He queued up the videos from all of the kitchen cameras then turned the screen so both men could watch.

Javi stood at his prep station chopping carrots and celery, tossing them into a container offscreen. Suddenly the rectangular stainless bin on Javier's left appeared on screen, flipping over and dumping cut vegetables across his workstation. Javi dropped his knife and scrambled to keep food from falling to the floor. Cam could see he was swearing a blue streak. Javier looked left twice, shaking his head as he scraped together the scattered food.

After replacing what he could salvage in the bin, Javi searched his area. When he turned right, Javi lurched, flailed his arms to keep his balance, but he fell out of view in front of his workstation.

"Do any of the other cameras show where he landed?" Jones asked.

"No," Cam said. "The other two don't cover the floor in that area."

The video showed Javi's coworkers swarming to assist him. Renard was the first on the scene, barking orders to the others as he disappeared from the camera's view.

"What happened when you reached Javier's side?" Jones asked Renard.

"I made everyone back off, told Jackie to call Mr.

Bennett, and then I checked Javi over for injuries. Javi refused to go to the hospital. He said he felt fine, and since there was no blood, I let him stay." Renard rubbed the back of his skull. "I was hoping Mr. Bennett would send him to the doctor."

Camden glanced up from the screen. "When you sent me the text, was Javi alive?"

"Yes, the second incident happened about twenty minutes later," Renard said.

Camden scrolled forward in the video searching for the fatal accident. Guilt choked him. *If I'd come straight to Sorcerie would Javi still be alive?* Cam fast-forwarded the grey video until Javier appeared carrying a stack of bins filled with prepared ingredients. He then pressed play and the story unfolded in real time.

Javi could barely see over the top of the containers he carried over to the walk-in refrigerator. He turned his body so that he could pull the handle on the door with his right hand while bracing with a knee and his left arm. He had just managed to unlatch the door when the tall, solid thawing cabinet to Javi's right toppled onto the small man. The containers started sliding out of his grip, and their weight prevented him from escaping the huge appliance. The cabinet slammed him against the edge of a steel table, which caught him under his left ear. His neck bore the entire downward weight of the appliance.

"Shit!" Camden shoved backward in his desk chair, twisting away from the screen.

Renard crossed himself. "Camden, it took three of us to lift the cabinet off him."

"Did the wheels snap?" Camden asked.

"No, sir."

"Should that appliance be anchored?" Jones asked, making a note on his tablet.

"No, it needs to be moved for cleaning, but the wheels are always locked otherwise," Cam said. The detective wrote this down.

"So you would consider this a freak accident, then?" Jones asked.

"Absolutely," Cam and Renard said in unison.

"I have never known such a thing to happen and I have worked in restaurants since I was fourteen," Renard said.

Camden checked his phone. He wished Sorcerie's lawyer would get back to him so they could start processing the worker's compensation for Javi's family. *What if they sue us for wrongful death?*

"We'll need a copy of that tape," Jones said.

"Renard can pull it." Camden opened the front drawer of his desk and picked up a new thumb drive. Then he surrendered the chair to his chef. "Give them the entire sequence between 9:35 and 10:55 from all of the cameras in the kitchen."

"Please include the footage from that time from all the cameras in the restaurant," Jones said. "We need to see if there was someone on the premises who did not belong here."

Camden heard shouts mingled with the shrill screeches of Watson and Holmes from the direction of the front foyer. *She's here.*

Camden led Detective Jones across the dining room to the source of the commotion. A lean woman dressed in a tailored navy silk dress stood in the center of the foyer. She flipped her long, dark auburn hair over a shoulder and whirled to face the officer trailing her. Her gold spike heels gave her a three-inch advantage over him.

"This is an affluent neighborhood," she barked at him. "I don't care who got hurt here, I demand that you exercise discretion. Move those vehicles!" She turned on

Camden. "Why is every godforsaken emergency vehicle in Pinellas County outside my establishment?"

The officer raised his hands. "Ma'am, you haven't been cleared—"

"What part of *my restaurant* didn't you understand?"

"Ma'am, *please*. I must verify the ID of anyone who comes in."

Camden grimaced. "Mother, please lower your voice. The officer is only doing his job."

She arched a manicured brow. "This is my restaurant which I share with you. Do not tell me what to do."

Camden turned to the growling, hissing macaws. "Boys, that's enough." The huge birds clumped together on the back wall of the cage, trembling and making sharp clicking sounds. "Mother, a member of our staff suffered a fatal accident this morning."

"Someone died? In my restaurant? How?" She strode into the dining room, grabbed a bottle from her personal wine collection above the bar, selected three glasses, and seated herself at her favorite corner booth. "This will be a PR nightmare. Will we have to close the restaurant down tonight? Do we also have to cancel reservations? What if we are forced to shut down for two nights?"

"We won't be able to open tonight. Renard will reschedule the reservations and offer a small discount for their inconvenience." Camden wanted to shelter his staff from her fury. "With all due respect, Mother, since you are so rarely here, why did you come in now?"

"It's on the news." She poured herself a generous glass of the dark merlot, then poured another for Camden. "There are onlookers and press outside. I will not allow a scandal to bring us to ruin." She poured the third glass.

Camden gestured the detective over. "This is Detective Jones, who is investigating the accident."

"Aerona Bennett. Sit." Aerona indicated the seat in front of her.

The buzz of adrenaline had begun to wear off as fatigue seeped in, leaving Camden overwhelmed, but it was best to see what his mother wanted and have her back on the road as quickly as possible.

"Mrs. Bennett—" Jones started to say.

"*Ms*. Bennett." His mother leaned back with a smile that didn't touch her green eyes.

"My apologies. I only have a few questions," Jones said. Instead of sitting, he flipped his notepad to a new page. "This won't take long. And thank you for the offer, but I can't drink while on duty."

"Very well." Aerona shrugged and pushed a glass toward Camden. "Your loss."

Less than twenty minutes later, after the detective gleaned all the information he wanted from Aerona, he excused himself and returned to the kitchen to confer with the coroner and her team.

"I need to be at the scene with these people, Mother. Is there anything else you need from me?"

"Make sure you contact our lawyers." Aerona swirled her wine in its glass. "Send condolences to Jose's family. Pay them what you must to keep them from suing us. I will handle the press. Do not speak to them."

"Javi, Mother." Camden sighed and massaged the space between his brows. "His name was Javier." *Could this day get any worse?*

"Whatever." Aerona batted a bejeweled hand in the air, her ruby encrusted bangles clattering on her slim wrist. "Just make sure this incident doesn't cost us."

"Yes, Mother."

Aerona pursed her red lips and studied Cam through

squinted eyes. Then her countenance lifted. "Drink your wine."

Camden shook his head, but this was his mother's custom whenever they were together. She insisted on one glass of wine over some sort of conversation. *Why would discussing a little emergency like an accidental death be any different?*

Aerona took a sip from her glass. Cam shrugged and did the same. It was getting harder, as he disliked her preferred merlot. Every bottle had the same odd note of frosty metal.

"Have you called the lawyers?" she pressed, swirling her wine in the glass and holding it to the light.

"I sent Samuel a text. He hasn't answered."

"What happened here today, Camden?"

"We had two accidents. Both involved Javier Martinez. In the first one, he slipped and hit his head, but Renard cleared him to return to his station. An hour later, in front of the walk-in, the thawing cabinet fell, crushing him up against the edge of a prep table and breaking his neck. Neither of them makes any sense. I can't figure out how they happened."

"When you hear from Samuel, direct him to me. I will handle the legal issues. You have a restaurant to run." She finished her wine and stood. Camden did the same. He came around the table, kissed his mother's offered cheek, and escorted her to her car. As soon as she'd spun out of the drive onto the main road he bolted back into Sorcerie.

He found Renard in his office calling guests and repairing the week's reservation schedule. Camden slumped into a chair. When his mother blindsided him like that, it took him some time to recover. Renard concluded his current call and turned to him.

"You missed my mother."

"I do my best, sir."

"Did you get the footage to Jones?"

"Yes. He asked that we join him in the kitchen when you were available."

"Alright then," Camden sighed and stood. "Let's see what we can do for Javi and his family."

7

SAM

"You're not fucking going on a date at night." Harper resumed his agitated pace, flattening a trail in the plush carpet of the living room. "There's a demon after you. No date. In fact, I don't want you going anywhere without supervision. You're only leaving the property to go to work."

"Don't tell me what to do!" I shot to my feet. "You abandoned us, now you just show up after *six years* of total silence, start shouting orders, and expect me to just obey? Oh, hell no."

"I'm *trying* to keep you alive." Harper pinned me with a glare.

"We all are, Harper," Leigh said. She sat on the floor, long legs crossed under her, sipping cocoa from that stupid cheery yellow mug she loved so much.

"Harper, watch yourself, son," Judy chided. She peered at him over her glasses. "You've just stepped into a role and don't really know your team."

Harper growled. His rage filled every corner of the room, but I would not back down. We'd been arguing in circles about the best way to handle our current predicament without Andrew at the helm, and I'd be damned if Harper thought he could treat me like a child. Yet Harper was hell-bent on doing exactly that.

"I'm a Warrior of Light," I said. "Trained in combat and strategy." I glared back at him. "I'm not some delicate waif that needs protection."

Harper stopped right in front of me. "You're wanted by a Demon-master. A new kind of demon visits you at work today, and you think—" He snorted in frustration. His fists opened, closed, and opened again. "Samantha, you insist on putting yourself in danger. You're smarter than that."

"It's *Sam*," I snapped.

"Harper," Leigh said.

"What?" His gaze flicked to her.

"Please be civil. There's more at play here than you know."

Harper's teeth clicked shut on a rebuke. He exhaled and tried again. "Talk, Kestler."

"This red demon not only taunted Sam, he threatened Cam's life. Isn't our primary mission to protect humanity, no matter the cost to our own lives?"

"That's right," I snapped.

Judy made a *zip it* motion across her mouth and glared at me with a severity that had me shrink back. Harper's upper lip twitched in a silent snarl.

"She needs to be able to keep tabs on him, right?" Leigh continued. "I say we let her go—"

"No."

Judy *tsked* at Harper's interruption. "Let Leigh speak."

Harper ran a hand over his face and shook his head. He resumed pacing.

"Sam should go on her date on Saturday," Leigh said.

"We need to know what it is about Camden. Her other boyfriends have never been threatened. Keeping her restricted to protected ground isn't going to draw all the players out onto the board."

Why hadn't she brought that up an hour ago? I thought.

"You don't know what you're up against," Harper said.

"You don't either," Leigh countered.

Harper flinched at these words.

"Besides, knowing Sam"—Leigh saluted me with her mug—"she'd probably find a way to leave the farm without anyone knowing, which would only put her in more danger. Is that what you want?"

There was that, too, I thought. Harper and Leigh stared at each other for several seconds.

Harper said, "Then she isn't going alone."

Leigh nodded and sipped her cocoa. I didn't like the gleam in Harper's eye.

"What's the catch?" I demanded.

"I'll trail you myself," Harper said.

"Definitely not." I planted my fists on my hips. "That—"

"That is unwise," Judy said, leaning forward in her chair. She set her teacup on a side table. "While I agree that Sammy shouldn't go alone, I rather think that Leigh is better equipped to be her back-up."

"I'll do it," Leigh agreed.

I saw a storm raging in Harper's sapphire eyes, one I didn't understand. Pain? Fear? Anger? Frustration, obviously. He took a deliberate breath, then exhaled in a gust. His fists were once again clenched, knuckles white. The muscles in his square jaw flexed.

What assurance could I offer him? I wasn't going to die without a hell of a fight. I was safe in Leigh's capable hands. I refused to cower and hide.

"I can follow her unseen, Harper," Leigh said.

"Fine," he snapped. "Don't get caught. And if Pops asks, I tried to stop both of you." He glanced at me, shook his head again, and left without another word.

I grinned at Leigh. "Nice save."

"I didn't do it just for you," Leigh said. "I need to know you're safe, too, and I'm not willing to gamble Cam's life."

"SAM!" Leigh roared from the back door of the store. I was out in the chicken coop collecting the day's eggs.

"Damn it all!" I stood and smacked my head on a roosting ledge. *Ouch. Busted.* I rubbed nestbox dust off of my hands and picked up the egg basket. "Better go face the music. Wish me luck, girls." The hens ignored me.

I'd skipped our Warrior training this morning because I'd had enough of Harper Tate and needed some breathing room. After our morning run, I'd told Leigh I didn't feel well and returned to the farmhouse. I showered and then left for work, texting to tell her that I'd open the store. I'd hoped that letting her know where I was would keep her from worrying, but no. By her tone right now, she was ready to flay me alive.

"You, get out." Leigh pointed at Liam, the warehouse runner boy, when she saw me enter. Leigh rounded on me. She hadn't taken even a few minutes to put herself together for work. Her hair was still damp and her blue shirt was rumpled; she hadn't bothered with her usual light touch of makeup.

"Sorry," I said.

"That's all you have to say?" she snapped.

"I just couldn't face Harper this morning. I have no

other excuses. You knew I was here." I sighed. "I promise I'll be back in the gym tomorrow."

Her gaze narrowed. "I covered for you. Harper is furious. He ranted *at me* for a good five minutes about your 'wanton disregard'—his words, not mine—for your safety. I took that lashing for you, Sam. You owe me more than a *sorry*."

She wasn't done. I'd give her a second.

"And because you left without me," she continued, "I had to drive my car. It's amazing I made it here at all."

"You could buy a new car," I suggested. "We don't have a lot of bills. Milton pays us well enough and rent's free."

"That is not the point!" She jabbed me in the chest with a finger. "And you know it, you brat."

"I just need some time, Leigh." I rubbed where she'd poked me. "I wish Andrew were here."

All of her defenses crumbled. "I do, too."

"Am I forgiven?" I asked after a quiet moment. Leigh stared at me for several heartbeats and then heaved a dramatic sigh before relenting.

"Yes. You know you are."

We stocked shelves, fed Buster, waited on customers, and didn't argue over the proper stacking of hay as we usually did. At the end of the uneventful day, I flipped the closed sign and Leigh punched in the security code.

"See you at home?" I asked as we walked to our vehicles. "What shall we do with our suddenly available evening, since there is no demon hunting until further notice."

She glanced up at me while unlocking her senile car. I felt bad that I'd made her drive that thing today. "Harper's just trying to do what Andrew asked and keep us safe."

"On a scale of one to ten, how mad do you think he'll be after my stunt this morning?"

"How about a fifteen?"

I groaned and ran my fingers through my hair. "I'm so in trouble. There is really no avoiding him, is there?"

Leigh sucked her teeth. "Nope."

"Damn."

"Don't swear." She got in her car without closing the door, and started the asthmatic engine. "I'm following you home."

"I'm stopping for snacks. Since we're going to be couch-bound, and all."

"I suppose demons don't prowl the produce section."

"I'll be in the freezer section. Ice cream, not carrots, for me, thank you."

"No longer than five minutes, promise?" Leigh held out her pinky for a solemn swear.

"Scout's honor." I hooked my pinky with hers. "No detours."

"Since you've given me your word, I'm gonna just head home. I don't trust Mrs. Crankyshanks to start again today."

True to my promise, I was in and out of the Winn-Dixie in four minutes and fifty-seven seconds armed with Peanut Butter Paradise ice cream, pretzels, and a two-liter bottle of root beer. I had taken the last bend toward the farmhouse when my phone chimed. I glanced down at the center console where I always kept it face up. *Bet that's Harper, ready to rip me a new one.*

"Watch out!" Letty's demand cut through my thoughts. I obeyed and looked up, gripping the steering wheel with both hands.

In that instant, the Civic spun out of control—around and around. On the second full circle, the car slid off the road. The tires dug into the gravel and grass of the shoulder. Traction let me steer the circle into a fishtail and then to a stop. In the stillness, clods of dirt and weeds thrown up by my skid plopped onto the hood. My chest ached where the seatbelt had kept me from flying through the windshield. I slumped against the headrest, my breath coming in spurts.

"You're okay. You're alive," I said, scanning my body for pain. "Nothing's broken. You're good."

I threw George the Civic into park; his engine hissed and clicked with his own trauma. I held my shaking hands out in front of me and curled my fingers into fists.

"One whole Sam, present and accounted for. No bits and pieces," I coached myself, unbuckling my seatbelt.

I glanced over to the passenger's seat. My groceries were strewn across the floorboard. I leaned over and tossed the items back into my shopping bag. The ice cream carton was dented, my pretzels were a little crushed, and the root beer was a bit foamy. Otherwise, my snacks had survived the ordeal.

I forced my eyes closed and took a soul-collecting breath before getting out. Either by dumb luck or Divine Providence, George had careened to a halt right on the edge of the farm's protected ground. I circled to the passenger's side and saw that both tires were flat.

"Oh, George." I braced a palm on the roof of the car. "We'll get you fixed up. Somehow. But can you tell me how the fire-fart we managed to accomplish this?" The Civic's engine hissed.

I scanned my immediate surroundings, looking for whatever had started that spin. The road glittered in the fading sunlight. I thumped George's hood. "What in the world—"

Where the grass met the road, at the property's edge, I

knelt and touched the asphalt. Gasping, I jerked my hand away. Ice. Freaking *ice* covered the entire street. In Florida. During the summer.

"What the hell?"

The car's rear end protruded past the boundary line, but it was off the road. Then I saw the rumpled bumper. There were four evenly spaced gouges marring the metal the length of the quarter panel. The edges of each line looked melted.

"This makes no sense——" My statement morphed into a scream as I felt someone jerk me backwards.

"Get off me!" I spun around, reaching for my Power. Its heat exploded into my bloodstream.

"Holy shit." Harper stepped back, his hands raised as if settling a wild beast. "Stop fucking screaming."

I laid a hand over my thumping heart. *Not you. Anyone but you.* "Didn't anyone ever tell you not to sneak up on a Warrior?"

He held my gaze for a moment before his focus slid to the quarter panel I'd been inspecting. "Are you hurt?"

"No." I shook out my arms. "But you could have been." Adrenaline and Power were a potent mixture.

His eyes roved over me in a clinical way. "Humor me." He grabbed my wrist, taking my pulse. "Any blurry vision? Headache? Follow my finger." He passed it from right to left and back.

"*I'm* fine." I did as he asked but jerked my arm from his grasp and gestured to my car. "George is not."

Harper scowled then side-stepped past me with panther grace. He inspected the damage just as I had. "You saw nothing?"

I should have. "Obviously not. I was going forward and then I wasn't. How did you know I was here?"

"I didn't." He examined the two deflated tires and pointed up the driveway. "Bear wouldn't shut up."

The squirming pit bull obediently waited about twenty yards away.

"Come here," I said, releasing the dog from his sit-stay. He bounded over to me with his typical exuberance. "You're my best boy."

I squatted and peppered Bear's head with kisses before burying my face in his neck and clinging to him. On a Warrior level, I knew what had caused this accident. The wreck had rattled me, but those gouges in my car freaked me right out.

Harper stood and surveyed our surroundings, staring hard at a cluster of palmettos across the road.

"A demon wrecked you," he said, voicing what I didn't want to acknowledge.

"But how?" I blurted. "And the ice? Did you see that?"

"I did." He studied me. "You sure you're okay?"

How did I not sense the demon? I turned a slow circle. There was no signature heat. No sulfuric scent. *How did the ice get there? How did all this get by* my *senses?*

"Sam," Harper said. "Would you fucking answer me?"

I waved a hand at him then pressed my palm to my forehead. "I'm thinking."

"You knew it was there," I said to Letty.

"Yes. But the demon's presence was so faint I almost missed it."

"What kind of demon has the power to mute its presence?" I wavered, squinting at the area Harper still studied. My head spun, my heart pounded, and my chest tightened. My vision went grey on the edges. *"Am I losing my abilities?"*

Harper touched my shoulder. He tipped up my chin, forcing me to meet his eyes. "Sam, breathe."

I inhaled and jerked away. Crossing my arms, I said, "I'm fine."

"Uh huh," he mused. Then he changed the subject. "I think it was your friend from the shop. Red. Impossibly fast."

I shook my head. "But *how* and where'd he go?"

Harper's gaze went back to that cluster of trees across the road. "I think he may still be around."

"Is that why you yanked me back over the boundary line?"

"Yes." That unreadable dark flame flickered in his eyes, like it had last night at the height of his fury.

"I didn't sense him."

"You didn't?" Alarm flashed through his stoic features.

"My inner Warrior said it was so faint she nearly missed it. Good thing she didn't, huh?" I let out a caustic laugh. "This is the third day in a row that Hell has tried to get my attention."

"I agree," Harper murmured. "Why do they want you and not Kestler?"

That's the million dollar question, you idiot. I uncrossed my arms and wiped my hands on my jeans. "The hell if I know," I snapped.

"You're goddamn lucky you ended up on sacred ground." He raked a hand over his short brown hair. "This is exactly the kind of shit I was concerned about, Samantha. Let's get to the house. If the demon is still around, I don't see him and you can't get a bearing on his whereabouts."

Andrew never used such a demanding, terse tone with me, nor was he one to limit my freedom. I would not allow Harper to continue that trend.

"You arrogant bastard," I growled through clenched teeth. "When did you become such a condescending asshole? I can't believe I ever thought you hung the—"

I inhaled, remembering that I wasn't fourteen

anymore, and notched up my chin. The dusky evening was loud with chirping crickets and screeching cicadas. An owl hooted in the distance. A light breeze rustled the Spanish moss in the Florida oaks lining the driveway.

"Hung the what, Samantha? The moon?" Harper asked. "I'm not that boy anymore."

"Ugh!" I snorted and shoved past him.

Harper sure as hell wasn't the same. It was like life had packed him into a five-gallon bucket filled with shrapnel, closed the lid, and shaken it. Whatever he'd been through scarred him. But that didn't give him an excuse for being a chauvinistic overlord. I retrieved my groceries from the car before starting up the drive without another word to Harper.

"Bear, come on dude." I patted my thigh. The dog leapt up from where he lay, bringing the stick he'd been chewing with him.

Harper fell in step beside me. I refused to look at him. If he couldn't refrain from talking down to me, we wouldn't be on speaking terms. *That* was about as adult as I could be when it came to him.

"I can't understand why you're being reckless with your life."

"Why do you care?" I snapped.

"Because I fucking don't want you dead. Jesus." He grabbed my arm, forcing me to stop and face him. "I'm not your enemy."

I stared down at his hand on my bicep. "You have a twisted way of caring, Harper."

Instead of an explosion of anger and disapproval, he muttered, "Your life matters, Sam."

And *there* was Harper I knew. The one he was before he went and screwed everything up. His eyes softened, worry brimming in their blue depths. He released his grip.

"Would you reconsider going out tomorrow night?" he asked, his tone still low.

And we're back to this again. At least he's consistent. "Sorry, that ain't gonna happen." I turned and continued my march up the drive. "I'm going on my date tomorrow and you're not going to be a raging bull about it."

He didn't miss a step, keeping in line with me. "Is this guy really worth putting your life at risk over? I'm trying to keep you safe. Staying on protected ground is the only way I know how to accomplish that."

"Is he really worth—" I jerked to a stop and whirled to face him again. "It's my *job* to make sure Camden is safe. When you left, you forfeited *any* influence you had over me." His earlier gibe about our past together still stung my battered heart. "And yes, you insensitive jerk, I thought you hung the moon."

I jiggled my grocery bag at him for added emphasis. "Why is that surprising to you? I never hid my feelings. Hell, I would have gone anywhere, done anything, killed anyone if you'd asked. But not anymore. Not now. There's too much damage here."

A few stupid tears slipped down my cheeks. Harper raised his hand as if he'd—what? Wipe away my tears? Ha! I took one step back. He dropped his arm and let out a deflated breath. His expression was enigmatic. Was he hurt or angry? Where I was an open book, he was a freaking locked safe, sealed with the blood of magical unicorns.

"Harper, you're not a Warrior." I kept my tone calm. "I am. I've trained hard, busted my ass, and fought on the supernatural frontline for two years."

He lifted his chin, eyes never leaving mine. His silence and self-possessed confidence could intimidate most people. Harper was a man that didn't need to use a lot of words to get his way. But I was no mere human being.

A part of me still wanted to hurt him, wound him like he'd wounded me.

"Don't let your emotion cloud your judgment, Brave One. Don't be petty. He's not offering any excuses," Letty cautioned. *"Harper is on your side."*

"He's got a shitty way of showing it."

Harper said nothing, standing in the middle of the gravel drive, his arms crossed. Bear laid back down with his splintered chew toy.

"I'm not going to apologize for any alleged recklessness," I said. "We might have to be civil with each other, but we're not friends. Don't make that mistake."

I'd taken five steps toward the house when I slammed to a stop. Something Harper said finally dawned on me.

"You can see demons?"

8

HARPER

My gut reaction was to lie. But this was Sam. I'd kept up the ruse that I was a normal human being for so long, confessing the truth felt like lying. Pops had worked with me as a child, teaching me to fly under the demonic radar. He had taught me how to hide my fear when they appeared and how to behave around them without revealing that I could see them. And Pops had shown me how to survive in a world where I could see the greatest danger and could do nothing about it.

Only Ma and Pops knew I was a Seer. Now there was no point in lying.

But when I tell her, which Sam will I get? The hurricane or the hurricane's eye?

"Yes, I can see demons," I said.

Sam gaped at me. Her grocery bag slipped from her fingers, its contents rolling out onto the driveway. She closed the distance between us in two long strides.

"For how long?" she asked. Her fists were clenched.

Hunker down, Tate. "My entire life."

"How?" She shook her head. "*How* can you see demons? Did you see them when we were growing up?"

"Yes."

"I don't understand."

"You grew up here." I gestured toward the safety of the farmhouse. "Pops trained me as if I was a Warrior. You watched some of my sessions with him. Hell, I'm proficient with every weapon he owns. Once you were chosen, didn't you ever wonder why he did that for me?"

"Why did Andrew never say anything?" she asked.

"I asked him not to."

She threw her arms up in exasperation. "But why?"

"Why hide that I can see demons? Come on, Samantha. You only became a Warrior two years ago. Before that, had you seen a single demon?" Just when I thought she would unleash gale-force fury on me, the wind shifted.

"Where is Andrew?"

Where did that come from? "Away."

"I know that!" she shouted. Bear lifted his head, ears perked.

"I'm right fucking here. No need to yell."

"Don't be a dick," she snapped. "We need him. What if something bad has happened to him?"

I almost laughed. Pops needed no protection. The man had been waging the invisible supernatural war for a *long* time, a fact that he hid from his Warriors. Pops had more power than most Warriors and had given me explicit instructions not to divulge this information. I didn't agree with his tactics, but I wouldn't break rank now.

"Pops is fine," I said.

"You've spoken to him? Where is he? What's he doing? When's he coming home? Why hasn't he returned my calls?"

I frowned. I would lie this time, but it was possible she

would see through me. While I hadn't spoken to Pops since he'd left, and I did know where he went and whom he searched for, I wouldn't tell her. Pops's orders. As for when he'd be home, I prayed it would be soon. Instead of answering, I glared at Sam.

The wind of Sam's temper shifted again. "You're definitely not a Warrior, right?"

"You know I'm not. Just a man."

"Who sees demons. And you kept that from me. That doesn't help me trust you, you know."

"That's your problem."

She huffed. "You have no other powers?"

"None."

Bear, bored with our conversation, turned his attention to Sam's groceries. She stepped back and shooed him away from the pretzels.

"I don't believe you're *just* a man," she said as she tucked her snack back into the bag. "You're some sort of something." She gestured up and down in my direction. "But human ain't it."

"What?" I said. Her words felt like a shove.

"Andrew's taught you a helluva lot more than you're saying," she said.

God, she's perceptive. I shrugged. "Sure, if that's what you want to think."

Sam studied me. "Fine. Keep your secrets." She shoved Bear's determined muzzle out of the bag. "So, what are we doing about George? We can't just leave him there, wounded and all."

How does she live in that mind of hers? But I didn't care how she'd arrived at this question; she'd downgraded to a tropical storm. I exhaled.

"I'll handle it," I said.

"Okay." Her eyes narrowed. "But I still don't trust you. And I still think you're a dick."

Sam wasn't wrong. Sometime after Molly's murder, I had mutated into a whiskey-soaked, full-blown asshole.

"*Huhmf*," she grunted, spun on her booted toe, and marched up the driveway.

Bear hopped up, realized I hadn't moved, and sat on his haunches. The dog huffed at me while I watched Samantha walk away. A very small part of me wanted to run and catch her.

I needed a moment to pull my shit together before going into the farmhouse, so I walked back to Sam's car. The Civic's engine, still hot, clicked as the motor cooled. The setting sun cast long, spiky shadows across the road. I crouched, examining the damage to the side panel, running fingers along the slashes.

Still squatting, I turned and surveyed the road. The sheet of ice had since melted, leaving wet asphalt behind. Even I had to agree with Sam that the ice was a bizarre turn of events. I scanned the treeline in the rapidly fading sunlight. An opossum ambled out of the palmettos across the street, froze at the sight of me, and scampered away as quickly as it could into a thick group of bushes.

Something cold touched my arm.

"Shit!" I scrambled, catching myself before I fell back on my ass. "Bear!" I scratched the pit bull behind an ear. "Thought you'd decided to go with Sam." The dog blinked up at me and licked my hand.

I heard a sharp snap of branches. Bear let out a small boof. Although it was dusk, I could still see the road, but the scrub across the street was all shadows. The hairs on the back of my neck prickled. Something more than a marsupial lurked nearby.

A red Greater Demon stepped around a saw palmetto

and sauntered onto the asphalt. His crimson skin contrasted with his tailored white suit, and he was impeccably dressed from his shiny black leather loafers to the fedora on his head. Aside from his skin tone and black eyes, he appeared human.

"Holy fuck," I said, leaping to my feet. I snatched Bear's leather collar to keep the growling animal from lunging at the interloper.

The demon strolled across the road, stopping short of where the grass met pavement. He took out a glass emery board from the inner pocket of his jacket and tended the nails on his left hand. He assessed his manicure, then tucked the file away.

"Good evening," he said, his voice smoky like barrel-aged scotch. "Where did Miss Fife go? Is she alright?" He craned his neck looking for her over my shoulder.

I shrank back. No demon had ever addressed me like this. I held my breath. My dinner threatened to come back up. I couldn't move. *You're on protected ground, you dipshit. Think. Study him.*

I dwarfed the red visitor. His stature was so average that he could disappear in any crowd, except that he radiated ancient self-assurance. *He can't touch you.* I squared my shoulders, meeting the demon's gaze.

"Why the hell does it matter to you? What do you want with her?" I was relieved that my voice sounded steadier than my hammering heart.

"I place a high value on information." The demon narrowed his black eyes. "There are rules to this game. If I answer your question, you must answer mine." He withdrew a pocket watch from his vest and glanced at it. "I am, however, pressed for time this evening."

"And the first one to refuse an answer?"

"Loses the game."

"Which means what for the loser?"

"You don't really want to know, boy. Now, where is Miss Fife?" He swung the gold watch in slow pendulum arcs.

"She's safe, away from you."

"You mean she is safe for now." The demon smiled and put his watch away. "I still want to know where Miss Fife went. She is highly coveted."

Bear's growl rumbled deep in his chest. His leather collar slipped against my sweaty palm but my grip kept him sitting. So many questions roiled in my head, jockeying for position.

"You're the one who visited the store yesterday. Why do you want to find her?" I asked.

His soulless eyes gleamed in wild delight. "A third question? My, my, aren't you delightfully greedy!" He grinned. "Yes, I am him. After what your Warriors did to my brethren a couple nights ago, I wanted to see these two for myself. And it is not *I* who wants your wee Warrior." He placed his palm on his chest. "My master does."

I stopped myself from blurting out my next question. He kept better count of my queries than I did. "Who the hell are you?" I growled.

"Ah-ah," he chided. "It's my turn." He tugged at the cuffs of his black shirt poking out from under his white jacket sleeves. "Tell me, where is Samantha Fife?"

"I won't answer anything about Sam." I scowled.

"No, boy. Either you play my way or not at all. It's no fun setting the parameters of what can and cannot be asked."

"You can't come in here so her whereabouts shouldn't matter to you."

"I believe you still owe me an answer," the demon snapped.

"Sam is in the farmhouse. Probably putting away her fucking ice cream."

"I was rather hoping I could speak with her," he said, "but you'll do in her stead."

"You had about ten minutes before she left. Why didn't you show yourself before then?"

He tapped the side of his nose twice. "Is that a question?"

"Yes." *Idiot. Don't waste your turn like that.*

He steepled his fingers, resting his chin on the tips. "I had a lovely time listening to the two of you go back and forth. Then she sprinted off and I am left with you." His gaze locked on me. "Does Kimberly Judith Shaw still live?"

Stay calm and be smart, Tate. "Yes," I said. "What do they call you?"

The demon sighed and rolled his eyes. "I'm willing to tell you anything you want to know, and you ask for my name."

I nodded.

"Very well." He lifted his fedora a few inches. "They call me Dominic. Where is Bernard Andrew Shaw?"

"He's not here and I haven't spoken to him since he left. He could be anywhere in the world by now. Who is this Master you answer to?"

Dominic cocked his head. "My kind call this being many things, but most refer to it as the Mage. *Why* did Bernard Andrew Shaw leave?"

I hesitated.

"Come now, boy, I thought we were past this."

"He left to find someone," I answered.

"Interesting." He stroked his black goatee.

"Where did you get the power to create ice on a hot Florida road?"

"I'm the Mage's favorite. What do they call you, human?"

"Harper. Why did you risk injuring Sam if the Mage wants her alive and well?"

The demon gave a small sniff and picked at one black fingernail. "Because I could."

I stepped up to the boundary line. The red demon peered at me with a curious expression. He tilted his head, studying me. "You have a familiar look about you, boy. From what bloodline do you hail?"

I started to answer, but he hissed, stumbled back, and wrenched the fedora from his head.

"You're a *Tate!*" he roared.

What the fuck? Dominic slammed his fists into the boundary veil. The invisible barrier rippled, burning the demon's skin and throwing him back several feet. He landed on his ass in the middle of the road. Black blood oozed from his burned flesh and his form flickered. He snarled something in a language I didn't recognize.

The moment his form stabilized he was on his feet, one hand sweeping toward me. A burst of dark energy rattled the barrier. The force of his rage made me flinch. Bear whined and pressed his thick body against my legs.

What did the Tates do to him?

"This is impossible," Dominic seethed. Abruptly, as if remembering who and what he was, he straightened his suit, dusted off his trousers, and plucked up his hat. The demon slapped the fedora on his thigh, then settled it on his head. He stepped back up to the line as if nothing had happened.

"I watched your parents die, boy. They must have hidden you well. Our scouts did not report that they had a child with them that day. Your expression tells me that you don't know what you are."

I almost crossed the boundary. Bear's weight held me in place. "How did you know my parents? How did you know I was a Tate? Did *you* kill them? What am I supposed to be?" *Shit. Shit. Shit. Shit.*

Dominic cackled and bounced on the balls of his shiny shoes. He pressed a red fist to his lips. "Oh, this is delicious."

Fuck.

The demon raised an inquiring brow.

"Fuck!" I took a quick breath and blew it out. "Yes."

Dominic held up four fingers, ticking off my questions. "Thomas and Elaine Tate were Bernard Andrew Shaw's alpha Warrior team. He sent them everywhere. Killed more of my brethren than any pair I've ever known." He folded down a finger. "The Mage killed your parents. I was present." Two fingers. "I know you're a Tate because you're the spitting image of both of your parents. You come from a deep bloodline of Light Warriors." Third finger. "You're supposed to be a Warrior of Light, boy, why aren't you?"

"I don't know," I answered through gritted teeth. With a handful of words, Dominic had flung me headfirst back into a childhood crafted by Hell.

I was six years old again, trembling in the kitchen pantry, peering out of the tight slats in the door. My father had swept me out of my chair at dinner and tucked me into the narrow closet. He had laid a finger over my lips and said, "Harper, Mommy and I need you to be as silent as a mouse, okay? Remember when we play hide and seek? Be quiet so no one can find you."

We'd played this game before, but this time Daddy was scared. I'd clutched his shirt. He'd kissed my forehead, plucked my hands away and closed the door. When I'd heard my mother's scream cut short, I pushed my fist into my mouth so I wouldn't scream, too. Daddy's tortured wails ended with a thump, and his body slammed into the pantry door. Even if I'd wanted to escape, I was trapped inside. I'd heard strangers laughing in the kitchen. Then heavy steps walked away. I'd been so quiet. Even when Uncle Andy had pulled Daddy away and opened the narrow closet, I made no sound.

Pops told me later that I didn't speak again for weeks.

"How curious," Dominic mused. "The child of two of the strongest Warriors of Light in history is impotent. It must be hard watching Miss Fife and her Warrior partner have what you've often prayed for. Am I right? Of course I am. That's not a question." The demon flicked road dust from his fedora's brim.

My chest ached. I rubbed a hand over my heart. *Be quiet so no one can find you.* I couldn't breathe.

"Come now, boy. Ask me your questions. I know you have them. Ask me why I think you're not a Warrior. You reek of untapped potential."

I slumped against the car and Bear stepped between the demon and me, snarling.

"Ask me about your parents," Dominic pressed. "Or about the Mage's plans. Ask me about Miss Fife. I know you want to, boy." He rocked back and forth on his heels, his rapid suggestions stealing my mental traction.

Then Dominic's face went blank. He stared off into the dusk, eyes intent on something not present. Annoyance overcame malice in his sneer. He rolled his eyes.

"You need me *now*?" he said. Dominic heard someone answer him. "As you wish."

The demon shrugged. "Alas, I must pause our game, but our little *tête-à-tête* is far from over." He rolled the fedora up his extended arm as though he were a departing performer and vanished the moment it settled on his sleek hair.

At Dominic's departure, my legs buckled. I caught myself on the Civic's bumper, using it to lower myself to my knees. Bear stopped snarling and snapping the moment the demon disappeared, but his short hackles were still raised. He sniffed the air, ears at attention, then he looked at me. I tugged the stout dog into my chest.

I pressed my forehead against Bear's wide shoulder and stroked his ears until my numb shock wore off and a new wave of emotion washed over me. Rage.

Dominic. He'd seen my parents die. He'd been there, for fuck's sake. Not only had demons taken my parents from me, they'd robbed me of my best friend, Teddy. They took his life when we were fifteen, snuffing him out with callous maliciousness. I'd seen a female demon standing over Teddy's body floating in the lake beside our campsite.

Demons also controlled the man who'd shot my fiancée, Molly, and then turned the gun on himself. All my paramedic training couldn't stop her from bleeding out from that bullet wound. Shock had stolen my voice even as she'd tried to reassure me.

"I just need to rest a spell, darlin'. Quit your fussin', it'll be alright," was what she said, and then she was gone. I'd fought my own EMT partner when he arrived and tried to pull me away from her. For four years I'd kept that pain sealed away, and in two minutes Dominic tore it wide open.

I was still powerless. Still so fucking useless.

What if I'm cursed? What if I'm doomed to always lose everyone and never have the power to stop it? Those thoughts lodged in my throat like a large pill refusing to go down. Above me, the stars appeared in the darkening sky.

I yelled at their Creator, "Do you hate me? Do you even care? What the fuck did I ever do to you?"

Bear whined and butted my chest with his broad head. "What am I gonna do, man? What use am I to Sam and Kestler? What if they die on my watch?"

Bear nudged my hand with his nose.

"I've got no powers to protect them."

The dog sneezed and glared at me, as if he understood and thought I was being a right little bitch. "You're right." I rubbed behind his ears. "Pops called *me*. He trusted his Warriors to *me*. Not sure why, but I'll do my damnedest to keep them safe."

Bear's tail thumped the ground, his tongue lolling as he grinned.

"Aren't you Sam's dog?"

Bear sprang to his feet, spun and bounced, then trotted a few strides toward the driveway. He glanced over his shoulder.

"Yeah, coming." I got to my feet, dusted sand from my jeans, and sighed.

Dominic had done a great job fucking with my head, but he wouldn't break me. And while I couldn't stop the enemy, I knew two Warriors who stood a good chance of doing just that. I would be there for them.

9

SAM

"Leigh," I yelled from my bedroom. "I need you!"

I was running behind at a quarter past five on Saturday, and struggling with a pair of black tights. Camden would be here at six. Guess who still had wet hair and wasn't fully dressed? I tugged a little too hard on one leg of the nylons and my finger popped a hole in them. Plopping down onto my bed, I huffed out a short breath.

"You know what?" I ripped off the tights and threw them across the room. "Not tonight."

I'd taken Max on a trail ride around four o'clock since mounting anxiety threatened to choke me. Being wanted by this Master and having its underlings threaten my boyfriend's life was one thing. Finding out Harper could see demons was a whole other level of what-the-hell. What I couldn't handle, what plagued my dreams, distracted me at training this morning, and had me on edge was that I hadn't sensed the demon who'd spun out my car last night. And that fear still prowled around my brain now.

"Am I being punished? Have I done something wrong?"

"Brave One, do not beat yourself up," Letty answered. *"There*

are greater powers at work here." Before I could answer her, Leigh popped into my room.

"What in God's creation are you doing just sitting there?" Leigh glanced at her watch. "He'll be here soon and you look like a drowned cat."

"I know," I moaned. "I'm a mess."

"Come on. Leave it to me to save the day." Leigh hauled me up from the bed. "What are you wearing tonight?"

"Not panty hose," I mumbled.

"What?" Leigh asked.

"Never mind." I went to my closet and selected the pewter one-shoulder dress I'd had forever, and never had a chance to use. "This, with those black strappy heels of yours, if you'd be so kind. And some sparkly jewelry."

"Perfect. Get dressed and meet me in my room. I'll do your hair and makeup. I've got the perfect dangly earrings you can wear. Do you have a clutch?"

I gave her a deadpan glare.

"Right. You'll use mine." Leigh headed back down the hall. "Make it snappy. I can work fast if you hustle."

Twenty-five minutes later, Leigh was putting the finishing touches on my face.

"You're so good at this crisis management stuff," I said.

"Oldest of five siblings, remember?"

"Life skills this only child didn't get." I ran my thumb over the glittering cubic zirconia bracelet in my left hand. Leigh's kind attention helped, but I was still frazzled. If I took Letty's word for it, I wasn't losing my Warrior touch. But that opened another can of demons. *How did they have the ability to mask themselves? Was it the master's influence over them?* The red demon from work had triggered my Power so hard and so fast that Letty had had to intervene. This one from last night hadn't even made a blip on my radar.

Leigh finished braiding my hair and settled the fishtail plait down the down the center of my back. She studied me in our reflection and tilted her head to the side.

"What's wrong?"

Everything. "Nothing."

"I've known you since we were five. You're a horrible liar." Leigh took the bracelet from me, circled my wrist with it, and closed the latch. "Does this have to do with Harper seeing demons or the fact that a demon spun out George by creating ice on a Florida road in summer?"

I startled. "He told you? When?"

"This morning." She shrugged. "When you came home last night and barely said anything to me after talking to him, I figured you two had had a fight. I let you have your space. But then when you didn't perk up with your coffee at breakfast, couldn't keep pace with me during our morning run, and did your target practice without music, I went to him. He told me what happened. Don't be mad."

"I'm not," I sighed. "Did he also tell you I couldn't sense the demon who attacked me?"

"Yeah," she said, sitting on the bed next to me. "Is that what's eating you?"

"Letty said it wasn't my fault. But I feel like my Powers are on the fritz."

"You bounced back like a champ after that black demon beat the crap out of you." Leigh gave my forearm a comforting squeeze. "Don't you dare lose your nerve now. Camden needs you to be on your game tonight. *I* need you firing on all Warrior cylinders. And let's not give Harper's obsession with keeping you under house arrest any more ammo. We need you to be Samantha Fife in all her glory tonight."

I chuckled. "That's a pep talk for the books."

"I've been reading up on motivational techniques." Leigh retrieved her high heels and handed them over by the straps. "Put these on."

I did as she instructed while she changed into black jeans, a black tee, and black boots. She was right, I had to turn this funk around. With shoes in place, clutch purse in hand, and best friend in tow I headed out of the room and down the hall. Cam would be here any minute. His fine qualities included punctuality.

We entered the den where Harper stood next to the kitchen bar. He had on a tattered pair of faded jeans and a greasy, holey, olive drab shirt. His eyes burned with some unreadable emotion as he stared at me, then cleared his throat and said in a raspy voice, "You clean up well."

"Was that a compliment, Tate?" I asked, halfway shocked and partially proud. "Where are you headed?"

"To fix your car."

"You already got it to the shop?"

"Yup."

"Oh. Thank you." *He's being nice. Not sure what to make of that.*

The doorbell rang. Like I said, punctual.

"That's my cue to leave," Leigh said. "I won't be far away and I'll text a check-in once or twice. Good luck and have fun!" With that she ducked out the back door.

Harper nodded to the foyer. "Gonna get that?"

"Yes." *What if I screw up? What if I can't sense a demon and people die tonight?* My feet became rooted to the floor. I locked eyes with Harper. He raised a brow when I didn't move. He crossed the room in large strides and headed right toward the foyer.

"You've got five seconds to get your shit together," he said under his breath as he passed by. "And Sam? Breathe."

I inhaled a sharp breath. He wasn't wrong. Now was

not the time to lose confidence. Camden's life depended on me. Humanity depended on me. *Letty's right. Leigh's right. I can do this. I'm still a badass Warrior woman.* I followed Harper.

He opened the door as I entered the foyer after him. "You must be Camden Bennett."

"That's me," I heard Cam say. "And you are——"

"Headed out." Harper stepped to the side, allowing Camden into the foyer, and hooked a thumb over his shoulder. "You're here for Sam, not me."

Harper ducked around Camden and jogged down the front steps. Cam watched Harper leave with furrowed brows. The introduction had been one-sided, and I didn't know if it was a power move on Harper's part or if he was continuing to be nice for my benefit. I didn't spare a second thought on the matter.

"Cam," I greeted him with a smile, setting aside my fears. "On time, as ever."

His eyes went wide when he saw me. "Oh, wow. You look——" Cam ran a palm over his mouth. "You look stunning."

"I told you I owned more than jeans." My Warrior worries were replaced with girly date jitters. He was quite debonair in that burgundy button down. It brought out the green in his eyes. "You're certainly no slouch either."

"Thank you." He kissed my cheek when I joined his side then offered me his arm. "Ready to go?"

"Absolutely." I took his proffered limb and we headed out.

At the car, being the gentleman that he was, he opened the door and helped me in. I'd won the jackpot when he'd walked into the feed store. He settled into the driver's seat and we made pleasant small talk while he drove down the driveway and turned onto my main road.

Ice on the road. Trees whipping in a whirl of green. Gouges in the metal of my Civic.

I shuddered, closed my eyes, and quietly willed my recent memory to shut the hell up.

"So, who was that guy who answered the door?" Cam asked.

"Uh." I blinked, stalling. "That was Harper. Harper Tate. He's—he's my grandparents' adopted son. Harper's parents died when he was six and they were the best fit to take him in. Been living in Savannah for the past six years. Just arrived home on Thursday." *Stop blabbering Harper's personal life, you ding-dong. He'll be pissed if you spill your guts.* "Hey, how's your employee? The one that hit his head?"

From my profile view of Cam, I watched his smile falter. "I guess I should warn you in case you overhear something from the staff tonight. When I left you on Thursday, I drove right to the restaurant. There were cops questioning my staff, a ton of first responder vehicles out front, and a freaking medical examiner. Javi died in my kitchen, Sam."

"No," I breathed. "Why didn't you tell me? I thought he was okay."

"There was a second incident I didn't know about. My phone died. I've been busy with lawyers and trying to keep morale up. I've watched the security video no less than fifty times and what I've seen has no explanation."

"God, that's—" I shook my head. "That's awful."

"You need to see the video," Letty said.

"What? How? Why?"

"I have a hunch. You must watch that video," she insisted.

"Ooookay." That was not going to be an easy task, but Letty was so earnest. Emphatic even. *"How do you suggest I do that?"*

"I have complete confidence in you."

Right. Sure. I cleared my throat. "Cam, I know your staff are like family to you. How're you holding up? How're the rest of your people holding up?"

He let out a caustic laugh and navigated his way onto the on-ramp of I-75. "They've been having a rough go. It's all been a living nightmare."

"Is this why you've been so distant?" I rested a hand on his shoulder. We'd texted and had a few short phone calls, mostly him just checking in to see how I was and to say hi. He was usually graciously attentive, but as I'd also had my fair share of distraction I hadn't noticed until this moment.

Cam stole a quick look at me, wearing a sad smile. "I didn't know how to tell you."

"Fair point." I gave his shoulder a squeeze.

"Let's talk about something else? Anything else," Camden suggested. "Something positive."

"Definitely." *He doesn't even want to talk about the incident. How am I gonna get eyes on that footage?* It was no simple task Letty had assigned me, but I had to honor Cam's request. "So you know my horse, Max? He's got a problem with cows and our neighbor's herd has taken to grazing near our fence line. Max refuses to go down there. Today, I convinced him they weren't there but he got one peep of the bull, spun, and bolted. I have no idea how I stayed on."

Camden laughed. "And that's positive?"

"Well, yeah. I didn't fall off and it's the best I could come up with on short notice."

Cam's mood lifted and the tension in his shoulders eased. We spent the rest of the drive trading my funny horseback riding fails with his humorous surfing mishaps. When we pulled into the lot of his restaurant, I was impressed.

Sorcerie was ginormous. She had a generous wrap-around porch decorated in a tasteful nautical theme with rope-wrapped columns, brass lanterns, wide paddle fans, and white-washed plant boxes. Camden steered me up the front steps. We passed by guests seated on luxury porch swings while they chatted with each other. In the waiting area inside, there was a floor-to-ceiling enclosure housing two huge birds.

"Watson and Holmes?" I asked.

"Yeah, that's the boys." Cam looked at his macaws with a fond half smile then turned to me. "You wanna meet them? I've got treats you can give them."

"That's very nice of you." I leaned up and kissed him. "But animals with beaks and talons make me a little nervous. Chickens are the only level of avian I can handle. Your guys are gorgeous though."

"Hear that boys? She thinks you're handsome," Cam said. He took my hand. "Let me show you around."

Camden introduced all of his staff by name, even the new bus boy who'd only been with them for two days. Each person responded to him with respect—several of them with clear affection—and they gave me the impression that I was welcome, not just as a dinner guest, but as Cam's date.

"They really are family to you, aren't they?" I asked as Camden slipped an arm around my waist and turned us down a hallway.

"I grew up working in my grandfather's restaurant in Connecticut. You know I lived with him after my father passed and my mother went AWOL. Anyway, it was a real ritzy place, more so than Sorcerie. I watched how good ol' Archie Bennett handled his people while he taught me the ins and outs of owning a white-table dining establishment. I wanted to be just like him, no matter what job I took."

"Sounds like Archie was a good man."

"The best." He stopped us right outside the kitchen. "I

want to introduce you to Renard and Jackie. It's a madhouse in there since it's Saturday night, so please watch your step. I don't want you to get run over or yelled at."

"Take me to your people," I said. Seeing Camden at ease in his natural environment endeared him all the more.

Inside the kitchen, Cam tucked me out of the way against a wall. I'd never been in a restaurant kitchen at the height of the dinner rush. The cooks and servers wove around each other like fish swimming on a coral reef. Everything ran with choreographed efficiency. It wasn't as loud as I'd expected given the level of activity and the number of people. Metal prep bins slid over steel tables, a girl rinsed and racked dishes with the care fine china deserves, stock pots bubbled, two men chopped ingredients with knives so sharp they slipped through food.

"Didn't that man die in here?" Letty asked. *"Sweep the room with your Power."*

"Well, hello there," I said. *"You've been quiet."*

"I was giving you your space. But this is the scene of the incident, so we need to find out what you can while your friend is away."

Warrior heat flooded my body as I extended my senses throughout the kitchen. *"What am I looking for? There's no demonic signature—Oh!"* An icy tendril of something dark and not-of-this-world lurked right in front of the walk-in refrigerator. I focused on that spot, my Warrior's perception assessing that alien cold for any familiar vibe. In my experience, leftover demonic energy felt hot, but this was something new.

"Letty, that's the same feeling the ice gave me last night. What is that?"

"It's ancient and it's evil. Be careful."

I took a small step in the direction of the fridge when a

waitress with her loaded metal tray whipped by me. "Watch it, princess!"

"Sorry." I skittered back to my place on the wall. Camden had put me where I wouldn't be in anyone's way, but I itched to inspect that area. I definitely needed to see that security video. With my Power on high alert, I sensed Camden behind me when he approached.

"I almost tripped one of your servers. Don't think I won any brownie points with her."

"If you're not used to a commercial kitchen, it can be intense." Cam put his arm around me. "I might get an earful later if you got in Brittany's way."

A petite blonde woman and a stout man stood behind Camden. They were dressed in white coats. Hers was splattered with dark sauces and tomato smears, but his was immaculate.

"Sam, this is Renard Bissett." Camden gestured to the guy. "He's my executive chef and a genius in the kitchen. And this is Jackie O'Rourke, my sous chef. She keeps us both in line. They are my closest friends."

I shook Jackie's hand and she winked at me. Renard's large hand engulfed mine.

"Pleased to meet you. Welcome to our home," Renard said. He spoke with a light French accent.

Jackie's blue eyes danced with mischief. "Bennett's never brought you around. We were starting to wonder if he made you up."

"Nope, I'm real." I grinned. "Nice to meet you both."

"And at the risk of embarrassing him," she continued, "he can't stop smiling when he talks about you. It's nice to see him happy for a change."

Camden tugged me close and spoke into my ear. "Let's get you out of here before they start telling embarrassing stories about me. You hungry?"

"Always," I said.

"Excuse us," Cam said to his chefs and guided me out of the kitchen.

I was very aware that he hadn't let me go and was even more shocked that I liked it. *The last guy that made me feel this giddy just being around him was*—I couldn't stop the name from popping into my head—*Harper. Dammit.*

"I hope you don't mind." Camden's voice heaved me out of my mental wreckage. "I took the liberty of ordering for us already. Renard has a few recipes he's been testing. Is that alright?"

"Ooo, surprises!" *Thank you, Cam, for being you.* "I'll eat pretty much anything except for raw oysters."

We started with amazing fried calamari with a spicy sauce, then the waitress placed a beautiful plate of sea bass stuffed with crab before me. I was used to fish fried or grilled, so this was fancy, and delicious. We chatted about younger Camden's world-traveling adventures with his grandfather and my summers at the Shaw property. Throughout dinner, I had to balance my supernatural concerns with the pleasure of our conversation. How was I going to view the security video? Where was Leigh? Had she found something? Was she okay? And what the fire-fart caused that evil cold spot in the kitchen?

A waitress took away our dinner plates.

"There we were," Camden said, "our private cruise ship dead in the water in the middle of the Danube. The captain was mortified and kept assuring my grandfather that this wasn't normal but that we were safe. We got a tow and stopped in this small German town for repairs. Anyway, while we were docked, I found this kick-ass sword in an antique shop that seventeen-year-old Cam just had to have."

"Do you still have it?" I asked. "Blades and weaponry happen to be a specialty—er, special fascination of mine."

"Yeah, I actually have it on display in my office." Cam chuckled. "I didn't know you liked that kind of stuff. You keep surprising me. Wanna see it after dessert?"

"Hell yes, I do!" *And maybe see if there is a way to get eyes on that footage.*

"I have a set of authentic Hungarian throwing knives in there, too," he said, waggling his eyebrows.

I busted out laughing. The man was speaking my love language and he didn't even know it. "And you keep surprising me, Mr. Bennett."

"Weapons are fun, Brave One, but I beseech you to check in with your Warrior partner," Letty reminded me.

"Excuse me, but I'll need to use the ladies room before dessert." I rose and placed my napkin on the table.

"Do you remember where the bathrooms are located?" Camden half-stood.

"Don't get up." I held up a hand. "I'll be right back."

I recalled the location of the restrooms from Cam's grand tour. For a place to take a crap, it was a fancy little joint with white marble floors, brass fixtures, and mood lighting. There were terry cloth towels in place of paper towels, for Pete's sake. I plopped down on the cream-colored couch situated along a wall and pulled out my cell.

Leigh had sent me a chain of text messages of her findings. She'd discovered a mysterious cold spot by the dumpsters with a trail leading down to the beach that had given her the heebie-jeebies.

I fired off a text. THERE'S AN ICY SPOT JUST LIKE THAT IN THE KITCHEN! LONG STORY SHORT, THAT EMPLOYEE WHO HIT HIS HEAD THE OTHER DAY WOUND UP DYING IN HERE. I THINK THE TWO ARE CONNECTED. I'M WORKING ON AN ANGLE SO I CAN SEE THE SECURITY

VIDEO. WHAT ARE YOU DOING? DID YOU FIND ANYTHING ELSE?

She responded promptly. THE GUY DIED?! WE'LL TALK AT HOME. OTHER THAN THE WEIRD COLDNESS, NOTHING ELSE HAS HAPPENED. I HAVEN'T EVEN SEEN A SINGLE DEMON ALL NIGHT. I'M SO BLOODY BORED. THINKING OF HEADING UP THE BEACH AND SCOUTING THE AREA A BIT.

I answered with, SOMETHING NEFARIOUS IS AFOOT, WATSON. DO WHAT YOU NEED TO, BUT BE SAFE. TEXT ME IN AN HOUR AND LET ME KNOW YOU'RE OKAY.

She sent a thumbs-up emoji and I put my phone away before heading back to Camden. I arrived just as our waitress set down a gold plate in the middle of the table. On it was a huge slice of seven-layer chocolate cake with some sort of caramel sauce drizzled over. My mouth watered.

"Did you miss me?" I asked, slipping into my seat.

"You know it," Cam said, doing that gentlemanly half-stand thing again. He met my eyes when we were both seated and gave me a genuine smile. My heart skipped a little when he looked at me that way.

Good grief, pull yourself together, Fife. "This is gorgeous, by the way." I pointed at our dessert. "But not too pretty to eat."

"Then I'll show you my weapons," Cam said.

I jabbed the nearest corner of the cake with my fork. "Deal."

As promised, Camden took me to his office. For a normal, human weapon the sword was a well-crafted *Messer.* I would know. I strolled around his office, looking at all the items he'd acquired from his travels, when my sights landed on a gold half-mask studded with diamonds.

I ran my fingers over one side. "This is pretty."

Cam came up behind me and put his arms around my waist. He dropped a kiss on the side of my neck and said,

"That's an authentic Venetian mask my father picked up at Carnevale. It reminds me of him, what few memories I have."

I leaned back, resting against him. He was warm and solid. "This is all so cool. I've only ever been to Ireland."

"The video," Letty prompted.

"You're persistent."

"You're stalling."

"I don't know how to ask this of him."

"So? I have faith in you."

I took a deep breath and turned around in Cam's arms. "This is going to sound morbid. Crazy, even. And so random. But—"

Camden searched my face and brushed the pad of his thumb over my cheek. "What is it?"

Remembering how sad he'd been in the car when he told me his cook died, I figured empathy and honesty were my best path to not making this request sound like I was insane.

"Here's the thing, I want to be here for you and I care about what you care for. You've been carrying around Javi's death alone. Will you show me the video of how he died?"

"Wow, that was not—" Camden cleared his throat. "Are you sure? It's gruesome and disturbing. It's not exactly what I'd like to show my girlfriend."

"I'm not squeamish and I don't scare easily."

Despite his trepidation, he moved to his computer and queued up the security footage. His hand hovered over the mouse, cursor arrow poised over the play button on screen when he looked up at me. There was a battle in his green eyes. "Are you *sure?*"

"Positive," I smiled and brushed my fingers through his curls. He started the video.

It started with Javi taking bins of prepped ingredients into the fridge. The impeccably dressed, crimson demon who'd visited us at work stepped into the frame from the right, hidden from Javi by a huge metal cabinet. He lifted it and threw it on Javi. The poor man never stood a chance. He fell sideways, and the edge of a steel prep table caught him under the jaw, snapping his head up as his body dropped. The cabinet lay on Javi so that only his left hand and skewed head were visible. The red demon grinned at his handiwork, then looked right up at the security camera. He straightened his suit. Then he winked and disappeared.

"Son of a bitch," I hissed.

"I shouldn't have shown you." Cam locked the computer, making the screen go dark. "Why did I show you?"

"No, you're fine," I said. "Poor Javi. That was—no wonder you're so upset."

"The police, my mother, Renard, and I have all watched the video and none of us can explain what happened with that thawing cabinet. Why would it fall that way? We checked and the wheels were all fine, and locked. It shouldn't have moved at all."

I stared at the blank screen. *This is bad, like, bad-bad. And Cam is in more danger than I thought.*

"Come on." Camden laid his hand on the small of my back and steered me toward the door. "I'll take you home."

The ride back was quiet. Camden, bless him, attempted small conversation, but my mind was billions of miles away. When he walked me to the front door, I yanked my attention back to him.

"I really enjoyed myself this evening. Dinner at your restaurant was phenomenal," I said. "Thank you."

"You're welcome. Next time we won't end the evening with a horror movie. I'm so sorry."

I looped my arms around his neck and looked in his eyes. "I asked to see it. And I have no regrets." I kissed him. "Promise."

"Then I can't argue with that." He kissed me again and rested his forehead against mine. "I'll call you tomorrow."

"You better." I stayed on the porch until his taillights disappeared down the driveway.

I sprinted to my room and changed into jeans and a T-shirt, brushed out my fancy hairdo, and took off my makeup. I went to Leigh's room. She wasn't inside. I checked my phone. No texts, no calls, no voicemails. My well-versed and talented imagination started feeding me worst-case scenarios.

What do I do? I closed Leigh's door, briefly rested my palm on the wood, and then left to go find Harper.

10

SAM

"**B**ear," I shouted into the night, jogging down the porch steps. "Bear! Where are you?"

Probably off chasing some nocturnal animal. Keeping my eyes peeled for the brindle dog, I headed to the gym. I slipped through the metal door and guided it shut so it wouldn't bang closed. The building's interior was dark, but warm light spilled across the floor from the gym office.

I could see through the open door that Harper's head was bowed, a folder of paperwork open before him. Bear had snuggled down in his dog bed in the corner. A small seed of jealousy sprouted in my chest.

"Focus on why you're here," Letty said.

"Harper?" I knocked on the door jamb and stepped inside. Bear's head popped up. He scrambled up, did a downward dog stretch, and lumbered over to me. His whiptail thumped against my legs. I patted his head.

"Samantha," Harper said without looking up. "What brings you out here?"

"Leigh's not home. She told me she was going to scout out the beach. I told her to touch base with me, but I haven't heard from her since our last check in around nine."

Harper's jaw tightened then he glanced up, looking past my shoulder—most likely at the clock on the wall—and then met my eyes. "Any chance you could have just beaten her home?"

"Not if she's riding Thad." I rubbed my hands down my face and melted into the guest chair in front of his desk. "She's not answering her phone, or text messages, or anything."

"Have you checked the barn?" Harper asked.

"No, I was on the way to do just that but"— I paused. Asking for Harper's help was foreign to me. "I was also looking for you, too. The red demon that visited me at work on Thursday is upping his game."

"Explain."

I related the supernatural stink that tainted my evening, careful to leave out any private Camden details. "Harper, he killed Javi just for the hell of it. And that damn demon with his tailored suit, perfect teeth, and silly fedora enjoyed it. He freaking winked at the camera."

Harper blanched.

"Fuck!" Harper slammed a fist on the desk, scattering pens, and making me flinch in surprise. He leapt up and blew past me to the door. Bear and I jogged after him. He hit the metal exit door with another "Fuck!"

"Harper, wait! Where are you going?"

Harper took the dirt path to the barn and was nearly there before I caught up with him. *How is he so damn fast? Good grief.* I tugged the back of his shirt. "Wanna tell me what all the 'fucks' were about? What do you know?"

He twisted his torso, breaking my hold, and shook his head. As if that were an answer. Before I could press him, Bear darted out in front of us and slammed to a stop—

forcing us to do the same—with his ears perked and tail vibrating in rapt attention. He boofed once, looked back at us, and tore off into the darkness.

Harper and I glanced at each other, and in unison, sprinted after the dog. We careened around the corner of the barn, only to be greeted by a dark, quiet interior. Harper hit the lights. I bolted to Thad's stall. He wasn't there. A few tears slipped out without permission. I dashed them away.

"Hey." Harper grabbed me by the shoulders and turned me to face him. "Stay focused. What can we do?"

Hannah, Andrew's retired mare, stuck her greying head over her stall door, bumping her nose against my shoulder. I patted her cheek. She watched me with dark, intelligent eyes.

"I have an idea." I crossed the aisle.

"Which is?" Harper asked, following me.

Max slept soundly on his side, all four legs extended. His calm, even breaths stirred the fine pine shavings by his nostrils. I opened his door and he lifted his head. *"Maximus Prime, I need you."*

He clambered to his feet, bits of hay and shavings stuck in his forelock. He blinked the sleep out of his eyes. *"What is it you want, my human?"*

I plucked the debris from his hair. *"Have you seen Thad?"*

"He left with his Warrior and has not returned." Max pressed his head into the center of my chest. *"What is wrong?"*

"Leigh is missing."

Max blew out a sharp horse snort. *"Do you think she is in trouble?"*

"I don't know buddy," I muttered, leaning my forehead against his. "Maybe."

Harper joined us, leaning on top of the stall door. He nodded at Max. "What's he saying?"

"Thad's been gone all night."

"Tell me your plan."

"We ride out and look for Leigh. Her last known whereabouts was Sorcerie. We can start there. You can take Hannah."

Harper's jaw flexed and his eyes burned a deeper blue. I was sure he was going to disapprove when he finally said, "I don't like it, but it's better than doing nothing. Let's go."

Well knock me over with a feather.

We tacked up Hannah in record time and I threw a bridle on Max. As we stepped out of the barn, Bear came bowling in, barking. He skittered across the concrete, looped behind Harper, and pushed against his legs. He did the same to me before heading back out.

"Gotta be Kestler," Harper said.

Illuminated by the blazing exterior barn lights, we saw a fully-armored Thad galloping through the night fog, coming in hot. I threw Max's reins at Harper and ran out to meet them. Thad slid to a stop, tossing his head and snorting. The grey horse's wide-open nostrils and heaving sides indicated he'd been going hard for a while. Leigh slid from Thad.

Her ball cap was gone, her brunette hair windblown-wild. Her black shirt was ripped across her abdomen and there was a tear in her jeans the length of her thigh. I could see she'd been crying, but there was no mistaking her Warrior rage. Fury still glowed battle-ready white in her right fist.

"Leigh, honey," I spoke low and calm. "Where ya been? I was worried about you."

She muttered to herself as if she were carrying on a heated conversation I wasn't privy to.

"Leigh, what's up?" I reached for her.

"No! Don't touch me!" she screamed and swept Fury up, warding me off.

"It's okay," I said, stepping back. "Just me. Just Sam."

"Careful!" Harper barked, rushing forward with Max and Hannah in tow. He met my eyes, nodded, and grabbed Bear's collar.

I turned back to my best friend. "Leigh, what's going on, hon?"

"So cold. In my head. I couldn't stop it," Leigh rambled. "We are not enough. Not at all." Fury burned brighter. Her whole body trembled. Thad remained in his armor watching her every move. "There were so many!"

"Can I reach her if I go full Warrior?"

"That will work," Letty said.

I called on the full Power of my mantle. White heat raced down my spine, wrapped around my bones, and settled into my muscles. My aura glowed golden and my clothes changed into our battle whites. Leigh's frenzied chatter stopped, her eyes widened, and she froze.

"Hey, it's me," I said, "your best friend." I stepped towards her, keeping tabs on the bright sword.

Leigh blinked several times, still struggling.

"You're on hallowed ground. You're safe. Thad's safe."

At last, her eyes locked on my face. Fury went dark and *thunked* into the grass as she let go of the hilt. She dropped to her knees. I picked up Fury and slid him into the scabbard on her back.

"Sam." Harper pointed. "Look."

I glanced over at Thad. No longer in Guardian mode, he now stood without armor or tack. I released my Power. Since I'd called on the highest level of my mantle and not acted on it, a gentle hum of residual Warrior energy settled in between my shoulder blades.

I knelt in front of Leigh. She had a bleeding cut along

one side of her jaw. I ran my hand down her arm. "What happened?"

"Sam," Leigh said before she started sobbing. I gathered her into my arms and let her cry. Only once she'd stopped shaking did I lean back.

"Leigh"—I smoothed tear-soaked strands of hair from her face—"you came flying in here like Hell was hot on your tail. You're bleeding. And Thad didn't stand down when he saw me. I need you to tell me what happened."

She sniffed and wiped her nose on her sleeve. "I'm so sorry."

"What on Earth for?"

"I hit a demonic hotspot when I patrolled the beach, and instead of listening to you to be careful, I followed the trail. Alone. And I screwed up."

"Kestler, what happened?" Harper asked from behind me.

"We gotta go," Leigh insisted. "Tonight. Right now. There is a demon nest right on the beach. People could be in danger."

"Is that such a good idea in your condition?" I asked.

Her eyes narrowed and she stood up. "This is our duty, Sam."

"You're in no shape to be going anywhere," Harper said.

"I'm fine," Leigh snapped but tears brimmed in her eyes.

I stood. "Are you sure?"

"Yes." She brushed past me, but Harper stopped her. She bristled. "We can't waste time."

"I'm not saying no," Harper said, "but we can't help if we don't know what's going on."

Leigh's jaw clenched. Harper stood firm. After a few

seconds of wordless debate, her shoulders slumped forward.

"We bolted for home," she said. "Thad was in Guardian mode so we could get here fast. When we were halfway here someone intercepted us." She snapped her fingers. "Like that."

I didn't know of anything that could match a Guardian's speed. "A *demon* stopped Thad?"

"No." She rubbed the cut on her jaw, smearing blood. "It was a being dressed in a black hood. It had white hands etched with red swirling tattoos. It was leading a slew of demons, including that one from the feed store."

"His name's Dominic," Harper said. "He's the Mage's right hand. I met him last night."

"Wait, you met him?" I asked. *So that's his name.*

"He introduced himself when I was examining George. We can talk about that later."

"Do you think you met the Mage tonight?" Harper asked Leigh.

"Yeah," she whispered.

"You're positive?" he asked.

"It introduced itself as the Mage. It yanked me off my horse, cut my jaw, and touched my forehead with a bloody finger. Everything went cold. Ice covered the ground and trees." Her voice shook. "I lost my connection with Thad and Rose."

I saw horror in her eyes. *I don't think she's telling us everything.*

"When the Mage let me go, the demons attacked. I jumped back onto Thad and he tore outta there." Thad stepped forward and nudged her. "We need to go wipe out that nest. Now."

"You're in no shape to go anywhere," Harper said.

"You need to rest," I said.

"This is our sacred duty, Samantha Grace Fife. I will not back down just because this Mage scared me."

Her bravery was admirable, but impulsive. It sounded like something I would do, not Leigh. She was shaken and, I suspected, scrambling for control.

"Are you sure you're up for this?" I asked.

"That nest could be gone, Kestler," Harper said.

"True, but at least we'll have done our due diligence."

I knew what made Leigh tick, what her tells were, what drove her to succeed. If she declared that she was good to go, I wouldn't argue with her. "Then we have a demon nest to visit."

"I'm going with you," Harper said.

"No," Leigh said.

"Are you nuts?" I asked.

"This isn't up for debate." Harper headed back to the barn. "I'll ride Hannah. I'll have no issues when she slips into Guardian mode."

I gaped at his retreating back. *He's not a Warrior but he can see the enemy. And now he can ride Guardians. What is he?* That question was for another time.

Leigh shrugged. She wrapped her fingers in Thad's long mane and swung onto his back.

Everything about this situation felt reckless, even for me. Harper handed Max's reins to me. Hannah trailed behind him. The mare *knew* something epic was afoot. Damn smart Guardian animals. Bear came from the barn and butted his head into Harper's leg.

"You stay here, man." Harper knelt in front of the dog. Bear whined. "Judy needs you. Can you protect her for me?" The dog's ears perked at this request. He barked, spun a tight circle, then took off for the farmhouse.

Harper and I joined Leigh. I vaulted onto Max's back. "Alright people, let's do this."

SAM

Leigh slowed Thad from Guardian's speed when we reached the sandy shore of the Gulf. We trotted, with her on point and me behind her. Harper rode up beside me on Hannah. He sat quiet in the saddle, unfazed that he'd sifted through time and space. I added his ease with Guardian travel to the growing list of skills Harper shouldn't have had.

Though it was well after midnight, beachfront hotel lights blazed bright in the moonless night. I whispered a thank you toward Heaven for Divine Intervention that masked us from late-night partiers, drunk resort guests, and beach security. All I heard was the shush of waves and our horses' breathing.

"How much longer?" I kept my voice low.

"Not too much farther," Leigh said, her tone terse.

"She's in a mood," I mumbled.

"The Mage fucked with her mind," Harper said, adjusting the chest strap of his sword's scabbard. He'd selected it from the gym armory before we rode out. His eyes never stopped searching along the shore. While he was a damn good rider, his fidgeting suggested he was worried.

"We'll be okay." *I hope.*

"Nothing about this plan is okay, Sam," Harper muttered. "And I haven't got a better goddamn plan of action except following Leigh's lead." He ran a rough hand over his head.

Leigh's abrupt halt wrenched my attention forward. "Heads up," she said, halting Thad.

Max stopped, his eyes and ears focused on the shimmering veil running up from the ocean to the beachfront properties. Leigh was on the other side of it.

"Holy shit," Harper murmured, reining in Hannah as she jigged sideways. "I knew these existed but I've never seen one in person."

"What?" I asked.

"This is a demonic veil. I've read about them," Harper said. "We can enter here but they can't enter our sacred ground."

"We can have this conversation later," Leigh insisted. "Focus on the mission." She set off at a walk. "Word of warning, passing through is a little disconcerting."

Harper shrugged and gestured for me to move on.

What have we gotten ourselves into? I thought. *Deep shit, that's what.*

The moment we passed through the veil, all the white noise coming from ocean waves, nearby highway traffic, and hotel nightlife snuffed out. Silence met my ears. There was a haze between us and the outside. Even the temperature changed from humid Florida summer into an oppressive, dry, Hellish heat.

My Warrior roared to life. *Disconcerting my ass.* My Power flooded me with fevered energy, tingling down my spine.

Max snorted. *"I don't like it."*

"Neither do I, Maximus Prime," I muttered.

"We are getting close," Leigh said from her front position.

"Fantastic," Harper said. "You're sure you want to do this?"

"We have to." Leigh lifted her chin with firm resolve.

"Of course you do." Harper looked up, as if pleading with Heaven for patience.

We rode another half mile in the hellish heat and reached a second shimmering barrier.

"Fuck," Harper swore under his breath.

"What? What's wrong this time?" I asked.

"When Hell wants to keep out intruders, they layer the veils like this. Basically, they're saying, 'Stay the fuck out of our territory.' You and Kestler will have to be careful. Stick together."

I had to hand it to Harper, he *was* useful after all. The moment we crossed through the second veil, the surrounding hotels and lights disappeared. Ahead of us, a lone building rose from the sand about a hundred yards away. It was the crumbling ruins of a derelict hotel, six stories high with a collapsed roof. Most of its windows were busted out. A bonfire raged outside.

"That's it. Follow me," Leigh said.

"Sure, let's ride toward the huge, haunted mansion," I grumbled, nudging Max on.

"Swear to me you won't do anything stupid," Harper said. "Scout around then get the fuck out. No reckless shit."

"Oh ye, of little faith." I laid a hand over my heart. He scowled and I rolled my eyes. "Yes, *sir.* It's not me you should be worried about this time." I glanced at Leigh, who'd set a determined pace towards the creepy building.

Harper shook his head. "This is a fucking stupid idea."

"I agree," I said. The sulfurous reek of a large demonic presence made me gag as we got closer.

"How many demons does it take to generate this level of Hell heat?" I asked Letty.

After a pause, she said, *"Hundreds."*

"Damn it all," I whispered. Adrenaline zinged through my veins, mixing with my Power.

"What did you say?" Leigh asked.

"Nothing," I said. "When you initially found this nest, did you know there were *hundreds* of demons inside?"

She shrugged. "I didn't stick around to count them."

"Right, awesome." *What have you gotten us into, Leigh?*

When we were fifty yards from the ruined hotel, Harper stopped next to a battered lifeguard stand. "You two go ahead, I'll stay here with the horses."

He had a sword and lethal skills, but he could only hurt a demon, not kill it. From his vantage point here, he was away from the den of the enemy but had a solid view of the nest.

I slid from Max's back, flipped Harper the reins, and laid a hand on my horse's forehead. *"Stay with him. He needs your protection more than I do."*

"You are my priority."

"Protect Harper," I insisted.

His reluctance filled my mind, but along with it, his acquiescence. I kissed his forehead and met Harper's determined gaze. "Take care of my boy."

"And Thad, too," Leigh said, passing her reins to Harper.

"The demons won't be expecting you since there's a third veil you'll have to cross," Harper said, pointing to a shimmering line in the sand close to the building. "They count on these barriers to keep wandering demons inside. You should be fine until you enter that third zone."

The closer we got to the ruins, the hotter it got. Every step we took toward the hotel dredged up dread and despair. Letty's calm presence kept me from losing my nerve. Leigh hunched her shoulders and powered forward, as if walking through an intense squall. Sweat trickled down my back and I breathed in ragged huffs. I stumbled. In the words of Dante, Hell's message was clear, *"Abandon hope, all ye who enter here."*

Just when I thought I couldn't take another step, we passed through the final veil. My gloom-and-doom lifted but the heat remained. I heard shouts, chatter, and the drunken disorderliness of a demon campout.

The crumbling hotel's courtyard was open to the ocean and a huge bonfire raged in the center. The fire illuminated everything around it with an orange, ghastly glow. The shifting light danced across the crumbling walls, and canvas-covered wagons flanking the rear entrance spawned deep, flickering shadows. There were iron-banded barrels, burlap sacks, and wooden boxes stacked in the space as well.

Hello, medieval time-warp. I stared at the encampment.

Leigh hauled on my arm. I hadn't been aware I'd stopped. We crept along the wagons, merging with the shadows. From the cover of a couple of barrels, we peeked inside.

The hotel was a shell of a building. Four towering grey stone walls enclosed a large square space of sand. There was no roof, no stairs ascending upward, no different floors. Rows of tents lined the barren brick walls. In the space between the bonfire and the back wall, they'd built a raised wooden platform.

At least two hundred demons milled around smaller

fires. They weren't the gangly ones we'd been used to fighting for the past two years. They were the same kind that we'd fought last Wednesday night. Every single one of the heavily-muscled demons was armed with multiple weapons.

My body pulsed with white-hot Power.

Some of them played cards at makeshift tables, others threw daggers at a target propped up in the sand, and nearly all of them were drinking. They were dressed in filthy, ragged clothes, looking like sea-weary pirates. Their general rabble-rousing was punctuated with the occasional bark of harsh laughter or sharp swearing in a language I didn't know. Two huge, black war-dogs with armor on their shoulders and canines as long as tusks snoozed next to the wooden platform.

"Hellhounds," Letty answered my unspoken question.

"Wait. There are actual, real hellhounds?"

"There certainly are."

Andrew never mentioned they existed. A dangerous spike of curiosity stirred in me. I raised a brow at Leigh, glanced at the sleeping dogs, and looked back at her. She mouthed a firm *No!* And if looks could kill, I'd be roasting in one of those fires.

I made walking motions with two fingers then pointed to a shadow near the tent rows. She nodded. We slunk inside, moving as ghosts through the field of tents. We stopped where we had a clear view of the action but with plenty of cover.

Two demons, one muddy orange, the other neon green, broke off from the main group and headed in our direction. Leigh reached for Fury and I stayed her hand without taking my eyes off the approaching pair. Leigh quivered. Was it from fear, restraint, or battle readiness? I wasn't sure.

The duo stopped at a tent just before reaching us. I rose to peer over the barrels, but Leigh grabbed the back of my shirt. I glared at her. She mashed her lips into a stern line. With more caution, I peeked around the tent instead.

"The Mage is in a foul temper tonight and I'm bloody tired of being yelled at," said the green guy.

"Careful with your words, Albert," the orange one said. "You know the Mage has ears everywhere."

"The mighty Mage is merely human, Cornelius," Albert sneered.

"A *human* that beat the shit out of you yesterday when you didn't bow," Cornelius said.

The Mage is freaking human? How? Leigh's face paled and she reared back. I rapped my knuckles against her shoulder and mouthed *Are you okay?* She gave a firm nod.

"A human," Albert said, regaining my attention, "who's protected by Hell itself, you dolt. You know where the Mage gets its Power."

"Too bad Dominic isn't in charge these days," Cornelius said. "I'm sick of taking orders from this outsider." The orange demon rubbed a spot on his chest, flinching.

Albert grunted in agreement. "It's also been so long since we've been allowed to hunt. I need to *feed*."

"Once the new Warriors are dealt with, the Mage promised to let us loose," Cornelius said, disappearing into the tent for a moment. He returned with a wineskin, took a long pull, and passed it to Albert.

"We'll soon have our feast, brother. Dominic *better* not fail us," Albert said.

I made to duck back behind our tent and froze. A shiny pair of dress shoes stepped into view. I followed the line of his leg to his head and stared into the crimson face of Mr.

Enigma, better known as Dominic. My throat constricted. My heart slammed into high gear. He sauntered forward with his hands clasped behind his back, but he wasn't focused on us.

"Cornelius and Albert," he crooned. "Frick and Frack."

The green and orange demons flinched at his voice and spun to face him. They scrambled to attention, some of their booze sloshing from the wineskin, and saluted.

"D-Dominic, sir!" Cornelius spluttered.

As the demon-master's righthand, he must be a high-ranking demon of some kind. Andrew's tutelage hadn't covered demonic hierarchy, or even hellhounds. *Why?*

"You weren't speaking ill of our master, now were you?" he asked, his tone charming. "The very same master responsible for your release from Hell? You'd still be wasting away in your underworld prison if not for the Mage's benevolence, you pathetic cretins. It would be such a tragedy if you were overheard being ungrateful."

"P-please forgive us," Albert stammered. "We just came to get a spot to drink." He bowed low at the feet of his scarlet superior.

Dominic smoothed his tie and picked at something on his lapel. He flicked whatever it was away and sighed. He returned his attention to Cornelius and Albert with something paternal in his black eyes. "Mind yourselves, boys."

Curiosity must have overcome Leigh's apprehension because at that moment she popped her head around the tent corner, joining me. Dominic's gaze snapped to us.

Shit! I grabbed Leigh's shirt sleeve. *All the shits!*

Dominic inhaled and a tight grin tugged at his lips. He looked like a cat who'd cornered his dinner. Without taking his eyes off of us, he barked at his underlings, "Get back to the fire before I gut you and send you to Hell myself."

Cornelius and Albert yelped and scrambled away, as they tripped over each other to get back to the main group. We slipped behind the tent. Leigh's lips moved in silent prayer.

Dominic meandered into view, stroking his black goatee. He kept his body half turned toward the main camp, giving us his profile. He didn't look at us.

"Why in the world would two Warriors of Light enter a Hell pocket without an army to back them up?" Dominic asked, his voice quiet. He rubbed his hands together. "Surely you're not so stupid, but alas, here you are."

We are stupid. What the hell were we thinking? Bile rose in my throat and I remained as still as a terrified rabbit. How were we getting out of this?

"Walking into a den of lions as you have, with your Power smoldering, snooping where you don't belong." He *tsked* then let out a dramatic sigh. "Do you know how long it's been since my brethren have been free on Earth? Samantha Fife, you *know* my master has plans for you. Why make this so easy?"

Dominic pointed to the platform. A lone hooded figure now stood there, situated behind a long wooden table. The Mage fiddled with bowls and a mortar and pestle, mixing ingredients for some sort of demonic hocus pocus.

We might as well have walked in here with our glowing weapons drawn and golden auras blazing. We were caught, well and good. Precisely the opposite of what Harper had asked of us.

I glanced at Leigh and saw her terror.

"What are our odds of fighting our way out of this and living to tell the tale?" I asked Letty.

"As long as you lived, Brave One, I would willingly give you my aid and whatever Power needed."

Well, then. *So that means the odds are zero.*

"And Miss Kestler, how do you know you won't be executed on the spot?" Dominic glanced at us, then looked back to the Mage's preparations.

Maybe we could escape the ruins, get through the veils, and get the hell out of Dodge. Not with two hundred demons milling around and Dominic aware of our presence. We were so screwed.

"Settle your pin feathers, wee sparrow. What my simpleton brethren fail to realize is that if Miss Kestler is dead, Samantha will not cooperate. I have no use for a dead Warrior of Light, and even less use for a noncompliant one." He flipped a hand as if dismissing the thought.

"Furthermore," Dominic continued, "capturing you tonight does not serve my long purposes. So I will postpone your inevitable recruitment. Be ready, for this favor comes with consequences."

Dominic disappeared and reappeared on the platform next to the Mage. Red tattoos glowed and swirled on the cloaked figure's hands. Dominic leaned in and spoke to the Mage.

"Cornelius and Albert." The Mage's shrill voice rang across the noisy crowd. "Come forward."

The heat from the roaring fire and massive demonic presence vanished in a frigid gust. Goose flesh rippled across my arms. My eyes stung. I grabbed Leigh's forearm. She jumped when I touched her.

Icy clouds of cold fog poured from the platform and flowed through the camp like a flash flood. The demons froze, their laughter silenced, games and sparring halted, and some toppled in mid-stride.

Only three demons were able to move. Cornelius and Albert took three hesitant steps toward the platform, and Dominic straightened his shirt cuffs. He glanced in our direction and pinched the brim of his fedora in an incon-spicuous salute. "Consequences," he murmured.

My sharp Warrior's hearing had no problem discerning what he'd just said. My grip doubled down on Leigh's arm so hard that she grunted. I let her go and flexed my cold fingers. *Why is he helping us?*

"Cornelius and Albert, you insubordinate, useless, pathetic *vermin!*" The Mage's voice was low. A red glow burned from deep under the hood. "You two think you can do better without my protection? Without my anointing?"

The Mage plunged its hands into a deep, brass bowl and withdrew them, a stream of thick, dark liquid draining onto the table. Then the Mage flung its arms outward, spraying drops across the crowd as it said one harsh word. Some ancient, evil power triggered the Warrior in me so strongly that I nearly changed into my complete holy ensemble.

A second later, every demon, every tent, everything—including Dominic and the Mage—vanished. Not even a single ash from the fires remained. The sound of waves, beach nightlife, music thumping in the distance, and night-time traffic met my ears. We were out of the alternate dimension and back on the Florida beach. Cornelius and Albert crouched back-to-back a few yards away, just as startled as we were.

"Oh, damn!" I exclaimed as I jumped to my feet, ready to fight. I let my Warrior Power surge and pulled Azira, along with two arrows, off my back. Leigh, already in her holy clothes, unsheathed the glowing Fury.

I nocked both arrows and fired before either demon saw us. Cornelius caught one shaft from the air, inches from his chest. Albert dived behind his buddy and the arrow intended for him sailed past into the dune.

Leigh charged them while they were dealing with my

arrows. She plunged Fury hilt-deep into Cornelius's gut. She opened him from navel to chin and his innards spilled onto the sand. He didn't even have time to collapse before he burst into bright splinters of light and disintegrated into dust.

That was the sort of good, solid demon death I was talking about. None of that flickering away bullshit.

I flung my bow aside and darted around Albert, who had grabbed at Leigh's sword hand. She stepped back and swung but he dodged. I kicked the back of his knees and he dropped with a grunt. I wrenched him into a headlock, turning away from the stench of filth and stale ale.

"Watch his head!" Letty shouted.

I was milliseconds too slow. Albert's skull slammed into my mouth with enough force to stagger me. My eyes watered in pain. I tasted blood.

"Bastard!" I snarled. Albert bucked against my hold. Leigh advanced, sword poised to gut her a second demon. Oh, no. This one was mine. "I got this, Leigh!"

Albert writhed in my grip. He nailed me with an elbow in the stomach that felt like an iron battering ram. He flung himself down. Albert roared in frustration when I pinned him to the sand, straddling his lower back.

"End of the line for you, *Albert*." I snatched an arrow from my quiver and shoved it down into his heart. I let go of his fracturing body, getting out of the way just before he exploded.

With our demons dispatched, I fist-bumped the night sky and whooped. Then I spit out a wad of blood and checked my teeth. All accounted for. Leigh knelt on the sand breathing hard, and we looked up at the sound of Harper's approach with our horses. I wiped my busted lip with the hem of my shirt.

"How did he catch my arrow?"

"I don't know," Leigh said. "But I think we need to get the heck out of here."

"You are so right," I said.

"Sam! Kestler!" Harper arrived in a shower of sand and horse snorts. He vaulted off of Hannah. "Are you two okay?"

His shrewd eyes scanned us, his mouth tightening when he saw my lip. Harper stepped closer to me and used a knuckle to lift my chin. The pad of his thumb grazed my busted lip with gentle pressure. My heart squeezed with apprehension and uncertainty. I looked at him sidelong and caught his blue eyes filled with concern.

"You're hurt," he said. There was no hardness in his expression. This was my old Harper.

"Demon headbutted me. I'm fine." I pulled away.

"I saw. What happened with the demons and the building, though?"

"Let's talk about this later," Leigh said. "I would feel better if we were back on hallowed ground."

Max leaned his long face against my chest and I ruffled his forelock. Thad had joined Leigh. The three of us mounted and our Guardians sped us home.

12

CAMDEN

"I'm an idiot," Camden muttered. He tossed his keys, wallet, and spare change in a brass bowl atop the foyer table beside the front door of the beach house he shared with his mother. He crossed the atrium living room, yanking off his tie as he went, and headed straight for the open kitchen.

Camden selected a beer from the fridge, popped off the cap, and rested his weight against the counter. He stared out the rear wall of windows at the now pitch-black beach.

"You ruin anything you touch," he said to himself and shook his head. He took a long pull from the bottle. Things had been going so well on his date. Sam had been at ease —engaging, funny, and charming. She'd even been interested in his medieval weaponry fascination.

Until he showed her that damn security video.

"What was I thinking?" Cam slapped the grey-veined marble countertop with an open palm. Even though Sam insisted that the horrific footage hadn't bothered her, she'd been quiet and withdrawn on the ride back to her place. He took another drink.

"You're home early," his mother's voice purred from behind him.

Camden flinched and gripped his beer tighter. *You've gotta be kidding me. Why is she up?* He watched his mother's reflection in the dark windows as she walked into the common room from the north wing. She tightened up her emerald robe as she strolled over.

"Mother," Camden turned around. *Do I have to deal with her tonight?* It would be easier to see what she wanted than to try to avoid the conversation.

"How was your date?" She wore no makeup, making the fine lines around her mouth and eyes more pronounced, and her long auburn hair was pulled into a ponytail.

"It went well." *Mostly.* Without taking his eyes off his mother, Camden picked at the bottle's label with a thumb.

"I didn't expect you until later." She smiled and laid a hand on his cheek. "Did something happen?"

"I'm fine, everything is fine." Camden pulled his head away from her touch. "Did I wake you?"

"No, I was waiting for you."

Oh, joy. What fresh hell does she want?

His mother flounced away to her Swedish secretary desk across the large room. She opened the hinged lid and withdrew a nine-by-twelve brown envelope. "This came today, addressed to you."

Camden raised a brow.

His mother often withheld documents, or omitted important information during a conversation, just so she could produce them at the time of her choosing. This pissed off Cam, so he had all his mail routed to Sorcerie.

Who would send him something here and why had his

mother been so forthcoming? *Is this a trap?* Camden sipped his beer. "You waited up just to give me that?"

His mother huffed. "I had to sign for it!" She thwacked the packet on the desk.

Curiosity overrode his annoyance. He strode over, took the unopened envelope from her, and sank onto the couch. There was no return address and the beach house address had been typed. His mother perched on the arm of the couch. Her cold green eyes pried like greedy fingers.

"Open it," she demanded.

Camden scowled but flipped over the packet and slid a finger under the sealed flap. Inside was a single sheet of heavy stationery. On it was a short, typed note:

> Javier Manuel Martinez was only the first.
> Who will be next?
> Don't you wish you knew?
> Won't this be fun?
> There is one thing for certain—
> Camden Remington Bennett, you will die last.

"What the hell?" Camden said, jumping up and flinging the letter onto the coffee table as if it were a snake.

"What is it?" Her prying question was faint behind the roar of his pulse in his ears. She swooped for the letter. Camden watched her read the note.

Javi's death was an accident, Camden thought. He ran a hand over his face. *How the hell could Javi have been murdered?* He'd watched it happen. There hadn't been anyone near Javi. Camden's breath caught as the rest of the note registered. More people would die.

"Oh, God! Renard. Jackie. I have to warn them!" Camden fumbled for his cell. His hands shook so hard he had to grip the phone tight against his chest. *Breathe, Bennett.*

"Camden, you're specifically mentioned here." His mother laid a hand on his forearm.

Despite his inner turmoil, he glanced at his mother's face. She wore a mask of concern, yet her eyes simmered with anger. She tossed the letter back onto the table and her grip on his arm tightened.

"Why would someone threaten you?" Her voice was frosty. "Have you been in contact with your former *employer?*" She dropped to a whisper. "Have you been fighting again?"

"No!" He jerked his arm away from her. "I swear to you, I honored my contract. I got out clean. And I haven't spoken to anyone from Connecticut."

She flipped her long ponytail over her shoulder and pursed her lips, studying Cam. It was all he could do to not squirm beneath her penetrating gaze. He clenched his teeth and forced himself to meet her eyes. *Show no fear.*

"You're telling the truth."

Camden exhaled when she looked away from him and withdrew her own phone from the pocket of her robe. "I'll handle the police. Who do you think this psychopath will go after next? Who do you care about?"

"My staff. They're family. Renard and Jackie, specifically."

"I will double security at the restaurant and put private security on those two. And you"—his mother tapped the center of his chest—"will not be going anywhere without a bodyguard."

He started to protest, then he thought of Sam. Dread slithered down his esophagus. "Shit."

His mother paused typing into the notepad on her cell. She tilted her head towards him. "Yes?"

"Sam." He pressed his fist to his mouth. *I have to warn her. I can't let anything happen to her. I have to protect her.*

"You just *now* thought of her? I guess I'll have to put cover on your girlfriend—"

"No!"

"She'll need protection, too, won't she?"

Camden bristled at her patronizing tone. "Let me talk to her first."

He wanted to protect Sam from whomever had sent the threat, but he didn't want her exposed to his mother's manipulations. "Let me tell her what's happened. I'll handle her security. If this catches her by surprise she won't —" Camden mashed his lips together. *She won't stay with you? Good God, Bennett, are you fifteen? Her life could be in danger and you're worried she'll leave your ass. What's wrong with you?*

Camden wanted to explain this situation. He wanted to ease Sam into the idea of a security team trailing her. He wanted to drive over to her house right now, drag her to his home, and keep her by his side. Camden winced. *How primitive of me.*

Allowing his mother to get involved without warning Sam was bound to end badly. She would definitely leave him, even though she might be in danger. Whether or not they were a couple, he couldn't let harm come to her because of his problems.

"Sam and I have only been together for a short time. Please let me talk to her first."

His mother's false compassion dropped, leaving behind a ruthless woman who snarled, "As you wish. I'll handle this threat, the police, everything but your Samantha. If any harm befalls that girl because you wouldn't let *me* protect her, her blood will be on your hands." She smoothed her auburn hair.

The way she turned off her cosmetic compassion, allowing her coldness to surface shouldn't have shocked Cam, but it did. *She's* got *to be some sort of drug kingpin or crime lord.* He could think of no other reason for her behavior and, if true, his mother would be the bigwig calling all the shots. Her reaction to this threat was too calm, too calculating to be normal.

"You've gone through something like this before?" Camden asked.

"Not exactly this. But it isn't my first dance with psychopathic thugs who think they can threaten what's mine." Her brisk tone guaranteed that she would castrate the sender of Cam's letter.

Then his mother had her phone pressed to her ear. "Detective, we have a situation. Come over?" Her jaw worked to rein in her rage as she listened. "Yes, I'm well aware that it's late. I pay you a retainer for this sort of thing."

She has a detective on retainer? Is that even legal? How often does she need discreet investigations?

"Good. Ten minutes," she snipped then hung up. She dialed another number and wandered away.

Camden exhaled, his mind focused on one person. *Sam.* He looked at his phone. It was late. *Do I dare call her?* Yes, he damn sure dared. The line went to voicemail: *You've reached Sam. You know what to do. But really, text me. Don't leave a message. 'K? Thanks! Bye!*

"Damn it," he muttered. In three months, Sam's line had never gone straight to voicemail. Logic told him that her phone was off and she was probably asleep. But in his panic, he imagined that she was already dead. "Get a grip, man." He pinched the bridge of his nose.

"As of two minutes ago," his mother said, rejoining

him, "Putnam Security has sent officers to the homes of Mr. Bisset and Ms. O'Ryan."

Camden dropped his hand and looked at her. Some of the tension left his shoulders. "Thank you. Honestly."

She ruffled his hair. "What mother wouldn't help her son?"

Fifteen minutes later, the doorbell rang. Camden's mother answered. "Paxton, you're late."

"Good evening to you, too, Aerona." A fit man with dark stubble and damp hair stepped over the threshold. He looked like a classic noir detective sans the suit. In its place, he wore a simple cotton tee and old blue jeans. "It's the middle of the night. I was asleep. So why the 911?"

Aerona turned her face from him. "I said ten minutes."

"I'm here now." Paxton ran a hand down one of her arms to cup her elbow. He then leaned in and kissed her.

"What the actual fuck?" Camden leapt to his feet. *She's sleeping with a cop?* Paxton startled as if he'd just noticed Cam and let go of Aerona.

"Camden Bennett, watch yourself!" she scolded. "Detective Lacey is here to help us with *your* predicament."

"You pay a cop to be at your beck and call and in return he gets—" Nausea swirled in his gut. "Never mind, I don't want to know."

"Careful." Aerona narrowed her eyes at him. She then looked up at the detective by her side. "My son's life is in danger."

"Your son," Paxton mused, glancing at Camden with renewed interest. The detective escorted Aerona to the seating area and helped her settle into a chair. He returned to where Camden stood at the edge of the common room.

"Tell me everything." Paxton eyed him, ready to enter notes on his phone. He had Camden go over his evening's activities three times. Camden could read nothing useful in the man's expression. The detective stowed his phone and turned away. Using a folded latex glove, he picked up the note, put it back into the envelope, then slid the packet into an evidence bag.

"Have you had any run-ins here? Anyone who might want to spook you or worse?"

"I've answered that question, detective." Camden raked a hand through his curls. His head hurt and his throat felt like the Sahara. "Not down here."

"And you've not had any contact with the crew you ran with up north? No one wants to get you back in the fighting ring? No one who bet on you and lost their shirt?"

"I haven't been in a fight in two years, man." Camden shook his head, trying to clear his weary mind. "My past has nothing to do with my now. I honored my contract, paid my debts, and cut out clean."

"From what I understand about underground fighting—"

This prick. Camden slammed his fist onto the couch. "Detective, someone killed one of my staff members and threatened the lives of everyone I hold dear. Anyone I care about lives here." *To hell with Lacey. To hell with this night.* "I've told you everything. We're done here."

Camden strode out of the seating area to the kitchen, ignoring his mother's terse demands to return. He was done being interrogated. *I'm not a liar.*

Detective Lacey followed Camden. "Any disgruntled former employees? A lot of drugs passed through Sorcerie until the Feds shut it down a few years ago, your mom bought it, and you took over management. Perhaps someone's pissed about that?"

"My restaurant is squeaky clean." Camden glared at the man.

"Look kid, I'm doing this as an unofficial investigation

and won't have my team to assist me. I'm flyin' solo here. How well do you know your staff?"

Camden turned his back on Lacey and got himself a glass of water. He checked his phone. *Sam's asleep. She's fine.*

"Aerona, a little help?" Lacey petitioned Cam's mother as she joined them in the kitchen.

"Camden, honey, answer Paxton." Her mask of compassion was back in place, but Camden saw the corner of her eye twitch. His compliance was not negotiable. "He's here to help."

Through gritted teeth, Camden said, "I vet every employee personally. We've had no turnover in two years. They are good people and I vouch for all of them."

"Paxton." Aerona turned to the detective. She slid her palms up from the detective's stomach to his chest. "Sorcerie is an upstanding business. We have a reputation to maintain, and apparently this death was a murder. If anything else happens, it'll be bad for business." She pressed herself into the detective's body, and Lacey brought a protective arm around her shoulders.

"I'll do the best I can," Paxton said. Detective Lacey let go of Aerona and gently tugged on her ponytail. He collected the evidence bag off the coffee table. "You know how long forensics takes to get through the system, but I will do my damnedest to get this processed as soon as possible."

Aerona smiled up at him. "That's all I can ask for."

The cold water hadn't settled Cam's stomach. *She's got him on a short leash.* He watched Aerona walk Paxton out the front door. *This whole evening has been a shit show.* Desperate to clear his head, Camden flipped on the porch lights and stumbled out the back door. He crossed the pool deck and leaned over a retaining wall in the courtyard. The clean beach air hit him and he drank it in. Then he doubled over, retching into the hibiscus hedge.

Cam swiped his face with his shirt tail. He concentrated on the whoosh of the surf below him and the scent of gardenias. His headache throbbed behind his eyes. *Could this be someone from Connecticut? I just don't think so. Who wants me dead? Why?* Camden had no straws to grasp at.

With Renard and Jackie under protective surveillance and no regard for his own well-being, Cam was left to worry about Sam. He called her number. Voicemail. *Do I drive over there? And say what?*

Camden shuffled over to a chaise lounge next to the pool. His mother approached carrying a bottle of her signature wine and two glasses. His stomach balked.

"Have some wine with me." She sat down on a chaise beside his.

"I'd rather not." To emphasize his point, he added, "Your gardener is going to find what's left of my dinner in the bushes tomorrow." His mother ignored him and poured red wine into each glass. *Does she ever listen?*

"Don't speak to me in that tone," she snapped. "Humor me." Her smile didn't touch her eyes. "Trust your mother. Stressing yourself is not going to solve anything."

"I *really* don't want any more to drink." Fatigue tugged at him, and he could have fallen asleep under the night sky, if only he knew that Sam was safe.

"What's one glass with your mother?"

Camden sighed, weary to his bones. He had no fight left in him after the night he'd had, so he held up a firm index finger. "One glass."

His mother tossed her ponytail over her shoulder. "Excellent."

She was the only person Camden knew to drink red wine ice cold. Maybe it was the temperature that gave it such a peculiar flavor. With the first sip, Camden's stomach protested. But with a few more sips a gentle warmth blossomed inside him, calming his queasiness and soothing his anxiety. His mother chatted about inconsequential things as Camden relaxed.

Old Mrs. Carlson kept letting her chihuahua shit on the Bennett's front lawn without picking it up. The pool guy wasn't power washing the patio to his mother's satisfaction, and she was tempted to fire him. Beverly Atwater, president of some committee down at the country club, wanted to partner with Sorcerie for a golf tournament benefiting a local hospital. His mother was thinking about adding onto her already massive beach house because the Duprees were building a mother-in-law suite.

Camden dropped the occasional "Mmhmm" and "Really?" in all the right places. Halfway through his glass he noticed his head no longer felt like it was being cleaved in two. The knot of worry lodged in his heart had loosened. He reclined in the lounger. He wasn't drunk, but he surely wasn't sober. *Numb.* He thought, closing his eyes. *I'm just numb.*

His mother's quiet chuckle made him turn his head in her direction. He opened an eye. She smiled at him over the rim of her glass. "I told you I would make everything better."

"You were right," he mumbled.

She joined him on his lounger and ran the back of her fingers down one of his cheeks. "You really shouldn't doubt me."

Camden sat up on the opposite side of the chaise. He stretched and let out a yawn. "If you don't mind, I'm going to fall into bed after this hellacious night."

"Of course, dear."

"Goodnight, Mother."

Camden trudged to the south wing of the mansion, through a long corridor, and tucked himself inside the safe confines of his room. Alone at last, he leaned his forehead against the cool, closed doors. He took several soul-cleansing breaths. Not bothering to turn on a light, he headed right for his bed.

He peeled off his dress shirt, unbuckled his belt, and shed his pants as he went. Clad in his boxers, he fell into his huge four-poster bed. Between his exhaustion, the fading adrenaline, and the anesthetizing effect of his mother's wine, he was asleep as soon as his head hit the pillows.

Camden woke hours later in a tangle of sweat-drenched sheets. He sat bolt upright, his heart hammering. Bits of his nightmare lingered. Sam, Renard, and Jackie had all been tied up while a hooded humanoid being with white eyes and red glowing tattoos drained them of their blood in some sort of ritual.

"What the hell?" Cam ran an unsteady hand through his tangled curls. Reality replaced the lingering grip of his nightmare. He recalled the menacing note. *Javier Manuel Martinez was only the first. Who will be next? Don't you wish you knew?*

"Sam!" Camden jumped out of bed. Wide awake, he padded over to his trousers on the floor and retrieved his cell. He had one text from Renard and one from Jackie. Both said they were safe.

"Sam, where are you?" In a moment of desperation, he called her. Voicemail. Again. If he didn't hear from her by seven, he would be driving to her house, even if she thought he was nuts for doing so.

On edge, he got dressed to work out. He placed his wireless headphones in his ears and stepped into the hall, scrolling through his playlists. He collided with a huge hulk of a man right outside his bedroom.

Camden dropped his phone, caught his balance, and slid into a fighting stance. His fists were up in a boxer's guard before he registered the intruder's severe military haircut, black and white suit, and coiled cord earpiece. He was taller than Cam, with a blocky jaw, mashed nose, and sun-weathered skin.

"Who the hell are you?" Camden asked.

"Mike Timmons. I'm part of your security team."

"Right." *Mother wasted no time.* Camden picked up his phone, stepped around Timmons, and continued down the hall. Timmons followed. *This is going to get old real fast.* Camden stopped outside the gym. He pointed at the wall next to the door. "Wait out here."

"Yes, sir. But if you leave this wing, I'm coming with you."

Cam flashed a smile he didn't feel inside. "As you wish."

Camden propped up his phone on the treadmill's shelf so he could see the screen in case Sam called. He started on the treadmill with a slow warmup. *How can I keep anyone else from dying? What if Sam leaves me and I can't keep her safe? What did I do to cause this? How long will I have a bodyguard?*

"Enough," Camden snapped, stopping his inner stream of questions. He ramped up his pace until breathing in and out was his only focus.

13

SAM

The ride back from the beach was quick and quiet, but the second we crossed onto sacred ground, Harper rounded on us. "What was inside those hotel ruins? Why the fuck did that demon nest vanish? And why the hell were only two demons left—"

Harper took one glance at Leigh and his inquisition trailed off. She had dark purple smudges under her eyes, her shoulders drooped, and she walked like Atlas carrying the weight of the world. She'd shoved down whatever trauma she'd experienced at the hands of the Mage so we could go on our mission.

"Kestler, go take a shower." Harper steered Leigh to the barn exit. "Get to bed. We'll take care of the horses."

"But—" She turned back towards the barn's interior.

Harper caught her shoulders. "Go." His voice was kind.

Leigh bit her lip and glanced at me.

I smiled. "We're good here. I'll be there in a bit."

"Thanks." She trudged toward the house.

Harper prepped the feed buckets for later, while I

turned out the horses and threw them hay. When I walked back into the barn, Harper picked up his inquisition. "What the fuck happened tonight?"

I had my answer ready. "It was so bizarre. Nothing harmed us inside the camp. Dominic, caught us snooping. He asked us why two lone Warriors would venture into a demon encampment without an army. Then he said that having the two of us caught by the Mage tonight didn't fit his plans. He caused a diversion, the Mage got pissed, and *bam*—they picked up and left. That dude's got some serious mojo."

Harper's eyes darkened. "Dominic is playing chess. What did you learn inside?"

I recalled the conversation between Corneilus and Albert. "These new demons are an elite army that the Mage freed from their prison. They're very ready to descend upon humanity and feed."

A muscle in Harper's clenched jaw twitched. Dominic may be playing chess, but Harper was playing poker. "Anything else?" he asked.

"The Mage is human."

Harper's gaze intensified. I resisted squirming. Harper was hiding how he felt, and maybe also what he knew. The way he'd rattled off information about the veils we'd gone through on the beach proved he'd read more than we had in Andrew's library. Never mind that he could see demons, ride Warrior horses, and handle Hell heat as well as we Warriors could. *Why isn't he a Warrior?*

"Why did Dominic let us go?" I asked. "Why did he suggest there was ever an army of Light Warriors? How is the Mage human? How can a human wield evil magic? Furthermore, why didn't Andrew tell us about hellhounds, imprisoned demons, and pockets of Hell on Earth?"

Harper picked up Hannah's bridle from the hook on

her stall and headed for the tack room. He stopped halfway there, kept his back to me, and said in a low voice, "Go be with Kestler. She needs you. If she tells you anything pertinent about her encounter with the Mage, come find me."

He walked into the tack room without another word. I stared after him, my fists planted on my hips. Of course Harper wouldn't answer my questions. I rolled my eyes and headed to the farmhouse.

I found Bear snoozing near the back door and herded him to Leigh's room. Her door was slightly ajar, so I pushed it open with a single index finger. "Knock, knock."

Leigh lifted her head from her pillow. She patted the mattress next to her. "Come in."

Bear bounded over and I followed him. The pit bull sprang onto her bed and flopped down next to her. Leigh sat up. Her hair was still damp and her face blotchy. Bear's tail thumped the mattress when Leigh looped her arm over his body.

"Thought you could use some canine comfort." I sat on the bottom corner of her bed.

"He smells a little gamey, but yeah, I'll take it."

I met her eyes. "Are you okay?"

"I'll live."

"Mmhmm."

"You were there." She rested her back against the headboard. "You saw what happened. Though I don't know why Dominic let us go."

"Yeah, that was weird. But you were a rockstar tonight. You'd already had one run-in with the Mage and you still led us back for round two."

Leigh scoffed. "I don't want to talk about that."

I got comfortable on the bed and crossed my legs. "You know I could annoy you until you do. It's my superpower."

She chuckled but the lightness didn't last. Leigh probed the cut along her jaw where the Mage had sliced her. "When the Mage touched my forehead with its bloody finger, it broke into my mind. It pilfered my thoughts and memories." Leigh wrapped her arms around her belly. "I couldn't fight it. I felt it rummaging through my head."

Oh, damn. I gave her leg a comforting squeeze. Bear whuffled and pushed his body closer to Leigh.

"When the Mage found memories of my family, it lingered there. Just taking in the information. Sam, it knows that to get to me, all it has to do is go after my family." Tears leaked down Leigh's cheeks.

Double damn. My heart felt like a wrung sponge. I hated to see Leigh cry. She did it so rarely. "Do you think they're in danger?"

"I don't know," Leigh whispered and dashed at her cheeks.

I gave her leg another gentle squeeze. "Do you think it knows *where* your family is?"

She sniffed and met my eyes. "Absolutely. The Mage saw where they live, right down to my mother's pink azalea bushes. But I don't think it wants to kill them. This felt more like a power move. As if it were saying, 'Look what I can do. And you can't stop me.'"

I glanced up at the ceiling. *Do not cry. Don't you dare. I can't believe she went through this alone* and *then went out on a mission.* I thought about Leigh's parents, Renee and Peter, and her four younger siblings. The idea that the Mage would harm a hair on their heads filled me with both violent fury and cold terror. *When I get my hands on this monster—*

"Sam," Leigh said, breaking into my murderous thoughts.

"Yeah?"

"No matter how concerned I am about my family, I'm more worried about you."

"Wait. Why?"

"Once the Mage found out that we'd been friends since kindergarten, it latched onto those memories and really tried to dig at them. It was so focused on getting information on you, its grip on my mind loosened. Rosewyn broke through the spell and helped me wall off all my memories of your family and our childhood. The Mage was furious, and you saw what happened tonight when it got mad. Imagine all that bitter, cold power filling your mind." Leigh shivered. "I thought I'd never get warm again."

"Oh, Leigh." I scrambled across the queen size bed and snuggled in next to her, sandwiching her between Bear and me. I wrapped an arm around her.

Leigh buried her face in my shoulder. "The Mage wants you so badly," she whispered. "It lost control when Rose and I wouldn't let it gain access to you. At that point, Rose booted the Mage out. And you know the rest."

Leigh shivered harder and her whole body racked with sobs. Her tears soaked my shirt. I held her close, kissed the top of her head, and rubbed her shoulder. Bear glanced at me with concerned brown eyes and laid his blocky head on her lap. Together we lent Leigh our strength as she cried. And this time, I didn't stop my own tears.

Sometime later, I awoke. Leigh slept on while Bear snored, his snout stuffed into her armpit. Careful not to jostle them, I got up. Leigh moaned when I shifted her, then she snuggled against her pillow. Bear's head popped up.

"Stay with her," I whispered, scratching behind his ear. "Keep the nightmares away, okay?" He tucked his snout in the crook of her neck and was out again in seconds. I pulled the comforter over her shoulders.

In my room across the hall, I plugged my dead cell phone on the charger. As soon as it had enough juice to power on, seven text alerts popped up and my voicemail chirped twice. They were all from Camden. The tenor of his texts got progressively more pointed when he couldn't reach me. This wasn't like him but given that I'd witnessed the murder of his prep cook, I could understand why he was jumpy. I answered right away: HEY! I'M OKAY. MY PHONE DIED. I'LL CALL YOU LATER.

I used the restroom, brushed my teeth, and washed my face. It was time to face Harper. He wanted information on the Mage and I had plenty. Leigh thought that the Mage intended to go after her family. *Not on my watch.* I saw light under Harper's door and gathered my wits about me. This was the second time I'd asked for his help in less than twenty-four hours. Hell must have frozen over. I knocked.

"Come in." Harper sat on his bed, a small laptop propped next to his right knee, a notebook resting on the other. His left hand tapped a ballpoint pen against the paper. How many times had I seen him like this?

"Did you get any sleep?" I entered his room, shut the door behind me, and leaned against the wall.

"Some." He'd changed into a plain white tee and black PJ pants, but it was the outline of a tattoo on his chest, visible through his shirt that caught my attention.

When did he get a tattoo? What was it?

"How's Kestler?" Harper looked up from his computer after several seconds of silence. He closed the laptop lid and set it aside along with his notebook.

"Funny you should ask." I shared everything Leigh had told me, then I said, "I need a favor."

"And what is that?"

"I need to go check on Leigh's family."

Harper crossed the room and stood in front of me. "I can't let you do that. It's not safe."

Despite Harper looming over me, I ignored the swoop in my belly and kept my wits together. "She's scared for her family but she won't ask for help. Leigh keeps putting me first. Making sure I'm safe. She suffers in silence. So, I want to make sure her family is safe."

Harper studied me. He smelled of sandalwood and cloves. I met his tired gaze and saw the flecks of silver in his blue irises. Harper shook his head, and without animosity said, "I can't risk you, Sam. Not after what happened tonight."

Tonight, Harper Tate had risen a few pegs up from scum-of-the-earth in my eyes. If he would agree to my next request, I might entertain that he could be forgiven.

"Can *you* do it? Can *you* look in on them? I'm sure Andrew didn't include babysitting Leigh's family in his orders to you. It's not in your job description, but I'm asking."

Harper peered down at me, his expression contemplative. He chewed on the corner of his mouth.

Please, I begged silently. I was trying to appeal to the Harper I remembered, not the broody, taciturn one. *He's gonna say no.*

But to my complete shock, he said, "I'll do it." He stepped back and nodded toward his door. "Now go get some rest."

Harper had called me Sam several times tonight. Each time his guard had been down. The way he looked at me now suggested he actually cared. This was hard for me to grasp. The Harper I grew up with was warm, fair, and always just. The Harper that stood in front of me now was withdrawn and cautious.

"What happened to you?" I asked. His eyebrows lifted.

"Sorry," I gasped. "That was inappropriate. I'm outta here."

Too tired to think, I went to my room and flopped backwards onto my bed. "Ahhhh, yeah. That's good." My memory foam mattress molded to my body.

I dreamed that I sat alone on a wooden stool in the middle of Milton's store. Two fluorescent bulbs buzzed and flickered overhead. The black and white wall clock ticked off the seconds, sounding louder than normal.

"You're a hard woman to get alone." A nails-on-chalkboard voice made me gasp.

"Holy Heaven!" I leapt up, stool clattering onto tile when I spun around. The Mage stood at the back of the store. It glided across the floor with its hands tucked into its hooded robe.

"Samantha, I came to speak with you as civilized, sentient beings. May I sit?"

"Be calm, Brave One. This dream is a mere projection into your mind. It can do you no physical harm." God bless Letty.

Fueled by my inner Warrior's reassurance, I crossed my arms. "No, you can't sit. We're not friends." The temperature dropped. I coughed, my breath visible. "And you can stop with the cold."

"You don't fear me?" The Mage asked, cocking its head. The interior of its hood was pure black.

I had a healthy dose of trepidation when it came to the Mage. But this was *my* dream. I held the cards. *Maybe.* But this freaked me the hell out.

"I'm asleep in my bed, in a house that's on sacred ground, so no." I smiled. "Now, turn off the tundra."

"The cold is a rather inconvenient side effect of my power. I can dampen myself, but my projection will be less solid. I did not want to seem as if I wasn't giving you my undivided attention."

"Please do." I righted the overturned stool and sat back down.

The Mage hissed. "Full of spitfire, aren't you?" Its voice became more like crystalline ice instead of a squally winter storm. "This is your own dream. You are safe from the reaches of Hell, demons, or my powers."

I growled and glowered at the Mage. It sighed and the store warmed about twenty degrees. The Mage's physical outline blurred around the edges. I bristled. "Why are you obsessed with me? Do you even know anything about me?"

"You're the daughter of Adam and Sarabeth Fife. You used to have a scar on the inside of your left calf from where you fell off your horse. The laceration took twenty-two switches, but the evidence was erased when you became a Warrior of Light. Your favorite color is purple or green depending on your mood. Your favorite—"

I threw up my hands. "Alright! I get it."

"You have a *very* curious bloodline." The Mage shrugged.

"And what of it?"

The Mage let out low, slow hiss. "You are much blunter than my informants told me. I would like to answer your questions, but in due time. Will you allow that?"

I pursed my lips and raised a brow. I was going to have to play by the Mage's rules. The thought rankled, but I nodded.

"We will have to do something about your incessant rudeness. I am here, young Warrior, because I want you to join me." The Mage gestured with one hand. Its red-tattooed arm wasn't glowing like it had been when I last saw it. I was aghast to see how human it looked.

"Did I hear you correctly? I *think* you just asked me to pull a Judas on my people. Why the *hell* would I do that?"

"Freedom. No Warrior laws to bind you. My dear, you

could develop into whatever it is you wish to become. And I can help you."

"You've confused me with someone who doesn't like being a Warrior of Light." I narrowed my eyes. "Find a different apprentice."

"You will not come willingly?" Cold seeped back into the room.

"You don't get told 'no' very often, do you?" I laced my fingers and settled my hands in my lap. "I'm guessing you don't know what rejection sounds like. Let me break it down for you: I am not joining you. Not now. Not ever." Frigid air sliced through me.

"You willingly choose the difficult path?" The Mage's tattoos glowed red.

"I like to make things interesting." I glanced at the clock. The second hand had stopped.

"I could kill you."

"My dream. My turf. How are you gonna do that?" How dare this bastard threaten me in my own head. I'd be damned if anyone was going to push me around. "I don't fear death. Man-eating spiders, great white sharks, and velociraptors are all more terrifying to me. But death? Try to kill me."

The lights flickered overhead. Shadows in the surrounding darkness shifted. "I could kill Leigh Kestler. And her family. I saw them in her mind. Rather quaint, really. There's also your Guardian. Max, is it? I would take him, too."

I gripped the edges of my stool. The Mage's words squeezed my lungs. I wheezed in the icy air. The Mage could beat, bruise, and freeze me, but threatening those I love was too far.

"I think you *need* me for something, don't you? You can't kill me to carry out whatever plan you have, but you'll go after those closest to me to get me to cooperate."

"Dominic told me you were intelligent. My goodness, you are exquisite."

"And you're creepy." My teeth chattered.

"Accept my offer," the Mage said. "Otherwise, I'll savor each of their deaths. They won't be pretty or quick or painless."

Images of Max, Leigh, the Shaws, my family, Camden, and even Harper flickered in my mind. "Andrew—" I started.

"Do *NOT* mention that man in my presence!" the Mage screeched. A coat of frost flashed across the counter-top, keyboard, monitor, and surrounding shelves.

I ducked. *What the hell?*

The Mage solidified, and its aura pulsed black. "Never speak that name! He is an arrogant, selfish hypocrite who has no regard for those he views inferior."

I stumbled off the stool. "How do you know Andrew?" Maybe I was batshit crazy to push the issue, but I had to know.

The Mage loomed over me, face still hidden in its hood.

"Clearly, you don't know him at all if you think he looks down on people. I've never known him to do that."

The Mage lunged forward, tattoos blazing. "You insolent child! Don't patronize me. Do *not* speak of that man. He is a duplicitous viper who lies to suit his need."

I scrambled back. *Space. I need space.* I vaulted onto the sales counter and stood, staring down at the Mage. I *knew* Andrew. Yet doubt crept in. Didn't I? He'd been gone for days, not checking in once. The Mage had to be wrong.

"You've hexed my best friend. You threatened my family. You insult the one man who's always been there for me. And yet you want me to join you? No. You're an evil sonovabitch and it's *you* I don't trust."

"It would appear that I have approached you prematurely with my proposition." The Mage said with glacial calm. "And perhaps altogether incorrectly. You are a fantastic Warrior with skills superior to those of your predecessors. Not to mention your fascinating bloodline."

This was the second time the Mage had mentioned my bloodline, but I refused to ask.

"Think about my offer, Samantha. I will leave you to your rest." A swirl of snow and ice whirled around the Mage. It raised an arm, tattoos glowing brightly in the dark. "Consider what I've said about your Adviser. Has he been completely honest with you? Does he know more than he's saying? Why doesn't he ever explain himself?"

"What do you know?" Whatever Andrew's sins may have been, he'd never let me down.

"I promise he's keeping secrets. But I offer you complete honesty and freedom. Until we meet again." The Mage faded.

"Sam, come on, wake up," Leigh said, shaking my shoulder.

I opened an eye. Bright light streamed through my window. I squinted. "I'm up. I'm awake."

"About time," Leigh said.

I groaned and sat up, peering at her through slitted eyes. She gestured to the corner of her mouth. "You've got a little—"

"Thanks." I wiped the line of drool from my mouth and looked down to see a damp circle on the pillowcase. "What time is it?" I rubbed my eyes, picking at the crust in the corners.

"You were sleeping like the dead."

"I had the weirdest dream." I glanced up at Leigh.

She'd done her hair so that it was straight and shiny, her makeup light, and she was dressed in khakis and a polo. The traces of her trauma from last night didn't appear to have lingered, so I thought better of mentioning the Mage at that moment.

"I'm hungry."

"You always are, but that will have to wait."

"Do you want to deal with hangry—"

"Andrew's home."

"What?" I jumped up, raked my bedhead-hair into a ponytail, and patted my body to make sure I was wearing important things like pants and a bra, then remembered that I'd fallen asleep in my clothes the night before. "Where is he?"

"Judy's formal room. He has news—" I'd already bolted out of the room and barely heard the rest of her sentence "—and wants to talk to us."

14

SAM

"My girl!" Andrew pulled me into a hug when I walked into the formal room. He kissed my temple as usual, then inspected me at arm's length. He hugged me once more before releasing me.

"You're really home," I said. *Thank God.* It seemed like weeks since I'd last seen him, not just days. He looked oddly rumpled, his silver hair uncombed, a shadow beard peppering his jaw, and his shirt wrinkled. *Had he even slept? Eaten?* Snippets of our recent troubles rose to the surface, and on the coattails of my dream, my initial elation faded. I felt queasy, my face flashed hot, then cold. I wanted answers. I wanted facts. And I wanted a plan.

"Where have you been?" I said, launching my word like a spear.

"Searching for an important friend," Andrew gave me a small smile. "Harper and Leigh briefed me on what's transpired in my absence. I'm sorry I left you without any answers."

"What friend? Where?" I crossed my arms.

"I started in Ecuador and worked my way home." Andrew's perceptive eyes studied me.

"You left the country?" I backed away. Andrew reached for me but I shook my head.

"Sammy, I will explain the whole situation soon."

"No!" My vision went hazy at the edges. "You left when I needed you most. There are holes in my training a mile wide. You brought in Harper, of all people, to stand in your place." *Without warning me.* "How could you just drop him into the mix? That wasn't fair to me." I flung an arm out. "Or to him, for that matter. How well do you think that went over? What were you thinking?"

Andrew frowned. "Harper is the most qualified—"

"Andrew, you're the most qualified. You should have been here. *You* should have told us about these new demons, hellhounds, dimensional veils, and the Mage."

"Samantha Grace, you are bordering on insubordination." Andrew's tone was sharp. "I will not explain myself to you. I promise you'll get the answers you want, but in due time."

I felt dizzy. Andrew was home, so why didn't I feel better? The dam of rage burst inside me. There were so many things I wanted to say, but he wouldn't listen. I stalked across the room and glared out the front window, seething. I heard Andrew approach so I whirled and glared at him.

"You must trust me, Sammy."

"We've been through some harrowing shit since you decided that leaving the country was a better idea than coaching your Warriors. Leigh's mind was hijacked last night by this thing the demons call the Mage. You know why? Because it could and because it's after *me*. This being is human. How is that *possible?*" I strode across to the couch, grabbed a throw pillow, and punched it hard. "How can anyone have that kind of power over Warriors?" I teetered on hysteria. "*Why* did you leave me?"

"*Brave One,*" Letty interrupted my tirade. She pushed her gentle warmth into my heart and mind. "*I know you're hurting. I know you're struggling. But you must remember this man is not only your elder, he's your Adviser. His position is superior to yours. I beseech you to keep this civil.*"

"That's *quite* enough," Andrew said. His brow was stern and his voice was so low that I had to focus to hear him.

I drew in a deep breath and squared my shoulders. "Dominic knows about Camden's connection to me. That damn demon popped into Milton's to make sure I knew that he knew and that Camden wasn't safe. I watched Dominic kill an innocent human, then grin at the camera as if he knew that I'd be seeing the footage."

Tears blurred my vision. I wasn't a crier, dammit, but I was so furious I didn't know what else to do. I sank to the floor. My voice cracked when I said, "I needed you."

"Sammy," Andrew knelt before me and reached a hand towards me. I shook my head. He withdrew.

"Do you know Dominic?" I asked.

"Yes."

"Do you know about these stronger demons? That they are an elite army?"

"Yes."

I trembled. "Do you know this Mage?"

Andrew ducked his head and rubbed his forehead. He sighed. When he looked back up, his eyes held an ancient tiredness. "Yes."

I knew he knew these things, but forcing him to answer gave me a sense of control. I loved this man. This man *knew* me. He knew my heart. So what bothered me more than anything, what broke me down inside, was that he hadn't believed that I could handle the truth.

"Why don't you trust me?" I whispered.

"Dear lass." Andrew reached for me once more and this time I let him. "I trust you. It's myself that I doubt." He gathered me in his arms, lifted me to my feet, and guided me over to the couch.

"Why?" I asked, sinking onto the seat cushions. Leigh sat beside me.

The front door opened and Bear trotted into view, nose up, sniffing the air. He looked at the tense humans, grunted, and dropped to the foyer floor. Harper entered after the dog, gaze resting on me. I was starting to get a clearer picture of Harper's point of view, so I gave him a small nod.

"My lad," Andrew greeted him.

Harper's eyes flicked to his father's face. "Pops."

"Good. You're all here," Judy said as she entered the room, drying her hands on a kitchen towel. She looked at Andrew. "When are we leaving?"

Andrew stepped over and kissed his wife's cheek. "Soon, my love, but I owe my Warriors some explanation."

Leigh stiffened beside me. She gripped my forearm, so I knew she was just as confused as I was about the whole situation. However, unlike me, she wouldn't say anything that questioned authority.

"Leaving for where?" I demanded. "Why are we leaving? What are you talking about?"

"Dearest," Andrew said to Judy, "could you please replenish my go-bag? Pack lightly for yourself but bring your full medical kit. You know he'll provide anything else we need."

Judy and Andrew had one of their silent conversations. She pursed her lips. Andrew tilted his head. Judy gave him a tight smile. "We'll be staying with him indefinitely then?"

"I'm sorry, I know you'd rather not." Andrew rested his forehead against hers. "But it's not safe to stay here. Not after what Leigh and Harper reported."

"Very well." Judy folded her towel. "I'll be ready in ten minutes."

I glanced at Harper; his expression was unreadable, as usual.

"Why is Judy packing?" I asked. "Where are we going? Who'll provide us with everything?"

"He's your Adviser," Letty said. *"Let him gather his thoughts."*

"Please, Andrew," I pleaded, "tell us what's going on."

"We're going to see a former associate of mine. His name is Xavier Gerena."

I raised my brows. "What kind of associate are we talking about?"

"Another Adviser and a dear friend. We trained Warriors of Light together for many years. After the slaughter—" Andrew cleared his throat. "Eighteen years ago, we severed all ties for the safety of any survivors."

Another Adviser? A slaughter? Survivors? The Mage had suggested that I didn't know Andrew as well as I thought I did. Years ago, Harper had left the Shaw residence after he'd fought with Andrew over something neither would disclose. And this week, Andrew had disappeared so quickly and had been unreachable by phone.

My Power flickered, tingling in my limbs.

"Be still." Letty pushed her gentle, soothing warmth outward. *"Don't lose your temper, Brave One."*

I didn't want to remain calm, but with all the restraint that my inner Warrior could lend me, I held my tongue.

"Warriors, I have kept information from you," Andrew said. "And in hindsight, that was to your detriment. My deepest desire has always been to keep the two of you safe."

Harper scoffed and leaned against the doorframe, his head bowed.

"I failed a lot of Warriors in the past which led to many deaths." Andrew sank into an armchair, his eyes haunted. "I've withheld truths from you that I shouldn't have. You are Warriors of Light. Your bodies can take hits that no others could survive, but you're not indestructible. I've kept you hidden, controlled your lives, and withheld facts. And I did so because of what lurks out there."

The buzzing in my ears rose to a crescendo. Andrew kept talking, his lips moving, but I couldn't hear him. Andrew wouldn't keep things from me. I *knew* him. Right? Who'd been there for me when my parents were too busy with their careers? Andrew. Who dried my countless tears, calmed my fears, and made me feel safe? Andrew. Who'd put me back together when Harper left? Andrew.

Then, there was the Mage's warning: *Consider what I've said about your Adviser. Has he been completely honest with you? Does he know more than he's saying? Why doesn't he ever explain himself?*

I looked from Harper to Leigh like I was outside my body observing the room with clinical detachment. Leigh had curled her long body into a ball on the couch. Harper studied Andrew. Letty's warmth seeped into my bloodstream, soothing me.

"Xavier and his team live about an hour from here," Andrew said. "We leave in a few minutes. I have reason to believe our border is weakening."

"Is that possible?" Harper asked, pushing his shoulders off the doorframe. "That the borders can fail?"

Andrew winced. "It's happened in the past. Yes, the

protection can fail under the right circumstances. Which is why we're in a hurry."

"Adviser Shaw, are you saying what's happening now has happened before?" Leigh asked, speaking for the first time. "How many Warriors were there?"

"I promise to tell you the story later. Right now——"

"But what about Bear and the horses?" Leigh asked. "They can't just stay here if the farm isn't safe."

The farm might be compromised? This made no sense. The invisible barrier protecting the farmhouse wasn't pene-trable by anything demonic. I gasped and grabbed Leigh's shirt sleeve. *The Mage isn't a demon. Could it enter unscathed?*

"Sam?" Leigh asked, peering at me sideways.

"Just a second," I said to her. Then I asked Andrew, "What about the feed store? Mr. Milton is still out of town. He left us in charge. We can't just leave the jobs you put us into. And what about Camden? He's not safe and that's on me."

"Being a Warrior is your first priority," Andrew said. "But part of being a Warrior is honoring commitments. You'll commute to work as usual until Milton returns. Sammy, since you've been targeted, don't go anywhere alone. Take Leigh or Harper with you. I'll look into what we can do for Mr. Bennett."

"Where will we be living?" I asked.

"I'll answer your questions once we're on the road. And Leigh, *all* of us will be going, animal and human alike. You'll summon your Guardians when we arrive and they'll come to you. Bear rides with us."

Judy entered the foyer with their go-bags and her medical kit. "Why are you all still sitting there?" she asked. "Go get your essentials, you have three minutes."

Leigh was on her feet first. She helped me up and steered us toward our rooms. We passed Harper, and anger smoldered in his eyes. He looked at me, said nothing, then jogged down the hall ahead of us. Bear scrambled to follow.

Outside our rooms, I asked Leigh "Are you alright?"

"I don't know. I guess so. I'm willing to see what this Xavier has to say." She pushed open her door. "Oh, by the way, Camden called while you were asleep. Your phone wouldn't stop ringing so I answered. He's got something up his craw, but I talked him off the ledge. You might want to call him back in the near future."

Oh, for the love of all things holy! I'd send him a text on the road with the promise to call when I could.

As ANDREW DROVE the gold Astro van containing five humans and one canine north toward Brooksville, he told us a bit more about Xavier Gerena. He was born in Spain, met Andrew in Rome, and together they immigrated to the States. Andrew also told us that Xavier was his trusted partner and longtime friend, but also that the man was a tinkerer, weapons master, and wealthy, eccentric fellow.

Xavier sounded fascinating.

Andrew turned onto a long, manicured private road which ended at a huge mansion. Xavier lived in an *actual* castle. Well, a modern mash-up of mansion and castle, borrowing bits of architecture from both to create a massive, sprawling estate of beauty, wealth, and excess. All I could do was gape, taking in the grey-and-white color palette of the stone walls, the black-lined glass panes set in Gothic windows, and a grandiose front garden with an ornate dolphin fountain.

Andrew stopped under a covered breezeway outside the main entrance of Casa de Xavier. Bear jumped out first, stretched, and walked off without permission, his nose pinned to the ground.

"He'll be fine out here. The property is fenced," said a slight man with a British accent. He wore a suit with grey under-vest and black overcoat. His hooked nose, keen blue eyes, and long triangular jaw reminded me of a hawk. I got the distinct impression he missed nothing and could probably move much faster than his age suggested.

"Nigel," Andrew greeted him, grasping the man's hand.

"Adviser Shaw." Nigel gave a shallow bow. He'd addressed Andrew by his title, not Mister or Pastor Shaw.

Leigh gawked at our surroundings. Harper's quirked eyebrow was all the astonishment he showed. Judy, on the other hand, pursed her lips as she glared off into the garden area behind the van.

"Adviser Gerena has been expecting you. Please follow me."

Nigel caught me watching him, like a hawk spotting a mouse, and held me pinned for a couple heartbeats. *Does he have superpowers?* He smiled at me and tapped the side of his hooked nose before his expression smoothed back to cool indifference.

He led us down a long entry hall lined with doors. Light streamed through high windows, making the wood floors gleam. We reached a large sunken common room filled with sunlight. About fifteen people lounged on leather sofas and wing chairs. Some read quietly by an unlit fireplace, others chatted and laughed with each other, and a few pairs were off in a corner playing chess at a long table. When we entered, the chatter stopped and all attention turned to us.

"What the fire-fart is this?" I whispered to Leigh. "Do these people live here?"

"I think so." She pointed to a blond boy, about seven, who wandered in with a glass of orange juice and a blueberry muffin.

"Ladies, please keep up. This is a large house; I would hate to lose you." Nigel spoke from across the common room. Andrew and Judy had already left the area. Only Harper remained. He met my gaze. I cocked my head as if to ask, *What do you think of this?* He gave me the tiniest half smile before turning to follow Nigel.

Do these people know what we are? Oh god, are they Warriors?

We ended our journey in a small, tiled room with a petite table in the center, topped by a vase filled with green and blue hydrangeas. There were two sets of elevators to the right and a fire exit door at the back. On our left was a plain block wall with no door or decorative touches. Nigel placed his hand flush against one brick and its surface came alive; a green scanner line scrolled down his palm from fingertips to heel. Leigh and I looked at each other, our eyes wide.

A section of the wall the size of a wide doorway sucked inward, then slid to one side with a soft whirr. It revealed a long hall lit by old-fashioned lamps every few yards.

I backhanded Leigh on the shoulder and mouthed, *No way!* This was so cool. We live in a humble farmhouse with a plain-Jane gym and these people—possibly Warriors—had access to this place? Just who were these people? But I knew one thing: Xavier was very possibly Batman.

As we followed Nigel, the hall sloped downward, taking us below ground level. Xavier had lined the passage with original paintings, many in ornate frames showing scenes of Spain and Italy. Others were more modern and abstract. I stopped at a picture where the artist had drizzled—or likely flung—an array of different colored paints at the canvas and swirled them together. In a weird way, I kind of liked the style.

"Keep moving," Harper said from behind me. His hand on my shoulder turned me back toward the others and we walked on.

"How can they expect me not to stare?" I whispered. "Are you seeing the same house as me? And those people?" I pointed up. "Who are they?" A painting of a splendid horse caught my attention and I slowed. Harper touched my lower back, reminding me to stay on task.

He whispered, "I'd rather not get left behind because you couldn't curb your curiosity. You know what they say about the curious cat?"

I kept marching forward. "Cats have nine lives, so what if I let curiosity take one?"

"I've seen *this* cat nearly lose a couple of them this week."

"Asshole," I grumbled, but lengthened my stride to catch up with the rest of the group.

At the end of the hall, we entered an enormous room that Xavier had made from one of Florida's many natural caves. The center was a spacious sparring area surrounded by circular support pillars. The same sort of lamps from the hall, equipped with brighter bulbs, lit the entire area. The gym included punching bags, a weapons wall, and archery targets. However, there were a few pieces of equipment I didn't recognize. I walked up next to Leigh. She pointed to a furnace built into a far wall and a blacksmith's forge sitting in front of it. Here was everything a Warrior needed and then some.

As I eyed the long wall of weapons, a delicious tingle of excitement trickled down my arms to my fingertips. The desire to touch every single white-metaled blade, bludgeoner, and projectile nearly overcame my good sense.

Letty purred when I spotted a pair of fighting daggers. They were nestled in a golden chest lined with velvet. I was drawn to them like a moth to light. Leigh snagged my sleeve before I could take a step.

"Och," Judy scoffed from where she stood, arms folded over her chest.

"My love," Andrew said. "I had no other option. We're stronger united." He kissed her cheek and drew her close with an arm over her shoulders. "You know this."

"Bernard Andrew Shaw, my brother, I'm glad you're here." A baritone voice steeped in a pleasant Spanish accent drew my attention away from Judy and Andrew. Xavier Gerena entered the gym. "Welcome."

15

SAM

"**M**y friend, thank you for having us," Andrew greeted Xavier. Judy scoffed. Xavier embraced Andrew in a hug, greeting him as a brother-in-arms. The Spaniard matched Andrew in height but appeared younger. His black hair greyed at his temples, and he sported a salt-and-pepper goatee. Where Andrew was long and lean, Xavier was broad-shouldered and trim-waisted. The air about him buzzed with a sort of energy I'd only ever sensed from Andrew. Strong and fit, he personified the tall, dark, and handsome cliché. He wore brown loafers, tan slacks, and a pressed red button down.

"Xavier, these are my Warriors, Leigh Kestler and Samantha Fife," Andrew introduced us.

Xavier turned his intense brown eyes to me. They held the same ancient wisdom as Andrew's did, as if he'd seen wars won and lost, love come and go, and Warriors live and die. He was secure in who he was and commanded respect with a single look. I felt like Xavier was staring into my soul, like I was a book he could read. The desire to protect my inner secrets made my Power flicker to life.

"Easy. Breathe," Letty said. *"Xavier will not harm you."*

"Pleasure to meet you, Adviser Gerena." I extended my right hand. Xavier gave me a firm handshake. With a nod and slight smile, he let go of me and greeted Leigh.

"And this"—Andrew motioned for Harper, who stepped forward—"this is Harper."

Xavier leaned away, fingertips to chest. *"¡Dios mío!* Is this who I think it is?" He glanced at Andrew who gave a sharp nod. "Thomas and Elaine's boy. I haven't seen you since you were—" Xavier held up his hand around waist height. "You're the spitting image of your father. He was the finest man I ever had the pleasure of knowing."

Harper went rigid, his jaw flexing. If there was one consistency about Harper, no matter what age, it was that he hated being taken by surprise. And while I couldn't confirm it, Xavier's confession had to have dropped a bomb that rocked Harper to his core.

It was out of empathy for Harper, not my own curiosity, that I gave him a moment of reprieve and asked, "How do you know Harper? How do you know his parents?"

I peeked at Harper. He closed his eyes and took a breath.

Xavier turned his scrutiny to me and arched a brow. "Ever the bold one, Miss Fife?"

Feeling compelled to answer, I stuttered, "S-sometimes."

"I suspect more often than that," Xavier said before looking back at Harper. "Where were we, Mr. Tate?"

"You have me at a disadvantage, sir. I don't remember you."

"I would be surprised if you did, as you were a young boy. Your parents were the finest—"

"Thank you, Xavier," Andrew interrupted. "I rather

think we have more pressing matters, do we not? I understand you have a couple of your own Warriors."

While I suspected as much since there were a billion
people living in Casa de Xavier, Andrew's lowkey confession that there were, in fact, other Warriors sent me
through a minefield of questions. I'd spent the entire hour's
drive to this place trying to get answers from him, and he'd
evaded every attempt. Typical. Andrew would give us
information when he saw fit.

"Right you are, brother." Xavier turned to his butler.
"Nigel, please show Judy to the infirmary. I'm sure she'd
rather be there than in my presence." He winked at her.
Judy glowered. "And please open the rear gate, near the
stables. Let Peter know to expect Warrior horses. They
should be arriving soon." To Leigh and me he said, "Now
would be a good time to summon them, ladies."

I prodded the space in my mind where Max lived.
*"Maximus Prime, please come to me. We're gonna be stationed some-
where else for a while. Apparently, there is a special entrance for you
when you get here. I don't know where because the whole property is
fenced in, but shouldn't be a problem for you."*

"No barrier is a hindrance to me," Max said, then asked,
"Shall we bring the wizened mare?"

Hannah. She couldn't stay alone. Since I had no idea
how long we'd be gone. It would be better for her to come.
Hopefully, Xavier had three stalls prepared. *"Yes. Come
quick. Be safe."*

Who had been Hannah's Warrior? Andrew told me his
Guardian had died long ago, so she wasn't his. Hannah
had always responded best to Harper, even when we were
kids, but he wasn't a Warrior so there was no need for a
Guardian. Then again, he'd ridden her in Guardian mode
just last night.

"You overthink much, Warrior of mine," Max said. *"Too curious for your own good."*

I chuckled under my breath. *"See you soon, bud."*

"Please follow me," Xavier said and started toward the doorway through which he'd entered the gym.

"But those daggers." This rogue thought came from Letty, a wistful breath within my mind, and it was almost as if she'd said it to herself. My eyes lingered on the gleaming white blades as we walked by, and I suspected Letty wasn't going to forget they were here.

We ascended from the Warrior gym on a flight of stone stairs. Nigel and Judy disappeared down a side hallway. Xavier led us to an industrial-sized, yet comfortable, kitchen. To our right, along a glass-paned wall overlooking the courtyard below, sat a four-seater table. The manicured castle lawn stretched out into a mixed terrain of grassy hill and scrubby Florida forest.

A man and a woman were seated at the table speaking with each other. They looked up as we entered, their conversation tapering off. Xavier motioned to them. They stood immediately. I suspected Xavier got what he wanted without delay.

"Andrew, I would like you to meet Leilani Kalakaua." The woman stepped forward and Xavier laid a hand on her shoulder. "I found her in Hawaii when I visited the islands three years ago. She's wicked with her chain whip and a superb gymnast. Brilliant surfer in her leisure time."

Leilani was my height, only leaner, with golden skin, and almond-shaped brown eyes. Of Pacific Islander descent, it was like Hawaii's coastal breeze wafted from her. Her jean shorts and an open-back shirt showcased her fit frame and chiseled muscles.

"Pleased to meet you." Her smile revealed flawless white teeth.

I pursed my lips. I wasn't self-conscious, but her perfectly applied makeup played up her beauty. And my hair never looked so stylish when I pulled it back into a messy ponytail, like she'd done with her jet-black hair.

"And this young man is Jackson Bozeman." Xavier indicated the giant fellow on his left.

Jackson towered over everyone, including Andrew. His arms and shoulders were well-muscled, straining the sleeves of his white T-shirt. He wore a snug pair of faded jeans and sported a belt buckle the size of a Texas. Shaggy blond hair curled out from under his ball cap and his soft blue eyes and kind smile pulled me in. Jackson had the down-home, grassroots vibe working for him.

"I found Mr. Bozeman six months ago near Asheville, North Carolina. He was working in a soup kitchen, serving the homeless. Took a bullet to the shoulder during a disagreement between two of the occupants. Saved a child's life in doing so."

"Y'all can call me Jax. Real nice to meet new Warriors." His southern drawl was as smooth as molasses in summer.

"Miss Kalakaua and Mr. Bozeman, this is Bernard Andrew Shaw. You will address him as Adviser Shaw. His Warriors are Leigh Kestler"—Xavier gestured to my best friend—"and this is Samantha Fife. They will be stay—"

"Sam," I corrected.

Xavier half turned towards me with pinched eyebrows and a pensive frown.

I grimaced. "I prefer 'Sam,' sir."

The corners of Xavier's lips twitched. He cleared his throat. "Going soft, brother? The Andrew I knew twenty years ago would have worked that out of her." Before I could dig my teeth into that comment, Xavier said, "This young man is Harper Tate. He is here as an honored guest.

Treat him with the same respect you'd show me or Adviser Shaw."

"Yes, sir," Jax said.

"Of course, Adviser Gerena," Leilani said. Her gaze wandered up and down Harper, lingering on his face; a faint appreciative smile graced her lips. She played with her right earring, caught one side of her lower lip between her teeth, and held Harper's gaze for a moment longer than I felt comfortable. My nostrils flared along with a jolt of territorial indignation. *Who the hell does this chick think she is?*

Xavier could make his little comments about me, and I'd deal with them because of his position. He held authority over me. But Leilani, this wench, had taken about three steps out of line. I opened my mouth to tell her just what I thought of her overt flirting when I remembered who I was, where I was, and who I represented. Any outburst would be a direct reflection on Andrew, so I choked back my indignation and crossed my arms.

Harper caught my eyes. He wore a faint smile, not quite amused, but not returning Leilani's attention. The look said he didn't need me to fight his battles but appreciated my effort. I'd have Harper's back despite our history, past sins, and turbulent feelings, because *nobody* was allowed to piss him off besides me.

"Everything okay, Miss Fife?" Xavier asked.

I smiled. "Peachy, sir."

Xavier's slow smile matured into a full chuckle. "Ah, Andrew, you know who she reminds me of?" He clapped Andrew's shoulder. "*You*, old friend. Before you learned to control that Irish temper of yours. It all comes full circle." He laughed even harder at Andrew's dissatisfied frown.

"Miss Kalakaua, please show Miss Kestler and Miss Fife to their quarters. Collect them in one hour for our

Warrior meeting." Xavier turned to Leigh and me. "I trust you'll find your accommodations satisfactory. I took the liberty of making sure your rooms were stocked according to your preference with information provided by Adviser Shaw. Please let me know if anything is amiss."

"Come with me," Leilani said, flipping her ponytail. She led us through a maze of hallways, passing a rec room filled with kids playing arcade games, a couple playing pool, and a group of guys playing some football video game.

"Who are all these people?" I asked Leilani, spinning in a slow circle as a man holding a toddler walked by us.

Leilani rolled her eyes. I glanced at Leigh. *Who is this chick?* Leigh shrugged at me.

"You're not joking, are you?" Leilani asked, her brows shooting up.

"Pretend I'm not," I said with a sardonic smile. *The attitude on this one.*

"They're Seers. This is a safe house. A safe haven from demons."

"Seers?" Leigh asked.

"What the fire-fart is that?" I asked.

Leilani stopped, giving the both of us a hard look. In condescending disbelief she asked, "Adviser Shaw never told you what a Seer was?"

Don't patronize me, flirty wench. I gave Leilani a flat glare, mouth mashed in a line. "Would we be asking if we knew?"

Leilani rolled her eyes again. "Seers are humans who can see the spirit realm, not unlike how we were able to do the same when we became Warriors of Light. These are humans who grew up being able to witness what demons do to people—usually the most vulnerable in society. Demons try to eliminate Seers first. Most here have lost loved ones in the most gruesome ways. Adviser Gerena has the means, the space, and the ability to provide them quarters. He gives them a chance at a normal life," Leilani explained. She spun around on her toe and continued down the hall. "We're wasting time."

Why have I never known about Seers? Not that Andrew's farmhouse could hold more than ten or eleven people total, but the church he pastored probably could house some of them. However, that I didn't even know Seers existed tugged at my slipping confidence in Andrew.

"Hold it together. We'll talk later," Leigh whispered in my ear. She asked Leilani in a friendlier tone, "How has it been for you to live with Adviser Gerena? He said you were from Hawaii, right?"

Leilani adjusted her shoulders. "It was difficult at first. I miss my homeland. But our calling has a higher purpose, doesn't it?"

"True," Leigh agreed. "What was it like fighting demons alone before Jax joined you?"

"Learning to fight as a team, after being on my own, was a challenge." She pursed her lips.

Was she annoyed that Jax was now her Warrior partner? Does she not like Jax? I wondered.

Leilani led us up a flight of stairs which opened into an arched, door-lined hallway lined with plush carpet that reminded me of a posh hotel. Crystal chandeliers overhead provided beauty and light.

"How'd you fight on your own for so long?" Leigh asked.

"Dedication. Diligence. Devotion."

"At least we know she can use alliteration," I muttered into Leigh's ear. Since Leilani was a Warrior, she probably heard me.

"Have you seen an increase in demon activity lately?

Or fought any demons that were different? Stronger?" Leigh inquired. Such good probing questions. I perked up.

"All questions will be addressed in the Warrior meeting. I don't know what I'm authorized to tell you."

"Authorized?" I quipped. "You're not our superior."

Leilani stopped in front of a solid oak door. I rocked back to keep from colliding with her. She spun around, glaring at me. We were the same height.

"*You're* petulant, arrogant, and immature. I may not be your superior, but I do have more experience."

My eyes narrowed, hackles rising, as Power flashed hot down my spine. Leigh slipped her arm around my waist, tightening her grip.

"I can read people," Leilani said. "You walk into *our* home like you own the place. You interrupt. You're rude. You lack impulse control. I suspect you don't follow orders well, either. You lack respect." Her tone turned saccharine. "Tell me, how has your Adviser let you get *so* out of control?"

"Let me—lack respect—" I spluttered. Never mind that Leigh and Harper had told me the same things about myself—valid, true things—Leilani's open assessment of my character flaws lit unmitigated rage in my belly. I stepped forward, and Leigh hauled me back, adding a touch of Warrior strength as a subtle warning.

"Don't," Leigh murmured.

"You're a bitch," I snapped at Leilani.

"Sam!" Leigh gasped, hauling me out of range so I didn't deck this chick.

"And you're precious," Leilani said, smiling.

Leigh threw her a you're-not-helping glare before rounding on me. Through gritted teeth, she leaned in and hissed, "You're proving her point. Hush."

Letty's gentle warmth bloomed in my chest. She

soothed my grated nerves.

Leilani thumped the door she stood next to with a knuckle. "This is your room, Samantha. Leigh, yours is over there." She pointed directly across the hall then laid a hand on a wall-mounted techy scanner next to the door jamb. "Adviser Shaw already gave Nigel samples of your DNA. These have been programmed to unlock when you touch your finger to the pad. As Warriors, you have open access to almost everywhere in the place except each other's private quarters. You can program who can enter at your leisure. Nigel will help you with that. I'll be back in an hour."

When Leilani was out of Warrior earshot, I said, "I don't like her."

"Why?" Leigh asked. "Because she appreciated the fact that Harper is easy on the eyes and told you nothing you didn't already know about yourself?"

I huffed. She laughed and pulled me into a hug. As a Warrior, I had to work with Leilani. But did that mean I had to like her? Nope.

"Yeah, yeah, yeah." I wiggled out of Leigh's embrace and grinned at her. I mashed my thumb against the scanner, the deadbolt unlocked with a clunk, and I grabbed the knob to open my door. "Let's see what's behind door number one."

The enormity of what constituted a bedroom at Casa de Xavier hit me like I'd walked into the Gaylord Palms in Orlando. My room at the farmhouse could have easily fit in this space three times.

"Whoa."

I heard Leigh make a startled squeak when she opened her own door.

I wandered into my room, across real wood floors, to a king-sized bed. Running a hand along the expensive bedding, its fabric rich and soft to the touch, I let out a low whistle. My small green duffle had been brought up and set next to a large, mirrored armoire. My scruffy bag looked pathetic compared to the extravagance of my new room. A small twinge of homesickness shot through me. *Is this my home now?* I missed the farmhouse's simplicity.

The wardrobe was fully stocked. Cocking my head and spreading open a section of garments, I studied the clothes. They were all my size. And probably cost twice the amount I would ever pay for a shirt.

I shut that door and explored further. The room had an entertainment center, seating area, a gorgeous view of the estate property, and a fully stocked bathroom suite. All the while, I wondered if everyone living in this place had rooms like this, or if it reflected my Warrior status.

When I had awakened this morning, all I'd wanted was answers from Andrew. Now I had all of *this* to contend with on top of my problems. Not that living in a ritzy castle in the middle of Florida was a bad thing, but I could've used a hefty dose of normalcy. I flopped backward onto the mattress, sinking several inches in its plush embrace, and laid there for a moment when Camden popped into my head. "Shit! I'm the worst."

I rolled over and pulled my cell phone from my pocket. I hadn't intentionally ignored him but a slither of guilt made my stomach clench. Cam had called a number of times but didn't bother leaving a message. When I saw the umpteen texts he'd sent, I buried my face in the duvet cover and groaned. I lifted my head. "Fife, you suck. On so many levels."

I called him back.

"Sam!" Relief whooshed from Camden's end of the line. "Thank God! I've been going out of my mind. You've no idea. Are you safe? Are you hurt? Have you seen anything weird?" A zing of panic shot through me. Here I was surrounded by a crap-ton of Seers, three other Warriors, Judy, Harper, and two Advisers all holed up in a ginormous fortress. Yeah, I was safe, but was he? *Did Dominic attack again?* I scrambled upright.

"Cam, I'm fine. It's okay. Andrew—er, Gramps—came home this morning and it's a really long story, but I'm totally alright. We're out of town for a while," I soothed. "But you sound like hell. What's wrong? No one else has died, have they? Are *you* safe?" I closed my eyes in silent prayer.

"Where are you? No, maybe it's better you don't tell me. Sam, I don't know how to soften this but—" He paused.

I pressed my fingertips to my closed eyelids. "Just say it. I can take it."

"This is gonna sound insane," he muttered. I waited. Camden took a measured breath then said, "I received a death threat last night when I got home from our date."

"A what?" I dropped my hand. "From who?"

"We don't know, but the police are looking for leads."

Is this Dominic's doing? Do demons send death threats? The Mage had to be behind this. After the dream I'd had last night, I had zero doubts. The Mage was going to fight dirty. I'd told it no, and Death hadn't liked my answer.

"What's going to happen now?" I asked.

"My mother stationed cops and private security at the restaurant. Renard and Jackie now have personal protection detail, as do I."

Something wasn't adding up. "If someone threatened *you*, why all the beefed-up protection for them?"

"The sender said others would die and Javi was only the first. Whoever threatened me is gunning for those I care about."

Comprehension hit like a sack of bricks. I was in Camden's life. I meant a great deal to him. He was worried I would be next. *Holy Heaven.* I leapt off the bed.

"What do I say?" I hadn't intended to ask Letty, but she answered anyway.

"Play along."

"Oh," I said out loud. I cleared my throat and tried again. "You're scared something will happen to me?"

"Terrified," Camden said, voice raw with emotion. My heart squeezed at his sincerity.

He cares so much. I almost laughed, the last of my coping abilities evaporating.

"Sam, I know this is a lot to deal with, and I would understand if—"

"Camden, what do you need from me to make you feel better?" *That's what good, normal girlfriends say, right?* It had been two years since I'd had to think from a non-Warrior perspective. *Or am I supposed to freak out? I should definitely be more scared.*

"As a human, you did take that news rather calmly," Letty said. *"However, as a Warrior, it was a diplomatic response."*

A bone-weary sigh met my ear. "I want personal protection on you, too. My mother has a very reliable security firm that she uses. They're discreet. Won't get in your way."

My heart tripped a beat. *No, no, no, no. That can't happen.* The idea of having some random human in a cheap suit, dark shades, and a comm device following me around was unacceptable. I'd have *way* too many questions to deal with if I Warrior-ed out in front of some hired bodyguard.

"I don't think so," I said.

"That is the opposite of playing along," Letty said.

"I mean," I clarified, "Am I in that much danger? What exactly did you have in mind?"

"Yes, I think you are. I care too much about you, and a simple dig into my life would show that," Camden said with conviction. "I'll get someone, a woman if you're more comfortable, to blend into the background and keep eyes on you. I promise you won't even notice them. Please."

Damn it all! I massaged my temple. *"What am I gonna do, Letty?"*

"You know, there is one person who may be able to help. His background covers security, he knows your true self, and he's more than capable in a combat situation."

My eyes widened. *"You beautiful, wonderful, intelligent inner Warrior. You're a ding dang genius. I don't tell you enough."*

"I know. But it's nice to hear sometimes."

"I have a better idea," I said to Cam. "I *am* uncomfortable with someone I don't know watching my every move. Male or female. Feels very stalkery to me. Can you trust me?"

"You know I do." He almost sounded offended. "What did you have in mind?"

"Give me like, an hour. I'll have the security you want and it won't be a stranger to me."

"I'll give you thirty minutes," he countered. "And Sam?" The words were gentle.

"Yeah?"

"You swear you're safe?"

Camden was a good man. He deserved better than what I could give him. His life was in danger because of me. "I promise, I've never been safer."

We said our goodbyes and I checked the time on my phone. Leilani would be here soon to collect Leigh and me for whatever this Warrior meeting was. Harper was bound to be in attendance.

And once I saw him, I'd ask him to be my fake bodyguard.

16

SAM

Leilani escorted Leigh and me to a library. That was a loose term of sorts; it was more like a miniature museum. A brass placard on the doors designated this space as *Warrior of Light Operation Command*, and just like the rest of Xavier's safe house for the demonically targeted, it was done with extravagance. Dark wood shelves, golden wall sconces, fancy gold trim, and two floors of old-as-dirt books lined the walls. A long table ran down the middle of the first floor with ten chairs on either side.

All the shelves contained a mix of books, old art, world globes, and weird knickknacks, *all* of which I desired to touch. I plucked up a spherical white metal trinket; it looked like a spiky Warrior grenade. I placed it back on the shelf just in case it *was* some sort of explosive. Wandering a little farther, I picked up a patinated copper goblet from its spotlit plinth. Leilani yanked the cup from me and glared as she set it back in its place.

I smiled at her, shrugged, and grabbed a seat at the long table. To provoke Leilani even further, I propped my flip-flopped feet on the top and leaned back in my chair.

Her delicate nostrils flared and sparks danced in her brown eyes. She said nothing as she zipped out of the room.

"Stop acting like a fourteen-year-old brat." Leigh shoved my feet from the table. "We're on the same team, fighting the same enemy."

I stood. "I can't help it. She's just so pretentious." Leigh got up to supervise me as I studied the bronze bust of some guy displayed in an arched alcove on the far wall. A black keypad mounted next to the alcove caught my eye. I went to stab the number four with a finger, but Leigh grabbed my wrist.

"Would you *please* act like an adult? For Heaven's sake, Sam."

"I'll behave. But only for you."

Voices came from the hall and we turned. Jax and Harper entered with Leilani in between them. She'd looped her arms through theirs. When she saw me looking, she peered up at Harper and her laugh became a giggle. Possessiveness coiled in my heart like a snake ready to strike. The only reason I didn't resort to throwing Xavier's priceless items at the perfect, polished Hawaiian Harpy was Harper's obvious indifference. He paid her zero attention as he took in the command center, his eyes roving over everything but Leilani.

I'd also just promised my best friend I wouldn't cause trouble. "Vindictive bitch," I muttered. One corner of Leilani's mouth lifted.

"Language!" Leigh hissed at me. She poked my ribs, prodding me forward. "Now's your chance to speak to Harper about your *predicament*." I'd told her about my call with Camden. She gestured to him with her head. "Do it fast. I suspect Advisers Shaw and Gerena will be here soon."

Striding forward, I snagged Harper's forearm, pulling

him away from the harpy. I kept pulling until we were in the hall. I felt Leilani's eyes boring holes of hate into my back. This time *my* lips curved in a spiteful smile.

"What the fuck, Sam?" Harper growled when we were alone.

Ah, that sound! Harper's gruff terseness was so familiar, so normal, and so comforting.

"Gimme a second," I said, dragging him, aware that he wasn't resisting. "There are too many here with perfect hearing." I tapped my ear.

There were a number of doors along the hall, and I stopped at one about fifty yards from the command center, pushing it open.

"Get in," I said, stuffing him through the doorway.

Motion-detecting lights flickered on, revealing brass instruments, a grand piano, a harp at least as tall as me, grey carpeted risers, and folding chairs. The music room walls were covered in grey acoustic panels. Eavesdropping would be hard even for a Warrior.

"I need your help," I said when the door clicked shut. "Specifically yours. No one else can know. Not even Andrew."

He lowered his chin, peering down at me. "Depends on what this favor is. I'm listening."

"Do you want the long version or the abridged story?" I asked.

"Seeing as you have to be in a mandatory Warrior meeting"—he glanced at his watch—"in ten minutes, talk fast."

"Camden got a death threat last night. Someone is targeting people in his life. They left a note saying Javi's murder was a warning, that there would be more deaths, and this would end in his. Due to all of that, Cam wants protection detail on me twenty-four seven." The burn of a deep embarrassment crept up behind my ears. "Obviously, I can't have one of his people follow me around. And we know Dominic killed Javi, so safe to say this is the Mage's attempt at coercion for my compliance."

"What do you need, Sam."

"I need *you* to be my bodyguard."

For the first time since Harper was dumped back into my life, a true smile split his hard features and spread to his blue eyes. He started laughing. Real, genuine laughter.

"Harper, this is serious!" I punched his shoulder. *"This was a dumb idea,"* I told Letty.

Harper sobered quickly and coughed, hiding a residual chuckle. His lips twisted, suppressing his smile.

"So glad you find this amusing." I scowled.

He met my eyes. "You *are* serious."

"Like a heart attack."

"Think he'd hire me?" He quirked a half smile.

"Maybe?" I ran a hand over my ponytail. "I don't know. Worth a shot."

"Let me get this straight. You want me to work for your boyfriend, the one you're hiding your true self from, so that I—a mere human—can pose as your bodyguard, when you are more than fully capable of defending yourself, thus perpetuating the lie that you are normal?" His raised eyebrows asked if he had missed anything.

For Harper, that was pretty verbose. And when he put it that way, what I was asking was quite absurd. Heat flashed up my neck, burned the backs of my ears, and brushed my cheeks. I didn't know which was more embarrassing: asking Harper to be my bodyguard, or having him plainly point out how ridiculous my request was.

"Yes." I sucked my teeth, annoyed, and looked away.

"Eyes right here, Sam." He hooked his knuckle under my chin and brought my face back to center. His expression was serious. "Do you think Bennett's in real danger, supernatural or otherwise?"

"Yes!" Tears welled in my eyes. I didn't want Camden to die because I refused the Mage. I jerked away from Harper and stared at my feet. Cam's blood was on my hands if anything happened to him.

Harper lifted my face once more and wiped away a single rogue tear from my cheek. "What aren't you telling me?"

The dam broke and I told him about the dream I'd had last night. I hadn't even told Leigh yet. "And the Mage said if I didn't hand myself over willingly, it would start killing those I love. One at a time. And from what I understood, they would be gruesome, painful deaths." I sniffed. "I feel like Javi's death is partially on me, too."

Harper cupped my shoulders. "His death was not your fault."

"But I—"

"It wasn't," he insisted. I sagged into his support. After studying me for a quiet moment he said, "I'll do it."

I jerked upright, relief washing over me. "You will?"

"Let me talk to Bennett. I'll hammer out the details." He guided me to the door. "You have a Warrior meeting to attend."

"Don't you need his number?" I asked.

"I have it."

Of course he does. Andrew had a file on practically everyone, odds were good that there was one with Camden's name on it. A file that Harper had access to. Any other time, in any other situation, Harper's breach of privacy might have irked me, but for once I was grateful for Andrew's thoroughness. I jogged down the hall.

"Letty?" I asked, my hands resting on the oiled bronze

door handles of the meeting room. *"You were right. Sorry I snapped at you."*

"All is forgiven, Brave One." A warm trickle of peace wove through me.

With my forehead pressed against the door, I took a deep breath and stepped into the library. All eyes focused on me.

"Thank you for joining us, Miss Fife," Xavier greeted me from the head of the table. "Miss Kestler said you had some urgent business to attend to. Anything your Advisers should know about?"

Probably. "No, all's well," I lied, keeping my eyes on the seat next to Leigh as I hustled over to her. "Sorry for the delay. We can start now."

"Harper's not coming?" Leilani asked.

"No, he has some things to take care of." *And none of your freaking business, Hawaiian Harpy.*

"He said——" she started.

"Something came up. He's not coming," I snapped.

"Sammy," Andrew's reprimand was subtle.

"Yes, sir," I answered. Andrew pointed downward, indicating I take a seat. I nodded. "Understood."

In the alcove behind Xavier, a large flat screen came down from above, hiding the bronze bust. I noticed a petite girl, no older than fifteen and no taller than five foot, standing off to the side of the silver screen tapping on a tablet. Her russet hair was pulled back in a short, straight ponytail. She looked up at me, her vivid green eyes full of life and curiosity. She smiled with a wide, full mouth and waved like she'd known me all her life. I hesitantly waved back. *Who is this fey child?*

"Now that Miss Fife has graced us with her presence, please pull up that presentation you created, Delaney," Xavier told the girl.

"You got it." She swiped two fingers across the face of the tablet and a picture popped up on the big screen.

Okay, that was very cool.

"May I have that little remote so that I can scroll as you speak?" Xavier asked Delaney while tapping his index finger in midair. The teen handed him a stack of folders and a black remote. "This young lady is Delaney Hayes. She is my daughter."

A what? I glanced back and forth between the Adviser and the pixie, trying to find some familial resemblance. She was white and light as the day. Xavier was Spanish bronze and dark. No way Delaney was his biological daughter.

She grinned at me again. "I'm adopted. Call me DH. Not Delaney. Only Dad gets to use my Christian name."

I found myself smiling back. "I completely understand."

"Do you need anything else?" DH asked Xavier.

"No, thank you."

"Hit the button to begin."

Xavier obliged and a second slide replaced the initial welcome picture. This new photo was a hieroglyphic scene which depicted a man with a flaming sword fighting a beast with a hefty set of horns and forked tongue. "While my charges know a little of their Warrior history, I understand the two of you haven't learned this material." Xavier's gaze flicked to Andrew, who gave a curt nod.

"There are reasons you've never heard of me and why my Warriors hadn't heard of Adviser Shaw. But I'm getting ahead of myself. Please hold your questions until the end. Delaney, let's begin."

I opened my mouth.

"Don't you dare," Leigh whispered.

My lips puckered and twisted, blocking what I'd been on the verge of saying.

"Warriors have existed since the dawn of time," DH began. "Our recorded history started around 400 B.C. but before that time, information was handed down orally."

Xavier flicked through pictures showing battles between demons and humans spanning the ages. Petroglyphs and cave paintings evolved into painted vases and mosaics, like one with a man in a toga wrestling a three-headed dog. Next was a marble sculpture of a gloriously naked guy holding the head of the Medusa. Then we moved into paintings, starting with a man at the entrance of a labyrinth.

"In the Greco-Roman area, men thought to be demigods such as Hercules, Perseus, and Theseus were all Warriors of Light," DH continued. "In Jewish culture, you had Moses, Gideon, Samson, and King David. All of them Light Warriors."

Depictions of Bible stories flashed on the screen: Moses parting the Red Sea, Gideon defeating the Midianites, Samson bringing down the temple, and David slaying Goliath.

I blinked several times. *How did Leigh and I not know this?* I glanced at Xavier's Warriors. Leilani doodled swirls in a notebook and Jax picked at the wooden tabletop. Next to me, Leigh focused on DH. I tried to catch Andrew's eyes, but he focused on the screen and nothing else.

"In time, these champions of humanity swelled in number, and they needed some form of structure. Elder Warriors were, in essence, retired and instructed to train small groups of new Warriors. Sage guidance made us more effective and let us develop faster."

The next picture was of a round table surrounded by men in armor. One guy standing to the side, dressed in a robe. He looked like a wizard, but not just *any* wizard.

"These teachers became known as Advisers. King

Arthur and his knights, all Warriors of Light, were trained by Merlin—who was not a wizard, by the way."

Then how did Merlin become known as a wizard?

DH didn't disappoint. "Advisers and Warriors allowed history to make up its own version of events." This made complete sense because no one knew Warriors of Light even existed. There was no mention of us in any literature or mythology. Divine Intervention always diverted curious eyes and astute minds.

"Each Adviser was in charge of a tribe of Warriors. These tribes, though they knew of each other, kept to themselves, working and fighting independently within their own regions."

"Uh, Dad." DH tapped Xavier's shoulder. "We're past the Middle Ages. We should be at slide twenty-two."

"Right you are, *mija*." Xavier sped through a few more pictures. "Right, you are."

DH smiled at him until he caught up to the image she wanted.

"Where was I?"

"Individual tribes. Kept to themselves. Fought in their own regions," Leilani prompted.

"Got it," DH said. "So, living apart and not working and learning together made them vulnerable. Each group took on strengths unique to their leader, but the enemy is smart. Hell realized it could capitalize on this weakness and targeted their attacks. As the Warriors of Light evolved, so did demons."

Xavier's next slides showed a post-battle scene with Warrior bodies strewn across a blood-soaked battlefield where colored demons dotted the landscape, black metal weapons raised in triumph. My stomach rocked at the carnage. I covered my mouth. This was *my* history. These were *my* fellow Warriors, slain. Bile burned my throat.

"Andrew," I hissed under my breath.

He wouldn't look at me, but Xavier did. I grimaced and settled back into my chair and stole a sideways glance at Leigh. Her jaw was clamped shut and her posture rigid. She drew in a shaky breath. Across the table Jax met my eye and smiled. Leilani sneered at me.

Xavier clicked to the next photo. It showed an ordinary joe clad in his holy clothes. There was nothing remarkable about his appearance.

"This is Sir William Archer, retired Warrior and Adviser of unique intellect," DH continued as if I hadn't interrupted. "Archer transitioned from Warrior into Adviser in the seventeenth century as we moved from the Renaissance into Early Modern history."

There was another painting of this Archer in nobleman's clothing, adjusting a student's fencing form.

Why hadn't Andrew told us any of this?

"Sir Archer created the office of the Adviser and was the first to cross train his Warriors with other Advisers' Warrior tribes. He's responsible for uniting all these factions, diversifying our holy weapons, and discovering that the children of Warrior parents made stronger Warriors.

"Archer realized that Warriors would be better off together. You could say he was like the Warrior equivalent to the Pope. His charisma, focus, patience, and background made him perfect for the position. He eventually died in battle, but he'd laid a solid foundation that produced Warriors of Light who were more powerful. Our kind flourished."

"Wait a second," I interrupted. Andrew grunted but still wouldn't freaking look at me.

"Miss Fife?" Xavier said evenly. "I asked that you hold your questions for the end."

"I know. Sorry. Does this mean that you and Andrew were Warriors?"

Xavier nodded once. "We were."

"How have you kept that hidden? And why?" I asked Andrew. He resolutely wouldn't look at me.

"Miss Fife." Xavier hadn't raised his voice, but the intensity of his tone silenced me. He stroked his goatee. And I cowered in my chair. It occurred to me that Xavier Gerena was probably not someone I should provoke.

"Sorry, go on," I said and glanced at Leigh. Her brow was furrowed and she had a white-knuckle grip on her chair arms.

Tendrils of my dream floated back to me. The Mage's voice echoed in my thoughts. *I promise he's keeping secrets.* What did the Mage know about Andrew that I didn't? Apparently everything. Doubt stirred in my chest and I tamped it down.

The next picture showed a depiction of Hell with a cavernous underground, a river of lava, and fountains of fires. However, the focus of the picture was a massive army in military-straight rows in front of a man outfitted in armor, black sword raised above his head.

"As the Warriors of Light unified and strengthened their resolve, so did the enemy."

Xavier leaned over to Andrew. I ramped up my Warrior hearing. "Do they know Hell's hierarchy?" Andrew shook his head and cast his eyes away from his old friend. Xavier's nostrils flared. "*Por Dios,* Andrew. Why?"

Andrew waved the question away.

DH glanced from Andrew to Xavier and asked, "Everything okay?"

"Yes. Please continue." Xavier advanced the slide. *Hell-hounds.* I inhaled. Unlike the snoring dogs we saw on the beach, these bad boys had flames burning on their feet and tails. They had blood dripping from their tusks.

"Hellhounds are the most animalistic creatures in Hell," DH explained. "They crave the taste of Warrior flesh. Used to cause chaos in battle, they can strike with fire and teeth. Their bite is as deadly as a demon blade."

The next slide showed the type of demons Leigh and I were most acquainted with. They had scrawny, gangly bodies in an array of garish colors. We'd fought many of them. A thin stream of Power started to flow in my bloodstream as I rubbed the pads of my fingers on the smooth wood of the tabletop before me.

"*Steady,*" Letty soothed.

"I'm sure you recognize these Lesser Demons. For the past eighteen years, they are the only type we've seen on Earth. They fuel and feed off of small crimes. While not strong, their swarming numbers can overwhelm Warriors in battle. Their chaotic nature means they can't unite for extended periods of time, but when they do, mass damage ensues."

Xavier advanced the slides yet again. That thin stream of Power turned into a white water rapid. On the screen were my new friends, the steroid demons. Huge, towering, with biceps the size of melons, and prepared for battle. Jumping to my feet, I sucked in a sharp breath. I looked at the faces of everyone in the room. DH stopped speaking and gripped her notes to her chest.

Andrew finally looked at me and his grey eyes flashed a warning. He motioned for me to sit and Leigh grabbed my arm. I righted my chair, reclaimed my seat, and didn't utter a word.

"Fascinating," Xavier mused, studying me. "*Muy fascinante.* A single picture ignited your Power." After several heartbeats, he nodded at DH. "Continue."

The faerie-child cleared her throat. "Greater Demons are the most powerful and intelligent beings among Hell dwellers. They have brutal strength, carry weapons, and are responsible for the worst in humanity. Their influence is powerful enough that they don't need the numbers Lesser Demons do. Greater Demons were the original angels who followed Lucifer to Hell, and the darkness mutated them into what you see here." She glanced at me. "And the stronger the Warrior, the more intense their reactions are to Greater Demons."

They have it wrong. Leigh is the better Warrior, I thought.

"Both sides, Warrior and demon alike, grew in power and abilities. All wars have roots in the battle of Heaven and Hell. Greater Demons have not plagued the earth directly in recent years, but their influence never loosened its grip on humanity."

Xavier clicked to the next photo which revealed a younger version of not only himself, but of Andrew. They stood on either side of a seated woman clad in a silk dress made of mauve fabric. Andrew, dressed in loose grey breeches with a black waistcoat over a blue linen shirt, had his hand on her shoulder. His white cravat poked out around the neck of his rich navy overcoat.

Xavier's flamboyant white shirt had ruffles on the ends of the sleeves and around his neck. His brown jacket had wide trim at the cuffs and along the lapels, stitched with elaborate gold flowers. Even his matching brown breeches had a thin band of gold at the knee.

"In 1776, shortly after America declared its independence, Heaven elected a trio of Advisers to oversee the Warrior network. These three Advisers were blessed with something none before them had: an extended lifespan to provide generations of Warriors stability and a strong source of knowledge. As you can see, they're still alive."

Leigh let out a quick gasp as she sat back, wide-eyed. "That makes you both nearly three hundred years old!"

"Are you shitting me?" I exclaimed.

"DH isn't finished," Andrew spoke with calm authority. "Please wait."

My hands trembled as adrenaline pumped through my body. The room was too small, too hot. I closed my eyes.

"I'm here," Letty said. *"We can do this. You're not alone."*

DH took my silence as cue to go on. "Adviser Shaw holds highest office; his left and right hands were my dad and Tabitha." She pointed to the lady in mauve. "Warriors of Light flourished under their leadership until—"

"A new evil was formed," Xavier said. He changed the picture to show a shirtless humanoid male with glowing purple whorls inlaid in his skin. Even his eyes glowed a malevolent dark violet. "Hell offered certain humans a contract: in exchange for unhindered power, they paid with their souls. They became the Warriors of Dark. It's every bit as devastating as you think. Warrior law gives no concession. No matter how twisted and mangled. If it's human—"

"We can't kill them," Jax said in his soft southern drawl. A mix of fear and rage pinched Leilani's pretty face. I might have wanted to throttle her, but in that moment, I'd found a common thread with the Hawaiian Harpy. This was news to them, too.

"Correct, Mr. Bozeman," Xavier said.

"That's what happened, isn't it?" Leigh asked. "These Warriors of Dark are responsible for killing off Warriors of Light. They're why we no longer exist as we once did, aren't they?"

"Yes, dear," Andrew said.

"Andrew, look at me," I demanded. He didn't. *Why won't he just freaking look at me?*

"In 2004," Andrew said, "we assembled the Warriors to discuss how we would handle these Dark Warriors." He ran a hand over his face. "I failed to protect them, and they were all slaughtered. Hell hunted down those not in attendance. Xavier, Tabitha, and I agreed to disband and go underground. But the world *needs* Warriors. Humans need protectors. As you can see, my plan to lay low hasn't worked."

His confession barreled into my chest. Hollow numbness consumed me. My eyes stung with coming tears. *I promise he's keeping secrets.* The Mage had been right. I didn't want to believe it then. But now? I had to. Choking back a sob, tears dampening my cheeks, my heart fractured into a thousand pieces.

I stood and confronted Andrew, "Look at me!"

He refused. I slapped my palms on the table. Leigh flinched. Xavier said nothing.

"Dammit, Andrew. *Why?* Why did you endanger Leigh and me by hiding this from us? Different classes of demons? Greater Demons are the original Fallen angels? And hellhounds? How could we make good decisions in the field without knowing all this? Ignorance almost killed us last night!"

My Power ignited. Did he think having a meeting with other people in attendance was going to soften the blow of his betrayal? I whirled, grabbed a book from the shelf behind me, and threw it at Andrew. I missed him on purpose. He finally met my eyes. I staggered back.

"Why didn't you tell us about Warriors of Dark?" I snarled.

"Sammy, let me explain this in private," Andrew said.

"No!" I roared. "You tell us now." I glanced down at Leigh. Tears flowed from her hazel eyes. Andrew lied to her, too. "The Mage almost got you because you didn't know the danger."

Leigh rested a hand on my side. "Yes, but—"

"Adviser Gerena told his Warriors damn near everything."

"Samantha," Andrew said, half rising from his chair. "Come with me."

"Don't you dare 'Samantha' me, old man." My vision blurred. "I've bled, gone to war, and fought for you. I've never questioned you. I trusted you with my life. And you couldn't trust me with any of this information?" Power zipped through me and my aura glowed. "Say something. Anything."

"Brave One." Letty tried to send her tranquil vibes through me, but I fought her. I could barely breathe.

Air. I needed air. My body trembled with Power and adrenaline.

"Be calm, Brave One."

"No!" I roared then sprinted for the library doors. Leigh yelled my name. I threw them open and bolted for the exit. To freedom.

17

HARPER

My phone buzzed, letting me know I'd gotten Bennett's email, which contained a copy of our signed contract agreement and nondisclosure form. I was now officially employed by The Bennett Family LLC. Sam's boyfriend had been reluctant at first, and it took more persuasion on my part than I liked. He'd relented quickly when I reminded him of his dire circumstances. I assured him that because I knew Sam personally, it was to his advantage. She wouldn't comply with just anyone.

Hell, she barely listens to me. And only because she wants to. I stowed my phone in a pocket and walked out of the music room. Sam blew past me in a woosh. Anger and hurt rolled off her in waves, and she gave no indication that she saw me. I heard a sob. *What the fuck?*

"Samantha," I called out. She kept going. "Sam?" I asked louder, raising an eyebrow when she hit the exit door at the end of the hall with full force. It exploded open.

"Damn." I followed her. In her state of mind, I couldn't let her run around Xavier's unfamiliar property alone. Keeping pace with her was like running behind a drunken panther. All power and grace in one body, yet she stumbled over the grass. In one fluid movement, she took a nasty trip, caught her balance, and stepped out of her flip flops.

I retrieved her shoes and stayed behind her at a light jog. She wasn't running with any clear destination in mind. It was aimless. While I hadn't been in the Warrior meeting, I had a pretty good idea what was discussed. Sam just learned some shit that she should have been told two years ago.

At a manicured circular clearing of trees, she finally stopped. I edged closer to her but kept a respectful distance a few yards off. From experience, I knew it was best to let her burn out her fury before approaching.

Sam hauled off and punched the massive oak in front of her.

Fuck! I jerked back, surprised at the amount of force she'd used.

"No, he lied to me!" she yelled in response to some unspoken question.

Everything in me clenched when she hit the tree a second time. I flinched, but remained in place and muttered, "Let her get it out of her system."

I looked away, not wanting to witness Sam coming apart like this. Yet my mind played the scene reel of four-teen-year-old Sam crying, crumpled in a heap, while eigh-teen-year-old Harper pulled out of the drive in his truck. I shut that shit down. While I devastated her as a kid, I could make it up to her now. *If she'll let me.*

Sam hid behind a mountain of bravado most all her life. She turned whatever she could into snark and sass. It was fucking irritating most of the time, but it protected her heart. I could count on one hand the times she'd truly broken down, waterworks, snot, and incoherent mutterings included. She *was* strong and she only cried when all her defenses failed. And it was in this state of mind that Sam wouldn't be able to tell the difference between hitting a tree or a person. If she used Warrior force to punch me, I wouldn't be able to bounce back like she could. So I waited. No matter how badly I wanted to keep her from harming herself.

"Come on, Sam, get it all out," I mumbled.

Without the same intensity as a few minutes ago, she stepped up into a roundhouse kick, and her shin connected with the rough bark. A defeated, strangled cry escaped her and she fell to her knees with her back hunched and head bowed.

Finally. I approached her with slow steps. She offered no fight when I reached down and gripped her by one elbow. I hooked an arm under her shoulder and brought her to her feet. She stumbled upright and met my gaze. Her eyes were red-rimmed and cheeks blotchy.

"Harper," she groaned. A few more tears leaked out before she sagged against my chest.

And as if it were the most natural thing to do, before I thought through my actions, I gathered her into my arms. To my surprise, she allowed this, blubbering into my shirt. I held her tight against me, cradling the back of her head with a hand. I closed my eyes. *I'm so sorry.*

Whatever had transpired in that meeting broke her. I held her while she cried it out. She was shattered, but not irreparable. At least, I hoped she wasn't. I was flying a bit blind at this point. I gritted my teeth.

"Sammy," I murmured into her hair. "I got you."

Her breath hitched. "Sammy?"

Shit. I grimaced. *Did I really just call her that?* Ma and Pops only adopted the nickname because I had used it originally. Glossing over my slip up, I asked "What happened?"

She pulled back and looked up at me with stormy blue eyes filled with thunder clouds. She bit her quivering lower lip. Under the welling tears, under the hurt, I saw mounting rage. There was a flash of lightning in her eyes as she gathered her wits.

Yes, there it is. I could handle her anger better than her hurt.

"Did you know?" she asked.

I hadn't a fucking idea what she meant, but in her state, I wasn't about to admit that. "Probably. But be more specific."

"About Andrew," she snapped. "About Warrior history?"

Fuck me. I let her go and took a step back.

Sam grabbed the front of my shirt in her left hand. Her eyes narrowed to slits. She knew I knew. It had been Pops's propensity for secret-keeping that drove a wedge not only between him and me, but also Samantha and me. Pops had taught me everything and taught Sam next to nothing.

I ran a hand over the scruff on my jaw, weighing my words. *If I say the wrong thing, she'll probably rearrange my face.* She'd been kept in the dark long enough that honesty would go a long way with her.

"Yes, I grew up knowing Warrior history. Pops had ingrained it into me by the time I was twelve."

Pain blindsided me from the left when she punched me. I stumbled sideways, fighting like hell for balance. Years of combat training kept my feet under me and overrode the urge to retaliate. Sam howled and fell to her knees, groaning in agony.

"What the fuck, Sam?" I probed my cheek and felt the slickness of blood. "Was that—"

She'd hit me with her broken hand. I touched my face again. And while sore, there was no cut. The blood didn't belong to me. It came from the crimson-coated fist that she had clutched to her stomach.

"I don't blame you for that." I squatted next to her, resting my forearms on my thighs. "But let's not beat the shit out of the man who's trying to help you."

She glanced up. Pale and shaking, she still managed to say, "Asshole."

"Absolutely." I eyed her hand. "Pops had his reasons for keeping things from you."

"Other than being a lying pile of horse shit?"

"Something like that." I traced down her arm from elbow to wrist, going slow like she was a wounded animal.

"How much do you know about Warrior history?" She jerked from me.

Dammit, Sam. I met her eyes. "Does it matter?"

She chewed her lower lip. "I guess it doesn't. But why all the secrecy?"

I tried for her hand again.

"It doesn't make sense," she said. "Why would he not tell me? *Me*, of all people?"

Let me see your goddamn hand. "He's always kept people on a need-to-know basis."

"Are you defending him?" She snatched her arm away just as I got to her wrist.

"Don't put words in my mouth." I sighed. I didn't want to fight her, not when she needed first aid.

She grunted and cradled her bloody fist to her chest. "Sorry."

While I had my own issues with the man, seeing Sam

so broken in spirit and angry with Pops, I couldn't let her lose faith in him. She'd idolized him her whole life.

"Pops has always treated you differently, and by proxy, Kestler. The man I grew up with was borderline cold-blooded. If I didn't know better, I'd say we were talking about two different people."

"Well, he sure did a hell of a good job keeping me on a *need-to-know* basis," she spat. "He didn't think I needed to know that there was an enemy I couldn't kill? Or that he was freaking old?" She ripped up a clod of grass with the roots attached and threw it.

Sam needed to have this conversation, but with a different person. Pops had to answer for his own sins, and I couldn't give her the kind of answers she sought. He had to heal the wounds he'd inflicted. I couldn't mend her heart, but I could tend her bashed-up fist.

"Show me." I held out an upturned palm. Her expression darkened and she regarded me with mistrust. I growled, "Don't be difficult. Give me your hand."

Without waiting for her approval, and with as much gentleness as I could, I pulled her arm to me. She flinched, gnashed her teeth, but otherwise gave no resistance.

"Can you open it?" I asked.

She nodded and extended her fingers, hissing as she did. Purple bruises spread across her pale skin. The flesh over her knuckles was bark-shredded. With careful, practiced skill, I felt around the delicate joints of her hand. Swelling had set in with a vengeance. I placed my thumb on the back of her hand, overtop of her middle finger.

"You broke it here. And may also have other hairline fractures." I met her guarded gaze. "Exactly how hard did you hit that tree?"

"Hard enough to know better." The corners of her mouth lifted sheepishly. "I put Warrior strength behind it."

"Fucking brilliant."

She hung her head instead of coming back with a quick retort, further evidence that her wounds went much deeper than I could fix. Holding her injured hand in mine, careful not to jostle it, I pulled a clean shop rag from a rear jeans pocket.

"We'll need Ma to look at this. Elixir will fix it," I said.

"Why are you being so nice?"

"I'm always nice."

"And I'm the freakin' Queen of England."

At least her snark isn't broken, I thought. Maybe all wasn't lost. I didn't answer and wrapped her hand.

"Cut the crap, Tate. Why are you being so kind and gentle? It's not your MO."

I finished the makeshift bandage and tied it off with a knot. "I know what you're feeling right now."

Sam's eyebrows shot up. "You know what it's like to be a Warrior who doesn't know all the players on the field? Please tell me—"

"Calm down," I growled. "Obviously I don't know what being a Warrior is like. I *meant,* I know how it feels to have Pops keep things from you. Important things. The day I left the Shaws' house—"

"The day you walked out on me."

I sighed. *She never makes anything easy.* "It wasn't about you. The day I walked out was the day I uncovered the truth about my parents' murders. I'd spent my whole life thinking six-year-old Harper had imagined how they died. But I hadn't. Pops conveniently let me believe what I saw was a product of my overactive imagination. He would never talk about it when I asked him." I stood and wiped my hands on my thighs, then helped her to her feet.

"What happened?"

"I'd been organizing his filing cabinet when I hit a

button underneath the top drawer. A hidden compartment popped open at the bottom. In it was a single manilla folder with my name on the tab."

"Mr. By-the-Book Tate looked inside?"

"I was more willing to act on my curiosity then, so I opened it. There were photos from the crime scene where my parents died."

Sam sucked in a breath. "Harper, I'm sorry. What happened? Were they killed in the Warrior of Light slaughter?"

"Not in the mass assembly coup." I'd suppressed this shit for a reason, but I'd suffer the painful memories only because it would help Sam. "Their bodies were splayed out on the kitchen tile. Their chests ripped open, hearts crushed, surrounded in pools of blood.

"Pops led me to believe a demon had killed them quickly." I rubbed a palm against my cheek. "The file said otherwise. It said their deaths were the work of a Dark Warrior. It wasn't until the other night in the driveway, when you spun out on the ice and I met Dominic, that I made the connection to which Warrior of Dark killed them. Dominic said he'd watched them die. Considering he's the Mage's right hand, I believe they were murdered by the Mage."

"Holy Heaven," she breathed, a flicker of a fear flashing in her eyes.

Yes, their deaths should scare you.

"I can't even imagine. I'm so sorry." Sam pressed her good hand to her chest.

Fucking pity. That's all I need right now. But she deserved the truth. Now that Pops had let the cat out of the bag, I no longer needed to carry this secret alone.

"The file contained newspaper articles telling the fabricated story of what happened. The truth of how they were killed was never made public. I don't think the real reason would have seen light of day unless I'd discovered it. The file was sixteen handwritten pages of what he found at the scene. His notes were meticulous and detailed. Long story short, he knew the Mage would strike them in the safe house. He tried to get there in time to warn them, but he was too late. Pops found me, grabbed me, and fled before the cops arrived."

"But why?" she asked. "Why did the Mage kill your parents?"

"The Mage thought my father was some sort of amplified Warrior of Light. Apparently, the Mage ranted about some bullshit that there would be a Light Warrior granted the ability to slay Dark Warriors. Pops refused to answer my questions on that one, too."

"But—" Sam shook her head. "How the hell did Andrew know this if he wasn't there? You couldn't have remembered that level of detail that young."

"You know how Pops can be. He can sit with someone for an hour and they'll tell him their life story. He has degrees in counseling, psychology, and therapy. Shit, now that you know how old he is, you know he's had a long time to perfect the art of extracting information from people. It's a talent of his."

"I had no clue," she whispered, closing the gap between us. With a tenderness I didn't expect, she touched my cheek. She rubbed the pad of her thumb over the spot where she'd punched me.

I circled her wrist with my fingers and removed her hand. "I don't want your fucking pity. Time and distance buried the wounds from that period of my life."

I turned Sam around, not letting her see me swallow against the lump that lodged in my throat. My parents were long dead and nothing would bring them back, there was no use in getting emotional about it. I gave Sam a small push forward.

"I was a scared kid hiding in a closet when Pops found me. I listened to my parents' torture and eventual murder through the vent slats of the pantry door. Pops was able to piece together everything from my perspective. He wrote it up in the report and filed the fucker with no intention to tell me the truth. Does any of that surprise you?"

Sam allowed me to steer her toward the castle. We paused so she could slip into her flip-flops.

"I don't get it," she said after a few minutes. "Why keep any of that a secret? Why lie? Do you think—" I felt her tense and stopped before she did. Sam spun around. "What's this business about a Warrior of Light with the Power to kill a Dark Warrior?"

I shook my head. *Can we do this later? You have a broken hand.* When Sam didn't budge, I sighed and said, "You know there's no such thing. It's a mythical idea. Now keep moving."

"Harper, your parents were straight-up murdered because the Mage seemed to think this *myth* was true." She speared me with piercing gaze.

I growled, trying to get her to drop the subject. She glared at me in defiance, so I turned her around one more time, gave her a stronger shove forward, and herded her onward with a little more force. I mulled over what she'd said while we walked.

Pops wouldn't have done a cognitive interview on the six-year-old me, written a lengthy report, and kept the truth hidden on a whim. The Mage and Dominic wouldn't have hunted my parents over mere hearsay. A Warrior of Light with the permission to operate outside of Warrior law *was* intriguing. *But what if it isn't true?* There would have been an entire network of Warriors and Seers with hope in a rumor. *I can't believe I agree with him, but Pops made the right decision to keep that quiet.*

We reached the castle lawn, where a group of Seers was finishing up their yoga class. They'd rolled up their mats and lingered in conversation. Since I had no idea where the infirmary was, I asked the instructor for guidance. She took one look at Sam's hand and agreed to take us where we needed to go.

I had a hunch Ma would still be in the hospital ward. That was confirmed when we rounded a corner. We heard her raised voice through a set of solid wood doors. The yoga instructor excused herself, leaving us on our own.

We stepped inside. The ward had ten windows lining the long side walls. A twin-size bed was situated under each window with a small side table placed beside each mattress.

"The sheets are threadbare," Ma was saying. "The beds might as well be made of stone. And your inventory system is manual. Surely your *employer* can afford upgrades to this place? Our Warriors and Seers alike already sacrifice so much, do we really need them uncomfortable during rehab? You"—she pointed to a willowy young woman with mousy features and a taut brown bun—"write this down. I want twenty sets of high-quality bed sheets and ten new mattresses. Put a rush on them. And get some quotes to update to digital inventory tracking."

The woman cowered in front of her. "But ma'am, Master Gerena—"

"If Xavier Gerena has an issue with how I run this infirmary, he can talk to me!" Ma snarled.

The thin brunette scurried away with her marching orders. Ma rounded on the second woman, a portly blonde nurse, and demanded, "I want you to make a thorough inventory of the supply closet. Do not miss anything from alcohol swabs to bed pans. Report back to me in one hour."

"Y-yes, ma'am. Inventory. One hour." The woman threw a nervous glance in our direction.

Ma followed her gaze and noticed Sam and me for the first time. She held up a finger. Looking back to the nurse, she said, "What are you waiting for? Christ to return? Go on." The woman fled into the closet at the end of the infirmary.

Ma wiped her hands on a white apron. "Xavier is many things but a doctor he is not."

"You're on the warpath," I stated.

"The only way I'll stay in this blasted monstrosity of a home is to work. Xavier's lifestyle is ridiculous." She puffed out an upward breath, the air ruffling her silver bangs. "That man has more money than some small countries, and he can't have the common decency to run a tip-top infirmary."

"We're in need of your medical skills." I dropped a kiss on the top of her head. "Samantha broke a few fingers."

She sucked her teeth and took in the sight of Sam cradling her arm. In much softer tones than she used with the nurses, she said, "Always getting hurt, aren't you?"

"Yeah." Sam shoved stray hairs from her face. "Kinda my specialty."

"Let's see the damage." Ma unwrapped Sam's hand and examined her injuries.

"I don't suppose either of you will tell me how this happened?" Ma peered up over the rim of her reading glasses. "You didn't hit him, did you?" She motioned to me with a head tilt.

Sam snorted. "I did. But not *that* hard. Amazingly enough, Harper is not the cause this time." She met my eyes. "He was an innocent bystander."

I'd deserved that punch, having been complicit in keeping my father's secrets. But I'd managed to gain some trust from Sam. The price was honesty. I avoided talking about my biological parents. I hadn't even discussed them with Molly, and I had planned to spend my life with her. It was a relief to tell Sam. At least now she knew I'd left for reasons other than her. *Maybe we have a truce?* Perhaps now I could start to repair the rift I'd caused. Perhaps she'd hate me less. Maybe she could finally understand me.

"Ma," I said, "she bolted out of the Warrior meeting and took off across the property."

Ma paused her ministrations and looked at Sam. "He finally told you, did he?" Ma cupped Sam's cheek before returning to the Warrior's injury.

"Are you—" Sam started to say.

Ma sucked her teeth. "I've been tellin' that man for years his way was going to backfire. Come sit." She steered Sam to a bed. "Let me go draw up a syringe of Elixir. I'll make you right as rain." To me she said, "Sammy will be here at least thirty minutes. These small bones heal quickly, not instantly. Go make yourself busy."

I waited with Sam while Ma went to gather what she needed. Sam stared down at her broken hand. *Do I let her stew on what she's learned today?* I wondered. *Do I encourage her to confront Pops? Or do I stay silent and let her fight her own battle?* I rubbed Sam's back between her shoulder blades. She inhaled a stuttering breath and leaned into my touch. Footsteps on the hardwood floor drew our attention and we both looked up. Ma was striding with purpose.

I patted Sam's shoulder. "I'll be back to get you."

"Don't leave me." Sam grabbed my hand and looked up at me with hurt-filled eyes.

Her quiet plea cracked my hardened defenses. I

squeezed her fingers and let go. "You know Ma will make me go. I'll be just outside. Focus on healing."

Outside of the infirmary doors, I paced. Telling Sam about my parents' murders started me down a path I'd refused to wander for so long. What would it have been like to be raised by them? Everything I ever read or heard about them had been positive. Xavier's words about my father were no surprise. They had been good people and Pops's alpha Warriors. The pictures I'd seen of them alive made it clear that they loved each other—and loved me. All the books said Warrior children became Light Warriors —there was never an exception. *So why the fuck wasn't I one now?*

"Stop. This won't help," I scolded myself. *What is taking so long?* I glanced at my watch. Five minutes. I pinched the bridge of my nose and inhaled. *I ought to give Pops a heads up on Sam's state of mind.* Wasn't that why he brought me back? To be his eyes and ears on the ground. But I couldn't do it. My mind told my feet to move, but I stayed rooted. I would no longer be the dutiful son who did Pops's bidding, no questions asked. No, I'd failed Sam once. There wouldn't be a second time.

"Fuck him." I pressed my back to the infirmary door and slid down to my ass. I'd wait for Sam and see what she wanted. I dozed there until I heard the click of a door-knob. I hopped up and got out of the way. Ma ushered Sam out. The color had returned to Sam's cheeks, she was no longer hunched over in pain, and the defiant glint was back in her eye.

"How's your hand?"

Sam waggled her fingers in the air. "Functioning."

Ma smiled at Sam before giving her a firm hug. I heard her mutter into Sam's ear, "Try to refrain from hitting solid oak trees and think over what we talked about. Andrew loves you, child." She then kissed my cheek. "Take care of my girl, will you? I have more work to get done in here, go on and be about your business."

"Will do," I said, arching a brow. *What had they discussed?* After Ma went back into the infirmary, I asked, "Do you want to find Pops? I'm sure you have more questions."

"Nope." She shook her head. "I'm not talking to him."

"I might not have amped Warrior senses, but my hearing is pretty damn impeccable for a human. Did I hear you say that you're *not* going to talk to him?"

"I would rather eat razor blades than be in the same room with him."

I almost smiled but squashed it. While I was thrilled to see her spark had returned, she did need to talk to Pops at some point, though now wasn't the right time. I stepped aside. "Very well. After you."

When we entered the hallway, Sam stopped and grabbed my arm. "Camden," she breathed.

"He knows you're with me," I said. I was on the clock, after all.

"He agreed for you to be my bodyguard?" Relief sagged her shoulders.

"That took some convincing, but he folded." I glanced at our surroundings, unsure where Sam had led us. "I had to send him a resume."

"That's just silly."

I nodded. *Fucking annoying, too.* Sam started walking again. I kept pace with her. "What's your plan since you're not going to talk to Pops?"

"I haven't got a clue. But"—she pointed a finger up in the air—"I will be speaking with Xavier about transferring Advisers."

We ascended a flight of green-carpeted stairs and

stopped in a circular alcove at the top. A suit of armor stood watch along the wall.

Leave it to Sam to find a way to avoid talking to Pops. "You sure you want to do that? You know he's far more strict with his Warriors than Pops is."

"What's the worst that can happen?" She faced me and put her hands on her hips. "Look, are you gonna have my back or not?"

I sighed. "Don't make me regret this."

"Thanks." She nodded, spun around, and looked around the alcove.

"You have no idea where you're going, do you?" I asked.

"I have a general idea where my room is, yes. I think. This place needs 'You are here' maps, but I'm positive we're headed in the right direction."

Sam plunged ahead up the next flight of stairs. I followed. *What the fuck did I get myself into?*

18

SAM

A s it turned out, I didn't know where I was going. After I got us lost, Harper asked for directions from a frazzled woman wrangling her toddler. I thought it had been a little insensitive of Harper, but Tammy was the only person we could find at the time. Our tour guide, along with her wailing blond child, showed us back to a familiar long hall. She'd called it Warrior Row and it ended with the very war room I'd fled from not too long ago.

I wanted to fall into bed. I'd lived a full lifetime from the time I woke up this morning to becoming a resident of Casa de Xavier. Maybe I was in some sort of weird, fevered dream that the Mage implanted in my subconscious, and when I woke up, all this would be a construct of my imagination.

"Let's see which door belongs to Xavier's office," I said.

Harper hummed low in his chest, which I took as confirmation, but he wasn't looking at me, he was watching someone further down the hall.

"Who are you—" Movement triggered my Warrior senses. Leigh pushed her shoulders off the grey stone wall, peeling herself away from where she'd rested. Her brows were furrowed and her mouth pulled into a tight frown.

"Hi," I said when we met in the middle of the corridor. Guilt wormed its way into my chest. I'd left her alone with Andrew and a group of people she didn't know.

"Where have you been?" she snipped. Harper hung back. There was an angry energy pulsing around Leigh that would give any wise man pause.

"I needed some air and to clear my head." My knuckles gave a phantom twinge of pain. Playing Rocky with a grandfather oak hadn't been a bright idea. "What happened after I left?"

"No, Sam," she said with forced calm. "You don't get to change the subject. I was worried about you! We looked all over!" She was livid, her hazel eyes snapping with fury. "Not to mention that leaving the meeting like you did was *entirely* disrespectful to our host and our Advisers."

What I did was disrespectful? My brows shot up and I rocked back on my heels. *What about what Andrew had done?* My hackles rose, not at Leigh, but at the whole damn situation.

"She's hurt too, Brave One," Letty said. *"Try to empathize. Have some compassion."*

My inner Warrior's reminder that my best friend was in the same boat as I was settled my puffed-up feathers. I looked past Leigh's wrath and tried to see what happened from her point of view. I'd wounded her by storming out and scared her when she couldn't find me. This was on top of whatever she had felt about Andrew's betrayal. That worm of guilt burrowed deeper, diffusing my anger.

"Leigh, I'm sorry." I reached out toward her but snatched my hand back when she snarled.

"Your outburst reflected on me, you know. We're a *team*. You made us look undisciplined. While Andrew is not off the hook, he *is* our superior. It made him look like he wasn't a competent Adviser." She shook her head slightly and shifted her feet.

Because he's not competent, at least not now. The man had crossed a line he couldn't come back from in my eyes.

"You mean, it made Andrew look like he couldn't control his Warriors," I said.

"Xavier made a comment along those lines, yes."

I gaped at her. *Is she defending Andrew?* "Were we in the same meeting? Did you not hear the same history lesson? Did you watch Jax and Leilani? They knew a lot more than we did. We knew *none* of it. Andrew didn't feel the need to tell us what we were up against when we were first attacked by Greater Demons. What did he do? He *left!*"

"He left for only three days and it was to get *help*," Leigh said.

White-hot ire—not at Leigh, never at Leigh—rose in me. I was furious at the man and angry at myself for my blind faith in him. I whirled and grabbed Harper by the front of the shirt, pulling him forward so he stood next to me. He didn't react or retreat. "Andrew brought in Harper to do his bidding, but he gagged Harper from saying anything. Andrew endangered us. Where do we draw the line, Leigh?"

"I don't know," Leigh said. "But I—" She bowed her head and then looked up at me. "I thought we could work the details out together. Can we talk about this?"

"Sure," I said. "*We* can talk about it." I motioned between me and her. "Right after I talk to Xavier."

"About what?" Leigh startled and raised her brows.

"I'm gonna talk about a trade deal," I said.

Leigh mouthed the words *trade deal*. She shook her head.

"Sam wants to switch teams," Harper clarified, eyeing

me. "We're not sure if that's a possibility, but she's hellbent on asking."

Leigh rubbed her forehead. "Are you for real?"

"Come with me and we'll find out together." I marched forward. When I brushed past Leigh, her right hand shot out and grabbed my left wrist.

"We *need* to talk about this." She took a steadying breath. "We *need* to speak with Adviser Shaw. We can't just make this change without seeking his council first."

I usually tolerated Leigh's gentle correction and appreciated her guidance. I had to be reeled in most of the time, I knew that. But she could be so rigid with the rules, not wanting to make a decision until Andrew agreed. Leigh's default was to toe the line, to dutifully follow instruction without question. Sometimes she needed me to rock the boat a bit. Our partnership worked because we balanced each other out. Hearing her use Andrew's Warrior title and her insistence that we seek his permission was too much, though.

"She needs grace right now," Letty said.

I stared at Leigh's hand on my arm. Her fingernails were neatly trimmed with a touch of clear polish. The veins on the back of her hand popped with the strength of her grip. Keeping my voice level, I said, "Please let go."

"A little help here?" Leigh asked Harper.

Twenty minutes ago, Harper had promised to support me. *Will he change his mind? Will he side with Leigh on this? Will he make me talk to Andrew? I can't talk to Andrew. I can't face him. Not now.* A zing of Warrior Power shot through my rising panic. I looked into Leigh's eyes and pleaded with mine. *Please back down. I'm not ready.*

"What do you want me to do, Kestler?" Harper said.

"You're here to help Adviser Shaw," Leigh said. "He would like to speak with Sam and me."

"I'm here," Harper said with clear authority, "because Pops needed help in his absence. Now he's back. My job is done."

Leigh gasped. "Sam, be reasonable," she whispered. "Please."

"Be reasonable? You aren't angry that he lied to us about everything?" I attempted to roll my wrist, but she clamped down. I grunted.

"Yes, Adviser Shaw withheld information. And I'm sure he had good reasons, which he'd tell us *if* we go talk to him. Together."

"You really believe that don't you?" My heart cracked and I gave her a sad smile. "Let me be clear, there is nothing he can say to us that will justify what he's done."

"How can she defend him?" I asked Letty.

"Her belief system has been shaken. Adviser Shaw is her comfort and sanctuary."

"He was mine, too!" I tried tugging my wrist away again. Leigh shook her head. Her fingernails dug into my skin.

"Leigh isn't you, Brave One. She's scared and doesn't know what to do."

A tear slid down Leigh's cheek. "He loves you."

"That's what Judy said."

"You spoke to Judy?" That threw her off, surprise loosening her grip. "When?"

In a swift motion, I freed my wrist. She stumbled past me. I took several steps back because she swung around angrier than she had been before. I raised my hands in front of me.

"I don't want to fight," I said. "When I left the meeting this afternoon, I ran into the forest on the back forty of the property. I punched a tree. Broke a couple of bones. Harper took me to have Judy mend it."

"Why do you have to make everything dramatic?" she

asked, exhausted. She rubbed her eyes and dropped her arms. "Andrew lied to me, too. He left me alone, too. I had a run-in with the Mage, who invaded and pillaged my mind, then threatened my family. I have *never* been so scared." She wiped tears away. "Newsflash, Fife, we're in this crap together, you *asshole*."

My body flushed hot then cold. I'd bet Harper could have heard my heartbeat. Shame seared my gut. I *was* a selfish asshole.

Leigh wasn't done. "You think that there aren't any consequences for your actions. You don't know the depth of repercussions that your impulsiveness, rudeness, and cavalier behavior cause. I clean up and cover for you over and over. Never once do I complain. I try to be a voice of reason. I try to make sure you're respectable. You never think, you just act."

I gritted my teeth to keep my jaw from trembling. Tears burned my eyes.

"You're dating a guy that knows nothing about you, and now he's on Dominic's radar. He's receiving death threats. You've put him in danger."

Her words were punches to my heart.

"You listen to no one. You disregard authority like you're above the rules. You stormed out of the first joint Warrior meeting in years because you didn't like how Adviser Shaw coached us. Did it ever occur to your bull-headed, stubborn brain that he has more life experience in his pinky than we have in our whole bodies? We're twenty, Sam, not even ten percent of his whole life!"

Either Harper had heard enough, or he saw something in Leigh's posture I'd missed through a blur of tears, because he stepped in front of me. He faced Leigh, his solid body blocking our view of each other.

"Kestler, that's enough," Harper said.

Would Leigh attack me? If she did, I deserved it. Everything she'd said so far was true. All of it. I couldn't form words, and my knees nearly buckled with the weight of my guilt. All I could do was stare at Harper's broad back.

"No, I'm not done." Her tone was resolute. I might not have been able to see her, but Harper's body couldn't stop her words. "We were invited into Adviser Gerena's home with open arms. Given luxurious rooms for as long as we need to stay. And you can't sit for an hour to let the Advisers explain the situation? Xavier has a war room! It contains so much history and knowledge. There are other Warriors of Light that we can get to know. Seers that we don't have to hide our true selves from. And you *ran away*."

"Back off," Harper growled. "Kestler, you're on the verge of losing control of your Power. Look at your hand. It's glowing."

"What does she expect from me, Harper?" Leigh asked.

"Grab Kalakaua and take a walk. Clear your head. Neither of you are in any frame of mind to approach Pops, let alone speak to each other."

I peered around Harper. Both of Xavier's Warriors had entered the hall from an adjoining wing. Leilani and Jax halted, taking in the scene.

"I love her," Leigh said. "She's my sister. We have fought together, bled together, and come close to dying together. But she doesn't care what I think, or how her actions create problems for me."

"It *seems* like that now," Harper said in a reassuring murmur. "You two process trauma differently. I think you need some time apart."

No one in my life was as loyal as Leigh. She deserved a sincere apology. "Leigh, I'm sorry I hurt you."

"I'm done," Leigh whispered.

Had she heard me? Tears dripped off of her chin.

"I can't keep doing this. My heart can't take it." She hunched her shoulders, turned, and walked away, leaving me in stunned silence. She disappeared into the war room.

"Can you go with her?" Harper asked Leilani.

"Of course," the Hawaiian Warrior said and jogged after Leigh.

I stared at the empty space where Leigh had stood. I didn't move until I felt Harper put a firm arm around my waist. I shuddered, my breath rickety, and looked up to see the hard lines in Harper's face soften, his serious eyes filled with something I couldn't place. I sank into him and blinked, trying to clear my eyes.

"Let's go for a run," he said.

I nodded. "That sounds good."

"I'll be right back," Harper said and let me go.

I swayed on my feet. *I shouldn't have left the meeting. Am I a horrible person?*

"Bozeman." Harper walked down the hall to the Warrior. They spoke for a moment.

Harper rejoined me, slid his arm around my waist once more, and nodded to Jax. He led us to my room. Harper's secure hold never slipped.

"Your room's next to mine, right?" Harper asked Jax.

"Yeah, in the next hall over," Jax said. "I'll wait for you if you need a moment." He nodded to me.

"Thanks, man. I'll be just a minute here," Harper said.

Harper turned to me. "Unlock your door, Sam."

I pushed a thumb to the scanner and opened my door. Harper ushered me in and set me on the bed. "Get changed. Don't go anywhere. I'll be right back."

Once alone, I tried to do what Harper told me to do. I really did. Leigh's words ran on a loop while I pawed through my duffle bag. I fished out what I needed. *Does she hate me now?* She had to know that I couldn't face Andrew. I changed shirts. *Would I ever be able to confront him?* Not today. Probably not in a week. Switching my jean shorts to running shorts exhausted me. *How do I fix this?*

I sat on the edge of my bed, tugged on my lucky purple socks, then my running shoes. I fumbled with the laces. I tried again and failed, my tears blinding me. Giving up, I rested my forehead against my bent knee. Harper was true to his word. I let him in when he knocked and went back to the bed.

"Sorry, I can't seem to pull myself together." I shuddered and more damn tears leaked out.

Harper knelt before me. His hands moved my fingers aside so he could tie my shoes.

Maybe Leigh was right. Maybe I should have gone with her to talk to Andrew. That idea made me flinch. Harper paused and glanced up. He searched my eyes. I just shook my head.

What have I done? What kind of person treats those they love like garbage? Me. That's who. Harper helped me off the bed.

"Why are you being so nice to me?" I asked. There was no fight left in me.

"Because I can. Bozeman's waiting."

I let Harper lead me. "Why him?"

"I don't know the area. We needed a guide and he could keep pace with us. Plus, Bozeman won't flirt with me." So Leilani's attempts at gaining Harper's attention hadn't gone unnoticed.

"I texted Adviser Gerena that you are okay," Jax said when we entered the hallway. He was ready for a run himself.

"Why are you helping me?"

The big blond Warrior lifted one shoulder. The dude

was huge. "I haven't been doin' this job too long. I reckon I remember my former life more than most. Sometimes this cargo gets heavy and you need a bit of a breather."

God bless Jackson. I caught Harper watching me. He gave me a closed-lip smile. I didn't know what to make of this new-and-improved Harper. *Could I trust him?*

"Y'all are in for a treat." Jax rubbed his hands with a fervent twinkle in his eye. "I'm gonna show you Shield Haven."

What the fire-fart was a Shield Haven?

19

SAM

J ax led us from the rear of the castle to a winding sidewalk which stretched on as far as the eye could see. He assured Harper that we would remain on hallowed ground the whole time. When we left the lawn, Jax opened his stride into a run and took us down the paved three-mile path. We ran side-by-side with me in the middle.

The manicured footpath wove through some gorgeous Florida wild land. However, I didn't have time to appreciate the scenery since Jax's long strides covered some serious ground. With my heart pounding in my ears, all I could do was focus on not getting left behind. I could have tapped into my Power, but that felt like cheating. Jackson Bozeman was a fast freak of nature.

Jax ran at his natural pace, and if he'd used Warrior Power, he'd be impossible to catch. I sounded like a puffing steam engine next to him. The pace challenged Harper, too, yet he still managed to scout our surroundings with a trained eye while I let my emotions burn off.

About the time I thought my lungs were going to burst,

Jax rounded a turn that dumped us into a small, thriving town. Startled, I dropped to a jog. Quaint shops lined both sides of the road. Jax hadn't slowed and pulled ahead of me. He glanced over his shoulder and took it down a few hundred gears.

A sign nestled in a well-tended flower bed said *Welcome to Shield Haven*. I stopped at the sign, leaned my hands against my knees, and sucked in as much air as I could. Sweat poured off me, stinging my eyes. Harper stopped next to me and propped both hands on the back of his head, elbows flared wide, as he attempted to catch his breath. Jax seemed a little worse for wear. Making sure I wasn't going to vomit, I straightened and lifted the front hem of my shirt to wipe my face.

"What is this place?" I asked.

"Adviser Gerena's town," Jax said.

Harper also wiped his face. "He *owns* it?"

"Kinda." Jax leaned and pulled his left leg into a standing quad stretch. "He created Shield Haven to give all the Seers who live in the castle a sense of purpose. The borders are protected here. Everyone free-leases their spot from Adviser Gerena, and everything they earn is theirs to keep."

"Do you actually get tourists coming through?" I asked. There was every type of business needed to keep a little town in the middle of Florida afloat. The shops were bustling with people coming and going.

"Yep, especially during the fall and winter seasons. Snowbirds and all." Jax started down the strip, passing a green Main Street sign. "Right now, we aren't as busy."

Not busy, my ass. The restaurant we passed had a packed outside seating area, the gas station had at least five cars in the parking lot and only two pumps, and the neighborhood grocery store had a revolving door with patrons coming and going.

"Jax!" came a chorus of children's voices behind us. The huge man turned and his face lit up with a wide smile. He squatted to the kids' level and held his arms open. A group of four, no older than seven, swarmed him in hugs. They laughed when they tipped him over onto his rear.

"Will you show us 'Zina?'"

He smiled. "Y'all know my axe is not meant for show-n-tell."

"Pleeeeeease," the kids begged in a collective whine. I stole a glance at Harper and had to choke on my laugh. His brow was furrowed, eyes tight, with a bewildered twist on his lips.

"Okay, okay, just a look," Jax said, chuckling.

"Who'er they?" demanded a redheaded boy, his face deeply freckled. He pointed his finger at me.

"That's Sam. She's like me. Harper is—" Jax looked at Harper.

"A colleague," he offered.

"What's a colleague?" asked the redhead, his little brow puckered in concentration.

Harper gave me a deadpan look. I snorted and covered my mouth.

"We work with him, Harrison. He helps people like Sam and me."

Harrison's little mouth formed an O. And with an attention span that made me proud, he asked Jax, "Do you have a quarter?"

"Nah, bud. We ran here. What did'ya want?"

"Just some bubble gum from Betty's Sweets." He kicked the sidewalk with the toe of his sneaker.

"Tell you what, run down there and tell Ms. Betty to put it on my tab." Jax winked at the boy, who grinned.

Harrison sprinted off without a backwards glance, leaving his three buddies behind.

"The kids like it when we come to town," Jax said. "Makes them feel safe. These boys are fascinated with our weapons. My war axe is actually called Tabarzina, but they have a hard time with that." He jerked a thumb toward the kids. "I'm gonna be a while. Why don't y'all head to the antiques store over there." He pointed across the street. "DH should be there. Get you some water and cool off. I don't know how long these kiddos want to keep me."

I paled. DH was Xavier's daughter. She'd witnessed my meltdown. *What if she summons Andrew somehow?* I wasn't prepared to face my doom.

With another genuine chuckle, as if he read my mind, Jax said, "She won't squeal on ya. She's good people."

"You're sure?" I bit my lip.

Jax drew large X over his chest with a finger. "On my honor."

"Thanks," I said and joined Harper as we crossed the street. In the middle of the street, I turned and walked backwards. "Hey Jax?"

"Yeah?" he asked.

"Why did you help me?" I asked. "I know it wasn't because of Harper's sparkling charm."

Jax's infectious smile faded. "Miss Sam, you ain't never done nothin' ill to me. I seen it in your eyes when I met ya, you've been fightin' battles in your head that no one really knows. Everyone needs a hand once in a while."

Is this dude single? Leigh hadn't been on a date in fifty-forevers. Ignoring the pang of regret that she probably hated me now, I waved at him. "Don't *ever* change."

"Don't plan to." He grinned at me before giving his full attention to his little fans. I watched him, letting the adorable scene be a soothing salve on my day.

We entered Xavier's Antique Emporium and the glorious A/C hit me like a merciful cold blast from Heaven. I let my head fall back and declared, "Sweet Jesus, thank you for the man that invented air conditioning."

Two elderly ladies with coiffed grey curls, wearing winged eyeglasses straight up from the '70s and pastel polyester slacks, gaped at me. One woman held a china plate, the other a porcelain cat figurine. Only then did I see DH seated behind the counter, handing a customer change. She'd paused mid-exchange, hand in suspended, as did her customer at my loud declaration.

"Sorry," I said. "It's a hot day." The shoppers went back to their business.

The shop was bigger inside than it had appeared from the street. Xavier had filled it with just about every type of antique you could think of, from tables and armoires to decorative signs and baskets. Instead of the weird mothball and musty, old furniture smell common in antique shops, I smelled cinnamon rolls and coffee.

There was a massive wooden staircase in the center of the shop leading to a second floor. The entrance to the stairs was rear-facing, leaving the cavernous underbelly of the stairs displayed to the main store floor. They'd added a marble sales counter to bridge the gap and an old timey cash register sat on top. There was even a rotary phone connected to a wall cable.

Harper mumbled something incoherent next to me, leaving me on my own to do God-knows-what. DH finished up with her patron, bidding him a good day. When he left, I sidled up to the counter.

Praying the girl didn't think I was as horrible a person as I was, I found a scrap of my bravado. "Hiya DH."

"Hi Sam!" She flashed me a huge grin. I found myself mirroring her cheer.

"You should apologize," Letty said. *"You ran out of the Warrior meeting in which she was the speaker."*

Well, shit. I sighed, wind in my sails dying. I ran a hand over the smooth surface of the marble counter. "DH, I owe you an apology. I left while you——"

The pixie waved her hand in the air, her smile not faltering. "Stop. You're totally not the first Warrior to lose her marbles in the middle of a Warrior meeting. You wanna talk drama? Leilani. Should've seen it when she found out Dad anointed Jackson. She wasn't the only child anymore." DH blew out an exaggerated breath and mimicked an explosion with her fingers. "Flipped her ever-loving mind."

Interesting. Some evil part of me wanted to see what happened if I provoked Leilani to her breaking point. I tamped that thought down before it could grow roots. "Thanks for not holding it against me. So, Xavier's daughter, huh?"

Her laugh was pleasant. "He found me in a foster home after a series of unpleasant incidents where I had to get away from demons. Went through six homes in two years. I might have run away a few times, too. Child prodigy or not, I was the crazy foster daughter no one wanted. Dad was my last hope."

No one could say DH was a shy teen. "Child prodigy?" I asked, picking up a pen from the mesh metal cup on the counter.

"I've got an eidetic memory and an IQ of 162. It helped me stay alive on my own before Dad saved me."

"How old are you?"

"Fifteen." DH went over to a small white fridge in the underbelly of the stairwell. She pulled out two bottles of water and held one in my direction.

"Yes, please, you beautiful human."

DH set one in front of me, the other at the end of the counter. "This one's for your boyfriend."

"He—what?" The pen fumbled out of my hand. "You think Harper is—" The pen rolled off the counter and bounced on the floor. I swooped so DH wouldn't see the spectacular shade of red I'd turned. Heat lanced up behind my ears.

"You mean he's not?" she said from above, peeping over the counter.

I righted myself and coughed. I broke the seal on the bottle and drank, gulping down the cold liquid. After draining half, I pulled it from my lips.

"What grade are you in?" I asked.

"I'm a sophomore at the University Florida, majoring in history and classical languages. I attend remotely, because demons."

"Damn," I said, feeling like a dumb ox next to a prized Narnian horse. My manners kicked in a second later. "Sorry you went through all that in your younger years." She *was* still a kid. "I can't imagine growing up that way."

"S'cool, Sam. Not too messed up in the noggin or anything." DH tapped her temple. "I'm just freaky smart and occasionally overshare information."

I found myself relaxing around her. "I like you. We should be friends."

Her face lit up like a child at Christmas. "I'd like that."

I drank the rest of my water and set the bottle on the counter, looking for a trash can. The plastic crunched under the pressure from my touch. "Tell me something."

"Anything."

"What's your Dad like as an Adviser?" Xavier ran a tight ship, but I wanted to know what I could expect should I be allowed to join his crew.

"He's tough, but fair. Doesn't tolerate drama with his

Warriors or Seers. He's patient but expects you to do what he says without asking a second time."

"So my epic meltdown was frowned upon?" *Of course it was. He must be so pissed at me.* Before DH could answer, the doorbell chimed. She glanced over my shoulder and her eyes widened.

"Miss Fife."

I froze at the curtness of Xavier's Spanish accent, my own eyes growing huge. In my peripheral vision, Harper appeared at the counter. DH held out the bottle of water she'd pulled out for him. He nodded his thanks.

"Your dad's mad, isn't he?" I asked DH in a whisper. "How do I know if he's mad?"

DH leaned her elbows on the marble countertop to get closer to me. "His eyes get all wild and like, have this reddish shine in them."

"His eyes turn red?" I asked.

"Pretty much."

"So, is he all fire-breathing dragon *right now?*"

"Nah, but he's comin' in hot." She gave me a closed mouth smile, released her elbows, and took two steps back to hop on a stool behind the counter. "Dad! What's new?"

Gathering my wits, I took a deep breath and swung around to come face-to-face with Xavier freaking Gerena.

"Xavi—"

"Stop!" Letty cut in. *"Use his proper title."*

"Right. Thank you."

"Adviser Gerena, didn't expect to see you here. Did someone tell you I was in town?" I offered a weak smile.

"Mr. Bozeman did not 'rat you out' if that's what you're implying." He appraised me, sweaty clothes and all. "I keep an office upstairs. You will join me there right now." Harper was at my side in an instant, moving with quiet stealth. Xavier eyed him. "Alone."

"With all due respect, sir." Harper's tone was cool. "Sam's whereabouts and wellbeing are of importance to me."

Xavier raised a brow. "Very well. You may stand outside. Follow me." He dipped his chin, acknowledging DH, but didn't spare a second glance at me.

Go, she mouthed. *Good luck.* She gave me two thumbs up.

I muttered into Harper's ear as we ascended the grand steps. "My whereabouts and wellbeing, huh?"

"Bennett's words, not mine. Wasn't enough for him to make sure you were safe at all times, he wanted to assure your *comfort* as well."

My heart bottomed out into my stomach and I stopped.

"Don't dawdle," Xavier called down to us.

"Coming," I said. I grabbed Harper, who was a couple steps up from me. I *knew* there was a reason he was being different. This had to be it. Camden was paying him to play nice with me in the sandbox. The feeling of being alone punched me in the chest. "That's why you're being nice, isn't it? I'm just a job."

Harper glared at me with furrowed brows, a darkness passing over his face, his sapphire eyes burning dark. I saw a raging fire that could consume villages in their depths. He clenched his jaw, trying to rein in his temper. I watched as the blaze came and went.

"How the fuck did you come up with that idea?"

More dadgum tears prickled in my eyes. I didn't want to fight with Harper, and I was one more harsh comment away from breaking into a million Sam shards. I wouldn't turn to Andrew. I couldn't turn to Leigh. Losing Harper for a second time would be the death of me. If this was just a job to him, I doubted I could put the pieces of my heart back together.

"Harper," I whispered. "I'm empty. Got nothing left. I gotta know, are you team Sam because you wanna be or because duty calls? Andrew's or Camden's."

To my absolute shock, Harper descended to my step. He took my face in his calloused hands and brushed away my tears with his thumbs. His expression was unguarded. A soft half smile eased the stoic hardness in his face. He leaned down and pressed a kiss onto my forehead. I stopped breathing. He rested his chin on the top of my head for a few heartbeats then he stepped away.

"My promise is to *you*. My allegiance is with *you*. The gig I'm doing with Bennett is because you asked me to. I don't give a fuck what your boyfriend thinks. And don't worry about Pops." Harper left me standing there as he ran up the last four steps.

I didn't follow. My brain blanking.

"Sam," Harper said.

I jerked out of my daze and looked at him. "Sorry." Harper made a gesture toward the second floor. "Right," I said. *What just happened?*

The evening summer sun washed the landing area with light. Xavier waited next to a door with a set of frosty glass panes. The elaborate black name plate with gold engraving labeled this room as his office. "I'm glad to see that you didn't get lost in here, at least."

I bet that toddler-toting woman told him what happened in the castle. Although, not much happened in Casa de Xavier or Shield Haven that he didn't know about.

"In you go." His tone wasn't friendly, per se, it was more 'I'm the boss.' I glanced at Harper before crossing the threshold.

"Mr. Tate will be right outside," Xavier said.

Harper nodded. I smiled, glad he was on my side. Then Xavier shuffled me into his office and closed the door. I was trapped.

"This was what you wanted, correct?" Letty asked.

"Yes, but I didn't come to him on my terms. He has all the power now."

Xavier strode through his tasteful, yet cozy office. The medium brown furniture matched his chocolate leather seating. His walls were lined with bookshelves containing old texts, old world decorative items, and a few displayed jewelry pieces. Just like his command center, the space had a relaxing, old world vibe to it. I ventured further in.

The Adviser stood across the room next to a tea cart. He busied himself scooping rich-smelling coffee into a glass French press. The soft bubble of boiling water came from an electric kettle next to it. He didn't say anything, so I started meandering around the room. On a side table, next to one of the leather couches, stood an iron statue which was about a foot tall. It looked like a tree branch.

What a weird piece of art, I thought.

"Coffee, Miss Fife?" He brought over a loaded tray with beverages, a cheese and cracker tray, and assorted jams. "It's a delightful dark roast with hints of caramel and vanilla."

"No, thank you." I had enough to deal with without adding a caffeine buzz.

"Very well." He went to the window and opened it before taking his seat next to that odd tree statue.

It's August in Florida. What's this man opening windows for? The place was gloriously cool inside. I watched Xavier toss a couple crackers on that side table with the iron branch, and then settle himself with his hot beverage. He reminded me of the Mad Hatter from *Alice in Wonderland*. All that was missing was his top hat, a dormouse, and an insane rabbit. Xavier said nothing and took a sip of coffee. He studied me with an intensity that curled my toes inside my sneakers.

"Miss Fife, do I need to invite you to sit? Let's chat."

I chewed on the inside of my cheek. A cool sweat prickled at my hairline. I wanted to know how deep my ass was in trouble. I was about to do as he'd asked when a raven flew into the office through the open window.

The black bird circled the room a couple times then landed on the iron statue. A perch. *Now it makes sense.* Eyeing the corvid, I made no move to sit. Realizing I'd backed myself against a shelf, I stepped forward and seated myself on the chair across from Xavier.

Xavier scratched the raven's head. "This is Nyx, Goddess of the Night. She's my Guardian. We've been together a very long time." Nyx closed her eyes and leaned into his touch.

"Oh." Because all Warriors had Guardian animals. "But she's a bird."

Nyx twitched her head and threw side-eye shade at me. Her sharp croak made me twitch. I felt thoroughly judged. Intelligence danced in the dark depth of her eye, reminding me of Max. She was a gorgeous cobalt black, though some of her tail feathers were the darkest of blue.

"Not all Guardians are four-legged mammals. Though most are." Xavier handed Nyx a cracker. "She can speak some human words. But she doesn't know you, so I doubt she'll say anything." Nyx took her treat with one of her feet and nibbled at it, crumbs dusting the side table. I watched her in silence, hoping Xavier would speak.

He didn't and I cracked first. "Am I in trouble, sir?"

Xavier tilted his head as he mulled over my question. He drew in a breath and adjusted his position on the sofa.

"I am still assessing your character. Andrew will decide if there will be consequences for your insubordination." He sipped his coffee. "I suspect you have some questions for me."

"Can I join your team?" I blurted.

Xavier had raised his cup again but paused. He studied me. Nyx let out another croak and flapped her wings. He finished his sip and lowered his arm. "You'd leave Andrew so easily?"

I didn't need to think about it. "Yes."

"And what about Miss Kestler?"

Shame shot through my broken heart. "We're not— she's not talking to me right now."

"She's your Warrior partner. You must make this decision together."

No wonder she was so furious when I'd told her that I wanted to leave Andrew. I'd have to deal with that later.

He took another sip of coffee. Nyx watched him, or rather his cup. "Henceforth, however, you will obey me."

"For sure." The man kind of terrified me. As long as he didn't hide things from me, no matter how intimidating he was, I would do what he asked.

"It wasn't a question, Miss Fife."

"I was just affirming, sir."

"Very well." He squashed a smile and set his cup on the side table. Nyx's eyes widened and she hopped off her perch. She plunged her beak into the dark beverage. "As Adviser Shaw has pressing matters to attend to, I will be taking over his charges for now."

"He what?" I hissed. "That is just like him to run off and not—"

Then I saw it, right there in his eyes, what DH had described. A red glint licked at Xavier's brown irises and an angry buzz radiated off him. This was his anger. And quite frankly, it was downright frightening. I shut my trap real fast. When I shut up, his temper simmered.

"You will be in the gym tomorrow morning at 4:30. Nigel will collect you at 4:15."

Nyx tipped her head back, relishing her stolen treat.

"What will we be doing, if you don't mind me asking?"

"I do not stifle curiosity. You are free to respectfully inquire about anything. Tomorrow, I will be assessing your proficiency with your Warrior weapon."

"Got it." *Fighting I can do.* "I'll be ready."

"You're dismissed, Miss Fife." Xavier twisted, reaching for his cup, only to find Nyx actively dunking a cracker in his coffee. "*¡Maldita pájara!* Stop that! Caffeine isn't good for ravens."

"No!" she squawked and clicked her beak.

And *that* was my cue to leave. "Thank you, sir."

Xavier, speaking rapid-fire Spanish to his Guardian, waved a hand at me. Nyx snapped and croaked right back at him.

I found Harper sitting in a plastic office chair. He'd propped his legs up on the wooden banister. When he saw me, he dropped his feet. "What happened?"

"Xavier is a modern-day Edger Allan Poe."

"What?" Harper cocked his head.

"Never mind," I said. My stomach snarled, feeling hollow. "I'm hungry and I have much to tell you but can't focus without nourishment. But I left my debit card at the castle. Do you have money on you? I will pay you back."

Harper said, "Yeah, I have cash."

"You're a gentleman." I patted his bicep. "I saw a pizza place down the road. I hope they have mozzarella sticks. And garlic knots."

"That sounds like a Band-Aid to a rough day."

"Ooh, and nachos. I plan on eating my feelings, telling

you all my woes, and then I'll drown my sorrow in ice cream. Maybe in the haze of carb overload, I'll be able to sleep tonight."

We walked through the shop and I waved goodbye to DH. She beamed at me and waved back.

Harper held the door for me. "Your coping skills are questionable."

"Possibly. I'll start working on it tomorrow." We headed along the sidewalk. "But just remember, Rome wasn't built in a day."

20

SAM

"I'm up. I'm coming. Keep your britches on." I padded over to my door and peered through the peephole. Nigel stood there, calm and collected in his suit at the ass crack of dawn. He'd come to get me exactly seven minutes before 4:15. Joke was on him, because after sleeping like absolute garbage, I threw in the towel and got up at four. I'd managed to brush my teeth and get on a clean T-shirt. I was pulling on a pair of pants when Nigel arrived.

"Up an' at 'em, buddy." I jogged over and scratched Bear's chest to wake him. He was on his back, all four paws hanging in the air. A loud snore ripped out of him. "Bear, you can't stay in here all day." I shook him. He rolled to his side and regarded me though half-closed eyelids.

"Do you want *breakfast?*" That was the magic word. He came to life, launched himself off the bed, and ran to the door where he proceeded to prance in place. Food, the universal motivator.

"Morning," I said to Nigel. "Is Leigh coming?" I glanced at her room. "Also, can you please tell me where I can get this mangy mutt some food?"

"Her appointment is at six. Master Gerena wants to meet with you separately." The Englishman beckoned my dog to him with two fingers. The pit bull obliged and lumbered up. "Master Bear's needs will be met. Let's go."

"Lead the way." I covered a yawn behind the back of my hand. "You wouldn't happen to have coffee in that suit of yours, would you?" I scrunched my eyes shut then reopened them wide and rubbed at the sleep crusted in them.

"Yes, right under my vest."

"You got jokes, Nigel?" I asked before another yawn overtook me.

"Mistress Fife, I am a British butler. I never *joke*." He winked, then guided me down through the castle to the subterranean gym. Xavier was seated at a desk in the corner with Nyx prowling along the ledge. DH stood over her father, holding a computer tablet.

"Good morning, Miss Fife. I trust you're well," Xavier greeted me without looking up. He was focused on what DH was showing him. So was the raven. Part of me wondered if Nyx could read.

"Hi, Sam!" The pixie beamed at me with alert green eyes and too much energy for this early in the morning.

With a sleepy smile, I nodded at her. "I've been better. But I'm present and accounted for."

"Did you get some rest?" Xavier asked and tapped his finger on the tablet.

Does nightmare-plagued, sweat-drenched sleep count as rest? I shrugged. "I slept."

"Excellent." Xavier looked up and pushed away from the desk. DH extended the tablet to him but he waved her away. "Confounded things. Can't I just use a pen and paper?"

DH sighed, like she'd had this conversation six hundred

eighty-two times. "Dad, we *need* to go digital. It's beneficial for preservation of texts, takes up less space, and it's easier to find information." Father and daughter stared at each other, locked in a silent stalemate. Xavier won the brief contest of wills.

"One day, Dad, one day." DH plunked the tablet on the desktop. Nyx pounced on it. DH hopped back in surprise and narrowed her eyes at the Warrior Guardian. "Good thing that sucker is in a case."

Nyx stared down, twisting her head back and forth, looking at her reflection. A genuine smile graced my lips. *That's kind of adorable.*

"Not while I have you, my darling," Xavier said as she set out a yellow legal pad and pen. "Now, go get ready for school. Take Nyx, too."

DH hugged him then ran a finger down Nyx's glossy back. The corvid lost interest in the tablet. She tilted her head, looked at DH, and made a throaty chirp. DH held out her arm; Nyx flapped her wings once and jumped on board.

"Bye, Sam!" DH said, passing me. Nyx's low croak sounded as if being with DH was the highlight of her day.

I waved at DH and yawned. *I could really go for some coffee.*

"Miss Fife." Xavier hooked a finger at me. We moved to the glorious weapons wall. He stopped next to a sword rack. "I spoke to Andrew and, given the circumstances, we've agreed to grant you a pass for yesterday's behavior. But just so I'm crystal clear, I will not tolerate any more insubordination. You will observe. You will listen. And you will learn. You will not lose your temper with me in such a manner. Am I understood?"

Heat flared in my cheeks from embarrassment.

Contrary to popular belief, I didn't want to screw up by running my mouth. I gave him a firm nod.

"Now, I understand Andrew gave you Azira."

"Yes, sir."

"Excellent. She's a fine weapon. Andrew also tells me you are a natural with hand-to-hand combat. In fact, he went as far as to say that you are one of the best he's trained." Xavier peered at me with something like skepticism. "That remains to be seen. However, I do trust his instincts. They haven't been wrong in the time I've known him. If he says you're one of the more preeminent of his students, then I'll not second guess him." Xavier studied me.

I rocked back and forth on my toes, swinging my arms for balance. "So are you gonna have me spar?"

"No, I trust Andrew's appraisal of your skill. I need to evaluate your proficiency with Azira." He walked away from me. "I want to see you shoot."

This was a test I could ace while half-awake. I hustled after him, stopping at a large circular track. There were six demon-like targets bolted to stands. Each stand was attached to a base that sat atop the track.

"From the center of the ring, you'll shoot nine arrows at moving targets." He pointed towards the middle.

I approached one of the demons and poked it in the cheek. The manikin's flesh yielded like it was real. *Creepy.* I moved to one of its neighbors and lightly punched its stomach. Again, it felt life-like. Xavier had captured the likeness of Greater Demons in perfect detail.

"This is legit," I muttered under my breath.

"I'll control the speed and direction the track moves." Xavier picked up a remote and moved behind a plexiglass shield. "Ready?"

"As I'll ever be." I went to the center of the circle,

closed my eyes, and reached for a stream of Power. My fingers closed around Azira, and I pulled her from her invisible spot. I held my weapon in front of me and slowed my breathing. I nocked an arrow and waited.

At the sound of the track starting up, I opened my eyes and focused all my attention on one of the demons, then released. It struck my intended target's chest. The rotation changed, going clockwise. I fired three consecutive arrows. *Thwack. Thwack. Thwack.* They all slammed into colored torsos.

Xavier sent the demons counter-clockwise, this time with greater speed. As the targets whirled by, I nocked an arrow, watching and waiting. I took a breath and aimed.

"Hold," Letty said just as Xavier changed the direction.

I paused, then shot my arrow. This one hit, but in a shoulder joint. *Damn.*

I tapped into my Power and with Letty's assistance, three of my remaining arrows pierced the demon chests. All would have been killing blows. With my last target remaining, I withdrew my final arrow. Just as I let it fly, Xavier changed the rotation. The arrowhead sliced a bicep on its way to the far wall. The circular contraption rumbled to a stop.

Damn. Damn. Damn. I jerked up out of my archer's position, pursed my lips, and glared at the demon's flayed arm. I'd missed some shots in the past week, too. Twice.

"Impressive." Xavier stepped from behind his safety glass shield. "Has anyone ever told you that the bow doesn't suit you?"

Perturbed at my botched shots, my defensive indignation flared. Azira had served me well. "What do you mean?"

"At ease, Warrior." Xavier went back to the wall of weapons. "When Andrew and I went our separate ways, he only took two weapons. We were under attack and needed to scatter. He took Miss Kestler's sword, Fury, and Azira."

I gripped my bow tighter. Fury was a part of Leigh. They made beautiful things happen together. I couldn't see her with any other weapon. That left Azira for me, and while I wasn't complaining, I wondered why Andrew only grabbed the two.

As if reading my thoughts, Xavier said, "It was not Andrew's fault. Our Warriors were being hunted and murdered. He dashed into headquarters, grabbed what was closest, and fled. You weren't provided with the weapon that best fit you because he didn't have the resources. Don't hold it against him."

Xavier placed a palm on top of a wooden chest encrusted with rubies and inlaid with gold. It was about two feet long and a foot wide. He withdrew a set of keys from his pants pocket and unlocked the lid, leaving it unopened. This chest was the one that Letty had been drawn to, and as if a cord were connected to my navel, I found myself standing before the box. I reached for it then snatched my hand back. Xavier hadn't given me permission to touch it, so I curled my fingers into a fist and dropped my arm.

"If the bow were your best fit, Azira wouldn't miss," Xavier spoke, breaking the spell. "This is not your fault."

For two years, Azira and I killed a lot of Lesser Demons. She was a close friend.

"As a Heavenly Armorer, my specialty lies not only in creating weapons, but also in pairing them to their Warrior. I made your bow, Miss Fife, and her ever-returning arrows." Xavier gestured to Azira. "And I forged what's in here." He patted the jewel-covered chest. "My instincts are never wrong when it comes to pairing a Warrior with a weapon. Now, if it is acceptable, I would like to offer you an alternative to your bow."

"She's been good to me." I clutched her to the front of my body. A wave of bittersweet nostalgia washed over me. Had he not just asked me to give up my bow, I would have focused on the *he made Warrior weapons* part. But whatever was in that chest called to me—called to Letty—like a siren's song.

Xavier smiled. "I've no doubt about that, Miss Fife. Nothing I've created would ever truly fail any Warrior. But there is an art to the perfect weapon pairing. Would you like to give them a test run?" He held out his hand. "I'll hold Azira for you."

I glanced between the box, Xavier, and back, not ready to relinquish Azira just yet. I looked down at the bow and stroked the long curve of wood. I ran my fingers over the white metal cap at one end.

"Go. Look," Letty prompted, her longing unprecedented.

"Here goes nothing," I mumbled under my breath and held my bow out for Xavier. When he grabbed hold, I refused to let go. "This isn't me surrendering her just yet."

"Understood," Xavier said. "She's still yours if you decide not to make the exchange."

I stepped up to the chest and ran my hands over the bejeweled top. The pull in my navel grew stronger.

"Open it," Letty insisted.

"I'm gettin' there. Keep your shirt on." I'd never felt her more excited. I opened the lid. Nestled in a navy velvet liner lay twin fighting daggers. The lethal white metal blades curved slightly toward each other. The smooth hilts had no crossguards. Small red crosses were etched onto the Heavenly steel, directly on the blades, just under the hilts—exactly in the same spot where Fury was branded. From tip to the

butt of the grip, the daggers were about a foot and a half long.

My Warrior Power resonated with the spirit of these daggers. I gasped and stepped back. Letty hummed her delight, sending radiant beams of warmth throughout my body. She was so pleased.

"Pick them up," Letty urged. Reverently, I did so. My grip on the hilts came as naturally as breathing. Their weight and balance fit my hands as though they had been made just for me.

Holy Heaven. I met Xavier's gaze. He was smiling, holding Azira. There was a *rightness* about the daggers that I'd never had with my bow. I hadn't had an instant, visceral connection with her. Still, she'd been solid for me. But there was no way, in time or space, that Letty would allow me to relinquish the fighting daggers. Nor did I want to.

"What's happening?" I asked.

"You feel the energy running from you to the weapon, yes?" Xavier nodded. "Miss Fife, there is a deep connection with the *right* weapon to the *right* Warrior. Finding these pairings has always been my job. You will instinctively know how to use your true weapon because it complements the Warrior inside you. I will not need to teach you to use the daggers, your Warrior will know what to do. Andrew said you'd trained with regular blades, if I'm not mistaken?"

"Yes, we did."

"Excellent." Xavier backed up several feet. "Try them out. You'll see what I mean."

He gave me an encouraging smile. I closed my eyes. Letty sent me rapid-fire flashes of myself wielding the daggers.

"Now it's your turn. I'll guide you," she said.

Power rushed through me. I launched into a series of

slashes, ducks, and stabs. Everything Xavier had said to me, all of what Letty showed me, was true. These bad boys were an extension of me, and we flowed with a natural grace. In one last move, I flipped into an aerial cartwheel and landed with the daggers pointed down in a power stance. I released a breath. I'd never felt this exhilaration with Azira. I *needed* these daggers.

"I presume they are satisfactory?" Xavier asked.

"Exceeds expectations. What are their names?"

"Sol and Helios." Xavier rejoined me. "Should you keep them, they will rest in the same invisible place on your back, stored in an X position. Give it a try."

Putting them where Azira still lived felt a little like betrayal. "I haven't given you my answer."

"I'm aware. Please do as I say."

I slid the daggers into place and they vanished from view along with their connection to my Power. I reached back to withdraw one of the blades, and the hilt solidified in my grasp. A pulse of Power flared in me. When I released the grip, the Power receded. At all times, I could feel their comforting presence. *Interesting.*

"Well?" Xavier cocked his head. "Have you made a decision?"

Chewing on the inside of my cheek, I took one final glance at Azira. Sol and Helios *felt* right, like they were a part of my soul. I nodded. "I'll keep them."

Xavier hung my former weapon on the wall in an empty spot specific to her shape. The quiver of arrows that went with her shimmered into view next to the mighty bow. I expected to feel a sense of betrayal or guilt, but there was no ache in my chest.

"You made the right choice," Letty said. The warmth of my new friends offset any sense of loss. They were the only change in my life these past two days that didn't come with

grief. Andrew betrayed me. Leigh hated me. I was a horrible girlfriend to Camden. The Mage thought I was dark enough inside to join Hell's team. My eyes burned with sudden tears.

"Everything alright?" Xavier asked, turning back to me.

No. Not at all. I cleared my throat. "I'm fine. Thank you, sir."

"It's my job, and my pleasure, to serve you in this area." Xavier crossed the distance between us and placed a hand on my shoulder. "You have such untapped potential. As soon as you match what's in here"—he pointed to my heart—"to what you have in here"—he pressed a fingertip against my forehead—"you'll be a force Hell cannot deal with."

That was *if* I managed to survive the Mage. "So, what's next on the agenda?"

"You're finished here. I'll call for Nigel." He headed for his desk.

"Wait a moment." I jogged over to him and touched his elbow. "Will you be doing the same test with Leigh?"

Xavier raised his brows. "Yes, but I've no doubt Fury is the correct weapon for her. It's a private session, just like yours. Was there something else Miss Fife?"

Since I couldn't watch Leigh's session, and I was in desperate need of coffee, I asked, "Actually, can you point me in the direction of caffeine?"

"Right up that flight of stairs. They end in the kitchen." Xavier pointed to the stairwell we'd used yesterday.

As I climbed the steps, I made a small to-do list. At the very top was seeing Camden. I'd been MIA, he'd been worried sick, and he deserved better from me. I'd try to smooth things over with him. At the top of the stairs, I stepped inside the kitchen and saw a familiar set of broad shoulders clad in a black tee. "Morning."

Harper pivoted, mug in one hand, and leaned his hips against the granite countertop. "Sam."

"You're up early."

I sat down at the round kitchenette table and shuddered at my reflection in the window. I looked like a girl who'd rolled out of bed and fought nine fake demons at four in the morning. Blonde flyaways stuck up everywhere and my ponytail drooped. I pulled out the elastic band and hastily put my hair up in a top knot.

"Camden called." Harper set down his mug, pulled a second one off a wall peg, and poured another cup of coffee.

Damn it. I definitely needed to make it up to him. "This morning? It's early."

Harper shrugged. "He was concerned when he didn't hear from you last night."

I propped my elbows on the table, burying my head in my hands. I'd been so lost in what happened yesterday that I'd let Camden fall last in line. It hadn't been intentional. He deserved an apology and an explanation. In person. He *did* matter to me. His life mattered. I glanced up at the sound of ceramic clunking down on wood and lifted my head. I let my arms drop and wrapped my hands around the mug of coffee Harper had placed in front of me.

"Thank you," I said. He also set a plate of buttered toast sprinkled with cinnamon and sugar in front of me. *How the hell did he remember I liked this?* He grunted and pulled out a chair, turned it around, and straddled it. He leaned his forearms on the back.

I bit off a mouthful of toast. "When did he call?"

Harper checked his watch while taking a sip of his coffee. "Five o'clock on the dot."

"Am I a miserable, no-good, terrible person? You'd tell me if I was, right?"

He laughed faintly through his nose. "Can you be infuriating? Frustrating? Yes. But I wouldn't classify you as a shitty person."

I sighed and tore off a piece of toast, shoving it into my mouth. After I swallowed, I said, "I've gotta see him."

"Figured as much. You have breakfast plans with him in a couple hours. His idea. Remember, I'm tailing your ass for as long as I'm employed by Bennett. But also because we're leaving the safety of this property, and we're not to go anywhere alone."

Butterflies did somersaults in my belly. Camden didn't hate me. He *wanted* to see me. Even after the wringer of worry and doubt I'd put him through. Even after my accidental blow-off of his texts, calls, and concerns, Camden was *still* trying to find a way to see me. I took a careful sip of coffee. When it didn't scald my mouth, I took a bigger gulp to wash down my guilt with a side of toast.

"How'd the evaluation go?"

"Fine. Xavier had me shoot." My heart raced thinking about my change in weapons. When I thought of my new blades, Helios and Sol warmed between my shoulder blades.

"And?"

"I missed a couple shots, so after the test, he made an offer, and as cliché as it sounds, I couldn't refuse. Check this out." I reached for one of my new daggers with my right hand.

Helios. Its name echoed in my mind. Power flared when I touched the hilt. He flickered into view. *Guess that means Sol is my left-hand man.* I set Helios on the table.

Harper let out a low whistle, eyeing the dangerous

curved dagger. He reached out just as I had when I first saw them, but he stopped. "May I?"

At my nod, Harper picked up my weapon, examining it. He flipped the grip in his hand, then took a test swipe. Everything Andrew had trained me in, he'd first taught to Harper. The man in front of me wielded my weapon like an anointed Warrior. I found I didn't hate the sight of him giving my dagger a go.

"That's a fine fucking blade Xavier gave you." Harper spun the blade so the butt pointed at me. I took Helios from him and slid the white-metal dagger home.

"I have two. They're twins." I rocked my head back to indicate I still had Sol sheathed.

"Suits you. I never thought a bow fit your style. What happens to Azira?"

"I guess she's sidelined until Xavier finds her 'true Warrior.'" I made air quotes.

"Hmm," Harper mused. "You should shower." He stood and walked over to an intercom. "She's ready. We're in the kitchen."

"Nigel?" I asked, pushing myself away from the table.

"Yes. Unless I'm mistaken, you still need some direction in this place."

I sighed. I missed the farmhouse, my room in said farmhouse, and my life at said farmhouse. Nigel arrived within moments. He was supernatural somehow, I just knew it.

I tapped my empty plate and said, "Thank you for the toast." To Nigel, I asked, "Where did Bear end up?"

"With a group of children in the common room. They are watching *Scooby Doo*. He's quite popular, it seems."

"Call your boyfriend." Harper raised his voice as I left the kitchen. "I don't want him harassing me when he can't find you." I gave him a thumbs-up on my way out.

I GRABBED the crossbar on the glass door to the restaurant, frozen in place with a bad case of nerves. "I can't do this. I can't face him. I've screwed up so bad. We need to go back." I whirled around, shoulders pressed to the glass. "Take me back to Casa de Xavier."

"What's with the cold feet?" Harper asked. "A man who hires a protection detail for his girlfriend, calls her bodyguard because the girlfriend isn't returning his calls, and schedules a breakfast date on the off-chance she'll say 'yes' deserves an in-person conversation." He leaned close to me. My breath hitched. He opened one of the doors. I stumbled to the side and he caught me by my armpit.

After spinning me around, Harper whispered into my ear, "You are a goddamn Warrior, Sam. You fight demons. I've seen you do some shit that requires a set of balls bigger than what most men lie about having. You can do this."

Harper was in the trenches with me, and that boosted my confidence. Camden's association with me put him in danger, not the other way around. I had to be strong. I blew out a short, hard breath and squared my shoulders. With my chin held high, I scanned the booths and tables for Cam.

A cheery bell jingled. Harper dropped his hold on me, like my skin had burned him, and took one step back. I turned and peered around Harper. Camden had entered. He removed his sunglasses and tucked them into the vee of his white linen button down. His blond curly hair was tousled just so.

My heart fluttered, and I smoothed the front of my silk shirt, taking a calming breath. *Big girl britches, Fife.* When Cam's warm eyes met mine he smiled, and all my reservations melted away. I stepped over to him. He wrapped his arms around my waist, pulled me close, and dropped his face into the crook of my neck. He planted a kiss on the sensitive skin there. I inhaled the fresh linen scent of his shirt mingled with the spicy notes of his cologne. He smelled good.

Camden pried me away and held me at an arm's length. "I was beyond worried when I didn't hear from you." He tucked a strand of hair behind my ear and laid a palm on my cheek. "I'm so sorry you're having to go through this. I swear, I will find who's—"

I put my fingertips to his lips. "I'm the one who needs to apologize. I didn't mean to disappear. And it wasn't fair that you had to check up on me through Harper."

Cam's smile faltered at the mention of my bodyguard. He glanced around. "He's here, correct?"

"Harper is taking his job very seriously." I twisted, looking for him, but the man had become a ghost. I craned my neck around in the opposite direction. My Warrior senses picked up Harper's scent of sandalwood and clove. I spotted him sitting in a dark corner booth. Harper gave me a barely perceptible nod and I turned back around. "He's around here. Doing what he was hired to do."

Camden had entered the restaurant alone. "Where is your security team, Mr. Bennett?" I tapped my fingers on his chest. "I figured your mother would have eight people trailing you at all times."

Camden laughed, then ran a sheepish hand through his messy curls. "I gave Adams the slip. My stalker said I would be last on the list. Besides, my safety is not what kept me up the past two nights. Yours did."

Whoops. "I'm so sorry." I hadn't intended for him to lose sleep over me. I chewed on my lower lip. Also Camden's disregard for his life concerned me. He should be more careful. I couldn't protect him at all times.

He smoothed his thumb over my frown, kissed me quick, and smiled. "I know I look like a frat boy beach bum, but I can take care of myself."

That's right. He had a past. I didn't have all the details. I entertained myself wondering what bad-boy Camden had looked like.

Before my imagination could take off, he interrupted my fantasy. "Shall we sit?"

My snarling stomach could have been my only answer, but I was polite. "Yes. I'm ravenous."

We were given a table in a quiet, sun-lit corner diagonally across the dining room from Harper. It gave him a clear view of us. I looked over the menu. We leaned back as our waitress came with water and coffee.

"What'll you kids be havin' today?" She pulled out a notepad from her apron and clicked her pen into action. We ordered and she left us with the promise of returning soon. The toast Harper had made me was long gone. My phone buzzed in my back pocket. I glanced over at Harper; he didn't have his out. My heart half-hoped it was Leigh texting me. I didn't want to be rude, so I ignored it.

"You're quiet this morning," Cam said after we hadn't spoken for a good five minutes. He picked up my hand.

"There's a lot going on that I haven't told you about." I looked away with a sigh. My phone buzzed again.

"You can trust me, Sam. I'm not going anywhere. I swear. We're in this together."

How did I tell Cam that my 'grandfather' was a three-hundred-year-old Warrior of Light Adviser who could kick ass and kill demons? And that he was a liar and kept secrets. I couldn't tell Cam the extent of my fight with Leigh because half her argument stemmed from the fact we were Warrior partners. He couldn't know the death threat and Javi's murder were supernatural.

My phone buzzed again. *For Pete's sake! Who's texting me?* By an act of God, I resisted pulling out my phone. Camden grinned at me.

"Let's talk about something else. Harper said you weren't staying at the farmhouse. Said it was for your safety, so I didn't question him, but I would like to know where you're staying."

Cam didn't need to know we were living in the middle-of-nowhere Florida, in a castle filled with Warriors, Advisers, and Seers. I returned his smile with my own. "Well, it wouldn't be a safehouse if I told you, would it?"

He chuckled. "Fair enough."

My damn phone buzzed another time. *Sonovabitch!*

"Look," Cam rubbed the back of my hand. "I know what I'm asking of you isn't easy. And you'd have every reason to bail on me. But I swear, Sam, just give me some time and I'll make it right."

"Cam, that's not what's wrong here. You're a *good* guy. I know you're trying to look out for me. I've just been going through some trying shit the last few days. I'm sorry if I made you feel like I was pushing you away, or that I didn't care about you." I squeezed his hand.

"I wish you'd tell me." His smile slipped a little.

"I wish I could." *Where would I even begin?* "How're Renard and Jackie? I know you were worried about them, too."

"They're dealing with it. They understand. And hopefully the restaurant guests don't notice the beefed-up security around Sorcerie. I'll admit having someone follow your every move like a shadow gets old quick."

My damn, freaking phone buzzed yet another time. "Christ Almighty, *what?*" I wrenched my mobile from my back pocket. "What do you want?"

When the screen flared to life, I stopped breathing.

Judy. My heart leapt from my throat. She didn't text. She said it was impersonal and made communicating more difficult. It wasn't that she didn't support technology, she just preferred verbal interaction.

"Everything okay?"

I'M AT MILTON'S, the text read. Milton's was closed on Mondays. My eyes narrowed.

NEED YOU TO MEET ME THERE. Judy left the safe house. *Why?*

ALREADY HERE. *When was the last time she drove?* I couldn't remember. Andrew and Judy ran errands together.

DON'T WAIT. COME NOW. For someone with a flip phone and who despised texting, she had a pretty good grasp on how to use punctuation.

I NEED YOU HERE IN FIFTEEN MINUTES. Nothing about these texts made sense. Something had gone badly wrong. I sprang to my feet. Our beverages sloshed over their rims.

"Sam, what's wrong?" Camden gaped at me, his eyes wild with confusion and hurt.

"I have to go." Adrenaline and Power ripped through me. The tips of my fingers glowed so I closed them into fists. My new weapons warmed my back. Harper appeared at my side.

I looked up at him. "I have to get to Milton's right now."

He nodded. And without further explanation to Camden, I bolted out of the restaurant, Harper on my six.

21

SAM

"The Mage kidnapped Judy," I said as Harper sped to Milton's. "That's the only explanation I can think of." Harper gripped the wheel and drove in grim silence. Dark thunder clouds had rolled in, peppering the windshield with raindrops, threatening to unleash their wrath. Judy had no reason to leave the safety of Xavier's fortress unless something—someone—drew her out.

In the thirteen minutes it took to drive from the café to the feedstore, I called and texted Leigh a billion times. Harper roared into Milton's empty parking lot, gravel flying as he rounded the side of the building. He slid to a diagonal stop, taking up two spaces.

I'd managed to keep my Power in check until now. It burst forth. My clothes turned into a white tunic and pants. I hopped out of the car and leaned in to speak to Harper.

"I don't know what I'm going to find in there. But if it's who or what I think it is, you can't help me." I met his dark eyes. "Keep reaching out to Leigh. Or Jax. Hell, I'd even go for Leilani. I might be too late. I have to go in *now*."

Harper grimaced. "I don't like it."

"Neither do I, but I'm Judy's best chance." While I'd love backup, Judy didn't have that kind of time. Xavier's place was well over an hour away. "I won't wait, Harper."

"Son of a bitch!" He slammed the steering wheel with both hands. "Fuck!" He leaned back against the seat rest, closed his eyes, and then pierced me with a burning blue gaze that shot right through my heart. "Be smart. Mind your back. Don't engage unless you have to. Get her the hell out of there. Don't be a goddamn hero."

His ferocity took my breath away. There was more emotion in his eyes, on his face, than I'd seen since he'd returned. Fear, love, determination, and boldness. Harper *cared* and he did so with an intensity so deep it burned him from the inside out. In that small glimpse, he'd let me in, allowed me to see a part of him that he kept guarded. He didn't want to lose Judy or me. And I didn't want to fail him.

"I'll get in and get out," I promised and withdrew from the car.

I needed Leigh. *How am I going to sneak in, scope out what's happening, and rescue Judy?* Leigh was the planner, the strategist. I didn't know how to do this Leigh's way. I ignored the pang of heartache and focused on my mission: Operation Rescue Judy.

My Warrior's hearing picked up a muffled scream coming from inside. I went to the front door. The lock and handles had been smashed in, and the metal hardware hung from two screws gripping the splintered wood for dear life. Someone had punched their way through. *Holy Heaven.*

With a single finger, I pushed on the door. It swung inward, opening with a long, creepy squeak. I paused, listening. There was no rustling, no beeping of the armed security system. The storm clouds outside hid the sun, so the only reliable light source inside Milton's came from a lone security fluorescent over the sales counter. Darkness cloaked the rear of the store.

"Stick to the shadows," Letty instructed.

I entered with whisper-light steps and sidled up to the alarm keypad. Ice crusted over the display. I glanced up at the security cameras I could see. They too had been iced. I swallowed hard and sent my Warrior senses throughout the store. *What if the Mage is here?* I was screwed. Judy was screwed. However, I didn't find the Mage's signature cold, but I did detect remnants of sulfuric demon heat.

Worry gripped me like a vice. I pushed my Warrior search deeper into the store. Then I heard it. My breath hitched. A good ol' fashion human heartbeat jerked me upright. *Please let that be Judy and not the Mage.*

Patience was not my virtue. It would have been a lot easier for me to come banging in, swoop up Judy wherever she'd been stashed, and get the hell out in a blaze of glory. But I'd promised Harper I'd be careful. Because I had no backup.

Sticking close to the long wall of the store, I ventured farther inside, peeking around shelves, saddle racks, and other store displays. A thin veil of demonic heat lingered like a cloud over the whole place. What did the demons do in here? Have a rave? This was *my* store. *Damn them.*

I found Judy in the dimmest corner of the shop. As silently as I could, I released a pent-up breath. She was strapped to the office chair with rope. Duct tape covered her mouth and a cut on her left temple bled freely. My spirits lifted when I caught the murderous glint of defiance in her brown eyes. Three centuries of being married to Andrew, healing Warriors in times of war, and living through some tough shit had molded Judy into a survivor. Judy was a Warrior in her own right.

I slipped through the darkness and crouched beside her. She flinched when I touched her arm. A frantic look flitted across her face, and she shook her head, eyes wide and nostrils flared. The wheels of her chair scooted and scratched on the tile. I turned the chair and forced Judy to look at me.

Her chest heaved when comprehension dawned in her eyes. *Sorry,* I mouthed and pressed a finger to my lips. She nodded. I motioned that I was going to remove her gag. Judy remained still as I peeled off the tape. She said nothing as I got to work loosening her tight bonds. I didn't have time or patience to pick them with my fingers.

"Hold still," I whispered into Judy's ear. I loosed Helios from his sheath; he hummed with energy. Power warmed my blade so it slid through Judy's ropes like butter. I helped her to her feet, feeling her tremble. "I know you wouldn't leave the sacred ground without a damn good reason. What leverage did they have over you?"

She gave me a stubborn look. "I'll tell you later. We must move." Judy was right, of course. She always was. I headed for the rear door with Judy in tow.

The unmistakable burn of a demonic presence flared to life behind us. The scent of sulfur filled my nostrils. I wheeled around, shoving Judy behind my back. In the light over the sales counter stood a dark blue demon with glittering black eyes. She wore a gleaming black breastplate and vambraces on her forearms.

"You came," she crooned, sashaying her way over, hand on her hip. The demon walked with sensual confidence. She drew a lethal-looking black scimitar, its curved blade begging to kill a Warrior. In the dim light, I saw an oily sheen on the blade's edge. My eyes widened.

Unlike Dominic, this demon didn't seem like a talker. I secretly wished he had come instead of this one. It was a

Real Bad Day when I preferred one demon over another. Judy gasped, spurring me back into action. I had to get her out of here. I extended my Warrior senses behind me.

The female demon smiled, her teeth perfect and straight. "Luring you here was so easy. Our master knew you wouldn't let your Healer come to harm. Our master also knew what to say to coax her out of her hiding place. Threatening a hospital full of your sick and dying young did the trick. All I had to do was get her across the boundary line."

I took a single step in her direction, anger burning in my gut. "What did you do?"

"Nothing." She shrugged with a Chesire cat grin. "The threat accomplished what I wanted, after all."

"Don't let her bait you," Letty said. *"Focus."*

"She threatened a children's *hospital, Letty!"* Of all the despicable, vile things to do. Of *course,* Judy wouldn't risk demons hurting the children.

"I'm sorry, Sammy," Judy muttered.

"I get it," I whispered. We needed to get out. I stepped back until I bumped into Judy. I herded her toward the rear exit. Judy turned so her spine pressed against mine. We moved in unison until the sound of squeaking hinges brought me up short. Demonic heat pressed in on me from the rear door. *We're trapped.*

Judy yelped and the contact of her body against mine disappeared. I bounded sideways so I could keep the blue bitch and whatever was happening at the back door in my field of vision.

"Shit," I breathed, my heart galloping. It was the black demon that had nearly killed me last Wednesday. He hadn't died when Leigh threw Fury into his chest, after all. He'd whooped my ass and this time Leigh wasn't here to rescue me. Today, it was one Warrior of Light, one Judy, and two Greater Demons. That was not good math.

The black behemoth held Judy pinned against his massive chest. She cried in pain as he wrenched her arm further up her back. She looked small and fragile in his arms.

Harper had told me not to engage unless I had to. *Sorry Harper. Engagement is happening.* I whipped Helios and Sol from their sheaths between my shoulders. The blades burned bright white. Holy Heat and Power flooded me.

In a loud voice, with more confidence than I felt, I said, "Alright. We can play." I pointed Sol at the black demon. "But first, you let her go."

He laughed, a menacing sound that sent goosebumps rippling over my skin. Fear clunked like ice into my stomach. On my right, the female shifted her weight. Helios flicked up, his light glittering over her armor.

"Not another step," I snapped.

She hissed and stopped. Malevolence rippled over her like a dark aura. She waved a casual hand at her partner. "Don't play with your food, Ambrose. You know our objective. We have a Warrior to collect."

"Can I get us both out alive?" I asked Letty.

"They're too fast." After a second, she added, *"The female is familiar to me, but I can't recall how. I also think her blade is tainted. Be extremely wary of her."*

Letty had never warned me about a specific demon before. The blue one was a dangerous unknown, and I already knew the kind of damage the black one could inflict. Fear kicked into a higher gear and dread sank deep into my bones.

They didn't care about Judy. She was just bait. They'd set this trap *specifically* for me. Had Dominic been watching me? Did they wait until I was out without my Warrior partner and then strike? Harper wasn't a threat to them and might even make additional bait. They'd played me perfectly.

Letty was good at her job, but Light Warriors fought in pairs for a reason. I had to claw my way out of this, but I couldn't take on two Greater Demons while also trying to protect Judy. I could throw a dagger at Ambrose's eye, praying he didn't move. Praying I didn't hit Judy. Praying he didn't yank her into my dagger's path.

I met Judy's bold brown eyes, expecting a measure of terror or alarm there. But no, not from Judy. I saw bravery, pride, and love shining from their depths. She nodded to tell me she knew what I knew. With a lionhearted smile, she notched up her chin. Kimberly Judith Shaw, Healer of Warriors, Survivor of Wars, Mender of Hearts. My arms shook but I held my daggers firm. Tears spilled down my cheeks, but Judy didn't cry. She was fierce.

"This is so touching," the blue demon cooed. "But, alas, we're on a schedule. Ambrose, get on with it."

"Give 'em hell, Sammy," Judy shouted.

Ambrose wrenched Judy's head to the side and ripped into her throat with his teeth, savaging her neck. Her blood sprayed all over him as he tore her apart. I couldn't look away, couldn't believe what I'd just witnessed. Judy went limp and Ambrose dropped her body to the floor. Looking up, he grinned at me, his teeth and chest coated in red.

"NOOO!" I screamed.

"Move!" Letty commanded, but I stood transfixed. *"Brave One, I said, MOVE!"*

Power roared through me so hard, my body pulsed with light, kickstarting me. I whipped my right arm across my body and flung Helios into Ambrose's chest. My blade hit its mark with a wet *thunk*.

The blue female charged. I whipped Sol up as her

scimitar came down, blocking her blade. She spun, leading with her sword. I tried to leap out of the way but was a fraction too slow. Pain lanced through my hip where she sliced through my Warrior tunic. *"It should have blocked that blow. Why didn't it?"*

"It's her blade. Whatever substance it's coated in is getting past your armor," Letty said.

Harper told me not to be a hero. I didn't need to fight this blue bitch, I needed to get the hell outta here. Ducking low, I swiped my dagger across her shins. She hissed and jumped back, black blood oozing down her legs.

Ambrose's body vanished just as it had when Fury struck him. He wasn't dead. He would return and hunt me again. I bounded over to snatch up Helios. I made the mistake of looking down. My dagger lay in a pool of Judy's blood.

I sucked in a breath, looking into Judy's glazed eyes. Grief clenched my ribs. I checked her pulse. Though she was still warm to the touch, there was no thump of a heartbeat against my fingers.

"Behind you!" Letty said.

I wheeled around from my crouched position and brought up Helios and Sol, making an X and blocking the blue demon's blow. She wrenched her sword back, steel screeching on steel. I rolled away, but not fast enough. She sliced my shoulder. I sprang up but the entire store tilted. I swayed in place.

"She's coming back," Letty warned. *"Move!"*

Pain from my hip and my shoulder throbbed, but I spun just in time, knocking her sword off course. The force sent her careening into the store's sales counter. I growled and took a fighter's stance, Helios and Sol at the ready, my Warrior energy in sync with my weapons, feeding energy back and forth.

The store tilted again and I staggered sideways. I shook my head, trying to clear my brain fog. My wounds throbbed and my tunic was sticky wet against my skin.

"Shit," I muttered. "Get out, Sam." I backed away from the demon.

"What's wrong little Warrior?" The blue demon cackled, righting herself. She cracked her neck and whipped her lethal black blade in an arc. "Not feeling so well?"

"Screw you."

"You *will* be coming with me. I thought you'd put up a better fight, but it seems you're quite susceptible to my poison." She sauntered forward.

"Her left hand!" Letty shouted.

I blocked two small objects the bitch flung at me, but a third grazed my neck. A burning sensation exploded where I'd been hit. I resisted the instinct to cover where the pain bloomed. I glanced down to see what she'd thrown. Shuriken. She had freakin' ninja stars.

I sprinted for the front door, shuriken flying around me —a couple made glancing cuts on my side and bicep. She wasn't trying to maim me, she was giving her poison time to work. I stumbled, my back slamming into a five-tier saddle rack. Leaning against it to steady myself, I glared at my attacker. She approached, her gait unhurried. The poison had me seeing several of her. My stomach lurched. My guts bubbled.

"Little Warrior. Let me introduce myself. I'm Enyo, Queen of War, and you *will* be coming with me."

Queen of War? I thought.

"Get. Out. Now!" Letty yelled. *"She is one of the most dangerous demons in Hell. SAMANTHA! MOVE!"* Letty's panic reverberated in my skull.

My heart slammed against my breastbone. The poison made my arms heavy, my legs sluggish. I blinked, unable to clear my vision, and looked up at the full saddle rack. It was loaded with roping saddles. Those suckers weighed at least forty-five pounds each, and with the heavy wooden rack, there was enough weight to slow Enyo.

Just survive, I thought.

I groaned, lifting my left arm over my head to slip Sol home. When Enyo was close enough, I heaved the entire saddle rack down onto her. It landed hard, squashing her. She screamed, flailing her arms and legs as leather, wood, and metal tangled her limbs. I hacked at any blue skin I could see, Helios flashing. The wounds he made smoked and stank. Enyo shrieked, raising the hairs on my neck.

Survive.

I stood. The room spun. I wavered. Vomit climbed my esophagus. The front door was too far away. I hit my knees.

Survive.

Crawling towards the sales counter, I clawed myself upright, and fumbled for the telephone. I managed to get the receiver off the hook and to my ear. The keypad numbers blurred. I strained to remember Harper's cell number. Every button I pushed took a herculean effort.

Survive.

"Harper," I whispered when the line picked up. "Help."

And then my world went black and I collapsed.

22

HARPER

Those two simple words from Sam robbed me of logical thought, and I headed into Milton's armed with only my Glock. I'd called in reinforcements, but just as Sam couldn't wait to go in after Ma, I wouldn't wait to go in after Sam. I had no idea if Ma was even inside. Warrior or not, I had to get in there.

When I stepped into the store, I saw a blue demon standing over Sam's limp body. She held Sam up by the hair on the back of her head. In her other hand was a knife, buried to its hilt in Sam's lower ribcage. The golden glow of Sam's Warrior aura flickered while the demon's pulsed a vivid black.

I fired. The bullet slammed into the demon's exposed side. She dropped Sam, screeching, her arms windmilling. Regular bullets wouldn't kill demons, but could wound them enough that they had to go back to Hell to heal—a survival skill Pops had taught me. I'd never needed to use that tactic until today.

The blue demon screeched, "I am Enyo, Queen of War. Who—"

I shot her a second time, hitting her in her shoulder. Oily blood flowed down her arm. She roared at me, then charged, swinging a black-metal sword. I squeezed the trigger a third time—a head shot. Enyo fell into a crumpled heap midstride. Her form flickered in and out and then she solidified. She got to her feet with jerky movements, her aura blinking like static.

"You inferior worm," she seethed. "We're not done. I'll come for you." With that, she disappeared, taking her sword and knife with her.

Not knowing how long she'd be gone, I sprinted over to Sam and dropped to my knees. Her blood pooled on the tile. I tucked the Glock into the waistband of my jeans and wrenched off my overshirt. Balling it up, I pressed it to her side.

"Fucking, fuck!" There was nothing in my vicinity that would help her. I closed my eyes and whispered a simple prayer. "Please help."

"Oh, my God!"

Fucking Camden Bennett. My eyes snapped open as he ran toward me. *Why are you here? How much did you see?* As far as I knew, Bennett wasn't a Seer. He skidded to a stop where I knelt over Sam's unconscious body.

"What was that *thing*? Why was it trying to kill Sam? She was—was she blue? And that smell. Is that sulfur?"

I growled. This was *not* who I wanted when I'd prayed for help, but Sam was dying. I looked up at Bennett. "Make yourself useful. Hold this shirt tight to her side, both hands. Apply pressure until I get back."

"We need to call 911." Bennett knelt next to me, phone in hand.

That would be a cluster fuck. "No," I hissed.

"She needs an ambulance, man!" Bennett started dialing.

With one hand pressed hard on Sam's side, I grabbed his cell and slid it hard across the tile towards the door. It slid over the floor, bumped over the front door stop, and thumped on the wooden deck outside.

"Just do what I fucking tell you," I snapped and pointed at Sam's hemorrhaging wound. Her blood had already soaked the fabric of my shirt. "Keep firm pressure."

"What the hell?" Bennett reared back.

"Worry about your goddamn phone later." I took a deep breath. *Keep your shit together, Tate.* I snapped my fingers in his face. "Look, Sam needs you. I know you're not used to taking orders, but don't second guess me. I know what the fuck I'm doing."

Bennett met my eyes then nodded. He scooted in and replaced my hands with his on Sam's side. I sprinted to the car, retrieved my med kit, and rushed back. Kneeling next to Sam once more, I wrenched open my backpack and rifled through the contents.

"She's bleeding through this," Bennett said.

"Then use your shirt. Add it over top."

We maneuvered so that I now held the pressure against Sam. Bennett took off his overpriced button down, leaving behind a white cotton tee, then moved me out of the way. I tugged my med kit to me and pulled out a roll of duct tape. I ripped off long strips and secured the bloody shirts to Sam's side.

"Continue with the pressure," I told Bennett.

I hissed through clenched teeth while assessing the rest of Sam's wounds. She had gashes on her hip, shoulder, neck, arms, and sides. Her pulse was too weak, respiration too shallow. I could fix her superficial wounds, but the stab wound concerned the hell out of me. *Had the knife nicked something vital?* She was losing too much blood.

Reminders of another blonde, from a different lifetime, surfaced. *Molly.* She'd been broken and bleeding before me just like Sam was now. I looked at my blood-coated hands. I couldn't save Molly. She'd been too human, too fragile.

"Harper," Bennett said, bringing me out of my flashback.

I can save Sam. I rummaged in my pack for a gallon-size storage bag and pulled it open, sifting the contents. Morphine. Lidocaine. Fentanyl. *There.* Three vials of amber liquid. Life Elixir. I glanced at Sam, grabbed all of them, and also took out a bottle of rubbing alcohol, three ten cc syringes, and three needles.

"What are you giving to her?" Bennett asked. "Are you sure we shouldn't go to the hospital? This looks way bad, man. I'm not disrespecting your abilities, but this is too much." Bennett's cheeks had a greenish tint to them and he wiped one bloody hand down his undershirt.

"Pressure. On the wound." I glared at Bennett. "How'd you get here?" I asked as I prepped and filled the syringes with Life Elixir.

"With a car?"

"No shit, Sherlock. What kind of vehicle?" I growled. The second syringe was locked and loaded.

"My Range Rover. Why does this matter?"

"The coupe we drove here is useless. Too small." I finished drawing up the final shot. "Go bring your SUV right out front. Keep it running and ready. Honk when you're there. And do it quickly."

"What the hell was that thing that stabbed her?"

We're back to this?

Bennett's eyes had lost some of their wild fear. "That thing wasn't human. What was it? I know you know."

"I'll explain later, just do what I fucking tell you."

"But—"

"Bennett," I cut him off and looked the guy square in the face. If this was his first demon encounter, what he'd witnessed would send any normal human into a mental spiral, but I needed his complete and total focus. "Sam is going to bleed the fuck out. She *will* die if you don't trust me. I know what I'm doing. Now pull your shit together and go get your goddamn car."

He drew in a deep breath. "This makes no sense, but sure, whatever you need me to do."

"Go now." I edged him out of the way and started rinsing off my hands with alcohol, then the creases of Sam's elbows, and the side of her neck. With gauze, I made quick work of cleaning up the blood.

I injected the Life Elixir into one arm, then repeated the process on her other arm. And only because Sam was a Warrior of Light, I injected the last syringe of Life Elixir into her jugular. I needed a shit-ton more Elixir and the only place close enough was the farmhouse. *Compromised borders be damned.*

Making sure Sam's dressing was tight, I stood and quick-called Xavier from my cell. The Adviser picked up on the first ring.

"We have a problem," I said before the Spaniard could speak.

When I finished relaying the situation, Xavier said, "I'll contact Andrew, he needs to know. We'll reroute to the Shaw's property. Have you located Judy?"

"No. I—" I turned toward the back of the store. "I haven't checked yet."

"Understood," Xavier murmured. "Try to find her, if she's even there. I'll send Nigel and Mr. Bozeman to handle the cleanup at the store. You focus your energy on Miss Fife. Is she stable enough for transport?"

I almost missed Xavier's question over the roar of

blood rushing in my ears. "Probably not, but we can't stay here. I drove off the demon that stabbed Sam, but she promised retribution. If I can make it to the farmhouse, I can give Sam a fighting shot."

"Tell me what you require, Mr. Tate, and I'll make sure you have it."

"Life Elixir, as much as you can spare. Ma has a supply closet but I don't know how much stock is in there. She'll have all the other supplies."

"Consider it done," Xavier assured me.

The blare of a car horn out front signaled Bennett was waiting. *Fuck. He's the other complication.* I let out a long sigh. "Sam's boyfriend showed up. He's not gonna let her out of his sight. He's got questions. Wanted to take her to a hospital. He can fucking see demons. Divine Intervention didn't stop him."

"*¡Mierda!*" Xavier swore. "You'll have to bring him. Tell him nothing."

No worry there. I thought, running a hand over my jaw.

"I'll speak with him," Xavier continued. "Godspeed, son."

I hung up and went looking for Ma. Bennett honked again. I hurried along until I saw a form lying on the ground. *Ma.* I took in her ravaged neck and massive dark pool of blood. My stomach lurched and my hands trembled. The jagged edges of her wound told me her death had been brutal. *Had she been bitten?* I shuddered. *What kind of demon does this?* I knelt next to Ma, checking for the pulse I knew wasn't there, then closed her eyes with a soft swipe of my fingers. I cleared my throat and swiped under my nose.

There was nothing I could do for her now, and Nigel would be there soon to tend to her as she should be seen to. Sam required all my focus. With a hardened resolve, I rose. Clenching my jaw, I sealed myself from feeling, but every step I took away from Ma was torture. By the time I reached Sam, I'd rebuilt my mental blocks.

I collected Sam's dagger and stowed it in my backpack. The hilt stuck out the top, but it wouldn't go anywhere. Sam's nicks and cuts had already started to mend, and the wound in her side hadn't soaked through the second layer of shirts.

Yet.

I checked her vitals. Her skin still had a grey pallor and her lips were ashen. But her heart beat a little stronger, and her breaths were less shallow. I slid one arm under her knees, the other under her shoulders, and scooped her up as if she were a feather, not the dead weight of an unconscious person. I cradled her against my body.

Bennett had laid down the seats in his Rover so I was able to slide Sam into the back. I hopped in and pulled off my pack. With one last look at the store, guilt over leaving Ma behind pierced my heart. *Nigel will take care of her.* I closed the hatch.

"Take us to the Shaw's farmhouse."

"She needs to go to the hospital." His reply was terse.

This again? Jesus. "Bennett, if you don't do what I say, you'll be eating through a straw and pissing into a bag when I'm done with you. Just drive."

Not bothering to see if he obeyed, I settled in a cross-legged position next to Sam. I checked her pulse. Her skin was hotter than it had been when I'd loaded her. I felt her forehead with the back of my hand. She was on fire. I flung my arm up, bracing myself as Bennett tore out of the parking lot. *She shouldn't be running a fever.* I checked her superficial cuts. Her skin was knitting itself back together. "What the fuck?"

"How's she doing?" Bennett asked as the Rover picked up speed. Trees and greenery whizzed by.

"Not good." I'd given her all the Elixir I had on hand. Her wounds were healing. This complication made no sense.

"Has she soaked through the second shirt?" Bennett glanced in the rearview.

"She's got a fever," I answered with a measure of disbelief. "Drive faster."

The sound of the Rover's engine purred louder and the vehicle sped up. After a brief pause, Bennett asked, "Why the hell is she running a temperature?"

"Worry about getting us to the farmhouse."

The man behind the wheel drove like a skilled maniac. He sped through lights, cut corners, wove through traffic, all while jostling as little as possible. I glanced up to make sure we were headed to the farmhouse and not the hospital. When Bennett took the exit off I-75 leading home, I leaned back against the side of the Rover, letting my head rest against the glass.

My phone rang and I glanced at the caller ID. "Sir."

"We're at Andrew's property. Nigel and Mr. Bozeman are on the way to Milton's now. They should know what they're walking into. Did you find Judy?"

"Yeah." I bowed my head and pinched the bridge of my nose. My voice cracked; I cleared my throat, then relayed how and where I'd found Ma's body. "The whole place is a bloody mess."

Xavier sighed. "I'm sorry, son."

I said nothing and blinked several times. My grief needed to wait.

"How's our Warrior faring?"

In the lowest whisper I could manage, knowing Xavier would be able to hear and Bennett couldn't, I muttered,

"Sam has a high-grade fever, and I don't know why. Any theories?"

There was a long pause. "Without running tests, I know of one demon who poisons all her weapons. It's her own concoction. Not only does it make any injury she inflicts fester, it attacks and compromises the Warrior's healing ability. Fever is a symptom, as are coma and hallucinations. But this demon hasn't surfaced in at least ninety-five years. Her name is—"

"Enyo," I said. "I shot her."

Xavier *tsked.* "She'll be in a towering temper, then. I'll warn Nigel, but you must get yourself and Miss Fife onto sacred ground before she returns. If the Mage has called Enyo up from Hell, it's personal."

Wonderful. "Do you have an antidote to Enyo's poison?"

"A steady stream of Life Elixir, prayer, and time," Xavier said. "Mr. Tate, I have several calls to make with this news."

"We'll be at the farmhouse soon." My eyes flicked to the bandage over Sam's ribcage, and I watched the slow spread of blood creep through the white fabric. *Dammit.* I leaned against Sam's wound, applying as much pressure as I could. Kalakaua and DH stood in the driveway when we arrived. When we stopped, the rear hatch popped open and I crawled out. I grabbed my pack loaded with Sam's weapon.

"DH," I motioned for her and held out my med kit. "Is Leigh here?"

"Yeah." Her eyes locked on the dagger sticking out of the top of my bag.

"Good, take these to her." I handed off the backpack and my Glock, making sure the safety was secure. "She'll know what to do with them." I had started getting Sam out of the vehicle when Bennett rounded the SUV to meet me.

He grabbed a fist full of my shirt. "If I didn't take Sam to hospital, there better be a fucking operating room in that house and one of these people better be a damn doctor."

Rage boiled my blood. Every moment this jackass wasted on doubting me was seconds off Sam's life. I snarled and plowed into Bennett's personal space, bumping his chest, standing nose-to-nose. "Back the fuck off, right now. I need to take care of Sam."

"Mr. Bennett." Xavier's commanding tone cut through the tension. He stood on the porch, hands clasped in front of him. "My name is Xavier Gerena. I will answer whatever questions you may have, so come with me. Allow Mr. Tate to attend Miss Fife."

Bennett took a reluctant step back. He pointed at Sam. "If she dies because you refused to take her to a hospital, I'll kill you myself.

I'd already turned back to Sam before he walked away. "I'd like to see you try."

"Where to?" Kalakaua asked.

"Dining room."

The Hawaiian Warrior jogged ahead and cleared chairs from around the heavy wooden table. So many Warriors had been mended on this table over hundreds of years. Pops made it for Ma, and it was built to last. I laid Sam down as gently as possible.

"Where does Healer Shaw keep her supplies?" Kalakaua asked.

"Tell us how we can help." DH appeared on my right, sans weapons. She'd put on an apron and a brave face.

"DH, stay with her." I hurried over to the swing door leading to the kitchen. "Kalakaua, with me."

I typed the code into the keypad leading to Ma's medical closet and opened the door. "You'll find everything you need. The fridge is stocked with undiluted Life Elixir. Bring it. All of it. And several IV bags of saline solution. Ma keeps bags of blood with Sam's name on them in the fridge. Start warming two in a water bath now."

"Got it." Kalakaua brushed past me and started loading up the metal equipment cart in the middle of the room.

I rushed into the kitchen, snatched a pair of scissors from a cup next to the phone, and hurried back into the dining room. DH had finished what Kalakaua started and lined the chairs along the far wall, out of the way. I checked Sam's minor injuries. They were already healed over.

"I'll be right back," DH said. "I'm gonna get warm water and washcloths." She backed herself through the open threshold from the dining room into Ma's formal room. "And get a sheet to cover this opening."

I nodded but my eyes stayed on Sam. I cut up the centerline of her destroyed shirt, set the scissors aside, and peeled the blood-soaked T-shirts from her skin, revealing streaks of black veins spidering out from her stab wound. I balked.

What is this fucking poison? Fear surged up my throat and anxiety bubbled in my gut. I stretched my trembling hands out in front of me. I'd stitched up many wounds before. I'd stabilized numerous poisoning victims. But this demonic toxin was unknown. *What's it doing to her?* At the sound of the kitchen door creaking, I dropped my palms to the table.

Kalakaua steered the cart loaded with supplies into the dining room. She got to work prepping what I needed and stayed out of my way. I snapped on the pair of gloves she laid out for me and got to work. She set up an IV stand, opened sterile tubing, and supplied me with whatever I needed. *What if I lose Sam, too? Ma and Sam in one day.*

DH reappeared and set down a bowl of water with several cloths on the opposite side of where I worked. She placed a blanket at Sam's feet then tacked up a sheet in the walkway from dining room to living room.

I suspected Enyo had hit Sam's spleen given the amount of blood loss. The Mage would be furious if the demon killed her outright. Kalakaua hung bags of fluids with Life Elixir and bagged blood on a pole while I put in Sam's IV. I turned my attention to her wound and focused on stitching it closed. Confident Sam was as stable as I could make her, I pulled off my soiled gloves and threw them on the ground. The dining room was littered with trash, discarded supplies, and bloodied clothes. Kalakaua retrieved the blanket at Sam's feet, and I grabbed it before she could flap it open.

"I got it." I took the cover out of her hands. "You can go. Thank you for your help."

She nodded, laid a palm on my arm, and said, "We're in the other room if you need us."

DH came through the swing door, trash can in hand. She started picking up the debris and tossing it into the bin. Kalakaua took her by the elbow. She glanced in my direction and said, "This can wait."

DH gasped. "Sorry, I didn't——"

"It's okay," I said. "You did good kiddo."

Kalakaua took the can from DH, set it down, and steered her out.

I covered Sam with the blanket, smoothing the fabric over her. DH had washed away the blood in Sam's blonde hair. Her vitals beeped on the monitor Kalakaua set up. I stroked Sam's head with my fingertips, feeling her raging fever.

"I'm sorry, Sammy. I fucked up." I grabbed a chair and sank into it. "I shouldn't have let you go in without backup. I'm the dumbass who let you go in alone. I wish you could tell me what happened. Hell, I wish I could have been able to fight *with* you."

A hole of despair yawned inside me. I took Sam's hand and brought it to my lips. "Ma's gone. She's dead."

I lowered Sam's hand to the table and leaned forward, pressing my forehead against our entwined fingers. Hot tears slipped out. The steel box that I kept my emotions locked in burst open. All my guilt twisted up with my grief. I was always a little too late to save the people I loved.

What will happen to Pops? They'd been married for centuries. Would the rest of the Warrior network look at me like I was a useless sack of shit? I was the son of Pops's alpha Warrior team, with no hint of being able to live up to their legacy. I didn't feel human, but I wasn't a Warrior. And I'd failed my parents' legacy.

I couldn't be still. I sprang to my feet, letting go of Sam's hand, and threw my chair aside. Seething, I slammed my fist into the wall, cracking the plasterboard. I prowled over to the trash can and threw it at the kitchen. The door swung back and forth a few inches, creaking as it did. I scooped up an empty Elixir vial and hurled it at the grandfather clock, shattering its glass face.

"Why?" I roared at Heaven. "You son of a bitch, you take everything!"

I punched the same spot in the wall again, and the weakened area gave way under my blow. I hit the wall over and over, in different spots, perforating it like swiss cheese. I continued until my knuckles throbbed and the skin split.

The makeshift curtain moved aside, and Kalakaua peered in. "Everything okay?"

"Leave me the fuck alone." *She doesn't deserve to be treated like this.* When she didn't move, I hurled an empty box of gauze rolls at the wall next to the Hawaiian's face. "Get out!"

The Warrior flinched, but didn't move. She started to say, "Sorry, we just heard—"

"Go. Away." I forced as much calm as I could into those words and leaned forward, bracing my palms on the edge of the table—my knuckles were bleeding. I met Kalakaua's brown eyes and glared until she flinched again.

"We're here if you need anything," she said and disappeared.

I sighed and looked down at Sam. There was no snark, no sass, no quick wit coming from her mouth. She didn't argue or question my authority. She would have dressed me down for destroying Ma's dining room. Or said something so ridiculous I'd roll my eyes. She knew how to disarm me and redirect my anger. It was irritating as hell.

A hollow ache replaced the emotional beast ravaging my insides. The soft beep of Sam's pulse oximeter combined with steady EKG/ECG readings spiking across the monitor offered me small solace. Sam was alive. For now. I'd saved her. I went to her side, righted my chair, and took her fevered fingers into my bruised hand. My tears came softer this time.

"Come back to me, Sammy. I can't lose you, too."

23

CAMDEN

Camden chewed the fingernails on his right hand to their quicks and winced when he drew blood. Shaking his hand, he paced the tile of the farmhouse's sunroom where he'd been told to wait. He stopped next to a floor-to-ceiling window. The rain clouds had blown through, and sunlight cast long shadows from the brown wicker furniture onto walls and floor. His stomach ached with fear, fatigue, and dread. The muscles in his lean limbs trembled from fading adrenaline.

Where is Sam? Is she dead? What is going on? What was that thing that attacked her? Camden smacked the glass pane with a palm, and left it there, bracing himself. *I should've driven straight to an emergency room. I should've listened to my gut.*

Sam needed a doctor. Instead she was being patched together by some rag-tag team of amateurs. Harper Tate had been so convincing, barking orders and commanding everyone around. Cam snarled and marched back to the other end of the room.

The door opened. He stopped mid-stride, spun toward the sound, and his heart climbed into his throat. The man that had introduced himself as Xavier entered. He had a raven perched on his shoulder. Leigh filed in behind him. She looked terrible, with hunched shoulders, blotchy cheeks, and haunted hazel eyes.

"How's Sam?" Camden asked, looking from Xavier to Leigh.

"Mr. Tate is tending to her as we speak. She appears to be stabilized for the time being." Xavier crossed the sunroom and sat in a wicker chair. Leigh gave Cam a small smile and nodded her encouragement. She settled on a loveseat, pulled her long legs up, and huddled into the cushions as if they would hold her together. She pulled her navy cardigan around her body.

Camden rubbed his burning eyes then crossed his arms. "What the hell is going on?"

"Mr. Bennett, please sit," Xavier said.

Camden's sanity clung by threads, but he did as the man said and sat opposite Leigh on the settee. He scooted to the edge of his seat. "Why are we here and not at a hospital?"

"Miss Fife can't be helped by human medicine," Xavier said. "This is the best place for her."

"Human medicine?" Camden ran a hand through his hair. "What're you saying? She's some sort of alien?"

"I assure you she's not from outer space. She's a Warrior of Light and quite human," Xavier said. The raven hopped into his lap, and he stroked her head.

"None of this is making any sense," Camden snapped, his patience wearing thin.

"Miss Fife heals at an accelerated rate, she can't be killed by human means, and Harper knows we cannot allow anyone to obtain a blood sample. Her DNA has two additional bases. Her blood cells have a protective protein that essentially acts as chainmail. You can imagine the hysteria that would cause."

"Two additional bases," Camden parroted, forgetting whatever he'd been about to say. He rubbed his face. "Are you implying she's superhuman?" He laughed at the absurdity.

"That's exactly what I'm saying," Xavier said without humor.

Camden swallowed, the muscles in his throat tight. "I don't understand. How is that possible? Is she the only one?"

"No, there are more of us," Leigh said. "Our gift comes from Heaven to fight Hell on earth. We have amplified strength and heightened senses, speed, and agility. We're physically flawless. And to the best of my knowledge, there are only four active Warriors, including myself. Advisers Shaw and Gerena are retired, but they used to be Light Warriors."

Cam's mouth gaped open and he shook his head. "This is ludicrous. Absurd. An insult to my intelligence." He leapt to his feet and glared down at Leigh. "I can't believe you, of all people, Leigh, are buying into this bat-shit crazy story. I should call the police and let the law sort you people out." *But what if it's true?* Camden clenched his teeth.

"Boy." Xavier stood to his full height, sending the raven flying. She screeched and Xavier's anger buzzed, his irises glinting red at the edges. "Do not think you can come into this home and make such egregious allegations. I'm a patient man, but I will not have you threaten those in my care. You will not speak to Miss Kestler so rudely and you will not question my judgment in how Miss Fife is treated. You will regain emotional control. Now, sit your *culo* down." The Spaniard reclaimed his seat.

Not used to being spoken to in such a manner, Camden obeyed. "This can't be real."

"When you arrived at the feed store today, did you see anything different about Sam?" Leigh asked. "What was she doing? Was she wearing white? Did she glow? Were there weapons in her hands?"

Everything had happened so quickly at Milton's, but one memory stood out to Camden. "Sam was stabbed by this *thing* that looked human. Only she was blue-skinned with completely black eyes. She hardly flinched when Harper shot her. In fact, she *stood up* after taking a head-shot. What was she?"

"That, Mr. Bennett, was a Greater Demon," Xavier said.

Camden blinked several times. "I must have heard you wrong. Did you say *demon*?"

"I did," Xavier said, crossing his legs. "As Miss Fife is a Warrior of Light, her duty in life is to defend humanity against Hell. If she had her weapons drawn when you saw her, and evidence suggests as much, she was battling the demon you saw."

Camden looked from Xavier to Leigh. *They've got to be lying.* "Sam knows how to fight?"

"We both do, Cam," Leigh said. "She's quite good."

"This is a lot to take in." Camden pressed the heel of his palms to his forehead.

"Miss Kestler, please show Mr. Bennett some proof. I think that would save us quite a bit of time and breath."

"Of course, Adviser Gerena." Leigh shrugged out of her cardigan and stood. "Cam, remember I'm just me. You're not in danger. "

"Show me *what*?"

"Just watch, Mr. Bennett."

Leigh's eyes fluttered closed. After a moment, an aura

of soft golden light flickered around her entire body, glowing around her. The illumination pulsed brighter, and her jeans and simple cotton tee transformed into a white tunic, pants, and boots.

"Holy shit!" Cam swore and bolted to his feet. Leigh reached behind her head with her right hand, grasping for something that wasn't there. *Sweet Jesus. She's not done.*

Leigh opened her eyes. "Don't be scared. I'm not going to hurt you."

"The hell are you talking—" Then he saw it, the hilt of a sword. "Holy shit," he swore again.

Leigh pulled a massive blade from some invisible place on her back. The raven screamed, took flight, and swooped around the sunroom. She landed on Xavier's leg. Camden stumbled away, putting distance between himself and the craziness before him. He pressed himself against the back wall by the kitchen door, too terrified to move.

Leigh brought the great sword over her head and held it out before her, its sharp tip pointed to the ceiling. She gripped the leather-wrapped hilt with both hands. Her aura grew brighter and the blade glowed bright white. A cross etched on the blade just below the guard flared red.

"One of the side effects from fully tapping into our Power is the refraction of Heavenly glory. It intimidates humans and demons." She shifted the weapon to her right hand and with her left she tapped the base of her throat and a silver skeleton key appeared in her hand. "Every Warrior receives a key. It unlocks the veil between what's visible and invisible. It locks us into service to Heaven." Leigh let go of the key and it disappeared. She took a one-armed practice swing with her sword then resheathed her weapon. It blinked out of sight along with her Warrior garb.

"Miss Kestler, that's enough," Xavier said, his tone

kind. "I know calling on your Power, only to absorb all of that energy, takes a toll on your body. And given your state of grief, you might need to go for a run and burn it off. I was hesitant to ask this of you, and I would have done it, but it's been at least seventy-five years since I went 'full Warrior.'" Xavier smiled at Leigh. "Go check on Sam. Nigel should be arriving soon."

"Thank you, sir." Leigh nodded, her eyes brimming with unshed tears. She grabbed her cardigan and headed out. Before leaving, she touched Camden's shoulder. "It's a lot to process. Imagine what it was like for Sam when she became a Warrior. Please don't hold anything you learn here against her."

Before he could answer Leigh, she was through the door and he was alone with the intimidating Xavier Gerena and his raven. Cam thought about trying for the doorknob, half expecting it to be locked, when Xavier spoke.

"To recap for you Mr. Bennett, demons are real, there's warfare going on around you, and there's a class of super-humans that battles against them. I'm on a tight deadline and don't have time to coddle you. For the second time, come over here and sit down. I have some questions."

Camden hauled in a soul-cleansing breath and sat on the settee. *Why am I obeying this man?* His heart still hammering, he said, "I don't even know where to begin. All of this sounds—"

"Pardon the interruption, Mr. Bennett, but I have a grave concern." The raven hopped off Xavier's lap onto the coffee table. She wandered closer to Camden, croaked at him, and clicked her beak.

Cam leaned as far back as the settee allowed. "What's that?"

"There are two types of people who can see demons.

Either you're born with the ability, seeing demons from birth, or you're a Warrior—either Dark or Light. Based on your behavior, this is your first demon encounter, so you're not a Seer. You're obviously not a Warrior of Light." Xavier's eyes took on that odd red tint again, his energy radiating in an angry buzz. "So convince me that you're not a Dark Warrior infiltrating our network. You put on a delightful ignorance act, but part of my job is to protect those under my care. Start talking, son."

Camden's stomach bottomed out. He flushed hot and cold. "I don't know what you're talking about."

Xavier's eyes narrowed. "Do *not* lie to me."

"I swear to God, man, I have no clue what a Dark Warrior is!"

Xavier raised a brow. "Then tell me how you are suddenly seeing demons."

Camden shook his head. "I don't know!"

"Out of all the women you could be dating, you were drawn to Miss Fife. How does one of your status and wealth simply stumble upon a humble feed store employee? I've been told she doesn't keep a boyfriend for more than a month, so how did you charm her to keep you around? I think you're trying to get close to our network, to infiltrate our ranks." Xavier's tone turned lethal. "You'll need to do better than 'I don't know.'"

Oh shit, will this man kill me? "Sir, I will swear on the Bible, the Qur'an, the Puranas, whatever book you want, that I'm not what you're accusing me of. I've never heard of any of this before today."

Xavier snorted and leaned back. He beckoned the raven with a finger. She ambled over to him, her talons clicking on the glass tabletop. She kept one eye pinned on Camden. "Do you think that because you have knowledge of various religious texts, that helps your case, boy?"

"My grandfather was fascinated with religion." Camden's voice went up an octave in his desperation. "He travelled the world and took me with him."

"What was your grandfather's name?"

"Archibald Oliver Bennett. Everyone called him Archie."

"Hmm," Xavier mused, still not looking convinced of Cam's ignorance or innocence. "What of your mother and father?"

Camden's brow furrowed. "Um, my mother is Aerona Bennett. My father's name was Micah, but he died when I was a baby."

Xavier stroked his goatee, studying Camden. Cam squirmed under his intense scrutiny. "Miss Kestler tells me you moved to Florida two years ago. Why? Miss Fife and Miss Kestler received their anointing around the same time. Did you have information that there were newly christened Warriors of Light?"

"What?" Camden gasped. "No! When my gramps passed away it sent me into a deep spiral. I was in a bad place. I got into the wrong crowd. Eventually, my mother demanded I come to live with her. She had me go to therapy for Christ's sake." Heat lanced up Cam's neck and behind his ears. He'd never told anyone that he'd been seeing a shrink.

Xavier pursed his lips then tapped his shoulder. The raven flapped her wings and settled where he'd pointed. She made low chattering noises with pops and clicks, as if conversing with him.

"Good point," Xavier said. He looked at Camden. "Nyx believes your story, but I'm not inclined to be so gracious. You may stay with us, unharmed, free to come and go, but I *will* be watching you."

Camden couldn't remember the last time he'd been so

unnerved by another person. *I'll do whatever you say, just don't hurt me.* "Are we done here?" Cam swallowed and added, "Sir?"

"No." Xavier's voice was crisp, businesslike. "I have another concern. Miss Kestler tells me you received a death threat and that one of your employees was murdered. She believes the crime was demonic in nature. I believe her. Tell me about these incidents."

Camden poured out the whole story from the moment he heard Javi was murdered until today's events. He even included ditching his protection detail. "How is this demonic?"

"I wonder—" Xavier looked off in the distance and rubbed his chin, lost in thought. Camden didn't dare say or do anything. When Xavier spoke again Camden flinched. "I'd like to see this security footage, and I want to watch it with you. If you're seeing demons now, I wonder if you'll see the demon who killed your employee."

"Sure, I'll have Renard email me the clip." At Xavier's nod, Camden took out his phone, wincing at the numerous missed calls and texts from his mother. *I'll have hell to pay for ditching Adams. She's probably tracking me, anyway.* Cam sent his head chef a text with Xavier's request. Renard answered immediately. "He's pulling it now. Said to give him about two minutes."

"You say the letter you received was typed? No prints, no trace?"

"Nothing, sir. The police are stumped."

Xavier tapped his finger in the air, as if scolding Camden. "I need to see that as well. If a demon sent it, I have equipment that can scan for supernatural evidence. Get me the note."

Camden grimaced. If he approached Detective Lacey

to ask for the letter, word would get back to his mother. "That might be difficult. The police still have it."

Xavier waved away this thought. "You live in St. Petersburg?"

Camden nodded.

"I have some connections that owe me a few favors. Who's the detective that worked your case?"

"Paxton Lacey, sir."

Xavier sucked his teeth. "*El tonto*. I've met him. While I have no evidence to prove it, I think he's dirty."

And he's sleeping with my mother, Camden thought. *Lacey is dirty, my mother is a mob boss. Why not?* He didn't dare say any of this out loud. God knows what Xavier Gerena would do. *Probably line up the firing squad for my execution.* Camden's phone flashed.

"This is it, sir." Cam queued up the video and handed his cell to Xavier. "Just push play."

As Xavier viewed the video, Camden watched a shadow of sorrow sweep over the older man's face, erasing the intense expression he'd worn while interrogating Cam. When the footage stopped, Xavier made the sign of the Cross on his body.

"*¡Dios mío!* It's him," Xavier whispered. "This poor man had no clue who was playing with him." Xavier looked up, as if he'd just remembered Camden was in the room, and handed the phone back to him. "Watch it."

Camden didn't want to. He'd seen it a zillion times. Each time he saw Javi die was as painful as the first, yet he wasn't about to argue with Xavier. He started the video. It started the same way, with Javi prepping vegetables. When it got to the part where the thawing cabinet fell on him, Camden gasped and almost threw his phone. There was a second person he'd never seen before, well-dressed and wearing a fedora. He watched in horror as this person killed Javi and then looked into the camera and smiled.

"Oh my God, oh my God, oh my God," Camden chanted, trying to wrap his brain around what he'd just witnessed. "Who? What? How?" he stammered, his thoughts an incoherent jumble.

"His name is Dominic. And if he's the one that sent you the note, you've become a pawn in whatever game he's decided to play."

"What are you talking about?" To his horror, Camden's hands shook with terror.

"All you need to know, son, is that I believe your story now. I think you're completely innocent." Xavier sighed from the depths of his soul. "Unfortunately, you're in more danger than you originally thought. If Dominic's come out of the shadows, his Dark Warrior isn't far away. And she's the most dangerous of them all."

SAM

My eyes popped open to a view I was familiar with but hadn't seen in years. A white popcorn ceiling with russet brown crown molding came into focus. Moving only my head, I took in my surroundings. Clear morning light flooded the room from the windows at the top of the bed where I lay. Woodsy camping decor accentuated the space. A rustic patchwork quilt covered me. I lifted the bedclothes and looked down at my body. Sure enough, I was dressed in what used to be my favorite pair of pajamas, covered in cartoon Dalmatians. The spotted dogs stared up at me from my boobless chest.

Impossible.

I knew where and when I was, but the how and why were super sketchy. I was in December of 2010. Nine-year-old Samantha Fife was present and accounted for, but twenty-year-old Sam's brain was at the wheel. Letting go of the blanket, I poked my head above the quilt and gathered it under my chin. This was the Shaw's vacation cabin, nestled in the Appalachian Mountains, just outside of Pisgah National Forest in North Carolina.

"What the what?" I asked. "How?" My young voice rose an octave. I flung the covers off, swung my legs over the side, and padded across the carpet. I wrenched open the door. Shiny pine walls and emerald-green carpet lined the hallway.

"No, no, no. This isn't possible." No one would have left young Sam by herself. She was too much of a daredevil. Evel Knievel with pigtails. I ran to the end of the hall and thundered down a rustic set of stairs that led to the main floor. The smell of bacon and coffee met me, and I hopped up on a kitchen bar stool. A familiar silver-haired woman was busy cooking at a stove with her back to me.

Im-freaking-possible. "Judy?" I asked.

She turned, one hand resting on a hip and her spatula cocked in the other. She wore a warm smile. "You're up early."

I held up a finger and then pointed to myself. "Am I dead?"

"Mmmm," she mused. "Not dead. The Inbetween."

"I'm in *purgatory?*"

Judy laughed. "No, baby, you're still alive. Only just."

Baby? I raised a brow. "Right." I glanced around, taking in the open concept living room, dining area, and kitchen. "Why am I nine again?"

She shrugged. "These are your memories. You tell me why we're here."

I pursed my lips and stared up at the elkhorn chandelier mounted high in the center of the living space. *Think, Fife.* As I tried to sort out what was going on, everything around me went dark, like I'd been sucked into a black void. Just as suddenly, a bright light flashed and I stood in an empty space with whiteness all around. And before I could take my next breath, I was back in the cabin. I hadn't moved.

I jerked in surprise, my scrawny ass nearly falling off the stool. "What the hell was that?"

Judy looked livid and stared into a bowl on the counter. The whites of her eyes flickered red.

"Oh, hell no. What was that?" I pointed at her. *This isn't Judy. The woman never called me "baby" in my life.*

Fake Judy's expression smoothed out and she looked up. "What was what, babygirl? Are you alright?"

"No," I snapped, shaking my head. "For the love of chicken biscuits, I'm *nine* again. Why would I be alright?"

"Perhaps there is some importance to this time in your memory?" Judy turned her back on me and scooped bacon out of her cast iron pan onto a paper-towel-lined plate.

I closed my eyes and massaged my temples. I was forgetting something. An important something. It felt like half of me was missing. Why did I ask if I was dead? *Come on Fife, use your head.*

I recalled reading some text messages, hurrying to Milton's, and pulling out my daggers. I remembered fighting a blue Greater Demon which ended in her stabbing me. The blade she'd used hissed and burned when she slid it between my ribs. The black metal had been coated in an oily substance. She'd said her name was Enyo. *Sonovabitch.* I opened my eyes. She *poisoned* me and now I was unconscious, stuck in this weird time-warp of memory.

"I'm gonna go for a walk," I told fake Judy.

She took the pan off the burner and flipped off the heat. "I'll come with you, dear."

Abruptly, we were trudging through snow. The evergreens were lightly dusted with white powder. I was clad in a heavy winter coat, jeans, and rubber duck boots. I glanced over my shoulder at the cabin and saw a friendly line of smoke coming out of the chimney. We walked to a cluster of leaf-barren sugar maples. I counted them, stopping at the fifth on my right, and ducked a low hanging branch.

I raised my nine-year-old hand and ran my fingers over two different sets of initials carved inside two crude-shaped hearts: LK + NJ and SF + HT. I rested my fingertips on the first set. Leigh Kestler and Nick Jonas. I snorted in laughter. She'd had such a huge crush on the youngest member of Jonas Brothers Band. I traced the S and the H inside the second heart. *Samantha and Harper.*

"Does this time or date mean anything to you?" Fake Judy asked.

Lie. The command was faint and distant. Like before, blackness enveloped me, followed by a flash, and I stood in a white space. This time, there was the silhouette of a person behind a frosted glass wall. And just as suddenly, I was back among the trees, but I trusted the voice that told me to lie.

"No, Leigh and I were just two kids with silly crushes."

Judy's expression faltered into something of annoyance, but her smile snapped back into place a nanosecond later. The crunch of snow and gravel caught my attention and I looked toward the sound. An old, red F-150 pulled up the drive. I knew that vehicle and so did nine-year-old Sam. Her excitement had us bouncing on our feet then running toward the truck as soon as it stopped.

Andrew's long, lean frame unfolded from the cab on the driver's side. His grey eyes were warm and welcoming, and a smile split his face when he saw me. His silver hair was parted on the side and he wore a red flannel shirt and jeans. Andrew swept my seventy-pound body into his arms, hugged me tight, and spun us around. He kissed my temple and set me down.

This was one of my all-time favorite memories. I

glanced around. Other people should have been here. There was no real Judy. Harper was nowhere to be seen. *Where is Leigh? Her family? My family?* The Shaws, Kestlers, and Fifes spent Christmas break together that year. There was only Andrew.

He grabbed my small, cold fingers and led me to the huge cabin. He didn't speak but I felt the love and kindness in his touch. As my snow-crusted, rubber-clad boot touched the wooden steps, the memory ended and the whole scene changed.

I was in a gym, but not one I recognized and not an average one, at that. There were the typical hardwood floors, weight-lifting equipment, and long wall of mirrors, but a copious weapons collection and archery targets declared it was a Warrior's gym. Twenty Warriors-in-training stood in a line along the mirrored wall, waiting.

My palms were sweaty and I had a bad case of nerves. But this emotion wasn't coming from me. This was not my head, my body, or my memory. The young woman I inhabited glanced at the mirrors and I nearly had a heart attack. An auburn-haired, green-eyed beauty stared back. She was dressed head-to-toe in black workout clothes and her posture was timid. I didn't have the control over this body that I'd had over young Sam. I could only move when she did, but at least I could think for myself inside her.

"You're late," hissed a female from my right. She grabbed my elbow and shoved me aside, away from everyone. Whoever's body I inhabited turned to face the other woman, but she didn't look up. I stared down at her tennis shoes.

"I can't keep covering for you," said the second female.

My chin lifted and I met a familiar set of sapphire-dark

eyes. They burned with annoyance. *Harper! But not. This has to be his mother.*

"Elaine, I'm sorry," Not-me said. "My alarm didn't go off. I set it last night. I'm sure I did."

Elaine glanced over her shoulder. Two girls giggled and whispered to each other. They kept stealing glances our way. "I'll murder them," she growled. *She even sounds like Harper.*

"No, please don't cause more of a fuss. I'd really rather not make waves."

"Cheryl, you've been late to training every day this week because those two keep changing your clock after you've gone to sleep. I'm going to tell Adviser Shaw."

"No, you have no proof," I—rather, Cheryl—whimpered. "Besides, he doesn't care about me anyway."

"That's not true," Elaine said, shaking her head, her chocolate-brown ponytail whipping to-and-fro. "He cares about all his charges."

Cheryl extricated her arm from her friend's grasp. "Last week, when he gave me double stall cleaning duty, do you know why?"

Elaine raised a brow and shook her head.

"Those two bitches put the manure I'd just taken out back in the stalls. When Adviser Shaw came around for inspection—"

"It looked like you hadn't done your job," Elaine finished. "You didn't tell him?"

"I set up an appointment to meet with him. He accepted it. But when I went to his office, he wasn't there."

Elaine scrunched her nose. "That just doesn't seem like him at all."

"That's because you're a strong Warrior. And you're popular." I felt Cheryl's bitter loneliness and deep ache that she was an utter failure. Elaine was the only one that treated her with genuine kindness.

"Oh, Cheryl," Elaine said and jerked Cheryl into a hug. "I'll help you."

And then the scene changed. There had to be some sort of long-term repercussion from head-hopping. I'd seen enough science fiction TV. I stood in a small room with lavender walls and laminate wood floors. A large purple rug covered most of the floor. There was a twin bed in one corner and a small work desk littered with Starburst wrappers in the other. I was inside thirteen-year-old Sam's head. This was my room in my parents' house.

I had full control of my body this time. I pulled open a closet door, the left one, and peering down at me was a movie poster from the 2014 movie, *Guardians of the Galaxy*. I yanked at the right door and Katniss Everdeen from *The Hunger Games* had an arrow aimed at me. Leaving both doors open, I squatted and unzipped my school backpack. A notebook slipped out and I thumbed the pages. There was a knock on the door. I startled, clutching my chest.

"Sweetheart," my mother called, "you need to hurry. Andrew will be here soon."

"Coming!" younger Sam answered. I stared at the full-length mirror mounted on the back of my door. My blonde hair had been curled and there was makeup on my face. I wore a tasteful knee-length royal purple dress made of satin, gauze, and rhinestones. Leigh had helped me get ready for homecoming. If memory served, my best friend was in the bathroom across the hall putting the finishing touches on her ensemble.

When I put my hand on the doorknob, everything in my vision went black. Then a bright light flashed and I stood in that stark white space. I looked at the frosted barrier. It was more like a glass-block wall now, and the figure on the other side was a woman. And then I was back in my room ready for the dance. I wrenched open the door. Fake Judy stood in my way, an angry sneer on her lips and her eyes solid red. When she saw me, she smoothed out her expression, appearing calm and placid.

"Okay Spirit Guide," I snipped. "What's going on? How is this possible?"

"The how doesn't matter so much, baby." She reached out and primped my hair. "The question is why. Why are we in this memory?"

"The how—the *how* doesn't matter?" I gaped. "I'm playing musical chairs with memories, some that don't belong to me, while unconscious, and possibly dying of poison."

"Don't be dramatic," fake Judy said.

"I'm being dramatic?" My brows shot up. The doorbell rang. I yelled, "I got it!"

Young Sam barreled forward and fake Judy dissipated into nothingness. I threw open the front door. Andrew stood there in khaki slacks and a green knit sweater, a twinkle in his Irish eyes. I grinned when I saw him. He was taking us to the dance since my father was out of town and Mr. Kestler had to work late.

"Samantha, you look so grown up." He pulled me into a side hug and kissed my temple.

Then my freaking memory shifted again.

I now sat in an unfamiliar bedroom with a vaulted ceiling and mussed waterbed made up with red silk sheets. *A waterbed? Dude, the nineties called. Wait, was I in the nineties?* Blackout curtains made the room feel like a cave, lit only by a small lamp on a night table.

I didn't have time to process this new scene because my vision went black, everything flashed, and I was back in the white void. The woman on the other side of the glass was completely visible now. She was otherworldly gorgeous, almost angelic. She pounded on the barrier, yelling, her crystal-blue eyes wide with panic. I heard nothing.

In less than the time it took for me to blink, I was back in the dim bedroom. *I'm losing my damn mind.* At this rate, I was going to have mental whiplash and need years of therapy. Whenever I figured out what was going on, there would be hell to pay.

I stared down at my lap, my face framed by auburn hair. My chest was more voluptuous than normal. I had no control over this body. I was back in Cheryl's memory. Her right eye throbbed and purple bruises spread over the skin on her forearms. Her ribs ached. *Did Cheryl get beat up? Who beat up a Warrior? Was it the mean girls?*

The door clicked open. Cheryl flinched. A guy hurried in, shut the door tight, and locked it behind him. He knelt before Cheryl—me—and ran his fingers down her face. He pressed a bag of ice to her cheek.

"Who did this to you?" he asked, taking her hand. Cheryl shook her head and tears welled in her eyes. She trembled like a leaf. The man held her hand tighter. He tucked a lock of her hair behind an ear. "Please tell me." This guy was a good-looking dude with short curly blond hair and calf-brown eyes. Something about his face looked familiar.

"Paris," Cheryl whispered. "She was my sparring partner today. Hit me with the hilt. She didn't pull her swings either." Her voice hitched but she continued, "Andrew asked what happened, but Paris lied. She said her hand slipped, or something." Cheryl plopped the ice next to her on the desk. "Micah, I can't do this anymore. I don't think I even exist in his eyes."

Micah gathered Cheryl into his arms and she pressed her good cheek to his chest. "This is the fourth time one of those girls has hurt you." He held Cheryl at arm's length, anger flaring on his face. "How does he not see it? You deserve better. Didn't you say there was someone else you could try to train under?"

Hopelessness overwhelmed her. "I asked. But he said he didn't have time to take on any new Warriors. I'm stuck with Adviser Shaw."

"This is bullshit. You have to stand up to him. Make your voice heard." Micah cupped Cheryl's jaw. "I believe in you. I know you can do this. I can't handle seeing you hurt like this." He kissed her forehead.

"You're not a Warrior. You don't know what it's like being under that man." Her rage and anger were bitter cold.

"What would he do if he found out you'd let me in on your little secret?" He kissed her nose.

"I doubt he knows I truly exist."

Micah moved her hair to one hand and trailed kisses down her neck. A soft moan came from Cheryl.

Oh God.

"I'm invisible to Andrew Shaw. No matter how hard I try." She moaned again when Micah kissed under her ear.

Dear, Heaven. No. I felt Cheryl's arousal but also her undying love for this man.

Micah pulled Cheryl to her feet and rested his forehead against hers. "Then he's blind. You're amazing. Now, let's help you forget your bad day." He slid his hands down her waist, her hips, and around to grip her ass. He lifted her up and she wrapped her legs around him. He captured her lips in a fevered kiss and walked them over to the waterbed. *Lord, have mercy.*

I did not want to be privy to this. Micah pulled off Cheryl's shirt and laid her down while kissing her. She arched into him. He reached over with one hand and pulled off his own shirt. *Oh, hell no. Spirit Guide Judy, where the fire-fart are you?* It was one thing to be experiencing Cheryl's emotions but a whole other beast to experience sex from within her head. *I get it. I get it! Andrew sucks. Micah is amazing. Now get me the hell out of here!*

Mercifully, I was deposited into a familiar, humble barn. When I let out a relieved breath, the body I was in breathed with me. I was back inside the right mind. But at what age? I was so going to need therapy.

The barn was decorated with purple, gold, and black streamers and balloons. There was a table at the far end filled with gifts and another piled with buffet-style food. There were four round tables covered with tablecloths and centerpieces in the same purple, black, and gold color scheme.

This was my sweet sixteen party. The Shaws had insisted on throwing it for me and made a big to-do about the affair. They'd hired a party planner. The decorator, catering, and DJ were all professional. Those in attendance had all been formally invited with an RSVP required. Andrew and Judy spared no expense.

I ran over to the third stall on the left. A copper-red horse stood gleaming in the barn lights, his neck bent down while he munched on alfalfa. I tried to reach out to Max with my mind and got nothing. He was my horse, only a younger version.

"He can't hear me because this was pre-Guardian, right?" I asked fake Judy as she joined my side.

"This is only a memory. And you weren't a Warrior yet either."

"I remember this night," I said looking down at my clothes. I wore a lavender dress and gold heels.

"What do you remember most?" Judy asked. "Why is this one important?"

That black-flash-white-void shift happened again and this time it stuck for almost a full minute. The gorgeous brunette woman was still screaming, still pounding on the invisible divider. I took a step closer to her, then another. She couldn't see me. This close to the pane I saw that she yelled the same word over and over. But before I could make out what she shouted, I was back in the barn.

"Judy, I keep seeing—"

Say no more. That same distant voice which had told me to lie echoed in my mind. I had a deep-seated conviction that it was important to do as I was told.

"Seeing what?" Judy asked, her tone a little too eager.

"Sammy," Andrew's voice came from the entrance of the barn. He looked sophisticated in his steel grey suit. He wore a black tie and loafers. As usual, fake Judy was gone. "How's my best girl?"

Young Sam answered, "I'm pumped. Tonight's gonna be *fire*." I grinned. "You clean up nice, old man."

"And you're cheeky." Andrew met me in the aisle and kissed my temple.

"You guys totally didn't have to do this."

"We have no grandchildren. You and Miss Kestler are as close as we'll get." He placed his hand in the space between my shoulder blades and directed me towards Max's stall. We both peered in at the horse, still munching on his hay. "I have a surprise for you before the festivities began."

Sixteen-year-old Sam was excited and curious. I knew what came next.

"This is your favorite horse in the world, right?" Andrew asked.

"He's the best."

"Well, my best girl, he's yours."

With a lurch, I was back in Cheryl's body. She was

sobbing. It was raining and she was shivering. She had her face buried in her hands. Since I couldn't move unless she did, I had no idea where we were. Cheryl rocked back and forth. And, oh my mercy, she was pregnant.

Toxic thoughts swirled in her mind. She was invisible, a nobody, a nothing. She was never good enough. The two girls, Paris and Julie, had made her life hell. Would Andrew ever believe her? Would anyone? She tried to be a better Warrior, putting in extra practice hours to no avail; she was still average at best. Maybe Paris was right and she was a waste of space—a mistake.

She felt like Andrew didn't see her, didn't think she was anything special as a Warrior. And now she was pregnant and unwed. The sound of shoes on wet pavement caught Cheryl's attention. She took a jerky breath, sat up, and swiped her nose with her long sleeve.

"There you are!" Micah exclaimed. "We've been looking all over."

"Who's we?" Cheryl asked, voice watery and unsure.

Micah ran to where she was seated on a bus bench. The only illumination in the misty darkness was a single streetlamp over the stop. A revolver sat next to her on top of a brown paper bag. Cheryl had loaded it with one bullet, spun the cylinder, and had already clicked through two shots. If I could have gasped, I would have. She was serious and was playing a deadly game. Cheryl was desperate, terrified, and felt completely alone. She thought this was her only option.

"Elaine and I have been searching for you for hours." Micah knelt and saw the gun. He popped open the chamber, tipped the lone bullet into his palm, and threw it into the woods behind the bus stop. Micah gathered Cheryl into his arms and rocked her, planting kisses on the top of her head.

"If I hadn't found you—" He leaned Cheryl back, smoothed her hair away from her face, and brushed the tears from her face. "There is another way out than this."

Cheryl shook her head, more tears spilling down her cheeks. She continued to shake. "No there's not. I'm not needed."

"But you *are*," Micah insisted.

"I don't know why I'm alive."

"Look at me," Micah commanded. The whites of his eyes were freaking red. "It's time to rise up like a phoenix, my sweet. You will *not* take any more abuse at the hands of the Warriors of Light."

Cheryl's breath hitched. "What do you mean?"

"I mean"—he stood, pulling Cheryl to her feet—"your life is of great value to me. And that's Micah's—my child you're growing. I love you both."

Hope blossomed in her chest. "Honest?"

"I'm going to offer you another choice, my sweet. Once the baby is born, of course. The change will be—unpleasant. You must accept of your own accord." He turned away but threaded his fingers through Cheryl's and led her down the sidewalk. "When we're through with your transformation, you'll be unstoppable. You'll be so powerful. And you'll have your revenge. Do you *trust* me?" He turned his red eyes on Cheryl.

I sure as shit didn't trust him, but Cheryl? Freaking Cheryl, *she* did.

"Yes, Micah. With my life."

My vision went black, the world around me flashed, and I stood in the blank white void. Instinctively, I searched for the beautiful woman. And there she was, screaming and kicking the wall between us. I put my hand on the invisible barrier.

Up close she had a light dusting of freckles on her face.

She had no harsh lines in her features and her nose was slender. From her forehead to brow line to chin, everything was in perfect proportion. She was the most gorgeous woman I'd ever seen.

I squinted. I couldn't hear her, but the woman screamed "Samantha!" over and over. I stumbled back and gaped at her. This wasn't a memory. Hell, it wasn't even a place I recognized. I had no cotton-pickin' clue who this woman was and why she was screaming my name.

Stop and think, Fife.

She was dressed in full Warrior white garb. She knew my name. And she was frantic with concern for me. The answer was right on the tip of my brain when the invisible barrier turned into obsidian. The temperature plunged. I spun around, eyes wide, expecting to see the Mage, but all I saw was Judy. Her image, and the now-black wall, flickered like a short circuit. *My brain is glitching.*

"Enough games," I yelled. "I know you're here! What the hell is going on?"

The seconds ticked by. Judy solidified and the barrier stabilized. The white space morphed into an elegant living room. The floor changed into warm walnut hardwood. The black pane turned into a great wall of windows. When the shifting stopped, a familiar voice spoke behind me.

"Hello, Samantha."

I spun and stood face-to-face with Dominic. "Are you doing this?"

He grinned. "Sit. Have some tea. We need to chat."

"Screw you. What are you doing in my head?"

He smoothed the lapels of his black suit and winked at me.

"Where's your boss?" I snapped.

"On the way," Dominic said and waved a hand over the coffee table. A tea tray appeared. I sneered. "No tea?

Ah, yes. I forget myself. Coffee is your preferred beverage." With a second pass of his crimson hand the tea pot turned into a glass carafe filled with dark liquid.

"Cut the crap. What do you mean, 'on the way'? My head isn't a public park."

"You're not wrong about that, my sweet. Your mind's defenses are the hardest I've ever encountered, and I'm ancient." He tapped the top of the carafe, turning it back into a kettle, and settled into a plush cream-colored chair, his red skin stark against the fabric color. "Blood magic of this magnitude only allows for the passage of one visitor at a time. My boss, as you phrased it, will arrive in a bit. In the meantime, sit. Chat with me. I won't harm you."

Dominic hooked an index finger in mid-air as if to beckon me, but a chair rammed into the backs of my knees. Gravity brought my ass crashing down onto the cushions.

"Get comfortable," he said. "I have a story to tell you."

SAM

I glared at the demon seated across from me. "You invaded my head, forced me to sit, and gave me no chance to ask you anything. Technically, this is my home and you're being a rude house guest, so before we have storytime, you're gonna answer a few questions."

Dominic leaned forward, dropped a sugar cube into a cup, and poured tea over it. "I suppose you're right and we do have some time. My sincerest apologies, Samantha. What would you like to know?"

I'd been so prepared for a *no* that I wasn't ready. I opened my mouth and shut it.

"Yes, my sweet?"

"Don't call me that," I spat.

"Very well, *love.*" His accent slipped into a British dialect. "Will this do?"

"Hardly." I gave him a flat look.

"You had questions, did you not?" He held onto the Brit accent.

"How is this possible?" I asked. We were in an elaborate living room straight out of a home decor magazine. I snagged a shortbread biscuit from the tea tray, sat back, and sniffed the treat. "How have you all infiltrated my head?"

"Blood magic. Specifically, your blood. As a Warrior, no one else's blood would have sufficed." The demon crossed his leg over his knee. "My *boss*, as you phrased it, had to take extreme measures because your mind is so heavily guarded. The plan was elaborate. Kidnap your Healer, draw you out, and then send in Enyo to obtain a generous sample of your blood. Although, I personally can't help but be impressed with you. You got a dose of Enyo's special concoction that would have killed a weaker Warrior."

"That's comforting, I guess." I nibbled the corner of my cookie. It seemed safe enough. I was locked in my own head, after all, and had no idea where my unconscious body was. *Well, that's terrifying.* "So you're here, your boss is on the way, and y'all have my blood. Who has my body?"

Dominic sniffed and adjusted his tweed flat cap. "Your people."

I breathed a sigh of relief. "So that means the Mage has a limited amount of blood and this rollercoaster ride through my head is a one-time trip."

"Aren't you clever?" Dominic's black eyes glittered with mischievous humor.

I shrugged. "Sometimes. Anyway, I know why the Mage wants me, but why did you let Leigh and me go the other night?"

Dominic took a sip of his tea. "You're fascinating. I have a vested interest."

"But why? Why does a demon go against his master's will? Is that even possible?"

Dominic's grin grew and he winked at me. I was getting nothing more on that topic. "Fine. Why has the Mage taken me down memory lane? And am I stuck with Cheryl's memories?"

"The first question I will let the Mage answer. As for the memories that weren't yours, those were implanted. They are rather permanent. The Mage has its reasons and you'll find out soon enough."

"That is a pretty hefty invasion of privacy. I'll send you my therapy bill." I didn't want him to know just how much it freaked me out that I was stuck with memories that weren't mine. I took a bite of the cookie. "So, who is the Mage?"

Dominic jerked his head up, his coal-black eyes focused on something outside this room. Then he looked back at me. "As much as I'm dying for you to continue your inquisition, love, I have less time than I thought I would."

He flicked his wrist and duct tape sprang over my lips. I clawed at my gag. *Who the hell does he think he is?* The adhesive stuck to my mouth with shocking permanence. I glared daggers at Dominic.

"Please, forgive my rudeness, love." He smiled and tapped his lips. "I have a lot to say in a short amount of time."

This was rude? Not the whole walk down memory lane? Not the takeover of my brain? Not the stabbing and poisoning of Samantha Fife? I was in a damn coma. But no, silencing me was considered rude. And the asshat hadn't even let me finish my cookie. I chucked the half-eaten biscuit at him. He let it peg him in the chest before sweeping the crumbs away with a few flicks of his fingers.

Dominic righted the watch on his wrist. "Listen well."

I threw up my hands. *Like I have another choice.*

"In the beginning, before the world began, there was a

war in Heaven. Lucifer, and those who fought with him, were thrown out of paradise. Lucifer was an archangel, second in command behind Michael."

This is the abridged version? I raised a brow.

"Right you are, I'll fast forward. When the angels that were cast out of Heaven morphed into The Fallen, there was a group of five that remembered the old ways. They had been high-ranking angels in Heaven and hadn't devolved over time. Their skin and eyes changed color, but they remained beautiful. These five created the Council of Infernal Order: Lucifer as the head, Azrael the Demon of Death, Deimos the demon of Fear and Panic, Bellona the demon of Destructive Warfare, and Tanda the Seer of Life and Death."

Oh, joy. Hell has a governing body. I wondered if Andew knew of this group. I grumbled behind my gag. Dominic spared a quick grin but continued.

"The Infernal Order provided protection, a system of structure, and kept everyone from turning on each other. Eventually, we all settled into our new underworld home. The Fallen, your kind calls them Greater Demons, shed their wings. They fornicated with each other." Dominic sneered as if the idea disgusted him. "These acts were not permitted in Heaven and the demons were now free. They did as they wished." His smile returned. "The Fallen birthed children, known to you as Lesser Demons, and they matured. These lesser creatures, while not the brightest, are loved by Lucifer. He allowed them to exist."

I don't want to hear about demons doing the dirty. I mumbled as such and Dominic chuckled as if he understood me.

"When Heaven realized what was going on in Hell, they panicked," he continued. "What of the human race? They were the demons' food source. This is when Heaven created the Warriors of Light to protect humanity." He said the title as if it were acid in his mouth.

"These super-powered beings were created to destroy Lucifer's children, and Lucifer hated what was being done to them." Raw anger formed on Dominic's face. "With the Order's assistance, Hell fought back. They created Hell's equivalent of a Light Warrior. Your kind calls them Warriors of Dark."

I huffed. *I know that.*

Dominic raised a hand with a patient smile. "I'll spare you the history lesson and jump into the heart of what I want to show you. Do you want to know how a Dark Warrior is created?"

Do I want to know? Hell yes. Not because I wanted to turn Dark, but because I was morbidly curious. I nodded, annoyed he'd gagged me.

"They are created much the same way as the Warriors of Light, with a twist." Dominic flicked two fingers and an old-fashioned movie projector sprang up in the middle of the living room. A choppy movie flickered on the white wall opposite the wall of windows. Every clip showed a Warrior of Light in transition.

A spear of golden Light raced from Heaven and slammed into each Warrior's chest. That Light raised each person so they hovered off the ground. Then the Light sprouted from their eyes, mouth, ears, fingertips, and toes, and transformed the humans into something superhuman.

My face was on the wall next, huge and in color. This was my transformation story. It was the summer after Leigh and I graduated high school. We worked at Andrew's church for a summer internship. In the scene before me, I stood outside that church in the pouring rain. It stormed like a tempest that night, with lightning splitting the sky every few seconds. Leigh and I had been heading out to the car, to go home, when Andrew stopped us mid-sprint. He shouted for us to come back.

"Here, I want you to have these now. You're ready," Andrew said, passing us each an old key. We'd thought they were for something in the building, but the moment we took them, our anointing began.

It was a peaceful transition on the inside. There was a comfort, a wholeness that the Light brought. Boldness replaced fear and my bodily scars were erased. My DNA changed, my body changed, and though it looked violent from a spectator's view, it was the safest, most comforting thing I'd ever felt in my life. I would go through that transformation every day if I could.

Dominic broke the spell by pausing the reel. He sauntered up to the wall and pointed at that golden ball of light just before it collided with me. "Your Power comes from Heaven through this. But do you know what that great shiny ball of brightness is?"

I rolled my eyes. *I can't answer, you nimrod.*

"That is an Angel." He unpaused the video and we watched the rest of my transformation.

I have an Angel living in me? I thought of the gorgeous woman yelling my name from behind that glass wall. She'd been frantic. I gasped behind my tape gag. *She's my angel!* My eyes widened. *My angel is—Leticia? Letty. Good God, I'd given an Angel of Heaven a nickname.*

My buddy Dom either hadn't heard me gasp, or he ignored me, because he continued speaking as if I hadn't just had a massive epiphany. "Conversely, a Dark Warrior's Power comes through a demon."

The projector imagery changed. Glowing balls of black light covered in writhing tendrils rose from the ground and grabbed hold of their hosts' ankles. The inky blackness swirled around their bodies, burrowing into them. "They must be willing, of course. Lucifer would never force this anointing on anyone." He turned and faced me. "Tell me, Samantha, were you given a choice? Or was this forced on you without your consent? Did Bernard Andrew Shaw even ask if this was what you wanted?"

"Really?" I mumbled from behind my muzzle.

Dominic crouched in front of me. "Those were rhetorical questions, love. But if you promise to not interrupt me, I'll remove the gag."

I blinked at him, giving my best deadpan glare, but he didn't move. "I promise," I swore, my words muffled. Dominic nodded and the tape vanished. I worked my jaw, opening and shutting my mouth.

"Behave," he warned.

I offered him a contemptuous smile and said nothing.

"Now, you may be wondering why there are no Warriors of Dark running around now."

That was one of my questions, yes, but I wasn't about to make a peep.

"The problem is that The Fallen are chaotic by nature. They are unpredictable, violent, and, perhaps, a bit insane. Living in Hell twisted their natures. Angels are steadfast, placid, and unswerving. Lucifer wasn't sure if the use of demons was wise. But he had to try, Samantha. Do you know what happens to a demon when he or she is slain by a Warrior of Light?"

"I have an idea." I shrugged. In truth, I had no clue.

Dominic chuckled. "They are sent back to Hell broken and destroyed—sick. Some bleed from their inflicted wounds. They become a shell of their former selves." His tone became forlorn and sad. "It takes decades for them to recover. Some never do. Lucifer had to create Dark Warriors because his children were being mutilated. He had to try to keep them safe."

I would *not* have sympathy for demons. They fed off humanity's worst behavior. Even as despicable as humans could be, I'd sworn to protect them. What demons did with people was pure evil. The more corrupt the demons could make someone, the more they could feed. Condoning their actions would be akin to saying that genocide, rape, murder, and theft were all a-okay because the poor demons were hungry.

"Unfortunately, the demonic energy was too chaotic and these Dark Warriors became too powerful. They soon turned on Lucifer's children. Enslaved them. Beat them. Treated them as dung. They used demons for atrocities I shall not mention."

Dominic closed his eyes, something like grief passing over his face, and then he looked at me. "Once the Dark Warriors killed all surviving Warriors of Light, Lucifer locked them away in Hell." He held up one slender, red finger. "Save for one. One who was highly favored. The one whose demon was much more stable than the rest. This Warrior alone has the power to command demon armies."

Dominic quirked a brow and I tried to understand what he was actually saying. I tilted my head. Then it dawned on me. "Ooooh!"

I'd asked him who the Mage was. Dominic had just answered me. The Mage was the one Dark Warrior allowed to be free. I swallowed hard. I'd sassed and provoked a being so powerful its friends had been locked away by Lucifer himself. *I am so stupid.*

"I'll allow you one guess as to who the Mage's demonic partner is." Dominic smiled, his teeth white and stark against his red skin. Teeth that weren't rotted like a normal demon's were. In fact, if not for the black eyes and crimson skin, he would have been a decent-looking fellow. He was always composed and there was nothing chaotic about him.

"You," I gasped.

Dominic's grin grew and he took a bow. "In the flesh."

"How are you so normal?"

"I never forgot where I came from, love." He tapped the side of his head then pointed up. "While my brethren reveled in what they'd become, I looked to the Order and modeled myself after them. I was selective about the sort of —*food*—I consumed in my new home. I kept my faculties. I bathed."

"And you were the only demon to do this?" I asked in disbelief.

"No, but there aren't many. The Order, Enyo, and a handful of other higher-ranking demons clung to the old ways."

"Hmm. Who's stronger? You or the Mage?"

Dominic's nostrils flared and his aura pulsed a tarnished bronze. I sucked in a sharp surprised breath. *That hit a nerve.*

"In this realm, the Mage is stronger. If we were in Hell, I would have significant power over my Warrior."

I had more questions, and I was willing to risk more duct tape to ask them. "You've been walking and talking with the Grim Reaper alongside you. So where's my angel? Why don't I see her like the Mage sees you?" I looked around expecting to see Letty. If what Dominic said was true, she should have been here. Unless she was still stuck behind that glass wall. I narrowed a glare at Dominic.

"You are fantastic." He studied me with something similar to pride.

"Thank you, but answer the question, Crimson Tide. Where's Letty?"

Dominic froze, eyes widening, then he sighed. "Our chat must come to an end. My Warrior comes."

That damn demon gave me two seconds' warning before the room in my noggin plunged into frigid temperatures. Ice climbed up the walls, shining like crystal in the sunlight. The Mage flickered into existence five feet in front of me.

"Samantha," it said, its cold voice like nails on a chalkboard. "How lovely to see you in person. I apologize for my tardiness and trust Dominic was hospitable?"

I glanced at him. He had reclaimed his seat in the cream chair across the room. His projector had vanished along with any hint that we'd had story time. With the Mage's focus on me, Dominic pressed a single long, red index finger to his lips, a duplicitous gleam twinkling in his eyes. I jerked my attention back to the Mage.

"Yes, he offered me tea and coffee. You're late to the party. Why am I in a coma?"

"I find it easier to discuss matters with you when you are unconscious."

I huffed. I reminded myself that the Mage was the most powerful Dark Warrior in existence, and I should keep my snark to a minimum. The Mage needed a teaspoon more respect than I'd initially offered.

"Do you know why I chose to show you the memories I did?" the Mage asked.

The common denominator in all of them was Andrew. Remembering how the Mage reacted to my Adviser's name during our first encounter, I didn't dare speak it aloud. "I think so."

"Why?" the Mage asked.

I didn't know there was a test. "I'm guessing it's because you wanted to show me contrasting views of An—um, my Adviser."

The temperature dropped even more and the Mage hissed. "You are correct. What did you learn?"

That I need stronger mental blocks to keep you people out of my damn head. I was tired of being told to sit, listen, and answer questions. This was my head, dammit! Instead of answering, I asked, "Who is Cheryl? And who was that man, Micah?"

The Mage rubbed the pads of its thumbs along the tips of its other fingers. Red tattoos swirled over the visible white skin—Dominic's signature. The Mage inhaled. "I will answer your questions, but first answer me. What did you learn?"

"For every good memory I had, you showed me one of Cheryl's bad ones. Andre—my Adviser gave me love and support. Showed me kindness and spared nothing to keep me happy. But Cheryl never believed he was there for her. She felt abandoned. From what I could see, she never asked for help, either. And she would have had it if she asked."

Snow swirled between the Mage and me. "Cheryl was a tragic Warrior of Light. Micah was her soulmate, her savior from *that man.*"

Something wasn't adding up. "Who is Cheryl to you?" My mouth formed an O as the thought hit me. "Are *you* Cheryl? That would make sense—"

"Cheryl is dead," the Mage snarled. "I watched her die, but I saved her memories, lest we forget the man we fight against."

"You mean, your fight against Heaven and Warriors of Light? Not against Andrew himself."

Icy rage billowed from the Dark Warrior, smoking and hissing like dry ice, and the Mage's aura pulsed. I knew it was risky, but I needed to push the Mage to see how much information I could get before the Dark Warrior lost its temper.

"You have a personal vendetta against him," I said.

"That man and his partner, Xavier, drove Cheryl into the arms of their enemy. An enemy that welcomed her without judgment and used Micah as her guide."

"Is Micah still alive?"

"I killed him," the Mage said, delivering this news with a cavalier hand flip. "I needed to show you what kind of men you've aligned yourself with. They don't care about the weak, the less fortunate, the average. Those men, Bernard Andrew Shaw specifically, only care about the strongest. Those with potential and talent. Now you'll *never* forget what they did to Cheryl. Her memory is with you forever. She won't be forgotten."

I thought of how Cheryl wanted to end her life. I felt her despair and her loneliness. I'd lived three of her memories in excruciating detail. I felt her heart break every time Andrew let her down. Or when Xavier didn't take her on as his charge. Micah had offered her a way out. Micah wanted her to live. Micah's eyes had been red in the last memory I saw. I glanced at Dominic.

He had a knuckle resting against his lips, elbow propped on the chair's arm. His black eyes studied me. I raised a brow and pointed at him. Dominic dipped his chin in confirmation.

Micah was *used* by Hell, possessed by Dominic himself.

Letty, where are you? I rubbed my eyes and then my whole face. *What am I missing?*

Realization struck hard and fast. "How the hell is it even possible for a Light Warrior to go Dark?" I was appalled and awed at the same time.

The Mage glided across the floor. "When a Light Warrior chooses the Dark, the angel they are tied to is burned and ripped from their body. It is a brutal transition, quite painful for both human and angel alike. One of The Fallen occupies that emptiness and mends the charred places in the Warrior where the angel used to be. I don't know what happens to the angel, but the end result is one Warrior of Dark where a Warrior of Light used to be.

"That is horrifying." *And Cheryl underwent that process. On purpose.* I placed a palm over my heart. The very idea of doing that to Letty was abhorrent. I couldn't—*wouldn't* —imagine doing what Cheryl had done. It would be like cutting out my own heart and setting fire to my body.

The Mage floated towards me. "Would you not have done the same, if you were in Cheryl's position? These people take and take, but do not care. They drive a Light Warrior to the brink of suicide. How can a woman as smart as you continue to support Bernard Andrew Shaw?"

I stared out of the wall of windows. Andrew had lied. He had hurt me. He had kept things from me that he *never* should have. But I wasn't suicidal. Bitter? Sure. Beat up? Definitely. But was I damaged enough to turn on my people? Turn on Leigh, Max, and Harper? No, no, and no. I suspected that the transition from Light to Dark was *deadly*, yet Cheryl had survived the process. Hurt, bitter rage, and revenge fueled her, deep in her soul. That begged the most important question: did I have that kind of hate inside me? Hell, no. But I wasn't Cheryl. I hadn't walked in her shoes or had to deal with the shit life threw at her. I was me. Samantha Fife. I didn't know how to be anyone else.

I looked at the Mage and then at Dominic. They'd trapped me in my own head. They'd sent demon after demon to get me. I was in a coma because of them. My memory of events leading up to this point was murky and scattered, but I knew who I was.

So, no. I would not have made the choice that Cheryl did. I'd never been truly alone. And no matter how angry and hurt I was by Andrew, he had to have a reason for keeping Leigh and me in the dark. And I sure as shit would *not* turn my back on my people. Fury burned hot in my belly. The thick ice started to melt from the walls of the living room. I'd had enough. I stood.

"What is happening?" the Mage hissed, anger in its cold voice. Dominic stood as well, but he was amused.

"You don't get to invade my head and call the shots." I took a step toward the Mage. "You will not continue to manipulate me here." I took another stride forward, sparks igniting the floorboards. "I will not be bought, coerced, or jaded into joining you." Supernatural flames climbed the walls, burning the wallpaper and sending fine ash into the air.

"Hell will not have me." I was toe-to-robe with the Mage now. Holy fire consumed drywall and burned down into the wooden studs. "This is your eviction notice."

With righteous indignation, I shoved the Mage's shoulders hard, flinging it towards the wall of windows. Before it crashed through the glass, the Mage dissolved into mist. The room spun, an inferno burning everything except me and the crimson demon before me.

"To be continued, love," he said, smiling, then he snapped his fingers and disappeared.

The whole living room swirled upward, flames and all, until the bright white infinite space of my mind remained. The invisible barrier that excluded Letty shattered, and she bounded toward me. Her crystal blue eyes found mine.

"Samantha," she breathed.

My body shook. I'd been trapped, stabbed, poisoned, and invaded. I could no longer bear my own weight. Too stunned to cry, I crumpled. A set of powerful arms swooped in and caught me. She lowered us both to the floor. I curled into the fetal position, laid my head in her lap, and trembled.

"You sent them away and they can't come back. I'm so proud of you." Her voice soothed me as she stroked my hair. "I've got you. Rest now, Brave One. You've earned it."

HARPER

"No change?" Xavier asked, entering Sam's room holding a piece of paper.

"Her stitches are holding this time. She hasn't had any more seizures since that first night," I said and finished hanging a fresh bag of fluids on the IV pole next to Sam's bed.

Xavier held out the sheet. "Here are the results from her latest blood test."

I adjusted the drip on Sam's IV feed and took the report. Sam had been in a coma for two days and was working on a third. She'd not fared well in her first twenty-four hours. Enyo's poison ravaged her body, kept dissolving her stitches, and jacked up her temperature. And, of course, the seizures. She'd had five or six in those first hours. Xavier had supernatural tests to measure the level of poison left in her blood. We ran them three times a day.

Reading through the new numbers loosened a knot in my chest. "This is much lower." I fell into my chair next to her bed. "I assume she's still in the coma because there's still traces of poison."

"I haven't seen any Warrior make it this far when Enyo attacked them, so your assumption is a good one." Xavier placed his hand over Sam's and rubbed his thumb over her knuckles.

"Fuck." I scrubbed at the heavy stubble on my jaw.

"Ah, yes. That was my sentiment as well."

"So we wait?" I tossed the paper onto the nightstand next to me.

"I'm afraid so. There is nothing we can give her to help the poison work itself through faster. Still giving her Elixir, I see." Xavier flicked the IV bag.

"Steady stream."

"How's our supply?"

"As long as she doesn't take any more wild turns, we're good." I leaned back in my seat; my eyes burned with exhaustion. I hadn't slept for more than a few hours at a time.

"I'll have Nigel make more just in case. God forbid, we might need it for other Warriors, too. You did raise the ire of a rather powerful demon, son. She may retaliate against someone other than you." Xavier looked back down at Sam. "I'm sorry this happened to you, Miss Fife." He checked his watch. "I have to go meet with the mortician about Judy's remains. You're in charge while I'm away."

At the mention of Ma, I gritted my teeth and swallowed the hard lump in my throat. "Where's Pops?" I'd heard him arrive in the dark hours of morning. "He hasn't come to see her yet."

"Andrew," Xavier sighed, "isn't well. Judy and Andrew were married by Warrior law. Warrior unions bring a level of permanence and connection that doesn't exist outside our world. Even within our ranks, not many take Warriors vows. Andrew lost a part of himself."

Xavier placed a hand on my shoulder. "I know you're angry and hurting, but do try to offer him a little grace. He's shattered. Allow him this time to process and grieve. He'll see Sam when he's able."

"Respectfully, why am I in charge? I'm not a Warrior and Nigel is my senior."

"I have my reasons," Xavier said and made his exit without further explanation.

I sighed. *One more thing to worry about.* I propped my feet on the other chair in front of me and closed my eyes. *Might as well take a nap while everyone's out.* I'd finally gotten comfortable when Kestler's voice interrupted my doze.

"Harper?"

Fucking fuck. I looked over at her standing in the room's entrance. She was already lean, but her cheeks were more gaunt than usual. Kestler had dropped weight. But it was the purple circles under her bloodshot eyes that softened the edge of my annoyance. I wanted to be left alone, but I'd permit her presence. We shared a common grief.

"You look like hell, Kestler. Take a load off." I dropped my feet and kicked out the corner of the chair.

"Have you seen yourself lately?" she asked and sat without a second invitation.

"I'd rather not." I crossed my arms over my chest.

"When was the last time you showered?" There was a mischievousness to her question. She leaned away from me and wrinkled her nose.

"When was the last time you ate?"

"Touché," she said, then glanced at Sam. Tears welled in her eyes and she pressed her quivering lips together.

I leaned forward and softly tagged her on the shoulder

with a fist. "She'll make it through this." *I hope to God I'm right.*

"Harper, I was so mean. I said things to her that—" A few tears escaped and she dashed them away. "What if she doesn't wake up, and the last thing I said to her was that she was"—she lowered her voice—"an asshole."

"Cut that shit out." I rapped her knee with a knuckle. "Don't play that game with yourself. She knows you love her."

"You were there." Kestler threw herself back into the chair and tossed up a hand. "I was cruel."

"You were *right*." She met my eyes. I pointed at her. "No one else on this planet could have said what you did and gotten through her thick skull."

She gave an unconvinced smile. Kestler had a way about her, and I finally started to understand the Sam-and-Kestler dynamic. We lapsed into silence, the lack of noise blissful.

"Where's Cam?" Kestler asked after a while, breaking the quiet.

That fucker. "I don't give a shit."

"You're still pissed at him? He's her boyfriend, Harper, of course he's going to be here."

I grunted. Bennett accepted Xavier's explanation with surprising swiftness, which made me suspicious. No one saw the shit he had seen and thought, "Okay, cool. This is fine," and kept going. I didn't trust him, and everyone seemed to give him the benefit of the doubt—save for Xavier.

Not trusting him wasn't what got Bennett on my shitlist. His place there was sealed when he plowed his way through Nigel and DH to get to Sam's room. Once she'd been stable enough to move, only Kestler, Xavier, and I were permitted in, but the entitled prick didn't think the rules applied to him. Bozeman kept me from ripping off Bennett's limbs and shoving them up his ass. Xavier and Kalakaua hadn't been at the farmhouse that evening since they were off dealing with funeral arrangements, but Kestler and Bozeman had talked me off the ledge.

Bennett wasn't going to let Sam out of his sight. I sure as shit wasn't either. In spite of her grief, Kestler had found it within herself to run interference. I relented. As long as his punk-ass didn't ask stupid questions, I promised that I wouldn't inflict bodily harm on him. Needless to say, I'd been fired from my position as bodyguard.

"He is her boyfriend, he saw that demon stab Sam, and he's being threatened," Kestler said. "He has a right to be here."

Rage rattled my ribcage. I glared at her. *Are you trying to provoke me?* She glared right back, not flinching.

"You may scare the crap out of everyone else with that look, buster, but not me. I'm the oldest of five children, my mother is an emergency room nurse, and my father is the toughest lawyer on earth. Beneath all your gruff alpha-male tendencies, you have a good heart. So change your face, sir. You can't glower me away." There were few people who didn't flinch under my scowl; I could count them on one hand, and Kestler was number five.

I scoffed. "He shouldn't be in her life."

"That's Sam's choice and you know it. And Divine Intervention didn't stop him from seeing what he saw." She shrugged. "Gotta deal with it, *bro*."

I coughed, covering my laugh, then sighed. "Bennett's in Pops's office. Either working or sleeping."

Bennett insisted on running his restaurant remotely, so not only was he allowed in Sam's room, he was permitted to invade Pops's office. Nigel had set up a cot for him in the study, and DH had provided him with whatever electronics he needed. And since Pops was in such bad shape, he wouldn't be using the office anytime soon.

"I see," she mused. "You should take a shower." I opened my mouth with a "fuck off" on my tongue, but she held up a hand. "I won't leave her side. I promise. If anything changes, I'll send in the cavalry." She reached over and squeezed my hand. "And you stink."

I rubbed my lower lip with my thumb and met her eyes. She had a stubborn set to her jaw and a stern brow. I shook my head. *I won't leave Sam.*

"When is the last time you slept?" She let go of me and leaned back in her chair.

"Last night."

"In a proper bed," she said. "And for more than a few hours."

I shrugged.

"Harper, for Sam's sake, take a shower and get some *real* rest." She gave me a soft smile. "You'll be better off with a full battery."

I'd rather cut off my left nut. But Kestler had a valid point —I was bone weary and would be prone to rash decisions. And if there was anyone I'd leave Sam's care to, it would be her. *Fucking-A.*

"Alright," I said, rubbing my eyes. "You win this one. This once." I placed my palms on my knees and stood up —my back, hamstrings, and joints protesting. "You know where my room is if anything changes."

"You'll be the first to know," Kestler promised.

I turned to Sam, rested my hand on her head, then brushed her forehead. *Don't do anything crazy while I'm gone, like seizing or dissolving your stitches.*

After a long, scalding shower, I found myself staring at the bathroom mirror. The face reflected back at me looked like shit warmed up and served on a hubcap. A beard had sprouted on my jaw, and I didn't have enough fucks left to give. I'd shave later. I went straight to bed. Kestler was right. I needed sleep. But there was a nightmare waiting for me when I finally drifted off.

Mounted on a horse, I stood on the sandy shore of an unknown ocean. Waves crashed against scattered boulders, and a cliff loomed over the beach. Ominous clouds blocked out the sun's warmth, and cold rain swirled around me.

My old EMS squad stood behind me, along with a massive corps of Light Warriors in full battle garb. Our enemy rose from the sea and lined the beach, trapping us along the cliff wall. They were inhuman with their twisted features, colored swirling tattoos, and dark power. Greater Demons filed onto the beach behind them, filling in the gaps and strengthening their numbers.

Lightning splintered the sky and at the crack of thunder, all hell broke loose. We charged. Swords flashed from their scabbards. Daggers lashed out. I heard cries of the wounded. My army's blood soaked the sand red. Demon ash floated in the air.

She was here. I felt it. My mare spun in a circle while I searched for her. The beach was littered with bodies and abandoned weapons, trampled into the sand by combatants. Pure carnage. I was losing men, Warriors, and Guardians like a hemorrhaging artery. My mare tossed her head and pranced.

Where was she? My panic rose. Then, like a lifeline thrown at sea, I found her. She fought like a classical heroine, her blonde hair braided long down her back. The rain plastered the loose wisps of hair to her face. Her head jerked in my direction and our gazes locked. She flashed me a smile, a hurricane raging in her blue-grey eyes. A fire ignited in my chest and hope filled my veins with electric fervor. My fog of confusion blew away.

I charged into the fray. As long as she lived, as long as I could feel her, I knew everything would be okay. I felt her passion, and it fed my muscles and filled me with fire-hot Power.

Abruptly, the world around me slowed while a black-hooded

figure rose from the sand. The temperature plunged, and my breath formed icy puffs. My metal armor became a frigid cocoon. I ignored the brutal cold. I felt no fear because of the connection to my Lifeline.

When the Mage stood before me, time snapped back to the frenzied pace of battle. My mare grew in height as she gathered herself for combat. Her ears swiveled forward and she snorted a warning.

"Mage." I nodded toward the hooded figure.

"Commander," it answered.

"Why do you call me that?"

"Is this not your army? Your men and women? Are you not the most powerful being here?"

I shook my head, sending water droplets flying. "I'm just a man."

"You are mistaken." The Mage glided in a circle around me. "Commander Tate, you possess something no one has had before."

"What's that?" I asked. My horse spun with the Mage, never letting the evil being out of our sight.

"If you don't know, I won't tell you. It works to my advantage." A red glow burned under the hood.

I glanced at my Lifeline, seeing her alive and fighting. Battle-lust kicked in and I charged the Mage, swinging my sword. The Mage evaded my blade. I kicked at its chest. The Mage flew backward.

Its hood fell back, revealing a human face tattooed with a swirling red pattern that matched her arms. The pattern continued down her neck and disappeared beneath her robe. Her eyes glowed crimson and her long hair was stark-white. Her pulsing black aura beat with the rhythm of her heart. The rain turned to snow. The Mage thrust her hands upward and an invisible force slammed into me, knocking me off my horse.

The Mage got up and glided away from me to the nearest melee. She punched her fist into a Light Warrior's back and withdrew a bloody hand. She clutched the man's heart. The Warrior dropped. Black power flared around the Mage and she turned to strike at me again. I ducked and rolled to my left. The Mage rushed me. I slashed my blade down the length of her arm, splitting robe and flesh. As her blood flowed, her black aura dimmed.

"Fool!" the Mage howled. She threw down the heart, lunged at another fighter, and broke the woman's neck without touching her. The Mage plunged both hands into the body and muttered.

Behind me, my Lifeline screamed. The Mage wore a wicked grin. I whirled to see three demons converge on my Lifeline. I ran toward her, scrambling through deep sand. She fought, clutching her side. I was almost to her when a black blade appeared at the base of her throat. Enyo pinned her from behind. The blue-skinned demon's troops disarmed my Lifeline and surrounded her.

She froze, and the hurricane in her eyes faded to terror. "Harper. Help."

"Move, and I'll slit the bitch's throat," Enyo said. I lowered my sword, my chest heaving, mind frantic. All I could see was my Lifeline's face. I had to help her.

A blood-curdling yell came from behind me. I turned and the Mage struck me in the face with the butt-end of a dagger. My nose crunched. She slashed my sword arm. I stumbled backward.

"Give up, Commander."

I hit my knees, blood in my mouth and flowing down my forearm. I started to rise but the Mage shoved me down without touching me.

"If only you knew what you were," she mused, hooking two fingers under my jaw, forcing me to look up. Her eyes and tattoos glowed red. She studied me with a longing that made me sick. The Mage didn't take her eyes off me and said, "Enyo, kill her. Then he'll understand."

"Don't—"

The Mage swiped the air with her blood-soaked hand, silencing my shout. I twisted and met my Lifeline's eyes. Hers pleaded for me to get up, tears streaking her face. I couldn't move, couldn't talk. The surge of energy inside me fizzled.

All three of her demon captors stabbed their blades deep into her body. My heart seized and I slumped forward with a gasp. That last bit of strength I had turned to cold ash in my chest.

Enyo's laughter rose above the sound of battle. I couldn't breathe. My Lifeline's murderers dropped her limp body. Waves splashed over her, dragging her blood into the ocean.

The snow turned back to rain as the demons, Warriors, and men vanished along with the carnage of war. All that remained was the Mage, me, and Samantha Fife's body. Tears mingled with rain on my cheeks and I shut my eyes.

"When you come into your Power, Commander, your life will be tied to hers. And if she dies, you die, too."

I jerked upright in bed, grabbing at my arm. My hand came away clean. I tested my nose and it was fine. I was in the Shaws' farmhouse. This was my room. It was solid and real. The bed I sat in was real. The bookshelf across the room was real. I was alive.

I covered my eyes and took in deep, slow breaths. It had only been a dream. *Or was it?*

"Sammy!"

Blind terror tore me out of bed. I jerked on a pair of pants and hit the door running. I barged into Sam's room. Kestler gave a startled yelp, dropping the book she'd been reading.

"What the hell is wrong with you?" Bennett snapped from where he was dozing near the closet.

I fell on my knees beside Sam. Only when I saw her peaceful face, the slow rise and fall of her chest, and felt the steady rhythm of her pulse, did I breathe again.

She was alive and I was losing my goddamn mind.

HARPER

"I am truly sorry about Judy," Mrs. Worthington said. "She was one of my dearest friends. I'll miss her deeply."

I walked beside the elderly woman, guiding her to the pews reserved for guests. My nose burned and my eyes itched. It took everything in me to remain stoic. Being reminded that Ma was actually gone triggered shit I didn't want to feel. *I don't want to fucking be here.*

"Thank you," I mumbled in a low rasp. Xavier caught my eye from the stage and he motioned for me to join him. "Excuse me," I said to the Worthingtons.

I met Xavier behind the pulpit. He handed me index cards. "Are you sure you want to speak?" he asked.

"No, but I'm obligated." Xavier and I didn't waste time with niceties.

"Very well. I'll deliver the Eulogy. Miss Kestler will say a few words and you'll close us out."

I glanced at Pops in the front row. With his vacant grey eyes and deadened expression, he could have been a walking corpse. DH sat beside him, rubbing his back. The pixie caught me looking. She offered an encouraging smile and gave a thumbs up. I nodded. She'd been good for morale at the farmhouse and she took care of Pops.

Nigel and DH had to tell him when to eat, to sleep, and to wake up. I kept waiting for him to snap out of this funk and see Sam. Day five of her coma and he hadn't so much as darkened her door. He'd turned inward, trapped in his own personal prison.

When Molly died, I drank too much, slept with too many women, and worked too many hours to avoid having to feel my loss, but never once did I shut down. I showed up at her funeral, withstood people's sympathies, and was one of her pallbearers. At work, my team depended on me and those whose lives I could save depended on me.

But Pops? He had Warriors that needed his expertise, his guidance. Xavier had told me to give him time, because of some Warrior marriage shit he never explained, but Pops wasn't the only one to lose her. Ma was the second mother I'd lost.

"He just sits there," I said.

Xavier placed a hand on my shoulder. "Judy and Andrew took a blood oath when they were wed. During the ceremony, they mixed their blood on a blessed altar. She became bound to him and he to her and only death could break it. There is nothing more binding than Warrior vows because they weave the two persons together spiritually and physically. They lived two hundred and seventy years together. So when Judy passed—"

"Part of him died, too?" Kestler asked from behind us. She'd put on a brave face but her black dress hung a little too loose on her lean frame.

She's still not eating, I thought.

"Literally," Xavier answered. "Give him time," he repeated the phrase he'd used days ago.

Kestler looked at Pops and sighed. "I can't even imagine how lost he feels right now."

"Sam?" I asked her, changing the subject.

"No change. Camden's sitting with her. Nigel's holding down the fort. Jax and Lani are on border patrol around the farmhouse since we don't know how strong the borders are these days."

I grunted. While I was loath to leave Sam alone, I was the adopted son of Andrew and Judy Shaw. My absence would stir up questions and drama if I didn't show up at Ma's funeral. I'd already heard snippets of conversation speculating how'd she'd died, and murmurs that I, the prodigal son, had returned. *If they only knew the fucking truth.*

"I should be with Sam," I said.

"Not this again." Kestler sighed. "You're paranoid. Cam is *not* gonna hurt her. We're all on the same side."

"Are we?" I had my doubts.

Xavier cleared his throat. "We're about to start. Find your seats." He pointed to a lone pew to the left of the pulpit. I knew Xavier had his suspicions about Bennett, but he had more tact than I did.

The ceremony went smoothly, for a funeral. Xavier did a great job of honoring the woman who'd raised me. Kestler's voice was clear despite the tears on her face. I managed to keep my shit together and delivered the closing. Afterwards, everyone filed out of the sanctuary and into the adjoining reception hall. There was no graveside burial. Hell, there wasn't even a body in Ma's ornamental casket. She would receive a proper Warrior-style send off this evening, at a private ceremony on the farmhouse property. I looked up from where I sat on the edge of the stage. Only Pops and DH remained.

"Hey kiddo, let me talk to him alone," I said to the pixie.

She glanced at Pops and ran a hand through her hair. "Um, I—sure."

"I'll try not to upset him. I just need a few minutes."

DH nodded and gave us some privacy. I knelt in front of him and looked into his eyes. "Pops, I know you're in there. You don't have to talk, just blink once if you understand me."

He lowered his lids and reopened them. *Good. A sign of life.*

"Look, I haven't needed you for a long time, and I've seen my fair share of death. But Kestler and Sammy? They haven't. And I get why you haven't seen her yet, but Sam—" I shook my head. "She's still in her coma. Xavier's tests showed there's no more poison in her blood. She's just not awake. I think—I think she needs to hear your voice."

A tear slid down Pops's cheek and he blinked.

"She needs you."

Another blink.

This is going fucking nowhere. I motioned for DH, who hovered nearby. She collected Pops and they went through the door leading to the reception hall. I couldn't stomach being around all these people anymore and found myself in front of Ma's closed casket; even though she wasn't there, I laid a reverent hand on top.

"This fucking blows, Ma. And I can't help but feel like this is my fault. If I hadn't let Sammy go into that store, if I'd made her wait for backup, and if I'd done that whole day differently, maybe you'd still be alive." I let out a bark of bitter laughter. "You'd tell me I was wrong, that I couldn't have known what would happen, and that I did the best I could. But I'm having a hard time believing that right now."

I bowed my head, resting it on the casket, and inhaled. I wanted solace and quiet. I wanted my brain to stop replaying Monday's shit show on loop. I wanted Sam to wake the hell up. I wanted a goddamn do-over. But Heaven had never done me any favors. So I stood, fired Kestler a text telling her where I was going, and left the church without a backward glance.

In SAM'S ROOM, I ditched my tie, tossed my navy suit jacket over the back of a chair, rolled up my sleeves, and undid the top two buttons of my white dress shirt. Her IV bag was full, her vitals stronger than ever, and her stitches held firm. Bear laid next to Sam. I stroked his head while we sat in the quietness of her room. Nigel sat in the corner, knitting, and watched me.

"How's she doing?" Bennett asked, tucking his phone into his front pocket. He leaned against the wall, arms folded over his chest. Bear rumbled.

"Fine," I growled.

"Xavier have any idea when she'll come out of this?" he asked.

"No. Now leave me the fuck alone."

"Come on, man, don't be a dick." Bennett settled in his normal chair at the end of Sam's bed. "What do you have against me anyway?"

Nigel looked at me with perceptive eyes. It was a fair question. And one I didn't have an answer to. Everyone else seemed to think he was a swell guy. I had no proof he was hiding anything. But the fact that he'd never seen a demon until five days ago didn't sit right with me. He was an outsider. One I didn't trust. Kestler and I had gone round and round with this.

"Sam's my girlfriend, man. I care about her, too."

Shut up. I suppressed a snarl. *And go away.* The funeral

this morning, dealing with Pops, and interacting with everyone here at the farmhouse had frayed my patience. I was fighting to keep myself from going to a dark-ass place.

"You don't just gain the ability to see demons, Bennett. I'm not buying your bullshit story."

"It's God's honest truth." He raised his hands in surrender.

"Stay with her," I told Bear. I so wanted to punch Bennett's naive face, but instead I stalked out of Sam's room. I went into Pops's office and threw down the books from the fourth shelf up by the window. A large emerald bottle came into view. I snatched the liter of Jameson, a tumbler glass from the desk, and prowled my way to the gym.

Not bothering to turn on the lights in the office there, I settled into the leather chair, set the tumbler on the desktop, and poured myself one finger of whiskey. I lifted the glass, swirling the amber liquid. *Do I want to go down this road?* I had a hard time keeping shit to myself when I drank. For two years I hadn't touched any of it.

Ma was gone, *really* gone. That was hard for me to fathom since she'd always been there. She raised me, gave me my first medical training, and taught me to drive. After I left, she called me every Sunday. A fucking demon had murdered her. My memory kept showing me Ma's savaged neck, her blood on the tile, and her lifeless eyes.

I wasn't sleeping because when I did, I saw Sam die over and over. Enyo stabbed her in each nightmare. Sam had bled all over my hands and then seized again, and again. I could do nothing to stop it. I was out of my fucking mind with Sam still in that fucking coma.

I put the glass to my lips and shot it back, baring my teeth as the whiskey burned its way down my esophagus. I poured a second measure and slammed that one, too. I rolled my neck one way and then the other, stretching the muscles in my shoulders. I tilted my chin to the side and closed my eyes, enjoying the silence of the dark gym. No one to bother me. No one to ask questions. No one to talk at me.

I drank small shots until my memories stopped hounding me. I let my head drop back against the desk chair. I didn't know how long I'd been alone in the office. But it was quiet.

"There you are!"

"Shit!" I scrambled upright, knocking over the tumbler but grabbing the Jameson. Kestler hit the switch on the wall and the fluorescent lights seared my retinas. She looked like absolute shit.

"You need a cheeseburger." My words slurred. "When was the last time you ate, Kestler? 2002?"

"Oh my gosh," she exclaimed. "Are you drunk?"

"Hell fucking yes, I am." I poured another shot only to have it snatched from my grasp. "The hell—"

"What about Sam?" she snapped. "What if something happens while you're—you're all schnockered up."

"She's in a coma." I waved a hand. "She's not going anywhere."

"What happens if she has another seizure? Or her stitches need to be redone again?"

"I don't have an answer for that one." I furrowed my brow.

"You're the best we have in the way of a doctor." She planted her fists on her hips. There were three or four of her.

"I kill everyone I love." I squinted, trying to focus on the one figure I thought was the real Kestler. "She's better off without me. Everyone is. I'm cursed."

"Oh, Harper," she said, her tone soft. "We've been looking for you. How long have you been here?"

"Ehhhh, not sure." I shrugged.

"We're going to give Judy her Warrior send-off. You want to be there?"

"Why the hell not?" I stood, wavered, but remained upright with the help of the desk. I grabbed the Jameson and took a drink from the bottle since I'd misplaced my glass. "You drinkin', too?"

"What?" She looked down. "No," she said acerbically and set the tumbler on the desktop. "And you're done." She pulled the green bottle from me.

Maybe she's right? I wavered on my feet. Kestler *tsked* and ducked under my armpit. She put her arm around my waist and grunted when she bore most of my weight.

"Good gravy," she muttered. "What are you? A tank?"

It was dark out now, and there was a small gathering of people in the clearing along the river. I recognized all but three: two women and a man. Xavier frowned when he saw us.

"Don't ask," Kestler said before anyone spoke.

Ma's linen-wrapped body lay on a pyre with burning torches placed every few feet, forming a half circle around the altar. I swayed and Kestler tightened her hold.

"I think you weigh as much as Thad," Kestler grumbled.

"Is he—" DH whispered.

"Yes," she growled.

"Where did you find him?" Kalakaua asked.

"In the gym with a bottle of whiskey. He almost polished it off."

I pushed off Kestler. "I would have had the whole damn thing if she hadn't interrupted me." Bozeman caught my woozy ass before I hit the ground.

"Easy, man," he said as he held me upright.

"We are gathered here to pay our last respects," Xavier began. "Judy contributed much to the Warriors of Light. She was a dedicated wife who raised four children to Warrior-hood over the centuries. She survived all of them. She mended many wounds and developed the Life Elixir. She took in Harper when he was a boy and raised him as her own."

God, I want another drink.

"Kimberly Judith Shaw was wife to Bernard Andrew Shaw, Head Adviser, and they were joined together by Warrior covenant."

I swung my head around looking for Pops while Xavier droned on—I tuned him out. Instead of Pops, my drunk ass focused on the petite woman I'd seen when Kestler and I arrived. She had two people flanking her. Bozeman must have seen me squinting at them.

He leaned in and spoke slowly enough that even my soggy brain understood, "The lady is Adviser Tabitha Holland. Advisers Gerena and Shaw located her in Ireland. Adviser Shaw was fetching her when Judy was killed. Adviser Holland was with him when he got the news. The two others with her are her Warriors. They all arrived this afternoon while you were—out."

"Huh," I mused.

"Let us honor the woman who loved us and healed us." Xavier lifted his sword. All the Warriors and Advisers, save for Pops, drew their weapons and hoisted them. There was a buzz of energy in the air that was trippy in my drunk-ass state. *Sam should be here. She should be with them.* In unison, they all repeated something that tugged at a fuzzy memory. *As you enter into Glory, be at rest. You have earned your peace.* I blinked and shook my head. I'd heard that at my own parents' funeral.

"Would anyone like to say a few words?" Xavier asked, as each person aside from Pops grabbed a torch. I raised my hand and stumbled forward.

"I'm not sure that's—" Kestler started to say.

"Ma," I declared, "never lied. She was fucking honest. And good." I ducked out of the way of Kestler's grabbing hand. "And she didn't deserve to fucking die." I finally met Pops's eyes, and with the massive amount of liquid courage I had on board, said, "It should have been you." I pointed to the pyre. "You should have been there for Sam."

"Harper," Kestler hissed.

"You're drunk, son. Don't do this," Xavier said.

"I can handle it," Pops answered.

My eyes grew wide in mocking surprise. "He speaks?" I wrenched away from Bozeman and Kestler and stumbled up to my dear old father.

"Mr. Tate," Xavier said, his tone sharp. Pops held up a hand.

"People are always dying for you." I poked a finger into Pops's chest.

"Son," he pleaded. "You have every right to be furious with me."

"I would say so." The whiskey had dissolved both my tact and my respect for this man. "What about my child-hood? You were a tyrant." I was nose-to-nose with him. He said nothing in his own defense. "You were a shitty father."

"It *is* my fault. All of this." He ran a hand through his silver hair. "I've been alive too long and made too many mistakes." He reached out for me, but I swatted him away.

"Don't fucking touch me. We wouldn't be in this"—I floundered for the right words—"this heap of horse shit if you'd done your job right."

"I know." His tone was solemn.

"Andrew, are you okay with this?" The new woman asked—Bozeman had called her Tabitha.

Pops nodded. "Let him speak his piece. He carries a heavy load that would have crushed most people."

"Kiss my ass," I growled. "Why haven't you visited Sam? Does she not matter to you? Are you wanting her to flip like Cheryl did?" Pops jerked as if I'd punched him. I grinned, the asshole in me emboldened with alcohol. "I remember her name. You forget, I have access to your files. I've read up on my Warrior history. Unlike"—I pointed at Kestler—"your Warrior charges. Hey Kestler, did you know—"

"Please don't—" Pops pleaded.

"Did you know, Kestler, that one of Pops's own became a Dark Warrior?"

"Harper," she snapped at me and held out her hand. "Come here."

"Don't believe me? Ask him. He won't tell you because he's ashamed. And it puts you all at risk."

"Judy wouldn't want this," Kestler whispered.

I rounded back on Pops. "All I ever wanted to do was please you. But it was never good enough. I should be a fucking Warrior, but you never got the call from Heaven on me, did you? Why? My parents were your Alpha team. I must be such a fucking disappointment to you. Is that why you were so cold and distant, you basta—"

"Enough!" Xavier demanded. Something hit me on the back of the head, and in blinding pain, my world went black.

I GROANED AND ROLLED OVER. My head pounded like a jackhammer. I eased myself up, swung my legs over the bed's edge, and sat there in my boxers. The aftertaste of Jameson lingered in my mouth. My fingers found a bruise on the back of my skull.

"Ah, fuck."

"Adviser Gerena hit you with the butt of his sword," Kestler said from where she sat in the dim corner of my room.

I winced. "How long have you been here?"

"Couple hours."

I buried my face in my hands. "How'd I get here?" I had no recollection.

"After Xavier knocked you out, he and Jax brought you up to the house. They got you into bed."

They undressed me. Fucking-A. How drunk had I been? "What happened?"

"You don't remember? You sure you wanna know?"

"No and yes." My stomach heaved when I tried to stand. "I should be apologizing if Xavier needed to shut me down." Closing my eyes, I pinched the bridge of my nose. "Fuck."

"Harper." She bumped my shoulder. I fixed one eye on her and she held up a T-shirt.

"Thanks." I took it and put it on, mortified at what my drunk ass might have done. "What did I say?"

"A lot. Mostly slurred and unintelligible. But you got your point across."

A wave of nausea hit me hard and fast. I bolted to the trash and puked. I heaved until my sides hurt then rolled onto my ass. I propped up my legs so my feet pressed against the carpet and my back leaned against the cool wall. Kestler stepped up next to me, towel in one hand and a can of Coke in the other.

I took them both and looked up at her. "Do I need to apologize to you?"

Her mouth lifted into a half smile and she relaxed. "Nah, you're good."

"Sorry," I said for good measure. She'd proven to be a good friend, and, if I drank as much as I thought I had, I'd probably made a right ass out of myself.

"Don't worry about it. You were quite verbose for someone that drunk."

"How's Sam?"

"No change. Thankfully she didn't have an issue while you were out of commission." She dug in her jeans pocket for a small bottle of ibuprofen. I held up an open palm as she tapped out four russet tabs. I washed them down with a long swallow of Coke. She joined me on the floor.

"I can't handle losing Sam, Kestler. I won't recover." A confession I'd only make to a select few. And if I didn't say it now, I was going to retreat to that pitch-black place in myself. History had proven how cold and distant I could be. I didn't want to be that guy again.

"I know," she said. "And no one blames you. This whole thing—" She shook her head, tears threatening to fall. "It just sucks."

"Yeah," I agreed, taking another drink of soda. "Sure does."

She patted my knee and we sat in silence. Even with my head pounding and stomach turning, I appreciated her presence. Pops'd fucked up being her Adviser, she'd lost Ma, and she loved Sam. If there was anyone on Earth that could empathize with me, it was Kestler. And for that, I was grateful.

SAM

"**B**rave One," Letty said, stroking my hair. "You took heavy damage but I think you're stable now."

I didn't know how long I'd been lying on the floor of my mental white space. She let me lie with my head in her lap and revived me with her gentle warmth, healing my ravaged mind and poison-damaged body. She smelled like fresh-cut grass, or the state fair, or coffee, or Max, or clean air after rain—all scents which soothed my soul.

"It's time to rise," she said, shifting me to a seated position. Her eyes were vast and blue, like a crystal sea. She offered a soft smile. Her quiet demeanor was the complete opposite of how she'd been when the Mage was here. I'd seen pure fear and desperate panic on Letty's face.

"You were so scared," I whispered.

Her smile faltered. "I thought I was going to lose you."

I crossed my legs. "Could you see anything I saw?"

"No." Her nostrils flared. "They found a way to block me with their abominable blood magic. I couldn't see, hear, smell, or feel you." She smoothed the front of her white tunic. "Their power is an abomination. It's vile.

One day they will pay for this trespass." Letty inhaled. "But you were strong enough to banish them from your mind."

"You're an *angel*. Why did you never say anything?" I cringed. "All the times I called you my inner Warrior."

She chuckled. "I knew you'd find out or ask me in your own time. You've never been one to get bogged down with details."

I mulled that over. "But if you're my angel, where are your—you know—*wings*."

This time she let out a genuine laugh. Letty stood, and with a grand sweep of her arms, a huge set of white wings unfurled with languid grace behind her.

From my seated position, I reached up and touched a feather then jerked my hand away. "Sorry."

"Ever the curious one." Her eyes twinkled. "They are not off limits, Brave One."

Her feathers were sturdy and had an opalescent sheen. Letty was so patient and gentle with me, even though I was a wild card who made questionable life choices. "Did you draw the short straw when they asked who wanted to be Samantha Fife's Warrior angel?"

"I volunteered." She shrugged. "Actually, I lobbied for your anointing. We do have some say in the matter."

I blinked. *Who would want to get stuck with me?* Sometimes I questioned my own sanity. To hear that I was wanted all the way up in Heaven was humbling. I rested my hands in my lap. "But why would you want that?"

"You're a perfect fit for my abilities, Samantha. I've never had a Warrior so align with my own strengths. We complement each other well." She was so matter-of-fact I didn't doubt her.

"I'm a little crazy. That doesn't bother you? I mean, aren't angels all controlled and disciplined?"

"I am those things, but I'm not a machine." She grinned.

"Have you had other Warriors besides me?"

"Two." Letty's wings snapped out behind her. "Those Warriors have earned their rest."

"But I'm the only one you asked for?"

"Correct." She tucked her wings back into a relaxed position.

I thought of Andrew, who had to be over three hundred years old. "So let me get this straight." I stood up and wiped my hands on my thighs. "You willingly joined yourself to me, argued for it, knowing that there is a good possibility you'd be stuck with me for *centuries*?"

"Oh, yes." She beamed and clasped her hands together, resting them before her.

"Well then." I ran a hand through my hair. "I don't know who's the bigger nutter. You or me."

But wait. Cheryl had been a Warrior of Light. Hellfire, some of her memories were mine forever now. After Dominic's description of how a Dark Warrior was made, he'd left me with unanswered questions.

"What happened to Cheryl's angel when she went Dark? *Who* was her angel? Are they okay?"

Letty hesitated, a flicker of grief crossed her ancient eyes and her smile faltered. She sighed like one carrying a great burden.

"Her angel's name was Ophelia. Ophie hasn't spoken a word since Cheryl turned. You must understand, Brave One." Letty took my hands in hers. "There is a level of love and trust that goes into each Warrior-Angel match." She tightened her fingers around mine. "We are not a silent bunch. We love to sing, and laugh, and talk. Except for Michael; he's broody. After what happened with Cheryl, Ophelia has not partaken in our joy—" Leticia shook her head, and her thumbs rubbed absently over the backs of my knuckles. "She has wounds that I'm not sure will ever heal."

Oh, my heart. Cheryl's betrayal of Ophelia robbed me of breath. I couldn't fathom turning my back on Letty. Even if everything in my life failed, she was there—strong and steady. "How did she do it? I can't imagine waking up one day and thinking, 'This is the day I go Dark.'"

"Dominic," she snarled. Her wings flared out to her sides and her crystal eyes blazed. She was once more an avenging angel and I took a respectful step back, extracting my hands from hers. She met my gaze. "Do not underestimate that one. He manipulates, and connives, and lies. He will weave whatever tale he thinks you need to hear. Since he's taken an interest in you, my Warrior, be vigilant. Never get complacent."

Hooboy! She didn't need to tell me twice. "But how did he get to Cheryl?" I thought for a moment. "Micah. Dominic possessed Micah, who in turn, seduced her with the possibility of revenge." I tapped my lips. "In the memories the Mage implanted, I don't think Micah was always under demonic influence. That happened later, right? After she was with child."

Leticia nodded at my guess. "Indeed."

"That means Dominic had to sit by and watch. He had to have invested *years* to pull Cheryl to the darkness." Dominic's patience floored me. His manipulation skills impressed me. He orchestrated every step needed to snare a Warrior of Light. He'd played the long game with Cheryl and *won*. I wrapped my arms around myself.

"Dominic works *everything* to his advantage. Never forget that."

My encounters with Dominic had puzzled me before. He was well-mannered and civilized, unlike any other

Greater Demon we'd met. Why would he let not one, but two Warriors of Light escape? Why would he defy the Mage? I chewed on my lip. After Letty's warning, I would be extra careful with that one.

"Why didn't you recognize him at first, like you did Enyo?"

Letty took a steadying breath, as if gathering her thoughts, then said, "He wears a different face than he used to."

"Hmm." I didn't know what to make of her statement before my curiosity took another abrupt turn. "You mentioned Michael. Are we talking about *the* Michael, as in the Archangel?"

"The very same." Letty nodded, her ire over Dominic evaporated with the change in subject.

My eyes widened. "Are you an Archangel? How many are there? How does that work?"

"Heaven, no!" She laughed. "There were only four of them. Three now, since Lucifer fell. Each of them oversees a third of the Heavenly Host. Michael's battalion is considered the elite of all divisions. The angelic partners for most Warriors of Light come from his ranks. I am Michael's—how do you phrase it—his second-in-command."

Fascinating. Does Andrew know this? Letty seemed open with her answers, so I felt free to ask, "Have any of the Archangels ever been a Warrior's angel?"

Letty's smile remained in place. "No, Brave One. Though it has been discussed, it has never been done. *Yet.* The Archangels' powers are much more intense and Michael's supersede all others. We don't know if a human could survive the transformation. We were created to protect, not harm."

She braced me by the shoulders. "If their own transformation doesn't kill them, the one who receives an

Archangel will be more powerful than any Warrior before him or her. Light Warrior laws will not pertain to that person. They *will* have the Power to kill a Dark Warrior without violating Heaven's laws."

Harper had said something about Andrew researching this very idea. The details of the conversation were fuzzy, but I distinctly remembered him saying that the Mage had slaughtered his parents because Hell thought Thomas Tate was this ultra-Warrior. Letty had just confirmed that there had been no Archangel pairings. Harper's parents were slaughtered based on a mistaken assumption.

I wanted to weep for Harper, but he'd tell me not to be a fucking pansy or something. Letty rubbed the sides of my shoulders. A tear slipped out before I could catch it.

Then, clear as day, I remembered Harper saying, "Come back to me, Sammy. I need you. I can't lose you, too."

I craned my head around, seeking him, as if he could appear inside my mind. *When had he said that? How long have I been here with Letty?* Faint colors appeared around the edges of my mental space. I looked back at Letty. Her outline blurred, but she still wore a smile.

"You're alright, Samantha."

I swallowed, not sure what the fire-fart was happening. "Did you hear Harper call me?"

My angel smiled, her form blurring, but her signature warmth settled into my bones. "How do you feel, my Brave One?"

I glanced down at my body, which was also fading. "Am I waking?"

"You are." She nodded, blue eyes twinkling.

"I'm scared!" I reached for her, but my fingers couldn't find her. She was more specter than corporeal now, but her comforting grace increased, flowing like a lazy river throughout my body. There was more color than white now.

"So long as you live, I'll never leave you, Samantha Grace Fife." My angel, Leticia, stepped forward and brushed a kiss to my forehead. It felt more like a warm breeze on my skin. "You are loved. Now *wake*."

My whole body twitched as I gained consciousness. Sunlight filtered through a window. *Too bright.* I turned my head, scrunched my cheeks, and shielded my eyes. A small plastic thing pinched my index finger. *Where am I?* I felt a nasal tube in my nostrils. *The heck is this?* I reached up with my left hand—an IV needle pulled against my skin. I looked over and saw all kinds of tubes and wires connected to me.

I tensed, gritting my teeth, as disoriented panic gripped me. The desire to rip off all these things attached to my person overrode any other thought. I jerked the blasted breathing tube from my nose. My fingers fussed with the tape holding the needle on the back of my hand.

"Stop, Brave One. You were in a coma." Letty's voice grounded me and I froze. *"These instruments are what they've used to help keep your body alive. Leave them be."* At my angel's insistence, I stopped pulling everything off me and licked my dry, cracked lips.

"Relax," she encouraged me. *"Take in your surroundings."*

The spring green walls. Grey and white bedding. A brindle dog curled in a ball at my feet. I was in my room at the farmhouse, in my old bed, with my pit bull Bear.

"That's it." Letty's soothing warmth eased my confusion.

The whole house was quiet as a library. Air conditioning pumped cool air through the overhead ducts. I heard a low, rhythmic beeping and glanced to my left. My heartbeat spiked across a monitor. Someone slept in the

room with me. I shifted onto my left elbow and pushed up
to get a better look at who was in my room. Pain lanced
through me, starting in my lower left side.

"Holy motherfu—" I bit down on my explosive curse.
My ribcage and entire torso felt like they were on fire. "Oh
Lord," I groaned and let myself drop back into the bed.

"Sam?" Leigh whispered. Bear's blocky head popped
up from where he was curled.

"Who else would it be?"

My best friend sat up on her rollaway bed, blanket
dropping from around her. Relief-filled hazel eyes locked
with mine. She looked like she'd been through hell.

"You're awake." She shot to her feet and rushed over.
Bear scooted up the bed and snuggled up on my right side.
He sighed then went back to sleep.

"How long was I out?" I asked, scratching behind
Bear's ear.

"Seven days." She mashed her trembling lips together.

"Shit."

"Don't swear."

We both laughed and she grabbed my hand. Tears
started down her face despite her best efforts.

"Nah, Leigh, don't do that." *Why is she crying?* "I've
been in a coma, not dead." I offered a smile. She shook her
head, not able to speak, and wiped her eyes with her
hoodie sleeve.

This wasn't the reaction I'd expected. "What's wrong?
What happened?"

"What's the last thing you remember?" Leigh busied
herself checking me over.

I squinted at my closet doors across the room and
pursed my lips, digging into my memory. The tiniest of
snippets came to me. A pool of blood. A black demon. A
blue demon. A flash of black steel. Pain exploded behind

my eyes and from my ribs, triggering a garbled burst of curses.

"Stop! You'll bust your stitches." Leigh splayed a hand on my shoulder.

I groaned, lifted my arm, and felt my left side. A large bandage covered up a wound. "I vaguely recall a couple demons."

"And?" she pressed.

"I got nothing." I shrugged my right shoulder.

Leigh nodded. "You were stabbed—"

There had been a black blade with an oily sheen, I remembered.

"—by a poisoned blade," she said. My face went slack, and I melted into the bed, fatigue hauling at my body. The mattress depressed where Leigh sat. "What about before you were attacked? Remember anything from then?"

I rolled my head to the left, meeting her eyes. "There was a restaurant. I went there with Harper for some reason—"

Harper.

I sucked in a sharp breath, a fresh round of panic kicking in.

Harper.

He'd called me Sammy. He'd been the one to ask me to come back. He said he couldn't lose me. My breath came short and shallow. The wound flared with every inhale. He'd been there for me. *Just like he'd promised.*

"Is he okay? Where is he?" I struggled to sit up but the pain stopped me.

"He's fine!" Leigh answered, pushing me back to the bed.

I massaged my eyes for a second. "I'm so confused."

"Sam, Harper's the reason you're alive. You were a

bloody mess when he found you. He never gave up. He saved you."

"Where is he?" I had an inexplicable need to see him. To make sure he was whole and unharmed.

"He's around the property somewhere. Lani and Jax made him get some fresh air. Might be in the barn. I'll go get him for you." Leigh smiled down at me. "I'm glad you're back. I missed you."

She jogged out before I could answer, so I settled back into the bed, hooked an arm around Bear, and said, "What am I missing, bud? 'Cause whatever it is, it feels like a whopper."

HARPER

In the barn, I heaved the last seventy-five-pound bale of alfalfa on top of a neat stack. Bozeman and Kalakaua had convinced me to leave the farmhouse, but a five-mile run ending at the barn hadn't dispelled my agitation and bad attitude. I'd ended up in the hay loft, finding it a complete mess. The bales weren't stacked with any order, and some idiot had opened one without finishing the other.

After sweeping the floors and making sure there were no more loose hay strings lying about, I took off my baseball cap, wiped the sweat and hay dust from my face, then settled my hat back on my head. The hay was now stacked with military precision, the wood-beam floors were clear of debris, and everything was where it needed to be. I'd restored order where chaos once reigned. *Too bad I can't do that with Sam.*

I grunted, hit the lights, then jogged downstairs to the barn aisle. Three horse heads poked out over their stall doors. Thad whickered and the other two stretched their necks toward me. "It's not dinner time. And I already gave you extra hay."

One horse didn't greet me. I frowned and crossed the aisle to the third stall on the left. Max stood in the back of his stall with his head down, velvet lips picking at his uneaten flake of alfalfa. This was how he had been for the past week and he didn't even flick an ear when I leaned on his stall door. His brown eyes were lifeless, his chestnut coat dull. The points of his shoulders and hips jutted out. I entered his stall and checked his feed bucket. His morning grain remained untouched.

"Max," I muttered, going over to him and rubbing under his mane. "You gotta eat, my man. For Sammy."

The cantankerous Thoroughbred lifted his large head, a flicker of sentient life in his eyes when he looked at me. I froze, a brief spike of hope clenching my stomach. That flash of acknowledgment in Max's brown eye sputtered and died. He lowered his neck down and sighed.

"Fuck," I hissed. Hope would be the death of me. "Fuck," I spat again.

I punched the stall wall. The unforgiving beam shuddered and I shook my hand out. Just like that, any solace I'd found from my run and throwing heavy-ass hay bales evaporated. I left the stall, scowling and prowling the length of the aisle. A punching bag hung at the end of the barn. *Perfect.* I needed something that could take my rage and not break my hands.

I fired off a fast series of jabs, crosses, and hooks. With each punch I landed, I imagined different enemies' faces: Enyo, who'd stabbed Sam; Dominic, who'd taunted me; the demon who'd killed Ma. The more I punched, the angrier I got, until I spun around and aimed a high kick at the bag. It rocked on its chain and dust motes exploded from the rafters.

They all could go fuck themselves. I rammed my shoulder into the bag, slipped left as it swung past, and then assaulted it with another series of blows. The punching bag creaked and groaned. Chest heaving, I grabbed the bag in my arms and squeezed it in a bear hug. My spike of anger and adrenaline faded.

The hair on the back of my neck prickled when I heard the soft scuff of shoes on concrete. I raised my head but didn't look behind me. I knew who it was by footsteps alone.

"Kalakaua," I growled. "If you're not here to see your Guardian, leave me the fuck alone."

"I wanted to check on you."

"I'm a grown man." I released the bag and turned around. "Why the fuck do you think I'd want you to do that?" Her brown eyes pleaded for me to not cuss her into next week. I glared at her.

She chewed her lower lip. "The farm's divine borders are compromised. It's not safe to go anywhere alone these days."

"Bullshit. You were keeping tabs on me." I raised a brow. "You think I need protection?"

"No, I just—I was doing my job."

A half-truth, I thought.

Then she followed up with a more honest answer. "I wanted to make sure you were safe."

"Because I'm a fragile human who needs to be babysat?" I crossed my arms over my chest. I wasn't being fair. She blushed. I sighed and rubbed my hand over my hair. "Go away, Kalakaua. I'll be fine."

"You can't know that, Harper," she snapped. "I wasn't singling you out. No one, Warrior or not, should go anywhere alone right now."

"It's one thing to keep tabs on someone and another to actively insert yourself when you're not welcome."

"Look, I know I came on strong when we met." The

Hawaiian Harpy—as Sam called her—looked contrite as she glanced up and wrung her hands. "I've always been too bold. It gets me in trouble. But I know now that there was never any chance for me."

My brow furrowed and I pulled back. "What?"

Kalakaua's lips lifted in a small smile. She gestured to the bag with her chin. "I'll hold for you. It's easier to hit when someone's holding."

I narrowed my gaze. "Don't deflect. What chance are you talking about?"

She laughed through her nose. "Exactly. What chance? You've only got room in your heart for one." Kalakaua tugged at her ear and shrugged. "Look, Harper, I come as a friend. Only a friend. You need more than one."

She was referring to Kestler, of course. *But maybe Kalakaua's right. Allies are good to have.* And if she'd really come in peace as she'd said, I was being a right dick. I gestured to the bag, squared up in a boxer's stance, and bounced onto the balls of my feet. Kalakaua held it and braced her feet. I fired off some combos and kicks, then repeated my earlier exercises with the benefit of her balancing the bag. Afterward, I grabbed a couple bottles of Gatorade from the fridge in the feed room.

"Thanks," I said, tossing a bottle to Kalakaua on my way to Max's stall. I had to check even though I knew there would be no change. Waiting for Sam to wake up and checking on Max had become fucking obsessions.

"Anytime."

One of the horses across from Max stuck his head over the stall door, watching me with intelligent eyes. He was a mahogany bay with a black forelock that almost came down to his muzzle. Kalakaua walked up to him and whispered a few words in his ear; he pressed his large head into her chest.

"What's your Guardian's name?" I cracked open my Gatorade and I took a long pull.

"York." Kalakaua scratched along the underside of her Guardian's cheek. He closed his eyes.

"The big palomino is Bozeman's then?"

"Yeah. Her name is Tatiana. Jackson calls her Ana." Kalakaua joined me at Max's stall. "He gonna be okay?"

"I don't know." Even I heard the rasp of desperation in my voice. "If I can't get him to eat, he'll fucking starve."

Kalakaua's face fell. "Surely he knows Sam's still alive, right?"

I clenched my jaw and ran a rough hand through my hair. "Who the fuck knows what Enyo's poison did to her internally. Xavier thinks it's blocked her from her Guardian, and probably her angel. If Max can't feel her or talk to her, he might think she's—"

"Max thinks Sam is dead." Kalakaua glanced at York. "I didn't even think of that."

I had a violent aversion to the words "Sam is dead." She'd come so close and wasn't out of the woods yet. I drained my sports drink. *If Sam woke up to find her Guardian dead*—I quashed the thought.

"It's why Xavier and I thought it would be best to bring the Guardians here," I said. "Honestly, I don't know how we even got Max in the trailer. We were hoping having them together would spark something in at least one of them."

"Did you try to bring him to her window?"

I glared at Kalakaua. "Don't you think that didn't cross my fucking mind?" She flinched. I jerked Max's hunter green halter off the hook, held it out to her, and flung open Max's stall door. "Go ahead. Try to get him out. Short of bringing Sam down here, which we can't do—"

"Harper," Kalakaua whispered, grabbing my shirt sleeve. She pointed at Max.

Max's head had snapped up, his neck arched high, and his ears swiveled forward. He blew out what sounded like an indignant breath. I gripped the door's ledge, my bruised knuckles turning white. He swung his head toward me, eyes filled with that preternatural spark of intelligence only Guardians possessed. His large nostrils flared. After a few heartbeats, he moved to his feed bucket and started to eat.

I tore out of the barn, Kalakaua keeping pace with me. I was halfway to the farmhouse when Kestler met me. She was smiling. Tears streaked her cheeks. I grabbed her by the shoulders and looked into her eyes.

"Is she—" My grip tightened. My heart thundered. Hope, goddamn hope, burned in my chest.

"Yeah, Harper," she said, breathless and beaming. "She's awake and she's asking for you."

"Then what the fuck are we doing out here?" I let go of Kestler and ran towards Sam.

ACKNOWLEDGMENTS

My eternal gratitude goes to author Katika Schneider for her developmental edit of this novel. You saw beyond many ugly rough drafts to what my story could be. Thank you for convincing me to not set off a bomb in that one chapter and for being Harper's mediator. He always trusted you first anyways.

To my writing coach, Anne Larsen. Where do I even start? Thank you for helping me with the broken parts of this novel that I couldn't fix on my own. More than that, you helped me find my unique voice. I'm a stronger, more confident writer because of you.

To Sarah, of Sarah Miller Creations, for my cover art: you took my stick-figure chicken scratch and turned it into a beautiful work of art. The weapons, the keys, the ice. It's so badass. PS: I ADORE the weapons. (It bears repeating!)

A massive thank you to all of you beautiful humans who beta read for me. Your input was vital to this publication, and I truly appreciate each of you. You are my people. A special shout out to Alex Perkins her final beta read through and to Kaitlin Kino for her diligent proof-reading!

Sam Parish, my fellow author-wizard-horse friend, thank you for formatting my book and adding those glorious chapter headers. We totes were meant to be friends. Dr. B, thank you for my logo. It means more than words can express.

To my husband, thank you for putting up with my creative crazy. And to my parents for raising me to believe I can do literally anything I put my mind to. I love you three so hard.

And finally, to Casey. You were the horse I didn't know I needed. You will always will be my bestest friend and my own personal Warrior Guardian. Thank you for listening to everything I ever told you, and teaching me to be a better human without using any words at all. Rest well, my fire pony.

ABOUT THE AUTHOR

Megan is Floridian by birth, Nebraskan by marriage. She currently lives with her husband and their two dogs in a little stilt house on the Anclote River in Florida. Megan has been obsessed with horses since she learned to walk. So much so that she quit nursing school to pursue something more horse-centric. In 2007, she graduated from St Andrew's University in North Carolina with a degree in Equine Business Management—doing things her way, as per usual.

Megan also enjoys coffee, memes, running, Denver Bronco football, Nebraska volleyball (#GBR), roller coasters, and theme parks.

As someone who has always had an overactive imagination and a love of reading, Megan felt like it was high time to put her creative juju to good use and pursue her next grand adventure: being a published author. She would love for you to connect with her on the ol' social media!

<ins>Facebook & Instagram:</ins>
@mmchromybooks
<ins>Email:</ins>
mmchromybooks@gmail.com